Praise for Robert Ellis's bestselling novel

CITY OF FIRE

"A gripping, spooky crime novel."
—*The New York Times* (A "Hot List" Pick)

"A no-holds-barred, barn-burner of a thriller that blends Los Angeles–style crime fiction à la Michael Connelly with pulse-pounding Dean Koontzian psychological suspense."
—*Chicago Tribune*

"My kind of crime novel. Gritty, tight, and assured. Riding with Detective Lena Gamble through the hills of Los Angeles is something I could get used to."
—Michael Connelly

"A scorcher."
—*Baltimore Sun*

"I just discovered Robert Ellis. This book is terrific."
—Janet Evanovich, *People*

"This book is fast, gruesome, and twisted, like a scary Jodie Foster movie. Ellis makes it easy to be terrified."
—*Library Journal*

"A complex portrait of the flawed but righteous Lena by Ellis makes this sure-footed police procedural something special."
—*Kirkus Reviews*

"Ellis vividly evokes Hollywood as a place of burning desires, where the boundaries between good and evil are blurred beyond distinction. Ellis' prose is crisp, and his plot moves at a good clip."
—*Booklist*

THE LOST WITNESS

R O B E R T   E L L I S

St. Martin's Paperbacks

This is a work of fiction. All of the characters, organizations, and events portrayed in this novel are either products of the author's imagination or are used fictitiously.

THE LOST WITNESS

Copyright © 2009 by Robert Ellis.

Cover photographs: of woman by iStockphoto.com/Nicola Scarmagnani; of city by iStockphoto.com/Niilo Tippler; of sky by iStockphoto.com/Shawn Gearhart; of badge by Jeff Costlow. Cover photo illustration by Shasti O'Leary Soudant.

All rights reserved.

For information address St. Martin's Press, 175 Fifth Avenue, New York, NY 10010.

Library of Congress Catalog Card Number: 2008036118

EAN: 978-0-312-36616-2

Printed in the United States of America

Minotaur edition / February 2009
St. Martin's Paperbacks edition / June 2010

St. Martin's Paperbacks are published by St. Martin's Press, 175 Fifth Avenue, New York, NY 10010.

10 9 8 7 6 5 4 3 2 1

For Deborah Conway Weber

ACKNOWLEDGMENTS

This novel could not have been written without the help and guidance of LAPD detectives Mitzi Roberts from the Robbery-Homicide Division, Rick Jackson from the Robbery-Homicide Division, Cold Case Homicide Unit, and Harry Klann Jr. from the Scientific Investigation Division. The author would also like to express a great debt of thanks to Arthur J. Belanger from the Department of Pathology at Yale University School of Medicine, and H. Donald Widdoes, for his work in firearms and ballistics. Although this story may have been inspired by real events, it is a complete work of fiction. Any technical deviations, exaggerations, or errors are the author's responsibility alone.

A very special thanks must also go to my editor, Kelley Ragland, for her contribution to this novel. But also for her patience and enthusiasm and keen insights. To my publisher, Andrew Martin, for his belief in the Lena Gamble series and his unyielding support. To Christina Harcar and Kerry Nordling, who introduced this series to the rest of the world. To Matthew Martz for his attention to detail, Ronni Stolzenberg for her marketing wizardry, and Helen Chin, my copy editor, for her special care. David Rotstein for his moody jacket design. To my UK editor at Pan Macmillan, Stefanie Bierwerth, for her contribution to the story and her encouragement and kindness. To everyone at Brilliance Audio, including Bill Weideman for his direction, and Renee Raudman for her wonderful interpretation and read. And to Emma Higgs at

Issis Publishing, and Regina Reagan, for another remarkable performance. To Sarah Melnyk for beating the streets and getting the word out, and Pat Schrevelius for managing the Web site so well. And to my agent, Scott Miller, a very special thanks for making all this happen.

The author is also deeply grateful to John Truby for his contribution to this story. But also to Joe Drabyak, Barry Martin and Mary Riley, Mark Moskowitz, Neil Oxman and Jean Utley. And to Nelson and Sharon Rising, who gave the author the experience and knowledge to keep this story balanced. Thanks to all for your advice and guidance and good friendship.

The author would like to thank Rayna Favinger, Kym Kegler, Naveen Mallikarjuna, S. Damon Sinclair, and Thomas "Doc" Sweitzer and Tam Heckel for their assistance and generosity during the writing of this work as well.

Contributions were also made by JJ Balaban, Marc Berzenski, Ezra Billinkoff, Lisa Cabanel, Jeffrey Confer, Michael Conway and Meghan Sadler-Conway, Peter B. Crabb, Peter and Terry Ellis, Chris Mottola, John Nelson, Raymond C. Noll and Deb Marciano, Bert Schrevelius, Jessica Shamash, Elaine Shocas, Jeremy Sykes, Rick and Michele Torres, Bill Wachob, and Kent Weber.

Last but really first, the author wishes to thank Charlotte Conway for her grace and understanding. Without her help and support, this novel would only be a dream.

Behind the darkness is another day.
Behind the day is more darkness
And another day...

—Johnny Cocteau,
from the *Blue Monday Sessions*

1

She glanced at the screen on her iPhone and groaned. It was 10:17 p.m. Exactly three minutes and twenty-one seconds since the last time she checked. Even worse, she had run out of people to call. No one was left on her speed-dial list.

She didn't like waiting. And it was getting late, so late that it felt like the entire night was slipping through her fingers. A total bust while all her other friends were having fun.

She took in a deep breath and exhaled, watching the vapor fog the windshield. She shivered in the cold night air. It was mid-December in Los Angeles. Twelve days before Christmas. Last week it actually snowed in Malibu. She had seen it on the news. Kids riding down the hills on pieces of ripped cardboard. Snowmen overlooking Santa Monica Bay. It seemed like the world was coming undone and no one on TV was saying anything.

She shook it off, found the keys on the dash, and fired up the engine. Checking the heat vent, she adjusted the driver's seat and tried to relax. After a while the fog began to clear from the windshield and she could see the motel and restaurant just past the Dumpster on the other side of the parking lot.

She could see the girls dressed in their sheer tops walking in and out of the place, the men eyeing them openly and hungrily as if they were riding cardboard sleds and had become little boys again. Faint bursts of laughter hidden in the wind began to push against the car. When she caught the scent of a wood fire, her eyes rose to the building's roof. A neon rooster was mounted to the chimney. Below the rooster another neon sign read COCK-A-DOODLE-DO, THE BEST CHICKEN PIECES IN L.A.!

She giggled, then caught herself. Two men were staring at her. They were leaning against the rail outside the restaurant, smoking cigarettes while they picked chicken out of their teeth. It didn't take much to guess that they were looking her way because this was the Cock-a-doodle-do, their stomachs were full, and now it was time for dessert. Even from a distance she could tell who they were and what they were. She moved her head into the shadows and looked at their low-rent faces. The creases on their foreheads and the deep lines around their eyes. Their cheap clothing from aisle seven at Wal-Mart. She wanted to tell them to stop looking at her. She wanted to tell them that she didn't fuck truck drivers or losers, only doctors and lawyers, movie stars and agents—but she didn't. Instead, she cracked open the window, fished her cigarettes out of her purse, and lit one. By the time she turned back, two blondes had approached the creeps and all four were purring.

Time to make nice, nice. Time to party and eat dessert. The best chicken pieces in L.A.

She watched them enter the motel—heard the door slam shut—dumbfounded that the Cock-a-doodle-do even existed. Nothing was hidden. One look and even the world's biggest loser could tell exactly what this place was. She had been sitting here for what felt like half an hour. Two cops had driven by. One even pulled into the lot and waited with the engine idling while his partner ran in for takeout.

For the love of money, she thought. Lots of money. Enough money to grease the wheel. Enough money to cook the chicken. And even more for that dessert.

She took another drag on her cigarette, carefully blowing the smoke out the window and hoping that she wouldn't catch hell for not stepping outside. Then she heard a truck pulling into the lot and smelled the exhaust. As the truck's fog lights swept through the car, she squinted.

It was a bright red Hummer, or maybe even a Land Rover. She couldn't tell through the glare, and either way, she hated both no matter what the color. She hated all SUVs and the stupid people who drove them. If she were cruising on the freeway right now and spotted the asshole, she'd give him the finger with the greatest pleasure.

SUVs were the reason it was fucking snowing in Malibu.

She listened to the oversized tires chewing up gravel as the machine lumbered by and pulled into a space somewhere behind her. The lights snapped off, then the gas-hungry engine died out. She could hear someone singing "Jingle Bells." A low, gruff voice cutting through the din. After a few moments the door opened and a man hopped out, but he didn't look much like Santa Claus.

The truth was that at some level he appeared handsome, even cute. He looked about six feet tall, maybe a little less, with short blond hair. And he was just about the right age for her, mid- to late thirties—the older type. But what she liked most about him was that he wasn't wearing a jacket in spite of the cold night air. All he had on was a pair of jeans and a T-shirt. She could see his muscles as he slung a bookbag over his shoulder. His tight stomach and sturdy legs, his smooth, tan skin. The more she looked at him, the more he reminded her of an actor she couldn't place. Someone on TV that had hit the wall, but bounced back on cable.

Rerun money.

She drew in smoke and tapped the ash out the window. The man must have noticed because he looked straight at her and flashed a dazzling smile. She couldn't tell the color of his eyes in the darkness, but she could see the spark. Before she could wave back he turned and crossed the lot, legging it toward the Cock-a-doodle-do.

He wasn't a doctor, she thought. And he didn't look like any lawyer she had ever seen before. Maybe not even a real actor. But he was hot. Totally hot.

She checked the time again, but didn't care anymore. Reaching for her iPhone, she fitted her earbuds in place and toggled through the menu. Late this afternoon she had downloaded the title track from the End Brothers new CD, *U All In?* When she found it, she hit PLAY, heard 187's voice and slipped the device into her pocket. Then she waved the smoke away from her face and got out of the car to finish her cigarette. Maybe she'd even smoke another one without worrying about what the smell was doing to the car.

> *U all in, pretty woman.*
> *U all in, little darl'n.*
> *That's right baby, u all in,*
> *'Cause u cheated on your daddy,*
> *And now u done.*

She listened as 187's brother, XYZ, began to chant— thinking about their rise to the top of the hip-hop charts. She took a last drag on the cigarette, rubbing the head against the Dumpster and tossing the butt in. Then she reached into her purse for a piece of gum and tossed the wrapper into the Dumpster as well.

And that's when she saw him.

The man who wasn't Santa Claus. The man who probably wasn't a doctor, or a lawyer, or even an actor living off rerun money. The hot man with short blond hair who got out of that fucking red SUV singing "Jingle Bells."

He was hiding in the shadows, staring at her. And he was close. He must have snuck around the row of cars when she turned her back. She could see the color of his eyes now, a vibrant blue, ice-cold and vicious. Even worse, he was holding something in his hand and pointing it at her. At first she thought it might be a squirt gun. But when he pulled the trigger, two barbs shot through the air right at her. She could see them clinging to her sweater. They looked like fish hooks, with two sets of wires running between her body and the gun. She could feel the fear. The confusion and panic freezing her in place. Her heart pounding as she scanned the parking lot and looked toward the Cock-a-doodle-do for help.

They were alone. All alone. Everyone was eating dessert.

The man started laughing at her, and then something

flashed through her body. The jolt. The juice. A bolt of lightning so painful that it felt like her body had been cut in half.

When she came to she was lying face down on the ground. The man rolled her over on her back as if she were roadkill. She couldn't move. Couldn't think. No matter how hard she tried—even with all her might—she couldn't scream. She couldn't even remember where she was.

She looked up and thought that she saw a jet lowering its landing gear in the black sky. When she turned back, the fish hooks were still clinging to her sweater, the wires tangled up with her iPhone. She saw the man holding the gun, staring down at her with those dead eyes of his. He said something she couldn't hear through her earbuds, but guessed from the look on his face that the news wasn't very good. Then he pulled the trigger again and she felt the electricity making a second jagged pass through her wrecked body and charred nerves.

When her mind finally bobbed back to the surface, she could see the man throwing her purse into the Dumpster. When he picked her up and tossed her into the backseat of his SUV, she couldn't feel anything. Not even the dread swimming through her stomach into her chest.

And then the SUV started chewing up gravel again. He was taking her away now. She looked through the window at the parking lot, but not much registered. After a moment she thought she saw someone hiding in the shadows between cars. If they were calling for help, she guessed that they were ten to fifteen minutes too late. But maybe it wasn't anyone at all. Maybe it was just a hope or a dream or a phantom born from the electricity inside her body that deadened everything.

The man turned from the front seat and smiled at her, but didn't say anything as he pulled out of the lot. Sensing that the truck was picking up speed, her eyes drifted back to the window. She could see that neon rooster on the roof. The Cock-a-doodle-do vanishing into the night. Another jet lowering its landing gear.

When the window went blank, she tried to turn off what

was happening and concentrate on her iPhone. She tried to use the music to gather strength. If she could just pull herself together and get moving again, she'd dial 911 and call for help. Maybe even push the door open and jump the hell out.

She listened to the music and tried to focus. She knew that the singer's legal name was Derek Williams, but he went by the number 187. His brother Bobby had changed his name to XYZ. She liked their voices. She liked them a lot. But about a mile or two down the road, 187 stopped singing, and so did XYZ. The track finally ended and the music ran out. . . .

2

Lena Gamble poured herself a fresh cup of coffee and walked it around the counter to the table in the living room. As she sat down, she took a first sip through the steam and gazed out the window at the city. It was two o'clock in the afternoon. The piping hot brew tasted rich and strong, with just enough kick to revive her. She had taken the day off and had done nothing but read the newspaper and listen to music. It was the first day she had worked at doing nothing in a long time and she was reveling in the vibe.

The repairs to her house were finally complete, and she was celebrating. The roof that had blown away in the Santa Ana winds eight months ago had been replaced—the work guaranteed for fifteen years. The ground cover around the house had been pushed back twenty yards in case of another wildfire. And her brother's furniture—and all of the evidence that went with it—had been removed and replaced. Yesterday the painters finally cleared out. All that remained was the smell of fresh paint and polyurethane. Nothing was left but silence. Emptiness. That feeling that she wished David was still with her. Still here to live and play his music in the small home they once shared on top of a hill overlooking Hollywood and the city of Los Angeles.

She turned and looked into the bedroom. Through the far window she could see the two-story garage on the other side of the drive. Just after moving in her brother had converted the space into a state-of-the-art recording studio, attributing the success of his band's third CD to the acoustics. But that was all over now. The studio had been dark for nearly six years. As her eyes fell away from the building, she wondered about the word *closure*—who invented it and why. It was one of the few words that had no meaning for her. No definition or purpose.

Lena realized that the reason she was probably thinking about all this was because last night had been the first night she hadn't slept in the upstairs guestroom since she closed the Romeo murder case and solved her brother's homicide. It had taken an entire bottle of wine to block out the memories and knock her down. But she'd slept through the night in her new bed without dreams, or nightmares, or any of the ingredients that taunted her and seemed to go with the word *closure*.

She had been dealt the low card. She knew that. Her brother's murder had been senseless. Something she would walk with for the rest of her days. But now it was time to turn the next card over. Time for a new table and another game. Time to fight the urge to cash out.

She pushed aside the newspaper, opened the slider, and stepped onto the porch. The winds had picked up, drying out the city after ten straight days of heavy rain. In spite of the sun raking the basin from downtown to the ocean, the temperature probably wouldn't climb out of the forties. Still, the view from the top of the hill this afternoon was stunning. The entire city appeared clean and polished, glistening in a wet light. Although she didn't heat the pool, vapor was rising out of the water and drifting toward the sun in a flush of color. She couldn't keep her eyes off it. The peace. The illusion of peace in the city so many people wanted to call their home.

She wondered how long the illusion would last. There had already been 478 homicides in Los Angeles this year. With only eighteen days left on the calendar, she wondered if they'd beat five hundred and expected that they probably would. Over the past eleven months, the prison population had reached 173,000 and become the twenty-fourth largest city in the state. Bigger than Pasadena, even though it was a city without a name, a football game, or even its own parade.

She wondered if the illusion of peace had the power to last.

The heat clicked on, the newspaper sailing off the table from the outdoor breeze. Lena stepped inside and shut the slider. As she picked up the paper, she noticed a photograph she'd missed on page three of the California section. A mansion in Beverly Hills was under a foot of snow. After thinking about what happened in Malibu last week, she started reading the article and realized that the photograph wasn't a result of the storm and hadn't been doctored by a special-effects house in Burbank. The snow was part of the city's grand illusion, manufactured and blown over the house and yard because the owner was rich and he wanted to give his kids a white Christmas. Instead of spending the holiday in the mountains, the house and yard would be sprayed with new snow every day at a cost of ten thousand dollars a pop. Lena did the math. The price tag for a white Christmas in Beverly Hills topped out at a cool $120,000. By all appearances, the illusion everyone knew as L.A., and the insanity that went with it, remained intact.

Her cell phone began ringing from its charger on the counter. Turning over the newspaper, she got up and checked the display before picking up. It was her supervisor, Lt. Frank Barrera from the Robbery-Homicide Division, calling on her day off.

"Good news, bad news," he said. "You cool, Lena?"

"I'm good. What's up? I can barely hear you."

"Hold it a second. Let me close the door."

Barrera was whispering. Lena spotted her coffee on the table and took another sip as she thought it over. Her supervisor's desk sat out in the open at the head of the bureau floor. If he needed to close a door, that meant he was in the captain's office and didn't want to be overheard.

For the past eight months, Lena had been fed a steady diet of Officer Involved Shooting cases. OIS investigations were time consuming, involved a lot of paperwork, and had nothing to do with why she loved being a cop. Even worse, the orders to pull her out of the normal case rotation were coming directly from the chief's office on the sixth floor. Lena understood that it was political fallout, that she was being punished for how the Romeo murder case shook out. That the last domino to fall had worn a badge, and the department's reputation had taken another hit. But what troubled her most was that the OIS cases didn't seem to have an end. The new chief Richard S. Logan, his adjutant Lt. Ken Klinger, and the bureaucrats on the sixth floor couldn't seem to let it go. After all this time she still didn't have a partner. And she was beginning to worry that the rumors sweeping through the division might be true. That the barrage of OIS cases would never end because they were waiting her out. Trying to make things hurt until she asked for a transfer, or even better, decided to quit.

Barrera came back on, his voice clearer but still anxious.

"Something's come up," he said. "A dead body in Hollywood."

"Why me?"

"Because you're close. The victim was found half a block north of Hollywood Boulevard. There's an alley between Ivar and Cahuenga."

"Behind Tiny's."

"That's right. The alley behind the dive bar."

Lena had started to reach for a pen, but stopped. There was no need to write down the location. She had worked out of Hollywood both as a cop and a detective before her promotion to the elite Robbery-Homicide Division last February. She knew the neighborhood, even the bar and alley off Ivar. The crime scene was in the heart of the city, just one block west of Vine.

"Do we have a name?" she asked.

"I don't have any details. All I know is that Hollywood's already at the location, and that they're gonna pass the case over to us."

Barrera was an ally. Catching the tremor in his usually steady voice, she sat down on a stool at the counter. Homicide investigations were usually handled by detective bureaus at the local level. For a crime to bounce up to RHD, the case was either high profile or particularly egregious.

"Why us, Frank?"

"It's bad, Lena. Real bad. It's a girl and she's all fucked up."

"So, after eight months I'm back in the rotation because I'm close."

Barrera cleared his throat. "That's the bad news. That's the reason I called, Lena. The order came directly from the chief. I thought it was another OIS case like all the rest, but this time it's different."

"Why?"

"That's what got me thinking. Either he's getting pressure from outside to use you, or it's some kind of . . ."

Trap, Lena thought. Her lieutenant didn't need to finish the sentence. She got it. The chief wanted her out and was hoping something might push her closer to the door. This case could be the fucking door.

"What about a partner?" she asked.

"You're on your own. I'll make Sanchez and Rhodes available if you need them, but you're flying solo. Your orders are to report directly to the chief and his adjutant."

"Klinger?"

"Yeah, Klinger. I just e-mailed you a copy of the chief's schedule for the day. He wants to be briefed after you've had a look at the crime scene. Doesn't matter what time it is. He wants a report in person as soon as you're done. Even if you've gotta wake him up in the middle of the fucking night, you need to show your face. You need to be there."

"I'm okay with that."

"Lena."

"Yeah?"

"I talked it over with Rhodes and told him not to bother you. But he's thinking the same thing I am."

"And what's that?"

"This smell's like yesterday's catch."

She turned away from the window and noticed that her fingers were trembling slightly.

"When I picked up, Frank, you said good news, bad news. When does it start to get good?"

He laughed, trying to cheer her up. "The crime scene's in Hollywood. You used to work with Pete Sweeney. He's your old partner, right?"

"Yeah."

"Well, Sweeney and Banks got the call. They already know it's your case. They'll work the day with you, then back off. You cool?"

She nodded, then remembered that she was on the phone. She was thinking about the sixth floor at Parker Center and looking through the doorway at her gun on the bedside table. A Smith & Wesson .45 semiautomatic. The sun was low in the December sky and had moved to the other side of the house. She could see the rays of light feeding through the window, her pistol awash in red and gold. She had killed a man this year, in the line of duty. A shot made as she reached the end of the road. She thought about it every day, that view into the abyss.

"I'll be fine," she said.

Barrera lowered his voice. "Good," he said. "Then go slow. Go safe. And keep me in the loop."

3

L ena tossed her briefcase on the passenger seat, jumped into her Honda Prelude, and fired up the engine. Adjusting the heat vents, she flipped the radio and found KROQ. But before she could even get the volume turned up, her cell phone began vibrating and she checked the display again. This time the news would be wall-to-wall bad. The call was coming directly from Chief Logan's office at Parker Center.

"This is Lieutenant Klinger, Gamble. Are you at the crime scene yet?"

She shrugged. Klinger had to know that Barrera just made the call to her, so this wasn't about information. This was about something else.

"I'm leaving now, Lieutenant."

"You need to hurry, Detective. Shift to a higher gear."

This is the way it would be, she thought: Klinger and the sixth floor watching everything she did from a spot somewhere over her shoulder. She wanted to tell him that there was no place in a murder investigation for micromanagers or know-it-alls. That crimes were created in the imagination and that's where they were solved. But she didn't say anything at all. As she listened to Klinger repeat just about everything Barrera had said ten minutes ago, she realized how little she knew about the man. Their paths rarely crossed. Klinger was about forty with fifteen years on the force. From what she'd heard around the division, he considered himself an expert at crime detection even though he had little if any experience as an investigator in the field. Instead, Klinger spent most of his career working outside Parker Center for the Internal Affairs Group, renamed by Chief Logan and placed under the supervision of the Professional Standards Bureau. There wasn't a working cop in any division that didn't have a natural distrust for IAG no matter what they called it these days. And Lena was as surprised as everyone else that the chief made Klinger his adjutant when he took the job. The chief may have been drafted from another city, but he had to be aware that the morale of the department was in play. No matter what Klinger's talents might or might not be, it didn't seem like the right move.

Her mind surfaced. Klinger had asked her a question, but all she caught was attitude.

"You there, Gamble? You still with me?"

"I'm here, Lieutenant."

"Then answer the question. Do you have a copy of the chief's itinerary or not?"

"I'm all set," she said.

"Then you know how to find us no matter what time it is. Get to the crime scene, Detective, and report back ASAP. The chief's keeping a close eye on this one. He wants to be kept up to speed on every aspect of the investigation. Is that clear? Every report. Every lead."

"Is there something I should know, Lieutenant?"

He hesitated a moment, as if he hadn't expected the question and was working from a script. "Every case matters," he said finally. "This is no different than any other investigation, Gamble."

Lena understood what Klinger was saying because she lived it. But something in the adjutant's voice didn't ring true. Not by a long shot. It suddenly occurred to her why the chief might be paying so much attention to this one.

It was the murder rate. He didn't want it to reach five hundred on his watch. He didn't want the black mark on his reputation. Yesterday they had been thirteen bodies away from the gold ring. Now they were only twelve.

It was spin.

The thought of it made her sick and she wanted to end the call. This was about appearances, not people. Numbers instead of lives. The chief and his adjutant weren't thinking about the victim at all. They wanted the case closed quickly so that they could shift the focus with the press. If the chief was asked about the murder rate, he could point out that the number of cases solved had risen. He could manipulate the dialogue, and sweep the murder rate and the victims that went with it under the rug.

"Anything else, Lieutenant?" she said.

"Just one thing, Gamble. You're a Los Angeles police officer. Act like it. Live the part."

She heard the phone click. Klinger had hung up on her.

A moment passed. She closed the phone, gazing across the drive at her house. A light breeze was pushing east and she could hear the palm trees rustling over the sound of the engine. She thought about why she wanted to be a cop. All the reasons she had signed up. She knew that she could handle this. No matter what she was feeling right now, she could handle this.

She switched off the radio, pulled out of the drive, and started down the twisting hill toward Hollywood. Opening the windows, she let the cold wind beat against the seats until the rhythm finally changed and any thought of Klinger dissipated in the rearview mirror. She could feel the anticipation of working a real case again. But she could also feel the fear.

The road straightened out when she hit Gower Street. As she passed the Monastery of the Angels, she glanced at the statue of the Virgin Mary on the hill, then grit her teeth and floored it all the way to Franklin. A few minutes later, she was rolling down Hollywood Boulevard and making the turn onto Ivar Avenue.

She could see the coroner's van pulling behind a row of black-and-white cruisers parked in the middle of the street. Yellow crime scene tape had been stretched across the sidewalk from the corner on Hollywood all the way up Ivar to Yucca Street. The Scientific Investigation Division truck was already here, backed into the alley and blocking the entrance. When Lena glanced across the street and spotted a news van and the video camera that came with it, she understood why. The SID truck had been placed strategically to hide the view.

She turned back to the road. It looked like the lot across from the Knickerbocker Hotel had been taken over by the investigation. When she spotted a cop with a clipboard at the entrance, she signed in and found a place to park.

That feeling in her chest was back, along with a moment of self-doubt that flickered off and on like a lightbulb ready to blow. As she started down the sidewalk with her briefcase, she glanced at the hotel. Marilyn Monroe and Joe DiMaggio had spent their honeymoon at the Knickerbocker. Elvis Presley had stayed there while shooting *Love Me Tender.* But that was a long time ago. Now it was a senior-citizen residence for Russian immigrants in a neighborhood that had hit the skids and needed a shot in the arm.

Someone called out her name. When she looked across the street she noticed that another news van had arrived. A third was waiting for the light to change at the corner. She looked for a familiar face, but didn't see one. As she turned back, she realized that it had been Ed Gainer, the lead investigator from the coroner's office. He was waving at her from inside the van.

"I'll be there in a minute," he said. "You hear anything?"

"Just the word *Go.*"

He nodded, acknowledging the media. "The chief's office made the call over the radio. Can't believe they didn't use a land line. They should know better."

Lena shrugged. Of course they knew better. Everyone who carried a badge did. If a radio was used, then the newsrooms were listening.

She swept past the SID truck, wondering why the chief and his adjutant wanted the press here and thinking about the word *trap* again. But as she entered the alley, it almost seemed like someone had turned off the lights. The entire space was cast in a deep blue shade, the air thick with fragrant smoke from the grill at Tiny's. Waving the smoke away, she spotted her old partner, Pete Sweeney, standing with Terry Banks halfway up. A handful of criminalists from SID were waiting off to the side as a burly figure with coffee-and-cream skin worked the crime scene with his Nikon and a motor drive. The photographer was Lamar Newton, another friend and ally she knew she could count on.

As Lena approached, she followed the path of the camera lens until it became blocked by a trash Dumpster. Picking up her pace, she looked back at the two homicide detectives from Hollywood. Although Sweeney was a big, wide man with an extra-easy manner, he appeared extra pale and unable to stand still. Terry Banks seemed just as uneasy, the rich color of his ebony skin and buffed head misted with perspiration in spite of the cool breeze.

Sweeney waved her closer. But when her view finally cleared the Dumpster, she didn't see a dead body on the ground. Just five green trash bags, the one up front ripped open.

"I'm sorry you caught this one, Lena. Real sorry."

Sweeney's voice was barely audible. All she could hear was the din of the city, cut against the rhythm of that motor drive.

She looked back at the trash bag. It didn't take much to figure out what was inside. Something horrific. Something so horrific the case was bouncing up to RHD.

Sweeney gave her a nudge and pointed to the black-and-white cruiser parked just behind them. A teenager was sitting in the backseat. The door was open, the boy handcuffed. His hair was long and brown, and Lena could tell from his soiled clothes and worn-out shoes that he was homeless. When he turned to look at her, she caught the zombie eyes and guessed that he was either a religious fanatic or a drug addict. When she saw his teeth rotting to the gum line, she knew that his drug of choice wasn't Jesus. It was crystal meth.

"The kid spent the day on planet X and worked up a real good appetite," Sweeney said. "Best we can figure, he went

Dumpster diving about an hour ago—fished these bags out and thought he'd landed his next meal deal."

"Merry Christmas," Banks said. "Enough food to last the week."

"Who is he?" Lena asked.

Sweeney glanced at the cruiser. "Danny Bartlett, sixteen years old from Little Rock, Arkansas. Ran away last August and ended up here. Only when he opened the first bag he was still fucked up. No meal deal and no nirvana."

"Just his own demons," Banks said. "The fucker freaked out."

Sweeney nodded. "The guy who runs the kitchen over at Tiny's heard the kid lose it and made the call. That's as far as we got."

Lena turned back to the Dumpster. As Sweeney pulled a bottle of water out of his pocket and took a shaky swig, Ed Gainer from the coroner's office finally arrived. Lena reached into her briefcase for a clean pair of vinyl gloves.

"Let's take a look," she said.

They stepped forward as a group. Slowly, but with determination. When they finally reached the green trash bag, Lena pulled open the plastic, spotted the long blond hair, and tried not to flinch.

It took a moment for the horror to register. Another moment to catch her breath.

The demons were all here. A young woman in her early twenties. Her body had been dismembered. Everything cut up. Even though her face had been damaged, her eyes were wide open. A bright golden brown.

Sweeney and Banks stepped away. Lena could hear her old partner taking another swig of spring water like it was a hundred proof. Someone lit a cigarette. As she heard Gainer murmur something to his maker, Lena turned back to the victim and let it sink in. She understood that this was another look at a place where evolution had reversed course. She wouldn't find humanity here. This case would be another walk beyond the last outpost of civilization. And she was without a partner. Flying solo and on her own.

4

Her first impression had been the right one.

This was not a crime scene. The alley between Ivar and Cahuenga off Hollywood Boulevard was nothing more than the location for a body dump. A convenient location just three blocks from two separate entrances to the Hollywood Freeway. They could search every inch of the alley and find no evidence. Not a wallet, a purse, or anything that might resemble a murder weapon.

Lena glanced at a criminalist from SID packing up his kit as she thought it over.

There was no linkage. Nothing found here would point to the perpetrator because the victim hadn't been murdered here. Instead, this was the place where she had been thrown out with the trash.

Lena could feel the anger in her bones.

If the perpetrator had made a mistake, she only counted one. The plastic bag the victim had been placed in didn't match any other bag found in any Dumpster within five blocks. The plastic was a commercial grade, thicker than any normal trash bag and a good 30 percent larger. Lena's father had been a welder. The Denver skyline bore its shape and beauty from his work. She knew from experience that bags like this were common on construction sites. The extra-thick plastic held more weight and was less likely to rip open if the bag contained sharp objects like glass and nails, or in this case, a young woman's jagged bones.

Danny Bartlett, the runaway from Little Rock, had stoked up his crank pipe and just hit liftoff when he fished the five green bags out of the Dumpster. Lena had gone through the four remaining bags with a criminalist, then again with the kitchen manager at Tiny's. The contents were from the bar and had gone out at 2:00 a.m. last night. According to the employee who tossed the bags, the trash had been picked up the night before, the Dumpster completely empty. None of the tenants sharing the alley had seen anyone drive through since they arrived at work this morning. So, it was a safe bet that the perpetrator got rid of the body between 2:00 a.m. and sunrise, then made the short drive north and vanished into the freeway system.

Lena shook it off, stepping aside when she heard the coroner's van backing toward the Dumpster. Gainer's assistants had placed the trash bag inside a blue body bag and were zipping it up. Once the victim was loaded into the van, Gainer handed Lena a receipt for the girl's corpse. The name of the victim was listed as "Jane Doe No. 99." Gainer included the date, time, and address, but nothing else to distinguish her identity. Lena was surprised by the high number, but didn't say anything. Like the murder rate, the number of unidentified victims would reset to zero with the new year. Still, the slate would never be clean.

"You're in luck," Gainer said. "I just spoke with Madina. He's changed his schedule. His plane lands at noon in Burbank. You're in tomorrow afternoon despite the backup."

She had been hoping for this. She wanted Art Madina to perform the autopsy, but knew that he was attending a medical conference in New Haven. Because the victim had been dismembered, she was counting on the pathologist's expertise.

"Did you bring him up to speed?"

Gainer nodded. "I told him that we left her the way we found her. That what's left of her is still inside the bag."

Gainer's voice trailed off. He had been on the job as a coroner's investigator for at least a decade. Lena figured that in those ten years he had seen all there was to ever see. Yet, she sensed something in his voice as he spoke about Jane

Doe No. 99 tonight. Something different in his eyes. Something she respected and admired in the man.

"We have to start at the beginning," she said.

"Madina knows that she's a Jane Doe. You're in good
hands. It's all set."

"Thanks, Ed. And thanks for hanging in this long."

"No problem. You know that, Lena. What happened to
Sweeney and Banks?"

"They took off with the kid. We're opening the streets
and shutting down."

They shook hands, then she watched him climb into the
van and drive off with the corpse. As she turned back to
the alley, she shivered in the cold night air and reached inside her jacket for the chief's itinerary. This was the first
time in the past six hours that she had thought about the
chief or his adjutant. For six hours she had been working for
the victim, free of the weight of department politics. She
unfolded the paper and moved beneath a street light. According to the schedule, Chief Logan was still at Parker
Center. The Police Commission was holding another emergency meeting on gang violence. Lena remembered seeing a
flyer posted outside the captain's office. A proposal was on
the table that called for the appointment of a gang czar, with
$1 billion to be spent on a Marshall-like plan that included
gang intervention programs and economic development.
Because half the homicides in Los Angeles were now attrib-
utable to gang violence, and that violence was spilling into
the wealthiest neighborhoods in the city, this was a serious
meeting and the chief would be tied up until ten or eleven. If
she left now and lucked out with traffic, she might be able to
catch him before the meeting ended.

She slung her briefcase over her shoulder and started down
the alley. As she stepped around the SID truck, she heard the
press shouting questions at her from across the street but
ignored them. The air felt raw and she couldn't wait to get
the heat on. When she finally reached her car and lit up the
engine, her cell phone started vibrating and she checked the
display.

The call was from Denny Ramira, the one and only reporter who knew her cell number. Ramira worked the crime beat for *The Times*. Even though they shared a certain history, she was reluctant to take the call. She stared at the phone for a while, then changed her mind and flipped it open.

"I know this is out of line," he said. "But I'm freezing my balls off out here and it looks like you guys are packing up. You've got nothing to say, right?"

"You're a mind reader."

"But this is *your* case, right, Lena?"

Something about the question seemed odd. Even out of place. She sat back in the seat, thinking it over.

"It's your case, right?" he repeated.

"What's going on, Denny?"

"I'm not sure. I got a heads-up about the murder. My contact wanted to make sure I knew you got the case."

"Who's your contact?"

Ramira hesitated. "Just some guy I know. But everybody out here got the same call. The question is *why*."

If it had been a multiple-choice question, none of the answers seemed very good. Still, this wasn't her main concern right now.

"Gotta go, Denny."

"Yeah, sure. I'm heading downtown to Parker Center. Maybe I can catch the end of that meeting. Maybe the night won't be a total bust."

Lena winced. "Maybe you can touch base with that guy you know."

She closed her phone before he could respond, hoping she wouldn't run into him at Parker Center. Pulling out of the lot, she made a left to avoid the media, then looped around the block and worked her way down to Gower and Sunset. She had skipped dinner, the view of the victim's lifeless eyes staring back at her from that trash bag still way too vivid. But she needed something. As she pulled into the lot at Gower Gulch, she didn't see a line at Starbucks and ran in. Five minutes later, she was back on the road, toggling through recent calls until she found Howard Benson's number. Benson had been a classmate at the academy and now worked in the Missing Persons Unit. Once they determined that the victim couldn't be identified, Benson had been her first call. But that was more than three hours ago and she hadn't heard from him. After six rings, he finally picked up.

"Sorry, Lena, but you didn't really give me much to go on."

"I'll have more tomorrow," she said. "I was just hoping something in the database would jump out."

"A white female in her twenties with blond hair goes missing in Southern California. I've got a lot of those. Nothing's jumping out."

Lena didn't say anything. The number she had dialed wasn't Benson's cell phone. It was his office number, and he sounded moody and tired.

"Lena, I'm sorry. All I'm saying is that we need more."

"What about limiting the search to the last twenty-four to forty-eight hours?"

"I tried that, but it's still a long list. Lots of kids come to southern California. And a lot of them are runaway females with blond hair. Only they're not living the dream. They're on the streets doing the nightmare."

Lena thought it over as she accelerated up the freeway entrance and hit the 101 heading downtown. If Jane Doe was murdered last night, then it was too early. A Missing Persons Report wouldn't be filed for another day, if a report was filed at all.

"I'm jumping the gun on this, Howard. I know that. I was just hoping for a little luck."

"We'll talk after the autopsy. I'm sure we can narrow it down. Height, weight—something will turn up."

"Thanks, Howard."

She tossed her phone onto the passenger seat and took a sip of coffee. It was hot and strong, and she needed it right now. She saw the long string of brake lights begin to glow through the windshield. Then the traffic slowed down to a crawl and finally stopped. Benson had triggered an unwanted memory without knowing it. Lena had been a sixteen-year-old runaway, along with her younger brother, David. After their father died, they had fled Denver before the Department of Human Services could scoop them up and dump them into the system. They had spent six months living in their father's car before they earned enough money to rent a small place of their own. They had left their childhoods in Colorado, and never turned back.

She took another sip of coffee. As the traffic started moving again, the memory vanished but not the loneliness. It was such an oppressive loneliness. So final and far-reaching. She tried to ignore it and to concentrate on the road.

The eight-mile drive downtown should have taken ten minutes, but turned into a grueling forty-five played out at ten miles an hour. By the time she found a spot to park in the LAPD garage and jogged across the street to Parker Center, it was almost eleven and people were beginning to file out of the meeting room on the first floor.

She pushed her way through the crowd. As she entered the room, she spotted the chief and his adjutant getting up from their seats. By Lena's count four of the five civilian commissioners were still here, fielding informal questions from the press and the thirty to forty people who stayed. But it seemed as if an energetic man with gray hair was getting most of the attention tonight. When he turned, Lena realized that it was Senator Alan West. West had been appointed to the commission by the mayor and approved in a unanimous vote by the City Council in an attempt to regain public trust in the department. He was three years in on his first five-year term. Although there was talk that West might make another run at politics, Lena had read in the newspaper that he thought his work overseeing the police department was just as important. While the chief handled day-to-day operations within the department, a civil rights attorney, a former mayor, two criminal defense attorneys, and Senator Alan West defined department policies.

Lena turned back to the chief. He was beckoning her forward. When she glanced at Klinger, he pointed to the alcove at the head of the room. Although she still wondered why the chief had picked Klinger as his adjutant, tonight they looked like bookends. Both men obviously worked out, their bodies lean, straight, and military tight. And their grooming was immaculate, verging on overprocessed, their hair short and gray. The only difference was in their eyes. Klinger's were a soft, even wounded brown without much catch. The chief's gave definition to his chiseled face and intelligence, but were as dark as night and at times uncomfortable.

She stepped around the conference table and entered the alcove, wishing she had better news. When Klinger started to say something, Chief Logan silenced him with a short wave of the hand.

"Let's hear it, Gamble. Who's your suspect?"

"We've got a long way to go," she said. "I know that's not what you want to hear, Chief. But that's the way it is. We're starting from scratch. Zero."

"What about witnesses?"

"We interviewed every shop owner on the block. Every employee. There aren't any witnesses."

She couldn't get a read on him with those eyes. All she knew was that the chief didn't take the news the way she thought he would. It was almost as if he'd been hit in the chest and had the wind knocked out of him. But his wheels were turning. She could see him thinking something over. If he'd been a suspect in an interrogation room, she would have guessed that he was guilty of something and holding out.

He shot her another penetrating look. "Then you don't even know who the victim is."

"We didn't find any ID."

"What about her clothing?"

Lena shook her head, remaining silent. The victim wasn't wearing any clothing.

"Here are my concerns, Detective. I don't want this to be a long, drawn-out case. If you don't have anything in the next forty-eight hours, chances are you won't have anything ever. You know that as well as I do. Your chances for success go to shit by fifty percent."

Lena didn't need the chief to give her the odds. When she glanced away, she saw Denny Ramira enter the meeting room and approach Senator West. From the way they shook hands, she guessed that they knew each other.

The chief must have noticed the reporter as well. When Lena turned to him, he was standing so close she instinctively took a step back.

The chief lowered his voice. "I don't want to read about this investigation in the newspaper, Detective. I don't want to see it on TV. You pull anything, and I mean anything like that, and you're out. All the way out. So far out nobody in law enforcement ever hears from you again. Do you understand?"

She gave him a long look.

"You're either a company man," he said. "Or you're a man without a company. You get the logic, Detective? Do you realize how serious this is? What will be tolerated and what won't?"

"I get it, Chief."

"This isn't another OIS case. This is a homicide, and I want a suspect. I need an arrest."

The chief came up for air, then Klinger stepped forward as if it were a tag-team match. Lena suddenly realized who made those calls to the press. It had to be Klinger, doing everything he possibly could to make things more difficult for her.

"We want reports," he said. "The chief's office is to be copied on everything. No one cares if it takes twice as long. Just do your job and do it by the book, Gamble. *We're* your partner now. And we're not a silent partner. You want to make a right turn, you ask before you make it. You want to go left, make sure you've got the order and it's signed by a judge. We're your shadow, is that clear? Please acknowledge that we have had this conversation and you understand what was just—"

Klinger suddenly became quiet. Everyone turned. Senator West was standing at the entrance, starring at them with a quizzical expression across his broad face.

"Sounds like a serious discussion, Chief. I hope I'm not interrupting."

Lena could tell in an instant that West wasn't sorry at all. From the look he gave the chief and his adjutant, it seemed they probably didn't get along. She remembered hearing a rumor that the chief's appointment had not been a unanimous decision by the police commission. That the water had been cloudy, and one of the five members voted against his appointment. Lena wondered if the lone vote of dissension came from West. From the look on Chief Logan's face, and Klinger's, they had heard the rumor and come to the same conclusion.

"We're finished here," the chief said. "It's no interruption at all, Senator."

"I'm glad, because I'm a fan of Detective Gamble."

West turned away from the chief and gazed at Lena. His eyes were clear and easy and filled with a certain wisdom.

"When Denny Ramira pointed you out," he said, "I couldn't believe that you were here. I followed the Romeo murders just like everybody else. I've wanted to meet you for a long time."

He smiled and reached for her hand. She could feel the tension in the room. But then Klinger turned away from the senator and stepped out of the alcove. As the chief began to follow his adjutant, he stopped at the entrance and shot Lena another look.

"There's been a change, Detective. The autopsy's scheduled for tomorrow morning—eight sharp—not sometime in the afternoon."

"What about the pathologist?"

"We can't waste time. I told Madina that if he needs to sleep, he'd better do it on the plane."

The chief didn't wait for a response from her. Instead, he marched through the meeting room and followed Klinger into the lobby. West watched them exit, then turned back and spoke in a voice that wouldn't carry.

"This is Los Angeles, Detective. Chiefs come and go. But

now more than ever, we need people like you to fill the ranks and take charge."

Lena didn't really follow politics, but had read enough to know that West was one of the good guys. The senator obviously had overheard the chief and his adjutant giving her the goods. He had interrupted them in order to help her. While she appreciated the gesture, he was slighting her commanding officer. No matter how great the compliment, it would have been out of line to respond. Instead, she was thinking about the autopsy. Only the chief could have forced Madina to shorten his trip in New Haven. Only the chief could make it happen so quickly. She wasn't upset. She was grateful. She was thrilled.

Her mind surfaced. Something glistened in the light, and her eyes flicked down the senator's jacket. He was wearing a pin on his lapel. Not the obligatory depiction of the flag, but something far more personal.

"Would you like to see it?" West asked.

She nodded. "The firefighters. They gave it to you after nine-eleven."

He flashed a warm smile—his blue eyes sparkling—then removed the pin and handed it to her.

"It was a gift," he said. "I wear it every day. It's something I'll never forget."

Lena rolled the pin over in her palm until the gold caught the light. It was a three-dimensional work of art depicting an LAFD fire engine set at ground zero in New York City. Nine firefighters stood on top of the truck raising a ladder toward the sun. Lena remembered when West had been honored by the Los Angeles Fire Department because her entire division participated in the ceremony. But she had never seen the pin before in real life, only pictures of the bright red and gold object printed in the paper. It was handmade by an artist living in South Pasadena. It was a very special pin given to someone who not only bent over backwards to help the rescue operation after the attack, but who also fought to provide medical treatment and financial aid years after when rescue workers started getting sick and hadn't received their due.

The pin was a gift to someone who didn't bounce from one story to the next like a cable TV reporter trying to steal money and ratings. It was a gift to someone who hadn't forgotten what happened and never would.

Lena passed back the pin and watched the senator carefully return it to his lapel.

"I'm going to ask you for a favor, Detective. And I already know that it's something you won't like." He had that quizzical smile going again as he passed her his business card. "I'm spending more time here than I am in Washington," he said. "If I can ever do anything for you, call me and I'll try my best."

"What's the favor? How can I help?"

"The press is out there. And I want a picture of me and you standing together for my office. Ramira's photographer would take that picture and send me a copy. But don't think that I'm naive. Everybody else in that room will take the picture, too. And that's why I said that you're not going to like it, but I am."

Lena thought it over. The senator raised an eyebrow, his warm smile becoming infectious. After a moment, she nodded.

5

Lena hustled down the stairwell at the coroner's office, too anxious to wait for the elevator. When she hit the basement, the smell of disinfectant and decomposing flesh hit back. Wincing at the harsh odor, she rushed past the long line of dead bodies waiting against the left wall without looking at them.

She hadn't been able to sleep last night, tossing and turning, and staring out the bedside window. She knew her anxiety came from the investigation being stuck in first gear. The heat from the sixth floor and the lack of evidence. Her inability to identify the victim or get past go. She couldn't shake the frustration, and now she was feeding on it.

She stepped inside the changing room. Pulling the scrubs over her slacks, she grabbed a pair of booties and sat down on the bench. When the door swung open, she looked up and saw Art Madina pulling the mask away from his face.

"How was New Haven?" she asked.

"A bit frightening."

"Lots of slide shows?"

"The conference was about the food supply. The Feds have cut the number of inspectors by half because of the war. No one's minding the store."

"What's the food supply have to do with pathology?"

"For the past twenty-five years, the first thing we looked for was HIV, Lena. But now it's Mad Cow disease. You can't kill it by cooking because it isn't alive. And there's no cure. No drug cocktail to see the patient through."

"It's that serious?"

"Like I said, no one's minding the store. You eat much beef?"

She gave him a look, then noticed the jar of Vicks Vapo-Rub on the shelf.

"Pass me the ketchup," she said.

Madina smiled, handing over a pair of goggles, a surgical mask, and the jar of Vicks VapoRub. He was a slim man, no older than forty, with bright, curious eyes and black hair cropped so short it probably qualified as a buzz cut. Madina had become the DA's favorite when presenting evidence at trial. Lena noted his one-day beard and the dark circles cutting into his cheeks. Although he may not have had much sleep last night, she still felt lucky that he was performing the autopsy.

"What did the chief say?" she asked.

Madina shrugged. "The plane landed at six-thirty. I didn't bother going home. The X-rays are done. She's on a table and everything's ready to go. You're a half-hour early."

"Yeah, I know."

They pushed open the doors. Three autopsies were under way in the same room with a staff photographer moving from one dead body to the next. Lena could hear a technician working the skull saw. The zap lights buzzing off and on as bugs hit the dense air, then crashed and burned. She took a deep breath, concentrating on the gel she had wiped beneath her nose. The mentholated odor wasn't working today and she wondered why. When she gazed across the room, she realized that the body closest to the rear door was in a state of heavy decomposition.

Autopsies were never easy. Not even when you really needed one.

Madina pointed to the far corner. Lena's eyes jumped ahead, and for a moment, she thought that they might have brought out the wrong corpse. The young woman lying on the steel operating table appeared whole, while the victim found in the trash bag had obviously been dismembered. But as she moved closer, Lena could see that Madina had pieced the parts together. The fit was so good, so tight, that by all appearances Jane Doe was a whole woman again. A twenty-plus-year-old woman with a small heart-shaped tattoo placed between her shaved vagina and her bikini line.

Lena counted the breaks where the body had been severed. Three in each leg, then cuts above the wrists, elbows, and shoulder sockets. After keying in on the decapitation wound, her eyes rose to the victim's face. Jane Doe No. 99 had been beaten, her face disfigured. Her soft brown eyes had been spared, but not much else. She was hard to look at, yet she seemed so vulnerable that it was difficult for Lena to turn away.

"Did you measure her?"

"Five-foot-seven," Madina said. "A hundred and twenty-two pounds. She's had a boob job and her belly button is pierced. The ring's over there on the table. I'm gonna guess that if we reconstructed her nose and cheekbones, she'd be beautiful. All-the-way gorgeous. And that whoever did this to her is very strong."

Lena stepped aside as Madina selected a scalpel and began opening the woman's chest. She remembered the first time she attended an autopsy. It had been in this room, and she found the process so difficult that she spent most of the time counting ceiling tiles. There were 729 before the lighting fixtures were changed last year. After that, the count dropped to 715.

Madina gave her a look, laying out the victim's lungs in an extra-large plastic container.

"She grew up in the city," he said. "Jane Doe's not a country girl."

"How can you tell?"

"The black spots on her lungs. Look at these carbon deposits. They're not from cigarettes. They're from air pollution. Thirty years ago, only a coal miner's lungs would've looked like this."

Lena examined the tissue. Jane Doe's lungs were pep-
pered with dark gray spots that had the look and apparent
texture of cinders.

"But she's young."

The pathologist laughed. "She's been breathing every day
for twenty years, Lena. Twenty years without a break. Why
do you think so many kids have asthma? It's not like it's a
mystery. Just follow the freeways."

Madina moved back to the body. Lena watched him complete the operation, then helped as he rolled Jane Doe's hands
with ink and made a copy of her palm and fingerprints.
Oddly enough, Lena thought that she could smell the clean
scent of the woman's perfume somehow rising above the
stench of the room. But the fragrance seemed to vanish as
quickly as it appeared. When they were finished—and the
house photographer made his final pass—the body was no
longer whole. No longer the sum of its parts. No longer a
pretty girl with her entire life ahead of her. As Lena gazed at
the victim's remains, she couldn't help but think of the murderer.

He had committed the ultimate violation and shown no
mercy.

"What about time of death?" she asked.

Madina shrugged off the question, then jotted something
down on his clipboard. "Yesterday," he said. "Right now
that's as close as I can get. But we've got a problem, Lena."

"That's one way of putting it."

"No, I mean we've got a *real* problem. This wasn't a sex
crime. And this wasn't done by some slime bag living on the
streets."

"What are you saying?"

Madina didn't answer her. Instead, he started piecing the
body back together until the breaks were almost invisible
and Jane Doe looked whole again.

"Let's start with the cause of death," he said. "There's a
laceration here on her neck. It's not just in any spot. The cut
was made in exactly the right spot."

Lena moved in for a closer look. "The right spot for what?"

"He didn't slice open the jugular vein. He went for the carotid artery. And he knew exactly where to find it."

"What's the significance?"

"You tell me."

"Arteries move blood away from the heart," she said. "Veins carry it back."

"Exactly. The man you're looking for cut the carotid artery because he wanted to move blood away from the heart. He wanted to drain the blood out of her body. You see the ligature marks around her legs and ankles. He hung her upside down and kept her alive, Lena. He kept her heart beating until she bled out. That's why I'm saying we've got a real problem."

Lena turned to the worktable and eyed Jane Doe's organs laid out in those oversized plastic containers. In every other autopsy she had attended, the internal organs were rich in color. Jane Doe's organs were a pale brown. It wasn't time that had changed the color. It was the lack of blood.

"You see it, don't you?" Madina said in an urgent voice. "Look at her liver. It should be a deep purple."

Lena glanced at the container, then turned back to the body. The killer bled her out while she was alive. She tried not to picture the moment, but the horror was sharp enough to cut through. This was a special kind of madness. A new brand drawn from the other side of the road.

"What can you tell me about who did this?" she said.

"I can tell you a lot. I can tell you almost everything you need to know except for his name and address."

She met his eyes, steady and even.

"Then you definitely think we're looking for a male."

"No question about it," he said, pointing to the ligature marks. "And he's strong. He was able to lift her by her ankles."

"What else?"

Madina pulled away his face mask. "He's a surgeon, Lena."

A moment passed—deep, and long, and rising out of the darkness. When Madina finally spoke again, his voice was tainted with bitterness and a mix of fear and disappointment.

The killer was one of his own. Someone who attended medical school and took the Hippocratic oath.

"He's a skilled surgeon," Madina said.

Lena remained quiet, watching the pathologist pull Jane Doe's body apart again as if the victim had become a mannequin.

"It's not easy cutting up a body, Lena. A lot of people try. More than you'd think. And most of them don't have a clue. They leave evidence behind. Hack marks. Saw marks. Ragged edges from the knife. Rips and tears that anyone could spot from a mile away."

Lena remembered her first impression of the body as she entered the operating room. Jane Doe's arms and legs fit together so well, she thought the pathologist had brought out the wrong corpse.

Madina pointed to the cut above the victim's left wrist, then the elbow. "This was done by someone who cared about what it looked like when he was finished. Only a surgeon would care about that because only a surgeon would be thinking about the scar."

"But she ended up in the trash. No one was supposed to find her. No one was supposed to see."

"That's irrelevant. The location for each cut is made exactly where it requires the least effort. He's a professional. There aren't any hesitation marks. See how straight they are. How clean. These are incisions, Lena. Incisions made by a skilled surgeon."

"So, what you're saying is that where she ended up doesn't matter. He wasn't thinking about it when he dismembered the body."

"Exactly. The two acts are unrelated. When he severed her hand away from the wrist, he was thinking about the incision and possible scar. He was keeping it clean and neat. It's in a surgeon's nature. His DNA. It's instinctual. He wouldn't know any other way."

"Because of his training," she said. "His experience. He's done amputations before."

"So many that I can't believe he didn't spend time over-seas. Iraq or Afghanistan. You don't get this good without practice. And this guy's had a lot of practice."

Lena took a step closer, gazing at the victim. The evidence was overwhelming. Jane Doe's body had been drained of blood and dismembered by someone who knew how to do it, and for whatever reason, had done it many times before. As she thought it over, a chill moved up her spine. Jane Doe's murder was performed by someone who liked it. Someone with a medical degree who cared about the quality of his work. . . .

6

Lena ordered an extra-large cup of Colombian, spotted an empty table by the far window, and cut across the room. Digging her laptop out of her briefcase, she found an outlet under the table, hit the power switch, and waited for the computer to boot up.

In spite of its close proximity to Parker Center, the Blackbird Café wasn't exactly a cop hangout. Nor did many tourists wander through the door. Instead, the café catered to artists and musicians who had migrated downtown over the past decade and sought a quiet place to sip what was probably the best cup of coffee in town. The place was hidden on a side street halfway down the block—an old brick building with vaulted ceilings that was originally built as a horse stable, served as an auto-repair garage for more than fifty years, and now had the look and feel of a community reading room. The lights were dim, the walls lined with books, paintings, and photographs. Last month a patron donated three prints by Minor White to the café's art collection, three views of the world cast in light and shadow that Lena couldn't stop looking at.

She had been a regular since her brother turned her on to the place after a gig at the Palladium. The Blackbird Café was open 24/7 every day of the year. Since her transfer from Hollywood to downtown, the place had become an oasis for her, and she needed it right now. One or two sips worth of high-end caffeine before she stepped back into the grind.

Klinger had called. Chief Logan wanted another briefing in an hour. Lena wasn't looking forward to the meeting and thought it a complete waste of time.

And the autopsy had been an ordeal. The condition of the victim, worse than anything she had ever experienced before. Lena had worked with Pete Sweeney at the homicide table in Hollywood for two and half years. Her introduction to the Robbery-Homicide Division ten months ago had been a brutal murder case with multiple victims.

But this one was different. A lot different.

As she thought it over, it was the murderer's expertise that made it different. The precision he exhibited with the knife. His obvious skills and physical strength. The cuts that weren't really cuts, but so well executed that Madina had called them incisions. It all pointed to a level of coldness and brutality that felt like it came from another world, a very dark and lonely world.

Lena glanced at her computer, still booting up. Lifting the lid off her coffee, she let the steam rise into her face and tried to forget about the foul odor she endured at the autopsy. The smell of death had permeated her clothes and ruined them. Even though she had showered and changed in the locker room at Parker Center, she could still smell it. Not in her clean pair of black jeans or her sweater, but lurking in the deepest recesses of her memory. She knew from experience that it would take two or three days, maybe even a week, before it faded into the background.

She took a first sip of coffee, glanced around the room, and turned back to her laptop. She had filed a preliminary report and created the murder book last night—a three-ring binder often called a *Blue Book* that would serve as the complete record for the case. But her concern right now was the chronological record. The program on her computer mirrored the first section in the murder book and amounted to a journal. Every step she made in the investigation—what she was thinking, planning, or had ruled out—would be included. And she wanted to update the file and print it so that she could give the chief and his adjutant copies when they met.

She had come up with the idea last night when she couldn't get to sleep. The only way to beat the micromanagers on the sixth floor was to flood them with paper. Keep them occupied with something tangible or nearly tangible so that she could work the case.

She checked her watch and started typing. After hitting the locker room, she had walked Jane Doe's fingerprints up to the Latent Print Section on the second floor. Someone must have prepped the way because SID agreed to make the run immediately. Lena was well aware of the backlog and assumed that the call to bump her to the head of the line had come from the chief, or even Klinger. Still, she would have the results within a day—not a week—and that's all that really mattered.

She wanted to push Jane Doe through the system as quickly as she could. Hit the speed bumps fast with the hope that just maybe something would shake out.

She wasn't counting on anything. She knew the odds of SID identifying the girl were handicapped. In order to get a hit, Jane Doe's fingerprints would already have to be in the system. One look at Jane Doe's clear brown eyes told Lena that she was an innocent. The chances of her committing a crime or working a job that required fingerprinting was just short of nowhere.

But at least she finally had an accurate physical description. Lena typed in the victim's height and weight from her notes jotted down at the autopsy. On the way over, she had made another call to Benson at Missing Persons and given him an update. Madina's office had already sent over the autopsy photos, including close-ups of the victim's belly ring and heart-shaped tattoo. Benson would make a run through the database and have results for her in an hour or two. But that only covered Los Angeles. The California Department of Justice would make a second, more extensive run. And with any luck, Lena would have their results in a couple of days.

She moved the cursor up to the menu bar and hit SAVE. When she reached for her coffee, she looked up and saw

someone walking toward her from the other side of the room.
It was Denny Ramira, the crime-beat reporter from *The Times*.

"What are you doing here, Ramira?"

"I saw you on the street," he said.

"You followed me?"

"Yeah. I've never been here before. Nice place."

"Don't make it a habit, okay?"

He smiled, still looking around. "Senator West digs you,
Lena. You made his day by taking that picture with him.
Did you see the paper?"

She shook her head. She had left the house early this
morning and didn't open the paper.

"You guys are friends?" she asked.

"His office is helping me research something on the side.
Maybe a book; we'll see. It's not that far along yet."

"A book about what?"

Ramira smiled again. "You might steal my idea."

"Yeah, Ramira. I've got a lot of time on my hands. I really
want to steal your idea."

"Okay, so I'll give you a hint. It's about crime. White-
collar crime. You know, the kind where nobody goes to jail
because everybody's rich enough to buy their way out."

Lena followed the reporter's gaze to her laptop. He was
trying to get a look at the screen, but his angle was off. As
he stepped to his left, she closed the file, shut down her computer, and started packing up.

"Sorry, but I'm not real sure I want to find my reports in
one of your stories."

"Hey, I wasn't looking. Besides, if you had anything real,
you'd give me a call. We've still got a deal, right?"

He gave her a look, and she shot it back at him. Ramira
was thin and angular, about her height, and probably five
years older. He was a handsome man with an intelligent face
framed by dark hair and a pair of glasses that seemed to
sharpen the light in his eyes. Although he may have been one
of the best reporters Lena had ever known, that didn't make
him any less dangerous. The deal he was talking about had
been struck after her last case. The doer had worn a badge,

and the brass on the sixth floor wanted to keep it buried at the expense of an innocent man's reputation. Lena needed an insurance policy and had given Ramira an exclusive "off-the-record" account of the investigation. Getting the story in print was the only way of ensuring that everyone involved lived up to the truth. When it was over—when the official record became straight and true—Ramira won an award, and Lena's plight with Chief Logan was born.

"What deal is that?" she asked. "You already got your story."

"You know what I'm talking about, Lena. You need me just as much as I need you. Even the senator said it last night. He saw Logan reaming you out. That's why he walked in on you and broke it up."

Lena slipped her computer into her briefcase without responding. Ramira checked the room, then sat down at the table and lowered his voice.

"You want me to say it straight out, then I will. You're in a rough business, Lena, and you need friends. Everybody knows that you're on the outs with the chief and his band of self-righteous Boy Scouts. It's all about your last case. You were right and he was wrong, and everything went down in public. I know that you didn't mean to embarrass him, but you did. The bottom line is that no matter how much he'd like to, he can't transfer you to the Valley and he can't fire your ass to oblivion. His hands are tied, and he can't get rid of you. But I'll bet he's thinking about it. I'd bet the city he spends a lot of time thinking about it. And that's why you need friends."

Lena relied on her ability to size people up quickly and accurately. As she stood up, she wondered if her read on Ramira had been off the mark.

"You need to chill," she said. "Take some time off. What you're implying is ludicrous."

"Is it, Lena? Like I said, you're in a rough business. Shit happens."

Ramira met her eyes. He looked tired and a little nervous. She wished that he hadn't followed her into the café.

7

As Lena crossed the lobby at Parker Center and started around the security line, one of the two cops behind the front desk called out her name. He lifted a package in the air, an eight-by-ten manila envelope.

"A messenger dropped it off five minutes ago," he said. "You saved me a trip upstairs."

"Thanks."

She glanced at the return address but didn't recognize the name. McBride. Navy Street. Venice Beach. None of it registered.

Stepping into the elevator, she hit the button to her floor, and took another look at the package. It was a padded mailer and she didn't think the contents felt like a book or CD. When the doors finally closed, the elevator shook and groaned and vibrated all the way up to the third floor.

Parker Center, aka the Glass House, was due to be leveled sometime in the next five years. Lena tried not to think about it because there was nothing she could do to make it happen any faster. Still, every time she stepped into an elevator, the question of her own personal safety crossed her mind. Parker Center hadn't survived the last earthquake, but city officials were saying that it did—pretending that it did. The replacement cost of the building was more important to city government than the safety of the people who worked here. At least that's the way it appeared to Lena as she did the math. The Northridge earthquake had rumbled through

Los Angeles almost fifteen years ago. The department would get a new building, but only after the people working here waited it out for a grand total of twenty years. For some, that was a life sentence. The length of their entire careers.

The doors opened and the thought vanished. Lena walked down the hall and around the corner, passing the lieutenant's desk at the head of the bureau floor. The Robbery-Homicide Division was comprised of twenty-four desks pushed together in four groups of six. Today was Friday, less than two weeks before Christmas, and it looked like just about everyone had left for lunch. Stan Rhodes was the only holdout, waving at her as he spoke with someone on the phone. She didn't see Lt. Barrera at his desk, or his computer, and guessed that he was working in Captain Dillworth's office across from the interrogation rooms. Captain Dillworth was taking an off-season Alaskan cruise with his wife, hoping to see the glaciers and polar bears before the ice melted and all the animals drowned. Although the crime logs had been moved upstairs to the Cold Case Unit, the only conference table on the entire floor was in his office, so he never locked the door.

Lena slid behind her desk, grateful that the bureau was nearly empty. She glanced out the window, still thinking about her conversation with Ramira. What he implied seemed so over the top. The chief and his adjutant may have given her a rough time last night, but that's all it was. That's all it had ever been for the past eight months. A steady diet of rough time. Not once had she ever sensed that it was anything more than that. Not once had she ever thought that she couldn't wait them out and survive with her career intact. She could still see Ramira measuring her after he finished. The fire in his nervous eyes.

She wondered why something so ridiculous was still on her mind. Why she found it troubling enough that it had followed her all the way to her desk.

She checked the time, then reached for her laptop. She still had fifteen minutes before her meeting. As the computer booted up, she found the tab on the back of the mailer and tore open the package. Holding the envelope to the window light, she gazed inside. And that's when she felt her pulse quicken.

It was an ID. Someone's driver's license. And there was something else caught in the corner of the mailer. At first, she thought it might be a key ring. But as she spread open the bubble wrap, she realized that it was a small storage device about the size of a cigarette lighter. Someone had sent her a USB flash drive.

She reached down for her briefcase, fishing out a pair of gloves. Pushing her laptop aside, she dumped the license and flash drive onto her desk. Then she flipped the ID over and zeroed in on the photograph. She noted the long blond hair. The soft brown eyes and high cheekbones.

Jane Doe No. 99 was no longer Jane Doe No. 99.

Her name was Jennifer McBride. And Art Madina had been right. If a reconstructed view of the victim's face had been necessary, it would have revealed a beautiful young woman.

Lena checked the return address on the mailer against the driver's license. Whoever sent the package used the victim's address. Jennifer McBride lived in an apartment on Navy Street, and had celebrated her twenty-fifth birthday less than two weeks before her death.

"Why are you wearing gloves?" Rhodes asked. "Is everything okay?"

She looked up. Rhodes was holding the phone against his chest and she could see the concern on his face. His partner, Tito Sanchez, had entered the room and was standing beside him.

"Where's Barrera?" she said.

Rhodes's eyes flicked to the captain's office in the alcove behind her, then moved back.

"Something's happened," she said.

Maybe it was the way she said it. Maybe it was Rhodes's instinctual ability to read her, their rekindled friendship, and that feeling in her gut that the case was about to lift off a blank page. Either way, Rhodes got rid of his call and within a few minutes, all three men were huddled around her desk. She brought them up to date, describing the location of the body dump in broad strokes. As she filled them in on the results from the autopsy, she pulled her computer closer and pushed the flash drive into the USB port. Then she clicked the drive icon and waited a beat to see what was inside.

It was a single file—a video file. Sanchez killed the overhead lights. Then everyone leaned closer as it began to play on her laptop.

The images were recorded at night and so degraded, Lena felt certain that the camera had been a cell phone. By all appearances, the photographer was more than nervous, hiding between two parked cars and unable to hold the lens still. The entire video only lasted five seconds, then looped back to the start and began playing again.

She could see a car parked in the shadows about twenty-five yards away. A building stood in the distance with a neon sign on the roof. A man with blond hair was tossing something in the Dumpster by the car, then turning toward the lens and bending over a large object on the ground. The man's face was blurred beyond recognition. The sign on the roof of the building, lost in digital noise. But as the shot ended, the last frame flashed a bright white. And in that instant, the large object on the ground took on definition.

The man was leaning over Jennifer McBride's body.

"Jesus Christ," Barrera said. "We've hooked a witness."

"Or they've hooked us," Rhodes said. "You think that was her purse going into the Dumpster?"

Lena glanced at McBride's license on her desk, then looked back at the screen as the video recycled to the beginning and the man tossed the object into the trash.

"That's her purse," Barrera said.

Lena agreed, her eyes riveted to the screen. When the man turned back toward the camera, she clicked the PAUSE button on the media player and the image froze. The man's face remained out of focus, but it was there. And he was wearing something around his neck. Something that glistened in the darkness. A medallion of some kind.

Barrera moved closer to the screen. "Madina thinks he's a surgeon?"

"Someone with military training," she said.

He shook his head, his face losing its color. "A doctor back from the war."

Barrera's voice died off. Lena could guess what he was thinking. After the autopsy, she had talked it over with Madina. If they were searching for a doctor with military experience, there was a good chance the man had passed through USC Medical Center. Since the beginning of the Iraq War, the Department of Defense had been training medical teams in the hospital's emergency room. Because of the city's high crime rate, this was the closest a surgeon could get to real combat experience. Saturday nights at the trauma center had all the living urgency of a mass-casualty war zone. More than two thousand people were carried into the hospital with knife or gunshot wounds every year.

USC Medical Center might be a step in the right direction, but they would need more than a guess or a hunch before they made it. Some way of narrowing down the man's identity.

Barrera glanced back at the video on the computer. "It looks like that could be a restaurant in the background. Any ideas where this is?"

"It could be anything," Sanchez said. "The quality eats shit."

Rhodes nodded. "We need to get this upstairs and see what SID can do with it."

Barrera stepped back, chewing it over and looking at Rhodes. "You and Tito are in court this week. You're on the same case, right?"

"We're due back at the courthouse in an hour."

"Who's the prosecutor?"

"Roy Wemer," Sanchez said.

Lena glanced at her watch. "And I'm ten minutes late for a meeting with the chief."

"About what?" Barrera asked.

"The autopsy."

"Forget it," he said. "We've got a victim and an address. You and Rhodes are on your way to Venice. Tito, you're going to the courthouse on your own. I'll run the video upstairs and check this driver's license, then talk things over with the chief. Anybody got an issue with that?"

Sanchez shook his head. "Shouldn't be a problem. I'm the lead anyway. I'll let Wemer know."

Lena gave Sanchez a look and knew that he meant it. Even more, she knew that he was used to it. Rhodes's sister had breast cancer. Over the last three months, Tito had been covering for him, working overtime while Rhodes took days off to drive up to her farm in Oxnard.

"What about the witness?" Rhodes said. "This video's only five seconds long. Whoever recorded it probably saw the whole thing from start to finish. And why is the envelope addressed to Lena? Why isn't there any postage?"

Barrera turned to her. "This didn't come through the mail room?"

"A messenger dropped it off at the front desk."

"I'll check on it," he said. "Now let's get started. Let's do it."

Lena met Rhodes's eyes. Everyone was in sync. But as she packed up, her thoughts returned to the victim—how she lived and who she was. Whether or not she had parents who might be waiting for her. A husband, or even a child. What it would be like to tell Jennifer McBride's family that she had been murdered. That their loved one had been mutilated by a madman.

Lena didn't need to eat lunch to keep going.

She jotted McBride's address on a piece of scratch paper, then looked over at Rhodes. He had returned to his desk for his keys and was getting into his jacket. He looked rough and ready and all wound up, just like she was. She could see it on his face.

8

They ran across the street into the garage. Rhodes pointed at the Crown Vic backed into a space beside the guard shack. The car looked like it had been to the body shop and returned before the job was done. It was primed, but not painted—the color of dusk, the color of junk—gun-metal gray.

"I'll drive down," he shouted. "You can bring us back."

They jumped in, and he fired up the engine. Hitting the strobes on the dash, he pulled onto the street and accelerated through the red light. Ten minutes later, they were rolling down the Santa Monica Freeway at a ragged eighty-five miles an hour. Bobbing and weaving their way through heavy traffic directly into the winter sun.

Lena lowered her visor. As she watched the city go by at high speed, her mind began to drift and she looked back over at Rhodes. He hadn't said a word since they left Parker Center. She could see him thinking something over. She could see the sadness in his eyes. Rhodes was a detective-three with ten years more experience than her. But he was more than that. If the timing had been different, they easily could have become lovers.

"You okay?" she asked.

He turned and glanced at her.

"You were on the phone when I walked in. Was it your sister?"

He nodded. "They've set a date. Her operation's on Monday."

"You going up?"

"Tomorrow night," he said. "I've been talking to her off and on all morning. I left a message on your machine at home. You just haven't gotten it yet."

He grinned at her, then turned back to the road. Lena knew his sister was all that he had left. His parents were gone and there were no other siblings. Like Lena, if his sister's health failed, Rhodes would be the last one standing.

"What did she say?"

He shrugged. "She was talking about bees."

"What do mean, bees?"

"Honeybees," he said. "The kind that fly around in the air."

"Okay. So why was she talking about honeybees?"

"She says they're dying. It won't affect her place because they grow lettuce. But her neighbor keeps orange groves. If all the bees die, then there's no way to pollinate the trees. She's not worried about her surgery on Monday. She's worried about her neighbor losing his farm. Kids growing up without knowing what an orange is. I guess that's why I love her so much."

Another smile spread across his face—warm, and quiet, and bittersweet. Turning back to the road, he took the Lincoln Boulevard exit, made a right on Ocean Park and a left on Main. They were driving through Venice now, two blocks from the beach. When they finally reached Navy, Rhodes killed the strobes and idled slowly down the narrow street. Jennifer McBride's apartment was in the middle of the second block on the right—a three-story brick building that had the look and feel of a halfway house.

He pulled in front of the entrance. As they got out, Lena gazed at the place and suddenly felt uneasy. She looked at the other apartment buildings pressing against the sidewalk. She could see the ocean at the end of the street. A single palm tree swaying in the cold and breezy air.

"You sure you really want to park there?"

She heard the voice but didn't see anyone on the sidewalk. It had been a man's voice—abrupt, verging on rude—the direction camouflaged by the wind. As Rhodes moved in beside her, he pointed to a window on the first floor. It was open but remained blank, everything inside concealed by a rusty screen.

"Is there a problem?" Rhodes said.

"You can read the signs better than I can," the man said. "That's a no parking zone."

"We're cops."

"Yeah, right. Driving a piece-of-shit car like that. Gives new meaning to the phrase *L.A.'s Finest.*"

They moved closer to the window. Although the man remained hidden behind the screen, Lena could see the light from a large TV in the living room. The man was watching cartoons.

Rhodes grit his teeth. "What's your name?"

"Lovely Rita, the meter maid."

"The one on your driver's license, I mean."

"Ted Jones. What's yours, champ?"

"Come closer so we can see you, Mr. Jones."

Rhodes opened his ID and held it up. After a moment, the man moved into the window light and that feeling inside Lena's gut began to glow a little. Jones was a burnout and anything but lovely. A small, troll-like man, about forty years old, who hadn't bothered to get dressed today. All he had on was a pair of boxer shorts and an old tank top. By all appearances he hadn't showered or shaved in a week. Although he was balding, thick waves of greasy black hair hung over his ears. His arms and back were carpeted with body hair as well. But it was his eyes that gave Lena pause. There was something wrong with them. His irises looked as if they were fading, like a rogue wave that washes up on the beach and dissolves into dry sand. She couldn't get a read on the color because it was slipping away.

She traded looks with Rhodes, then cleared her throat.

"You the manager?" she asked.

"No, I'm not the manager. I own the place."

"You spend a lot of time by this window?"

"What's with the fifty questions, lady?"

"We want to take a look inside Jennifer McBride's apartment," she said.

"Why don't you try ringing the bell? If she's home, I'll bet she'll answer."

Lena moved closer to the window. "We're from Robbery-Homicide," she said. "Jennifer McBride's not home. Now get some clothes on and open the door."

Jones remained quiet, staring at her with those eyes. She watched them flick down to her waist and spot the gun. After a moment, the reason why they were here finally seemed to register on his face and he let out a gasp.

"She's dead."

"Open the door," Lena said.

"Give me a second."

Jones vanished into the room. When the door buzzed, Lena pushed it open and they entered a small lobby. The carpet was threadbare. The place, cheap and rundown. As she eyed the staircase, the door to apartment 1A opened and Jones walked out in a pair of tattered jeans. He was wearing eyeglasses now and jiggling a set of keys.

"Follow me," he said.

They climbed up to the second floor, the steps creaking below their feet. When they reached the landing, Jones led them across the hall to apartment 2B and inserted the key.

"When was the last time you saw her?" Lena said.

"A couple of days ago, I guess."

"Wednesday?"

Jones nodded. "She walked out, heading for the beach. Must have been around three in the afternoon."

"How well did you know her?"

"She paid her rent on time."

"Did she have a lot of friends?"

He turned and looked at her through his glasses. The lenses were scratched and dulled by fingerprints, yet still magnified his damaged eyes.

"I never saw her with anyone," he said, pushing the door

open. "Now what am I supposed to do? Rent's due in a couple weeks. Who's gonna pay for this?"

Lena suddenly became aware of the man's body odor.

"We'll let you know," she said. "And we'll need that key."

"I've got half an idea to pack her shit up and move it down to the basement. I could have the place rented in an hour. This close to the beach, there's a waiting list."

Rhodes turned sharply. "You wouldn't want to do that, Jones. You wouldn't even want to walk inside this place until we say so."

"But I own the building. I want my fucking money."

"Forget about your fucking money," Rhodes said.

He took a step toward Jones. Lena could see him sizing up the vile little man, trying to bridle his emotions. She was struck by the differences between the two. Rhodes towered over Jones by at least a foot and was dressed in a light brown suit, a crisp white shirt, and a patterned tie. His presence was raw and powerful, his voice, dark and quiet.

"How long has she lived here?" Rhodes was saying.

Jones paused a moment, his eyes shifting back and forth. "About a year," he said.

"You run a credit check?"

"Nobody moves in without one."

"Then give us the key and get McBride's paperwork. Wait for us downstairs."

Jones started to say something, but looked at Rhodes and stopped. He removed the key from the ring and handed it to Lena. When he was finally gone, they stepped into the apartment and closed the door.

A moment passed. Rhodes shot her a look, but didn't say anything. He didn't need to. Jones was a bottom-feeder. A lot of bottom-feeders migrated to Venice. As the silence began to settle in, Lena pocketed the key and tried to focus on the victim. Jennifer McBride's presence.

They were standing in the foyer with a clear view of the entire apartment. She could see the living room and galley kitchen through a set of French doors. To her right, the bedroom and bath. She turned and noted the table beside the front door. One or two days' worth of unopened mail sat in a basket next to a lamp and a copy of the *L.A. Weekly* that had been folded in half. She turned back to the living room and calculated the floor plan: it couldn't have added up to more than three hundred square feet. A small one-bedroom at the beach. But unlike the rundown building, the apartment was clean, the paint was fresh, and there was a certain peace here. An innocence that seemed to match the innocence she had seen in the victim's eyes.

She held on to that image as she slipped on a pair of gloves and followed Rhodes into the living room. She glanced at the hardwood floors, taking in the couch and chair. Although the TV appeared new, everything else looked as if it had come from secondhand shops and yard sales.

"She lived modestly," Rhodes said. "She didn't have much money."

Lena turned and noticed the shelves built into the near wall. While the top shelf remained empty, the bottom two shelves were stuffed with at least fifty paperbacks.

"And she was a reader," Lena said.

She moved closer and scanned the titles, recognizing most of the authors. Every book on the shelf was a mystery published within the last year.

She glanced back at Rhodes and saw him moving toward the double set of windows on the other side of the couch. The curtains were drawn but were made of sheer lace and provided a soft, even light that filled the room. When he pulled them open, Lena looked past the fire escape at the close-up view of a brick wall and understood why the curtains had been closed.

She crossed the room, spotting the ashtray outside the window. The next building was so close it barely covered the width of the fire escape. She gazed at the rusty steps, following them down to the first floor and the narrow alley that ran between the buildings. As her eyes rose up the brick wall on the other side, they came to rest on a window. She hadn't seen it until now because of the angle. There was a man in the window. Another deadbeat like Jones, only this one was wearing a wool cap and had a pair of binoculars. This one seemed to get off by peering into other people's windows.

"Nice view," Rhodes said.

"He's staring at us. You think he's waiting for Jennifer McBride to come back?"

"She's not coming back," he said. "And this is Venice. Let's keep going."

They moved into the kitchen. As Rhodes checked the cabinets and drawers, Lena examined the refrigerator and what was left in the coffeepot. When she didn't find any mold beginning to collect on the coffee's surface, her mind turned to Art Madina. The pathologist couldn't give her an accurate time of death, but thought that the murder occurred the night before the body was found. Between this and what Jones had told them, Lena now had tangible evidence that the pathologist was right.

Jennifer McBride was murdered on Wednesday night.

Rhodes followed her out of the kitchen. They worked methodically, scouring the small apartment without talking. Lifting seat cushions, searching the foyer closet, sifting through the mail and finding a utility bill and three credit-card offers from a bank that advertised on television and got people hooked on high interest rates. Reaching the bathroom, Lena noted the shower curtain fastened to the wall and scanned the tile for blood spatter. When she knelt down to examine the tub, she found a thin film of soap residue and took a swipe with her gloved fingers. The fragrance matched the bar of soap set on the wall tray, not a detergent that might be used to clean up after dismembering a body.

Rhodes closed the medicine cabinet and they stepped into the bedroom. There was a window on the right, the curtains open. This time the view didn't face a brick wall or some lowlife trying to sneak a peek. This time Lena could actually see the Pacific Ocean. Although much of the view was blocked by a condo in the distance, the bed appeared to be set at just the right angle so that McBride could wake up in the morning and see the beach.

As Rhodes started rifling through the chest of drawers, Lena stepped back and took in the rest of the room. She noted the iPod docking station on the bedside table. Another paperback was beside the clock radio and cordless telephone. When she went through the closet, she didn't find anything but clothes.

Jennifer McBride had been abducted in a parking lot and taken somewhere before she was murdered and dumped in Hollywood. But this wasn't the place. This wasn't the crime scene.

Lena watched Rhodes search through the bottom drawer as she thought it over and tried to quiet her disappointment. They hadn't found much. Jennifer McBride may have only been twenty-five-years old, but all she owned was a single set of sheets. A single set of towels. Her kitchen was stocked with minimal accessories, just enough to get by. She didn't have a CD player and speakers. Instead, she relied on an iPod. She didn't read hardcover books, but went through paperbacks at about one per week.

Money may have been an issue in her life, but there was something more here. Something trying to break through the surface. After a moment, it dawned on her.

Everything in the entire apartment was portable.

With the exception of the furniture that came from secondhand thrift shops and probably cost less than a couple hundred dollars, everything else could have fit into the trunk of a compact car.

But there was something else. Something more difficult to pin down.

Her eyes made another sweep through the room and stopped on the bedside table. There was a snow globe sitting beside the lamp and telephone. She hadn't noticed it before.

"Is something wrong?" Rhodes asked.

She didn't say anything. She didn't want to lose the thought. Instead, she moved around the bed and picked up the snow globe. Inside the heavy glass sphere was a detailed model of Las Vegas. When she shook the globe, a thick cloud of snow whirled around the Bellagio Hotel and Caesar's Palace, then settled down to the bottom where the streets were painted a bright gold.

She looked over at Rhodes as that stray thought finally jelled.

Everything was portable. But even more important, there was nothing personal here. They had made a first pass through the entire apartment and found nothing personal at all.

Not a single photograph. Not a letter or postcard from a friend. Nothing that would point to the victim's life. What she cared about or who she loved. Just the books she had read since moving in a year ago and this snow globe.

The phone began to ring from the bedside table. Lena glanced at it and realized that the message light was blinking. After two rings, the machine clicked and went silent. Thirty seconds later, the speaker lit up and the caller's voice filled the room. It was a man's voice, and he sounded old and more than a little nervous.

"This is Jim, uh, Dolson," the man was saying. "I'm trying to reach Jennifer. I'm in town from Cincinnati and, uh, saw your ad in the *L.A. Weekly*. I'm definitely interested in some of that massage therapy—if you know what I mean. I'll be here for a couple more days. If you're available on short notice, please call me back. I'm staying in Century City at the Plaza."

The phone clicked. Then the room filled with dial tone, and all the innocence was gone.

9

Rhodes pulled the telephone closer, examining the keypad. "It's digital," he said. "Looks like six messages."

Lena moved within earshot as Rhodes found the right button and hit PLAY. Except for the voices, the first five messages were pretty much the same as the last. There was Jim Dolson from Cincinnati. But there were three more men from out of town staying at various hotels on the Westside. The fourth was from some guy claiming to be on vacation with his wife and asking if McBride did three-ways. And then the fifth, this time from a woman, wondering if McBride was bisexual.

All six messages referred to the victim's ad in the current edition of the *L.A. Weekly.* According to the time stamp, all six calls were placed after McBride's body had been discovered in Hollywood.

Lena grabbed the *L.A. Weekly* off the foyer table and quickly returned to the bedroom. Paging through the back of the paper, she sat down beside Rhodes and began sifting through what appeared to be several hundred classified ads for escort services, phone sex, and massage parlors. McBride's ad was in the middle of the pack on the second page.

Massage Therapy. Hot young blonde with magic hands and knockout body seeks men who want to relax under my spell. For pure joy call Jennifer at . . .

Lena reread the ad, then opened her cell phone and entered the number printed in the newspaper. When McBride's phone rang on the bedside table, she didn't close her cell even though she had confirmed the match. Instead, she let the machine pick up and listened to the outgoing message. It wasn't the default message that came with the phone. It was Jennifer McBride's voice. She wanted to hear it. Absorb it. The voice of the victim before she was murdered.

Lena could feel the hairs on her neck standing on end. An ice-cold chill fluttered up her spine. It was a simple message. Direct and to the point. McBride greeted the caller using her phone number rather than her name, then promised a call back to anyone leaving their contact information. The message ended with an easy *Thanks*.

Lena paused a moment before closing her cell—McBride's voice now seared into her memory and a part of her being.

"Jones told us that he never saw her with anybody," she said. "And I'll bet he spends a lot of time by that window."

"She didn't bring them here," Rhodes said. "She went to them. Somewhere around here she's got a bag of tricks."

"I didn't see it when we went through the place."

"We weren't looking for it," he said. "If she didn't take the bag with her, then it's here."

They checked underneath the bed and behind the hamper in the bedroom closet. It took them ten minutes to find it. A small black duffel bag in the foyer closet right beside the front door. Rhodes carried it over to the coffee table in the living room. Ripping the zipper open, he turned the bag over and shook the contents out.

Lena knelt down on the floor, picking through the lingerie and thinking about the small heart-shaped tattoo she had seen between McBride's shaved vagina and her bikini line. She counted three transparent baby-doll negligees with matching G-strings, a variety of push-up bras, a sheer robe, and a pair of black panties. But there was something else here: a white skirt and matching top. Lena held the blouse up for a better look, eyeing the low neckline and the red cross that had been embroidered over the left breast pocket.

"She wore a costume," Rhodes said. "She played a nurse."

"Looks like it, huh."

Lena returned to the duffel bag, giving it a lift and measuring its weight. Spinning the bag around, she opened the first side pocket and fished out an array of scented oils, three different kinds of condoms, a vibrator, and an extra package of batteries.

She looked over at Rhodes on the couch. He was reaching down for a cosmetics case that had fallen on the floor. As he unzipped the case and split it open, his eyes danced over the contents and widened some.

It was a cache of pills.

Rhodes cleared a spot on the table, shaking the plastic bottles and reading them off one by one before setting them down. The list was impressive and seemed to cover a client's every want or need. Viagra and Cialis were here. But so were ample supplies of Xanax, Valium, Vicodin, and Oxycodone.

"She knew somebody," Rhodes said.

Lena eyed the labels. Jennifer McBride's name wasn't listed, nor was the pharmacy. She played the victim's ad back in her head.

Hot young blonde with magic hands and knockout body seeks men who want to relax under my spell. For pure joy call Jennifer at . . .

The words *relax under my spell* seemed to have a new meaning. A darker meaning. She looked back at the lingerie and costume, at the condoms scattered across the table. She remembered the belly ring Madina had removed from the corpse at the autopsy. Jennifer McBride had been more than a masseuse. As Lena mulled it over, it seemed clear that the young woman's apparent innocence was an asset to her business—something she probably flaunted.

Lena glanced over at Rhodes. His eyes were turned inward; his face, troubled. She wondered if he was thinking about his sister again.

"What is it?" she asked.

"I was just thinking about how this will play with the chief."

"You mean because of who McBride turned out to be?"

"Yeah. The chief and Klinger. You know what I'm saying. When you're so straight you're bent, who gives a shit about a whore on dope?"

"You and me," she said quietly.

"You and me," he repeated, still thinking it over. He got up and crossed the room to the window, rubbing his neck and gazing outside. "That guy's still sitting by his window," he said. "Still waiting for McBride to come home."

"Now we know why. She knew that he was out there and probably liked to tease him."

Rhodes turned toward her and leaned against the sill. "There was this case in Atlantic City," he said. "Four prostitutes were raped and strangled to death a couple years ago. They were found in a drainage ditch. I remember it because the details were so bizarre. The bodies were laid out in a row fully clothed. But their heads were facing east and their shoes had been removed. I remember it because another murder case was making headlines. Not here in the States, but from a small town outside London. This time it was five prostitutes. Their bodies were found over a period of ten days."

Lena knew where Rhodes was going. She actually remembered reading about both cases after an article popped up during a Google search. The story appeared in *The New York Times,* which had recently opened their archives and made them free of charge. After her last investigation ended so violently, Lena began researching past cases in an attempt to better understand the man she had chased down and killed. It had been part of her recovery. Dealing with the aftermath of taking a human life. The article in *The New York Times* was a side-by-side comparison of the two cases Rhodes was talking about.

"In the UK," she said, "the detectives asked for help and the community came together."

"That's right. They put up billboards at the soccer stadiums. They blanketed the streets with flyers. Even the prime minister offered his sympathy to the victims' families. What these women did for a living was irrelevant. The community came together because the victims were from their neighborhood and needed help. That's all that mattered to them."

"I read about it," she said. "They closed the case. They caught the guy."

"He's going on trial next month. In New Jersey, they don't even have a suspect yet because no one at the top gives a shit. They didn't process Missing Persons Reports. They wouldn't even let vice detectives knock on doors. They wouldn't let them do their jobs. The victims were whores, right? Streetwalkers who used drugs. Did you know that all four victims were mothers and left behind young children?"

Lena nodded.

"Well, no one else did," Rhodes said. "No one else knew because no one put it out there. The detectives' hands were tied. Bad things happen to bad people—the victims probably deserved it, right? And even if they didn't—even though the guy's still out there—our neighborhoods are better off without them. Our lawns are greener. There's more room on our streets for more luxury cars. If we keep quiet, the casinos won't lose any money and people will still come to play the slots."

Rhodes became silent, but Lena knew why he seemed so bitter. Jane Doe No. 99 counted because she was an innocent victim, but Jennifer McBride wouldn't because she was a whore. If they worked the neighborhood, no one would care because no one would think that it had anything to do with them. The victim would be seen as irrelevant. The investigation, a needless interruption in their busy and important lives. Even worse, when the chief reviewed his list of unsolved cases and cut it against the murder rate climbing to five hundred, there was a good chance that he might reevaluate his resources and spend them somewhere else. The case might be shot down the divisional highway, then dropped altogether and put on ice.

She could feel her heart beating in her chest. The anger

that came with the possibility that Jennifer McBride might not count at Parker Center if your office was on the top floor.

The phone began ringing again—another two rings before the machine picked up. Thirty seconds later, another shadowy voice filtered out of the bedroom. Another potential customer who had read McBride's ad and anxiously awaited her spell. Another willing subject who didn't realize that his fantasy—the hot young blonde with magic hands and a knockout body—had been dead for two days and was lying in a plastic bag at the morgue.

When the call finally ended, the silence came back. The anger. As Lena considered the evidence, she realized that they were still riding the train without a ticket. Still making their run in the dark. She looked over at Rhodes staring at the pills lined up on the coffee table. After a moment, his eyes seemed to clear and he headed for the bedroom.

Lena found him sitting on the bed by the telephone. He was holding the handset and gazing at the LED screen.

"Does it strike you as odd that she only had one phone?" he asked.

Lena shrugged. "I'm sure she had a cell. We just haven't gotten there yet."

"I mean here. There's only one phone in the apartment."

"It's cordless. This is a small place."

Rhodes paused to think it over. "Makes sense, I guess. Today's the fourteenth, right?"

"What are you doing?"

"Her address book must have been in her purse. I was hoping maybe she programmed the automatic dialer, but she didn't. When I picked up the handset, I realized that she had Caller ID."

Lena moved closer. Rhodes had found the menu and was toggling through the caller list. He was moving backward, and she recognized her cell number and the two calls that had come in while they were here by the time and date. Some of the numbers farther down the list were blocked, and most were from area codes that she didn't recognize. When

Rhodes reached the first number with a name attached, he stopped and became very still.

"What is it?" she asked.

He turned the screen toward her so that she could get a better look. A moment passed, and the glow in her stomach returned.

The call only lasted for thirty seconds, but it was from a doctor. Lena checked the area code and zeroed in on the name. Joseph Fontaine, MD had called at 7:00 p.m. on Wednesday, December 12, from somewhere in L.A.

"We're looking for a surgeon, right, Lena?"

She met Rhodes's eyes and caught the sharp glint. "That's the night she was murdered."

Rhodes turned back to the handset and continued toggling through the Caller ID list. He didn't have to go very far before Fontaine's name popped up on the list again. The call had been made at 4:00 p.m. that same day and lasted another thirty seconds.

"He's hitting the machine and hanging up," Rhodes said. "Trying to reach her, but not leaving a message."

Lena dug into her pocket for her notepad, found the first clean page, and wrote down the doctor's name and number. When she finished, Rhodes clicked through the list until he reached the end. Of the thirty-six calls McBride received this month, seven belonged to Joseph Fontaine, MD. Three were hang-ups made on the day McBride was murdered. But the remaining four were spread over the previous ten days, each lasting for almost an hour.

Rhodes placed the handset on the cradle and turned. She could feel his breath on her face. The heat emanating from his skin. His eyes on her.

"You bring your computer?" he asked.

10

Lena pushed aside the lingerie and condoms, clearing a space for her laptop on the coffee table. While Rhodes logged the pills into evidence, she switched on the wireless broadband card and within a few seconds had a secure connection to the Internet. She found her bookmark for Auto-TrackXP and clicked it. When she arrived at the Web site, she typed in her user name and password, and the information gate to billions of current and historical records swung all the way open in a single instant.

She typed Joseph Fontaine's name and phone number into the search windows and hit ENTER. In another instant, the man's entire life was rendered before her eyes.

"I'm up," she said. "I've got him."

"Who is he?"

This was where every background check began. Lena studied the screen, grateful that the department had an account and that she had access to such an extensive database: names, aliases, every job ever worked, every address ever used, every phone number, all registered vehicles, all property owned, his relatives, neighbors, associates, credit history, and tax records. She scanned through the list. Dr. Joseph Fontaine's life was three and a half pages long.

"He's got an office on Wilshire in Beverly Hills," she said. "His house is in Westwood on South Mapleton Drive."

"He's got money. What kind of car does he drive?"

"Two Mercedes."

"What about a wife?"

Lena clicked to the next page. "He's got two of those, too. But he's been divorced for the past ten years. Looks like his second marriage only lasted eighteen months. He's fifty-six years old and single now. No kids. His address hasn't changed since he was thirty-five, so the house couldn't have been part of either settlement."

Rhodes sealed the evidence bag. "Let's pack up," he said. "We need to roll."

It was a tactical decision filled with risk. Depending on how they handled things, confronting Fontaine could tip their hand.

Lena made a left on Wilshire Boulevard and started picking out street numbers. Rhodes sat in the passenger seat, reviewing McBride's credit history and the rental agreement that Jones had given them on the way out, and trying not to look at the glove compartment. Lena knew that there was a pack of cigarettes inside. She had found them on the drive to Venice. Rhodes called them his emergency pack and said that they had been there for three months, but remained unopened.

They were driving through Beverly Hills, about six blocks south of Cedar-Sinai Medical Center—stop and go for the past forty minutes. She checked the clock on the dash, then looked back at the traffic. It was 4:30 p.m. and already starting to get dark. The trip from Jennifer McBride's apartment probably covered less than ten miles. But Lena didn't mind because it had given her a chance to think.

Talking to Fontaine wasn't the right move or even the best move. But this was a case that had been speeding into the big nowhere ever since they found McBride's body. Talking to the doctor seemed like their only move.

She spotted a parking lot just this side of Fontaine's building. As she pulled in, Rhodes slipped the rental agreement into her briefcase and climbed out. Five minutes later, they were in the lobby scanning the building directory. His name was listed in the center column. Joseph Fontaine,

MD, leased more than an office in one of the most exclusive business districts in Los Angeles. The Joseph Fontaine Pediatric Center occupied the entire fifth floor.

They traded looks as they stepped into the elevator and the doors closed. But when they finally reached the fifth floor, they found themselves in a reception area that didn't seem much like a doctor's office. Particularly a doctor who treated children. The woman behind the counter was dressed in a cool gray Armani suit and appeared too well manicured. There was too much mahogany and frosted glass, and the place was too neat and too quiet.

"May I help you?" the woman asked.

Rhodes pulled out his ID. "We'd like to speak with Dr. Fontaine."

Lena studied the receptionist's face, guessing that she was about thirty-five. The woman glanced at the badge, then looked up as if it didn't have any meaning. As if it might be a mere toy. Lena had never seen anyone react this way and had to remind herself that they were in Beverly Hills.

"Do you have an appointment?" the receptionist was asking. "Is he expecting you?"

Rhodes didn't answer the question. "We're from Robbery-Homicide," he said.

Lena followed his eyes to the reception area and noticed two men in dark suits sitting on the leather couch. Both held copies of *The Wall Street Journal* in their hands and had looked up. While the badge didn't seem to have an effect on the receptionist, its effect on the two men staring this way was more than clear.

She reached for the phone. "Let me see if he's in," she said. "Who shall I say would like to speak with him?"

She had just looked at Rhodes's ID, but either hadn't retained the information or couldn't help being difficult. Rhodes gave her their names and she jotted them down on a pad. After someone picked up on the other end, she turned away from the counter and lowered her voice. A few moments later, she hung up and told them that Dr. Fontaine's assistant would be out in a minute or two. Rhodes thanked her, but didn't offer an apology or any explanation for barging in.

Ten minutes passed before another woman wearing another Armani suit entered the lobby from the hallway beside the front desk. But this one was different. Five years older, five years smoother, and higher in the food chain—with more to lose. Lena could see the concern in her eyes as she glanced at the receptionist, then turned toward them with an outstretched hand. She introduced herself as Greta Dietrich, Fontaine's assistant. Her smile was completely forced, but well done. And she didn't look at or acknowledge the two men in suits still watching from the leather couch. But Lena could tell that they were preying on Dietrich's mind by the way she and Rhodes were whisked away from the front desk and ushered down the hall.

Dietrich was a blue-eyed blonde. Educated and attractive with a hint of the street hidden beneath her makeup. Her steps were quick and choppy. Under any other circumstances, Lena would have laughed out loud. But not tonight. Not now.

"I'm sorry," Dietrich was saying. "Dr. Fontaine is on a conference call and will be tied up for several hours. The call is terribly important. A matter of life and death. Is there anything I can help you with? Would he even know why you are here?"

They were passing office suites and conference rooms, not examination rooms. As she steered them into her office, Lena realized the jam Dietrich was in. She didn't want two homicide detectives anywhere near the two men in the lobby, but she didn't want them in her office, either.

Lena glanced around the room. The closed door on the far wall had to lead to Fontaine. And that light blinking on Deitrich's telephone wasn't attached to an outside line. She could see it from six feet away. The intercom was open. Fontaine wasn't on a conference call, or saving anyone's life. He was hiding in his office. He was eavesdropping.

She turned to Dietrich. She'd had enough.

"We're working a homicide investigation," she said. "We don't have time for this. Tell your boss to get off the phone."

Dietrich looked back in disbelief. Before she could say anything, the light on the phone went dark and the door at the far end of the room swung open. It was Dr. Joseph Fontaine, asking all three of them to come in. His voice was subdued and quiet and he knew exactly why they were here—Lena was certain of this the moment she set eyes on the man.

As they entered his office, she looked him over more closely. Like the women who worked for him, Fontaine was well kept. Lena noted his graying blond hair and the Rolex on his wrist. His strong arms and straight back. His eyes were almost the same shade of blue as Deitrich's, but were less transparent and reflected the outside world like a pair of mirrored shades. As he offered them a seat and stepped around his desk, Lena traded looks with Rhodes. There was no question that the doctor was nervous.

"What can I do for you?" he said.

Lena didn't answer the question, watching his assistant move around the desk with her boss and lean against the credenza as he sat down. They had matching tans. December tans. The kind that came from Mexico. As Lena took it in, she noticed the cut of Dietrich's jacket. She was showing a little too much cleavage for an executive assistant. A bit too much of her black bra. For some reason Lena thought about the nurse costume Jennifer McBride kept in her duffel bag, and wondered if maybe Fontaine made his assistant wear one, too.

"I'm just curious," Lena said, "As we walked to your office, I didn't see any examination rooms."

"I see patients at the hospital," the doctor said. "But most of my work involves research. That's what we do here."

Fontaine turned to Rhodes, probably thinking that he would be asking the questions. Rhodes pulled out his notebook and pen without saying anything. They had made the decision as they walked from the parking lot to the building. If Rhodes could get them past the gatekeepers, Lena would handle the interview. She had an easy way of talking to people. Rhodes had more experience and wanted to watch the way Fontaine handled himself.

"What kind of research?" Lena asked.

The doctor paused. When he finally turned back to her, she could see the irritation on his face. Arrogance cut with resignation. Clearly, the doctor thought that he was the smartest one in the room.

"All kinds of research," he said.

"Then you don't concentrate on anything special."

"Just pediatrics."

"Do you write many prescriptions, Doctor?"

"Of course."

"Do you perform surgeries?"

Fontaine turned to Rhodes, watching the detective flip the page in his notebook and continue writing.

"Where is this going?" Fontaine asked.

Rhodes stared back at the man but didn't reply.

When Lena repeated the question, Fontaine gave her another look—colder this time—and finally said, "Yes. I perform surgeries."

She paused a moment and made a point of looking him over. "You're what? Fifty—"

"I'm fifty-six years old."

"So in nineteen-seventy-two you would have been twenty."

"This isn't nineteen-seventy-two and I'm a very busy man. What is the point of all this?"

"Did you serve in the military, Doctor?"

His face changed as he considered the question. "Vietnam. The last two years of the war."

"What was your role?"

"Survival. I was drafted. I was a grunt."

"Did you see much combat?"

His eyes flooded with more irritation, his voice becoming higher pitched. "I was working at a medical station in the jungle ten miles west of the Cu Chi tunnels. Yes, I saw a lot of combat. It's the reason I went to medical school. Now, would you please tell me why you are here?"

Lena didn't respond, letting the silence work on the doctor's nerves. He fit the profile. He could be the *one*. But Fontaine fit a lot of profiles. He could have been McBride's drug supplier. Or just one of the clients reveling under her spell.

"We were wondering about your relationship with a young woman living in Venice. Jennifer McBride."

Fontaine cleared his throat. "Who?"

Lena repeated her name, then watched Fontaine think it over and shake his head. His performance was more lame than convincing. He was shooting quick looks at Rhodes, and seemed concerned that the detective was writing everything down.

"I don't know a Jennifer McBride," he said.

Lena crossed her legs. "Maybe you should take a moment to think it over, Doctor."

"I don't need a moment to think it over. I don't know her."

"You're sure?"

He slapped his desk. "Absolutely. Who was she?"

Everything stopped. Fontaine had just used the past tense. Everyone in the room knew that he'd slipped up. Even Fontaine.

"She was a prostitute," Lena said.

The doctor let out a nervous laugh that died off quickly. His eyes were jerking back and forth as if something was clicking in his head. Lena noticed the sweat beginning to bead on his forehead. His cheeks, a bright red. As much as she wanted to look at Dietrich and measure her reaction, she kept her gaze fixed on the doctor.

"I don't know any prostitutes," he managed.

"She might have called herself a massage therapist."

"I don't know any of them, either."

His right hand began to quiver. When he noticed, he pulled away his arm and hid it behind his desk. The conversation was no longer beneath him. All of a sudden he was in over his head.

Lena wanted to seize the moment, amplifying the pressure with another measured dose of silence. She glanced at Rhodes in the chair by the window. As she took in the office and noted the expensive furnishings, she realized that there was only one photograph in the entire room. A picture of an older woman with white hair set in a silver frame and placed on the credenza by the phone. The resemblance between Fontaine and the old woman was striking.

She lowered her voice. "You need to be careful, Doctor. You're speaking to two police officers. And you've got a lot to lose."

"I know who I'm talking to."

"We have phone records," she said. "I never asked if you knew Jennifer McBride because we already knew that you did. All I asked was *how* you knew her."

"Maybe you should think about who *you're* talking to," he said. "You've made a mistake, Detective. Your records are wrong. I never called her because I didn't know her."

Lena met the doctor's eyes. "Then how did you know that she was dead?"

A beat went by. Thirty seconds of empty air billowing into the room. He glanced at his assistant without answering the question. Lena kept her eyes on the man.

"You called her three times on the day she was murdered, Doctor."

The strong man with the athletic body wilted in his chair, still staring at Greta Dietrich for help.

"Where were you two nights ago?" Lena asked.

He looked confused, anxious. When he didn't respond, Dietrich cut in.

"He was at the Biltmore," she said. "A reception and dinner. The invitation's still on my desk."

"Dinners like that are usually over by nine or ten. What time did it end?"

The doctor turned back to her. His eyes were hollow now, his anxiety evolving into anger fully realized. He flashed a mean grin.

"You know what?" he said. "We're through here. Call my attorney, Greta, and show these good people the fucking door."

11

"He's doing her," Rhodes said.

Lena nodded. It had been obvious the moment Dietrich followed Fontaine around his desk, the moment she spotted the matching tans. Dietrich wasn't supporting her boss. She was standing beside her man. Even after hearing about McBride.

Rhodes held up his hand and Lena tossed him the keys. As she climbed into the passenger seat, she understood how difficult it would be to interpret Fontaine's shaky behavior. She didn't buy anything he said. Fontaine knew the murder victim, looked them in the eye and lied. But he had a lot of reasons besides Dietrich to want to keep hidden his relationship with a young prostitute. He was a doctor who worked with children. McBride wasn't much more than a girl. Even worse, she looked young for her age. Innocent.

The possibilities, the secrets, suddenly appeared more than grim.

Rhodes pulled out of the lot into a sea of cars inching their way down Wilshire Boulevard. She looked out the window at all the brake lights. The twelve-mile trip downtown would probably take a couple of hours. When her cell phone vibrated, she checked the video screen, saw Lieutenant Barrera's name and flipped it open.

"Where are you guys at?" he said.

She turned on the speaker so Rhodes could listen, then gave Barrera an update in broad strokes, what they had found at McBride's apartment and who they had met in Beverly Hills.

"This is L.A.," he said. "Sounds like a start."

She tried to smile, but couldn't. "What's going on with the video?"

"SID's working on it, but it's still hard to see his face. We checked everything for prints. McBride's license and the USB drive—not even a smudge. Everything had been wiped down."

"What about the envelope?"

"Another strikeout," Barrera said. "And we're having trouble locating the messenger service. Sanchez got out of court early and made some calls. There's no record of the delivery anywhere in town. And the guys behind the front desk didn't get a receipt."

"What about the messenger?" Rhodes asked.

"A kid in a leather jacket wearing a Dodger cap. That's all they remember. He didn't ask them to sign anything. But here's the deal. I ran McBride through the system, Lena. No priors. Nothing that stands out at all. Her only living relative is her mother, Pamela McBride."

"You get an address?"

"She lives in Van Nuys," he said. "Odessa Avenue. Just north of the airport and east of Northridge Military Academy."

"We'll need to talk to her tonight," Lena said. "I don't want her to hear about this on the news."

"I agree," Barrera said. "And don't worry about the chief. I straightened everything out."

"What about Klinger?"

"I don't give a shit about Klinger. Do whatever you have to do. Just do it right."

Barrera gave her Pamela McBride's address, and she wrote it down. As Rhodes made a U-turn, heading north toward the Valley, she slipped the phone into her pocket and fought off an anxious yawn. She was beginning to feel the weight of a long day that had begun with an autopsy at the morgue and hadn't included much food. A day that would end with the difficult task of a next-of-kin notification. Telling Jennifer McBride's mother that her only child was dead.

She thought about Fontaine and the front he had created for himself, wondering if his assistant meant anything more to him than a prop. She thought about appearances and perversion, and about the man's guilt that she could feel creeping into her bones. And she thought about those cigarettes Rhodes kept in his glove compartment. She thought about them two or three times over the next hour until they finally reached Odessa Avenue.

It was a small California bungalow standing in the middle of the block. The kind you could have bought out of a Sears Catalog in the early 1900s and had a local carpenter assemble. The design was an offshoot of the Arts and Crafts movement and so popular it swept across the entire nation. Clean and simple and easy on the eyes with gardens on both sides of the stoop.

Rhodes pulled to the curb and they gazed at the windows. Lena could see a TV flickering through the linen curtains. McBride's mother was home.

"Let's get this over with," she said.

"You want me to tell her?"

"I'll do it," she said.

They glanced at each other and got out, watching a private jet brush the treetops overhead on its approach to the regional airport one block south. As they climbed the steps, Lena noted the empty rocker on the porch. When she knocked on the front door, she took a deep breath and thought about that pack of cigarettes again.

A beat went by, and then the door finally opened. Lena met the woman's eyes, recognized the pain, and knew in an instant that Pamela McBride had been expecting them.

"Please," the woman said. "It's cold outside. Come in."

Lena hadn't been aware of the temperature until she stepped inside and felt the warmth of the house. Although the light was off in the kitchen, she could smell the remnants of dinner in the air, a rich tomato sauce that had probably been simmering on the stove for most of the afternoon.

She turned back to the living room. McBride's mother was offering them seats and asking if they would like something hot to drink. Lena thanked her, but shook her head, spotting the candle over the fireplace as she sat down.

"I've been lighting it every night," the woman said. "Hoping things would be okay again and Jennifer might come home."

She sat on the couch, picked up the remote, and switched off the TV. As Lena studied her face, she guessed that the age she was wearing came from fatigue and despair, not the passage of time. McBride's mother couldn't have been more than forty-five years old, but she looked closer to sixty. She was a small-boned woman with delicate features. She wore a pair of corduroy slacks with a black V-neck sweater.

"You were close?" Lena asked.

The woman offered a weary smile, her mind drifting into the past. "We used to be. We sure did. Things used to be real good."

"When did they change?"

"I guess when she was about fifteen. That's when she started looking more like a woman than my little girl."

Lena concentrated on her breathing and tried to relax. She could tell that Pamela McBride sensed why they were here. But the woman appeared willing to talk, and Lena wanted to find out as much about her daughter as she could before she gave her the bad news. She knew that she would lose the mother at that point. And any background information they might learn before that moment might prove invaluable to solving the case.

"What about your husband?" she asked.

"I raised Jennifer on my own. Her father walked out before she was even five. I don't think she had any memories of him. Just what I told her. I didn't know much myself, so I tried to keep it positive. For her benefit as well as mine."

"Did you ever reconcile with her?"

The woman leaned forward with a sense of expectation and appeared visibly nervous now. "When she moved out things got a little better. She found a good job, but things were never really the same. I always felt like I wasn't getting the real story. Like she was keeping secrets. You know how kids are."

Lena tried not to think about what Jennifer McBride had done for a living. Tried not to think about what they found in her duffel bag, or the men waiting for her in their hotel rooms. Still, she had to ask the question. It was part of the job.

"What did your daughter do for a living?"

The woman took a deep breath and shuddered when she exhaled. "She said it had something to do with advertising. I knew that she was making money because I saw how much she was paying for rent. There wasn't much left for anything else. But she seemed to like her job, that's all I cared about. She seemed happy."

"Did you see her very often?"

"About once a week. Usually for Sunday dinner."

"Did she ever come with a friend?"

"A boyfriend?"

Lena nodded.

"No. She never did. I always thought it was odd. A girl with her looks. There should've been a line around the block, but there never was."

The woman's voice died off and the room became so quiet that Lena thought she could hear the sound of the candle burning on the mantel. She looked at Rhodes staring back at her and caught the gentle nod. This was the right time to tell her. The right moment. She tried to put the words together in her head. Find some way of saying it that wouldn't feel like a knockout punch. In the end she realized that it was hopeless, that she couldn't protect the woman from what she was about to learn.

"I'm sorry to have to tell you this," she said. "But your daughter Jennifer has been murdered. She's dead."

The woman didn't move or say anything for a long time. Instead, she stared at Lena, studying her face. After a while a tear dripped down her cheek. Then another.

"If there's anything we can do," Lena said. "Anything at all."

McBride's mother finally turned away. "It must be some kind of mistake," she whispered.

"I'm sorry. There's no mistake. It happened Wednesday night. Her ID was missing. It took us this long to find you."

Another long moment passed. Lena could see the woman struggling to put it together.

"But I've known she was dead for two years," the woman said.

Lena's eyes snapped across the room to Rhodes, then rocked back.

"What do you mean you've known for two years?"

The woman began to tremble, her voice barely audible. "There was a bank robbery in North Hollywood two years ago. Three men wearing ski masks. Jennifer was at the bank. I thought you came here tonight to tell me that you finally caught them. The three men who shot Jennifer."

12

If fuck-ups could be measured, if records were kept on a fuck-up's size and weight and the number of people ruined or lost, this was the mother lode.

Lena and Rhodes legged it around the corner onto the bureau floor at Parker Center. It was a Friday night in mid-December and no one was here. She spotted Barrera's jacket on his desk chair. Rhodes pointed to the captain's office, the overhead lights still burning. When they reached the door, they found Barrera at the conference table with an open three-ring binder and a can of Diet Pepsi. He looked up as they entered. Lena could see the worry in his eyes.

"That background check was good," he said. "It may have been total bullshit, but everything about it was good."

He turned around the binder and pushed it across the table, then got up from his chair like he had just been served rotten food. Lena didn't say anything, her eyes zeroing in on the binder. It was a murder book. They had made the call to their lieutenant as they sped back into town. Barrera had been able to pull the files on the bank robbery in North Hollywood—the case so grisly that it had been bumped up to RHD a long time ago. She scanned through the case summary, but already knew the details because Pamela Mc-Bride had shown them press clippings from her scrapbook. Her daughter had been twenty-three when the robbery went down. Making a deposit while on a lunch break from her job at a local ad agency. She had been shot in the back as she tried to run away. Even though the three men wore ski masks and couldn't be identified, the bank manager and two tellers were led into the vault and murdered as well. One shot each with a .38 revolver to the back of the head.

"Where's Tito?" Rhodes said.

Barrera loosened his tie and opened his shirt collar. "Upstairs working with SID. We have a decision to make. If we release the video the witness sent us in the next thirty minutes, the stations have agreed to run the story on the eleven o'clock news."

Lena glanced at her watch. It was 9:00 p.m.

"How are they making out?"

"I checked an hour ago," Barrera said. "I don't think it's going very well."

"Are they trying to enhance the entire video or a single frame?"

"They've pulled a frame, but it's still blurry. I wouldn't be able to ID the son of a bitch if he was my brother."

"What about the driver's license," Rhodes said.

"It went to Questioned Documents after it was dusted for prints. Irving Sample says it's legit."

Irving Sample began his career as a document analyst for the Secret Service. When he took a job teaching at U.C. Berkeley, the department actively recruited him to move to Los Angeles and run the unit. Sample had played a key role in Lena's last case. If he called the driver's license legit, then there had to be some other explanation.

"I've got some calls to make," she said. "Can I take the murder book?"

Barrera nodded and they broke up, Lena and Rhodes heading for their desks on the floor. Any closer look at Joseph Fontaine would have to wait until tomorrow. Tonight was about favors. Cashing in on past relationships because it was a Friday night. Rhodes knew someone at the DMV. Lena had only worked out of Bunco Forgery for six months while in Hollywood, but managed to make some friends.

She opened her computer and switched it on. While she waited for the machine to boot up, she dug into her briefcase and pulled out the credit report and rental application the victim's landlord had given them. The documents were one year old, but even at a glance Lena could tell that Jones had made a thorough sweep of his tenant in apartment 2B. All three credit agencies had issued reports. Jane Doe No. 99, aka Jennifer McBride, had a checking account and credit card over at Wells Fargo. A little less than ten thousand in cash. A little more than five hundred on the card.

Lena flipped over the credit report. When she picked up the rental application, she noticed a blemish on the paper and tilted it into the light. The victim's rent was two grand a month. She paid first-month, last-month when she signed a one-year lease. But it looked like she had also paid a one-month security deposit. While Lena and Rhodes were upstairs searching the victim's apartment, her landlord had been working overtime with a bottle of Wite-Out making the security deposit disappear.

Lena felt a tinge of anger flicker in her belly. She had seen it before and knew that she would see it again. Life sinking to its lowest mark. Life finding the drain. Jones had wiped out the security deposit, hoping that no one would notice. The little man with the damaged eyes was two grand richer and feeding off the dead.

Two grand richer for a while.

She took a breath and exhaled. Rhodes sat at his desk on the other side of the room, taking notes while speaking with someone on the phone. Pushing the papers aside, Lena checked her Internet connection and logged on to Auto-TrackXP. She typed Jennifer McBride's name into the search window, along with the address on Navy Street that appeared on her driver's license. When she hit ENTER and the information rendered on the screen, she confirmed that Barrera's background check had been righteous. But also, she could see what Jones had missed with just a credit check—no matter how complete.

Jane Doe hadn't just borrowed Jennifer McBride's name. She'd ripped her entire identity out of the record books and glued it on her back.

Lena grabbed the murder book and opened it to Section 11, combing through the real Jennifer McBride's background information. Then she checked it against the rental application and compared both with the search made on the Internet.

The real Jennifer McBride opened her first and only checking account at a small independent bank in the Valley. The same bank she died in two years ago. She rented an apartment in Burbank. As Lena looked at the address she figured it was about a ten-minute drive to her mother's home in Van Nuys. But after her death, everything went dark. Anyone looking at the data would have assumed that she moved back home. Then, one year later, another Jennifer McBride surfaced. A new account was opened at Wells Fargo. A new apartment rented in Venice. A new phone number and a new driver's license issued for a new life that wouldn't last very long.

Lena turned back to the rental application in Venice. Jane Doe had used the same social security number. The same date of birth. The same place of birth. Even the same occupation.

The stolen identity was so well executed that Lena wondered if Jane Doe might not be a phantom. Someone who borrows an identity for a few years, then drops it and moves on. But as the image of the victim's face surfaced in her mind, it didn't seem to fit.

She pulled the murder book closer, leafing through the section dividers until she reached the crime scene photographs of the real Jennifer McBride. She was lying on the floor in a pool of blood, her eyes glazed over and lost in the stars. Her delicate features had come from her mother. She had probably inherited her light brown hair from her as well. Obviously, there was no resemblance between her and the victim left in the Dumpster two nights ago in Hollywood.

Lena opened her address book, found Steve Avadar's number over at Wells Fargo, and picked up the phone. Five rings went by before she heard the line click over to his service. But instead of hitting an outgoing message, Avadar actually picked up. Even more surprising, he recognized her voice. They had worked together on a forgery case that led to a conviction. But it was a small case, something she closed out more than three years ago.

"It doesn't sound like you're in your office," she said.

"I'm forwarding everything to my cell. Hold it a second. It's loud here."

She could hear music in the background. People talking and laughing like they knew each other. Avadar was at a holiday party, but still taking business calls. After a moment, the noise began to fade and she heard a door close.

"That's better," he said. "How can I help, Lena?"

She gave him a summary of the case, along with Jane Doe's financial history. Avadar understood what she wanted immediately.

"I can pull her account statements and get you everything by nine tomorrow morning. If she wrote checks online, you'll have more than a name. You'll have each account's address and phone number. Would that be okay?"

"It would be great. What about her credit-card statements? Is that doable?"

"I'll pull everything. Should I call this number when I'm ready?"

"Better use my cell."

She gave him the number. When she spotted Tito Sanchez entering the bureau floor with a file under his arm, she thanked Avadar for the favor and hung up. Sanchez stopped at his desk. Then Rhodes got off the phone and pointed to the captain's office, and all three headed back. Barrera was still sitting at the conference table. But now that can of Diet Pepsi was empty, the aluminum flattened into a makeshift ashtray for his half-smoked cigar.

"Let's see them," he said.

Sanchez opened the file and placed two photographs on the table. The first was a blowup of the victim from her driver's license. The second, a single frame from the video recorded by the witness on the night of the abduction and murder. No one said anything—everyone's eyes riveted to that second photograph. Lena moved closer, trying to cut through the blur as she thought about the doctor's face.

"Does it look like Fontaine?" Barrera said. "Is he the one?"

The hair color was close, she thought. And so was the jawline. But the image remained lost in a hazy, midnight blur.

"I can't tell."

"I can't, either," Rhodes said. "But Fontaine knows the victim and lied about it. He even knew that she was dead. When Lena pushed him, he lawyered up so we know he's involved. The man's guilty of something."

Barrera leaned forward. "Everybody's guilty of something."

"Fontaine's guilty of more than that," Lena said. "But I can't tell from this image. It's still out of focus."

Sanchez cleared his throat. "Rollins says it'll get better, but he needs more time. Another day or two. Monday at the latest."

"We don't have a day or two," Barrera said. "We've got five minutes. Do we release the pictures tonight or not?"

Lena thought it over. There were a lot of reasons to release the photographs no matter what their condition. The case was running out of time. Fast-tracking its way to archives and the deep freeze of every other cold case in the open/unsolved drawer. The victim had been murdered two nights ago—not just murdered, but mutilated and thrown out with the trash. Two days and all they had was her body and a stolen ID. No crime scene and no real name. Releasing the photos would put the story out there. And even if no one could tell who the murderer was, someone might recognize the victim. Someone who knew her. Most people keep track of beautiful women. There was a good chance someone was keeping track of Jane Doe before she stole McBride's identity. Before she became a prostitute.

"Okay," Barrera said. "We're releasing the photographs. Maybe we'll get lucky. Anything else before I make the call?"

Lena thought about the snow globe they found in the victim's apartment. "We should probably run these photos in Vegas as well."

Barrera looked at her. "Why Vegas?"

"Because she may have been there. Because of the way she made a living."

"It can't hurt," Rhodes said.

"Okay," Barrera said. "I'll make the calls. Anything else?"

Lena turned to Rhodes. "What happened with the DMV?"

"They're sending over a certified copy of her photo and fingerprint," he said. "We should have everything by Wednesday. She owns a car registered in California under Jennifer McBride's name. A black Toyota Matrix. If it's on the road, we'll find it. But this woman's off the charts. Her driver's license looks legit because it is. She walked into the DMV and gave them her social security number. They snapped her picture and she took the test."

13

Lena pulled into the drive, grabbed her briefcase and made her way through the darkness to her front door. It had been a long day. The kind of day that began with an early morning autopsy but was fueled with hope by a witness. The kind of day that ended with a next-of-kin notification that went so wrong she would never forget it as long as she lived. A day filled with ups and downs and packed so tight it didn't include taking a break for food. But as she sifted through her keys and opened the front door, she wasn't thinking about details or any of the people she had met along the way.

She was thinking about Jane Doe. The woman who stole a dead girl's identity and placed sex ads in the *L.A. Weekly*.

The woman who cast spells.

Lena switched on the lights and glanced at her telephone mounted over the counter between the living room and kitchen. When she saw the message light blinking, she hit PLAY and listened to Rhodes's voice. He was telling her what he'd already told her in the car this afternoon, that he would be driving up to Oxnard tomorrow night to spend time with his sister. She let the message play even though she knew how it ended. She liked the sound of his voice. Liked knowing that it was on her answering machine.

When the house finally quieted, she turned up the heat, checked the time and found the remote on the coffee table. As she sat down on the couch and peeled off her shoes, she switched on the TV, toggled up to Channel 4, and muted the sound. She had a few minutes before the news started. A few minutes to think.

There was something about Jane Doe she couldn't shake. A feeling she couldn't place. A certain curiosity and fascination. She had been wrestling with it ever since she walked into the woman's apartment, ever since she went through her duffel bag and heard her voice on the telephone answering machine. The connection seemed inexplicable, yet it was there—dark and out of focus like that photograph of the man they were hunting. The one who killed her.

As she mulled it over, she realized how many of her own memories had been triggered by the victim. Her mother walking out on them after her brother was born. Her father's early death and what it meant to be orphaned at sixteen. Grabbing her younger brother and fleeing Colorado before the Department of Human Services could get them. Arriving in Los Angeles. Living out of their father's car until she found a job and made enough money to rent an efficiency apartment smaller than Jane Doe's. Going to sleep hungry once or twice a week in a city where the streets were paved with gold.

Lena looked through the slider at the vast basin below Hollywood Hills. It was a clear night, and she could see the lights of the city shimmering from downtown all the way to the Pacific Ocean. She found the Santa Monica Freeway in the distance. The traffic was so thick, the lights so fluid, it took on the appearance of a fifteen-mile-long lava flow.

The connection was loneliness, she decided. Living life on her own. Floating through time on a raft. Seeing the sharks in the water and doing whatever it takes to survive. She had handled herself differently than Jane Doe. She had made her own choices—and her memories, no matter how bleak on the surface, were good ones. Yet the connection was still there because it felt like they had started out in the same place. They had been spoon-fed from the same empty bottle. She didn't understand why the chief assigned her the case, but knew deep down in the marrow of her bones that no matter how bad things got, how cold the trail grew, she would never let this one go. The woman laid out on a gurney at the morgue was her client. No matter who she was. The connection was irrevocable and she wouldn't let go.

Her mind surfaced, her eyes focusing on the TV and a news broadcast that had just begun. Although she knew that Jane Doe's murder wasn't the first story, it took a moment to figure out what was going on. A live remote had been set up from somewhere on the Westside. From what Lena could tell, a man had bought his wife a new Lexus for Christmas. After pulling into his driveway, he attached the large red bow the dealership had given him to the roof. As he adjusted the ribbon from inside the car, a chunk of ice the size of a basketball fell out of the sky, crushing the vehicle and killing the man. Nothing was left except the big red bow and a story that would probably run for most of the night. The house and driveway were flooded with camera lights. The reporters that came with the cameras were fighting off grins and struggling to put on their game faces.

Lena turned up the sound. A scientist from Caltech was being interviewed from his office in Pasadena over a shot of the police line and pile of rubble in the driveway. Either it came from a passing jet, he was saying, or the more likely theory—the chunk of ice was really an atmospheric meteorite, the tragedy a result of global warming.

Christmas in the Palisades . . .

If the murder was broadcast at all, it would be so brief no one would notice.

Lena tossed the remote on the couch and walked around the counter into the kitchen. She didn't watch much television, particularly since the networks had been invaded by the pharmaceutical companies, bludgeoning their audiences with all those idiotic TV ads the same way candy, cereal, and fast-food makers tried to brainwash kids. Watching television these days carried unmeasurable risks, yet no one cared enough to say anything.

She opened the fridge and looked around, but still felt too unsettled to eat. Moving to the pantry, she spotted the case of wine on the floor and reached for a bottle. As she opened it

on the counter and poured a glass, the wine triggered another series of memories, this time good ones. It was a bottle of Pinot Noir from Hirsch Vineyards, and the price was
way out of her league. The case had been a gift from someone she met at a restaurant downtown, a stranger she shared
a meal with last month while sitting at the chef's table in the
kitchen. Lena had become friends with the chef at Patina
exactly one year after moving to Los Angeles. It had taken
a year for her to realize that the easiest way to a full stomach was working at a restaurant, and she lucked out when
she got the job. Ever since her graduation from UCLA, the
chef had invited her into the kitchen and served what was
undoubtedly the best food she had ever tasted. The invita-
tions came two or three times a year and had never stopped.
Last month she sat at the table with a developer whom she
had read about but never previously met, the man most people
considered the prime mover in reshaping the City of Angels.
Because Lena had majored in architecture, they had a lot to
talk about. After the dinner ended, the man asked her to
pull her car around to the kitchen door and threw the case in
her trunk. When she tried to object, he laughed and told her
that he was a new grandfather of twins. His wife was helping his son and daughter-in-law at the house. He didn't
smoke cigars anymore, so she had to accept the wine as his
gift.

It had been an act of generosity and grace from someone
who loved the city as much as she did—the kind of thing
you don't hear about very often. As she sipped the red wine
and savored its clean, smooth taste, she felt her stomach
glow and finally began to relax. After a second sip, she returned to the living room and opened her briefcase.

Before leaving Parker Center, she had stopped by SID and
picked up a second eight-by-ten photo of the victim pulled
from her driver's license. Lena would meet with Steve Avadar from Wells Fargo Bank in the morning. But she also
wanted to show Pamela McBride the photograph on the outside chance that her daughter and Jane Doe knew each
other. Although Jane Doe's knowledge of the identity she

stole was crystal clear, Lena still considered the possibility unlikely. This was a case about people feeding off people who couldn't fight back. The law of the technological jungle. The iJungle. The me-jungle. The fuck-everybody-else-jungle. As she thought about the mother's scrapbook, more than enough information had been published in the newspapers for Jane Doe to get started. If she had any computer savvy at all, it would have been easy to fill in the blanks over the Internet. Still, the idea needed to be checked out and crossed off the list.

She took another sip of wine and looked at the TV. A commercial had just ended and they were cutting back to the newsroom. After the picture faded out, she saw a graphic that included Jane Doe's photograph and the help-line number.

They were doing the story.

As the newsreader summarized the case, Lena realized why the station wanted so much lead time with the photographs. They had set up another remote, not on the Westside covering a crushed Lexus, but in an alley just north of Hollywood Boulevard. And this time there wasn't even a hint of a smile on the reporter's face. It was all business as the man stood beside the Dumpster where Jane Doe's body had been found.

The station had done their homework. They knew the condition of the body even though the details had never been released. They cut to a series of shots from last night. The camera operator must have paid off someone because he found a position on a rooftop and recorded the body being loaded into the coroner's van. They even included a shot of Lena walking away from the crime scene, along with a brief history of her role in the Romeo murder case.

She didn't care about the leak or about being singled out. They had spent five entire minutes on the story and ended it with the two photographs set side-by-side—the victim and her killer. Lena couldn't have hoped for more.

The phone began to ring. Moving to the counter, she switched on the small table lamp and read the name off the Caller ID screen. It was Rhodes.

"I think Barrera did good," he said. "Tonight was the right time to release the story."

"You hear anything?"

"Only that I'm still working with you. At least through tomorrow."

"What about Tito?"

"He made plans, so he's not that happy about it. He'll be there, though."

"You guys will start with Fontaine, right?"

"I'll run him through the system," he said. "Tito's geared up to interview the doctor's neighbors. What about you?"

She thought about her meeting with Steve Avadar in the morning. That just maybe the victim's bank statements would shed some light on Fontaine's involvement. She didn't say anything because it was only a hunch. Still, it had been the single reason why she'd called Avadar on a Friday night. The reason she didn't want to wait until Monday to see the statements.

"I'll be in later," she said. "I'll call from the bank when I'm done."

"Sounds good. What are you drinking?"

She smiled. "How do you know I'm drinking?"

"Your voice," he said. "It changes. It gets deeper and cracks."

She set the glass down on the counter. "Ice water," she said.

Rhodes laughed. "I'll bet it's really good ice water. Try and get some sleep. I think we're gonna need it. I've got a feeling about this one."

"Me, too," she said.

He hung up. Lena stared at the phone, thinking about what Rhodes said for a moment. Letting the words sink in. Then she switched off the TV, crossed the room to the slider, and opened the door. The thermometer on the wall read thirty-nine degrees, but it felt much colder than that. As she stepped outside and walked down the steps to the pool, she could feel the cold penetrating her socks from the concrete.

She sat down at the table and lifted her feet off the

ground. Gazing over the lip of the pool, her eyes swept across the city below. She could see the world moving, but she couldn't hear it.

She took another sip from her glass. She was beginning to feel the wine now. The ebb and flow of her breathing. As her mind quieted, she thought about Rhodes and wondered if he was alone tonight. She could tell that he still had feelings for her. Although she felt the same way, she was torn because she liked working with him so much and didn't want it to end.

A moment passed, her thoughts lingering. Dreams. Fantasies. The smell of his skin. And that's when she heard the sound of a car door.

It was close. Too close. The sound had come from right in front of the house. Her closest neighbor was through the brush on the other side of the hill. There was no reason for a car to be parked there. The road was too narrow, the twists and turns through the hills too sharp.

She got to her feet, glancing at her socks and wishing that she had a pair of shoes on. Checking the driveway, she slid into the shadows and followed the path around the other side of the house. She moved slowly, silently—her feet burning from the cold. As she reached the clearing, she paused a moment and looked around the corner. Satisfied that she was alone on the property, she kept to the darkness and started through the brush. There was a bluff between her house and the road, about twenty feet high, and she could hear voices now. Lowering her body to the ground, she crawled to the top and peered over the other side.

It was a Caprice, parked across the street underneath the trees.

A man in a suit was leaning against the door, smoking a cigarette, and whispering to someone through the open window. They were laughing about something. She noted the chiseled young face and short brown hair. She could see the gun strapped to his shoulder and knew that he carried a badge. Even though she couldn't place the name, she remembered seeing him around and knew where he worked. He was one of Klinger's friends—someone Klinger was bringing along before he left Internal Affairs. She was having trouble with the name because the bureau wasn't housed at Parker Center. Instead, they were over on Broadway several blocks away.

It looked like Klinger and Chief Logan were trying to keep in touch. Close touch. Although she had skipped the meeting after the autopsy and hadn't called either one, Barrera had said that he talked to them this afternoon and everything was cool.

She backed down the hill, trying to control her anger and see the situation for what it really was.

If they wanted to keep an eye on her, which was insane, why would they park in the only spot that didn't offer a view of her house? Why would they park behind the bluff? The man she saw smoking the cigarette looked young and stupid. All the same, he probably wasn't that stupid.

As she considered the possibilities, the answer seemed obvious.

She looked up and followed the telephone line through the air. The wire crossed the front yard, then made a run along the side of the house she'd just passed from the pool. She moved down the path to the utility box and swung open the plastic door. As dark as it was, she didn't need a flashlight to spot the tap and wireless transmitter.

They didn't need to keep watch because they were listening. Listening without a judge signing off on a warrant.

Lena closed the box without disturbing the tap. Grabbing her wineglass, she returned to the house and locked the door behind her. She was glad she'd skipped dinner, but thought she might have trouble getting to sleep tonight.

14

Nathan G. Cava watched the Mercedes pull into the drive and vanish behind the grove of oak trees. But it was the Ford Explorer with darkened glass following the Mercedes onto the property that he found so disturbing. As the gate closed, he pulled into a construction site just across the street. Someone wanted a new mansion, so they tore down the old one. Nothing was left but a ten-foot wall protecting a bunch of dirt.

Welcome to the Westside. Swimming pools and movie stars.

Cava made a loop, his Hummer grinding up the loose soil. When he had a reasonable view of Fontaine's place, he slammed on the brakes and watched the cloud of dust rake across the hood. Then he reached for his binoculars, steadying his view through the trees with his elbows pinned to the steering wheel.

Fontaine and his girlfriend from the office were heading for the front door. The two men riding in the Explorer were walking around both sides of the house, sweeping the property.

It looked like the Beverly Hills doctor had hired a pair of bodyguards. All of a sudden things were getting dramatic. And Nathan G. Cava didn't like dramatic.

He wondered what had spooked Fontaine, and figured that it must have been that story they ran on the news last night. Cava had seen it on one of the stations when it was rebroadcast at 1:00 a.m. He'd just returned to his apartment, popped an Ambien CR, and was lying in bed waiting for the drug to take. That's when he learned that there had been a witness. That part one of his three-part Hollywood deal wasn't exactly done yet. There was another loose end. Another screwup, just like all the other screwups he'd endured while overseas.

Someone had been hiding in the parking lot Wednesday night and had the balls to take that picture. The quality of the photograph ate shit and wasn't worth worrying about. But someone had been lurking in the shadows. Someone had been watching him. No matter how dark it may have been that night, odds were that the witness saw his face and probably knew the make and model of his car. As he played back the night in his head, he had to admit that he'd been a little nervous, a bit rusty and not exactly up to par. He hadn't expected her to be so young or pretty. And he hadn't expected her to smile. He had seen her do it through the window when he walked by. He could see the spark in her eyes.

Even worse, he wasn't really sold on the reason he had been given to talk to the pretty girl and to take her life. It felt a lot like the reasons he had been given during his three tours of duty. When he did the math, it never really added up. Especially the two additional years he had spent in Eastern Europe, where he had been given the nickname *Dr. Neat*. The truth was that he considered himself a physician—not an information specialist who interviews people and delves into their past with the aid of special tools. Although he had followed orders, he hated the nickname and the people who gave it to him. It felt more like a burden than anything else. A burden placed on him by people he couldn't trust because he knew that they didn't have souls and were using him.

Cava needed reasons to do the things he did. The more personal, the better. And if he couldn't be given a reason, he needed to find one on his own. Something with more resonance than money. Something more real and less tarnished than *For God and Country*. Sometimes, he found the reason the moment he looked at a person. But usually it took a couple of days to smoke out and feel true. It was part of the creative process. The thing that kept him sane in a world that had stopped spinning eight years ago. The thing that protected his core deep inside. The core no one could get to, that no one could catch or reach or run a jetliner through.

His mind surfaced and he lowered the binoculars. A double-decker bus filled with smiling tourists pulled to a stop in front of the Playboy Mansion at the end of the block. After everyone got their pictures, the bus would stop before the house they'd used to shoot the movie *Scarface*. Five mansions up the yellow brick road and they would make a third stop in front of Humphrey Bogart's old house. The place where Sam Spade hung his hat and played with Lauren Bacall's tits in bed.

Cava knew the route because he'd taken the tour yesterday, shooting pictures like a dumb ass from the upper deck as he tried to get a better feel for the neighborhood. It had been worth the hassle—a reconnaissance mission wearing light touristy clothes purchased directly from Tommy Bahama's store at the Grove on Third Street earlier that morning. Despite freezing his ass off, he seemed to fit in and managed to get a good first look at Fontaine's house. The property may have been the smallest on South Mapleton Drive, but still included a pool, tennis courts, a guest house, and a garage big enough to get lost in. But unlike his neighbors, Fontaine only had two cars. This surprised Cava—not ten cars, just a pair of Mercedes. And the convertible looked a little old, like maybe the Beverly Hills doctor was living beyond his means, trying to hold on in a neighborhood where everyone else had enough cash to let go. Still, the house was perfectly placed, the backyard opening like a gate to the Los Angeles Country Club. It seemed to meet Cava's every need. Getting to Fontaine would be easy when the time came, especially at night.

The tour bus lumbered by, spewing a thick blue cloud of diesel exhaust into air that already smelled like a truck stop. Cava recognized the driver from yesterday and lowered his head, thinking about the growing list of potential witnesses and those two bodyguards.

He had followed Fontaine and his girlfriend home from the office last night. Kept an eye on them until midnight before driving across town to his apartment on Barham Boulevard overlooking Universal Studios and the Warner Brothers lot. When he returned this morning, he noticed the Ford Explorer leading the way to a 7:00 a.m. breakfast at Nate'n Al's in Beverly Hills. Although he didn't enter the deli, he glanced through the window in passing and saw Fontaine and the blonde seated with the two men. Probably working out terms and doing the deal.

Cava checked on the tour bus again, watching it wheeze slowly up the hill. Raising the binoculars, he took a last look at Fontaine's house and wondered if the bodyguards were smart enough to ask for their money up front.

Probably not.

He grinned a little as he kicked the idea around and watched someone lowering the blinds on the first floor. It was beginning to feel right. Beginning to feel true. But first he needed to get rid of his car. He checked his watch. He wanted to hit the dealership before nine.

15

She was standing by the window in the second-floor bedroom and could see the left front fender of the Caprice over the crest of the hill. At some point during the night Klinger's friends from Internal Affairs had moved their car farther down the road. They may have been anticipating daylight, but they were still there. And when Lena checked the utility box this morning, the tap and wireless transmitter were still in place as well. They were listening, or at least trying to. After returning to the house, Lena had programmed the phone to forward incoming calls to her cell. The tap on the outside lines would no longer be able to pick up a signal, just the initial ring before the phone company's computers rerouted the call. It would be a series of long, cold nights for both detectives from Internal Affairs, nights spent in futility and silence. She wished she could see Klinger's face when they called in their report.

Her cell phone vibrated and she glanced at the LCD screen. It was Steve Avadar from Wells Fargo Bank, calling at 8:30 a.m.

"Lena, when was the woman calling herself Jennifer McBride murdered?"

His voice was quiet. Maybe too quiet.

"Wednesday night," she said. "Why?"

"Because the account's still active. Her ATM card has been used every day since the murder to get cash."

"How much has been taken?"

She could hear papers rustling in the background—Avadar cupping the phone and saying something to someone in his office. After a moment, he was back.

"Whoever's using the card is pulling her daily limit. Five hundred a day. Two thousand so far. Someone used the card at seven-twenty-three this morning."

Lena turned away from the window, thinking about the witness. She had received the victim's driver's license and the video clip of the abduction, but the witness had kept the victim's purse and everything inside it, including the ATM card.

"How much is in the account?" she asked.

"More than fifty thousand dollars."

It hung there. The weight and breadth of the money. Along with the reason why the witness wanted to remain hidden.

"That's serious money," she said.

"You bet it's serious."

"Where was the withdrawal made this morning?"

"On Fourth Street in Santa Monica."

"I know it's Saturday," she said, "but is there any chance we could meet there instead of downtown?"

"I've already made the arrangements. The ATM's been shut down and we're pulling the video."

"I'll be there as soon as I can."

Five minutes later she was easing her car out of the drive and checking the road to her right. The Caprice remained hidden around the bend. As she made a left and hit the accelerator, she rolled down the windows and kept her eyes pinned to the rearview mirror. She could feel the cold air beating against her face, the heat in her blood, but the road behind remained empty.

The bank was at Fourth and Arizona, one block north of Santa Monica Boulevard. Lena entered the lobby and found Steve Avadar in the manager's office combing through a stack of papers.

She tapped the door on her way in. Avadar was alone and grinned as he rose from the chair.

"We're still working on the ATM video," he said. "We're pulling the first three withdrawals. They're from local branches, so it should only take another ten minutes."

"Thanks for doing this, Steve. Let's start with the victim's account."

"I've been going through her monthly statements," he said. "I think we've got something."

"Show me."

Steve Avadar may have been a vice president directing fraud investigations and risk management for the bank, but today he looked anything but corporate. His dark brown hair was longer than she remembered. And he'd left his suit behind for a pair of jeans and a fleece pullover. Although his appearance was young and athletic, casual and laid-back, she remembered his mind being tack sharp. And when he quickly arranged the statements in chronological order, she could tell by the expression on his face that he wasn't driven by worry. It was all about discovery now—a certain fascination for what they might find underneath the next rock.

"Okay, Lena, it's our lucky day. We've got thirteen statements. The woman calling herself Jennifer McBride opened a checking account thirteen months ago with ten thousand dollars in cash. For the first month there was no activity. The money just sat there. When we get to month two, her address changes and money's moving in and out."

Lena checked the address printed on the first two statements. Although the town and zip code bordered Santa Monica and Venice, the block number at Lincoln and Ocean Park wasn't residential. It was a major intersection in a part of town she had driven through many times. When she remembered that a Mail Boxes Etc. was located on the same block, it made perfect sense. Jane Doe was in the process of stealing an identity and becoming Jennifer McBride. She needed a mailing address to get started—a safe address where she could receive mail until she rented the apartment within walking distance over on Navy Street.

Avadar pointed at the statements. "I've gone through the checks she wrote and nothing stands out," he said. "Rent and

utilities, cable TV, telephone bills for the house and a cell—
it's all routine stuff. Same with her credit card. Just gas,
groceries, and restaurants. Did you guys recover her checkbook?"

Lena shook her head and gave him an overview of what
they thought had been in the victim's purse at the time of her
murder.

Avadar thought it over. "So maybe she kept an address
book or memo pad with her. Maybe she wrote down her
password."

"I think she wrote down a lot of things. She was living
two lives and juggling the details for an entire year. She
couldn't trust it to memory. She was too smart."

"But not smart enough to not get killed."

A moment passed as Avadar's words settled into the
room. Then he cleared his throat and continued in a quieter
voice.

"Whoever's using the ATM card knew the password from
the very beginning, Lena. On the first withdrawal, there were
no mistakes. No second or third tries. They inserted the
card, punched in the magic number, and took the cash."

"Let's get to the deposits," Lena said.

"Do you know what she did for a living?"

Lena hesitated a moment, deciding not to answer the
question unless it became necessary. "Why?" she asked.

"I'm just curious. She's not depositing a payroll check.
Look at the third statement. Six deposits. Four or five hundred bucks each. All of it's cash."

"How does this add up to fifty thousand dollars?"

"It doesn't. Every statement here is exactly the same.
Small cash deposits amounting to about twenty-five hun-
dred dollars a month. Just enough to pay her bills. The fifty
grand came in last Friday, six days before she was murdered.
The deposit won't appear on her statement until next month.
It came in as a single chunk."

"Cash?"

Avadar shook his head. "We would have noticed that," he
said. "It was a check from Western Union. I'm gonna make

a wild guess that whoever sent it didn't want to leave a paper trail."

"And that the fifty thousand started out as cash."

"All they needed to do was show an ID and fill out a form, Lena."

"Then Western Union cuts a check at this end and the victim deposits it into her account."

"Right," he said. "Let me see how they're making out with the video."

Lena watched him exit the room and sat down in the chair. This was what she had hoped to find, what she thought she would find, but had held back from Rhodes last night on the phone because she wasn't sure. This was the only thing that made sense and explained why a Beverly Hills doctor like Joseph Fontaine could be involved. Why he knew the victim and lied about it to detectives investigating a murder case.

She turned back to the bank statements, reviewing the small cash deposits made at the end of each week.

The best Lena could figure, Jane Doe would have had three good reasons to steal McBride's identity. First, she grew up in Los Angeles and wanted to hide the fact that she was placing sex ads in a city paper and had become a prostitute. Second, she really could have been a *phantom*— someone who lights up a stolen identity and moves on after the candle has burned out. The fact that everything in her apartment was downsized and portable seemed to support this. And then the jackpot: the possibility that both were true and she was blackmailing Fontaine. Threatening to expose the Beverly Hills pediatrician with their relationship unless he paid up. Rather than risk losing his career as a doctor who worked with children, Fontaine probably bought time with a small first payment before deciding to lash out. Either he paid someone to murder the woman or he killed her himself.

Avadar walked into the room holding four unlabeled DVDs. "I've got them," he said. "I'll burn you a single disc after we take a look."

He copied the video files from each disc onto the computer's hard drive. When he finished, Lena moved around the desk for a better look. The four files were on the monitor, each labeled by the date of the withdrawal. Avadar highlighted the group and hit PLAY, running the clips back-to-back without interruption. Although the images were degraded, it was obvious that the same person had accessed the ATMs and stolen the cash at five hundred dollars a shot.

But Lena wasn't really thinking about the money anymore. She was playing back her telephone conversation with Lieutenant Barrera in her head. The one she'd had after leaving Fontaine's office last night. The one that included a brief description of the messenger who walked into Parker Center with the package from the witness. The kid in the leather jacket wearing a Dodger cap, who didn't ask the cops at the front desk to sign a log book and didn't bother to leave a receipt.

She studied the monitor, watching their witness work the keyboard and rip off the cash. His head was lowered, his face partially concealed by the bill of his cap. He knew where the camera was, and he knew that he was committing a crime. Still, she could see enough of his mouth and chin to know that he was young. Eighteen or nineteen with long dark hair. She could see enough to know that it was him.

16

Nathan G. Cava strode down the long row of cars in his suit and tie, worrying that maybe Vinny Bing the Cadillac King had been the wrong choice in a dealership. He could feel a punk salesman tagging along, nipping at his ankles like a stray dog. And something was going on in the main showroom. He hadn't been inside yet, but he could see some sort of commotion through the glass and sensed that there was a problem.

He glanced back at the salesman—the mealymouthed man jabbering away on autopilot—and regretted giving the idiot his name.

He had chosen Vinny Bing's dealership because it was on the south side of town. Poor people lived here, and he hoped that he might get a better deal. He already knew which car he wanted. An SRX Crossover. Not as big as his beloved Hummer, but enough car to feel at home in. He particularly liked the size of the sunroof. The retractable glass extended from front to back, taking up most of the roof of the car. Cava thought it might come in handy for surveillance work. Still, he would be sorry to see the Hummer go. It was almost new, and he liked the way it drove. The fact that people got out of his way and left him an open road. Even those creeps in their BMWs.

Cava continued his march down the aisle, ignoring the salesman. He knew the car he wanted, but couldn't decide on the color. In the best of all worlds he would have chosen black. But for someone in his line of work, he thought that it might be safer to go with something less stark. Something that would blend a little better in the neighborhood. He had narrowed his choice down to two, and as he continued walking, he spotted them parked side by side.

He stopped and gave the two cars a long look, then turned to the salesman and waved his hand in a call for immediate silence.

"What color is that car?" he asked.

"Oh, you've picked a good one, sir. That's an SRX, and it's priced just right. It's on sale today. If you buy it in the next hour you'll save even more."

"What color is it?"

"We call that one 'Light Platinum.' And it's the best."

Cava pointed to the second car. "What color's that one?"

"That's 'Radiant Bronze.' You couldn't make a better choice, Mr. Cava. It's the best."

"How can two cars be the best?"

"They're all the best. That's all we sell here. Just name your price and I'll run it by Vinny—simple as that. Want the keys? Let's test her out."

Cava turned and looked down at the salesman. He was dressed in a ratty suit and his wrinkled shirt needed a hot iron.

"I don't want a test drive. I want the car and I want it in Radiant Bronze. Now, go get Vinny."

"We need to do this inside, Mr. Cava. We've got a deal room."

Cava paused a moment. He didn't know what a "deal room" was.

"I'm okay with that," he said finally. "But I don't work with a translator. If you want the deal, bring Vinny."

"Okay, okay. But don't come in until I give you the signal."

The man winked at him, then cantered ahead and disappeared into the showroom. Cava didn't get it. But then, he hadn't understood anything the man had been saying for the past ten minutes.

He started walking toward the showroom, worrying

again. Thinking that maybe he should head back to the Hummer and bolt. Take his chances that he wouldn't get stopped. The witness probably saw his face and knew that he drove a Hummer, but that's as far as it would go. No one had his plate numbers because he had taken the precaution of lifting a temporary set from the C Lot over at Los Angeles International Airport earlier that night, then switched back.

He could split right now and take his chances. But was it worth the risk?

He held out his hands and realized that they were trembling. Not enough that anyone would notice, but not rock steady, either. Not kill steady. He heard the salesman call out his name and looked up.

The little guy was holding the showroom door open and waving at him. Cava guessed that this was *the signal.*

He took a deep breath and stepped through the door. Heard Ray Charles singing "Rudolph the Red-Nosed Reindeer." Saw the bright lights hanging from the ceiling, and a man moving in from the right with a video camera. A second camera was pointed across the room at a man with a grotesque smile slowly descending a staircase from the management offices on the second floor.

Cava tried to keep cool and focused in spite of the confusion. The man making his runway entrance down the stairs was wearing some sort of weird costume. At first, Cava thought that he might be dressed up as Santa Claus or maybe even the Burger King. But after a while he put the scene together with the cameras and music and decided that the bizarre-looking jerk was just Vinny Bing, the Cadillac King.

Cava turned to the camera in his face and covered the lens with his right hand. When the cameraman tried to pull away, he tightened his grip on the lens. Then, a kid in jeans and a T-shirt ran over and started hyperventilating in his ear.

"Be cool, man. You're on the show."

"What show?"

"Vinny's show. We're shooting the second season. We're on cable TV, man."

Cava met the prick's eyes, ready to snap the lens off the camera. "This is *live*?"

"No. It won't be on until next year. The season starts in January. Not this coming January, the next one. If you wanna make the cut, you gotta be cool. You cool?"

Cava's eyes swept across the showroom as he thought it over. He spotted the tent pitched in the middle of the floor— the neon sign that read LET'S DO DA DEAL blinking over the entrance. The king was still working that staircase, his smile growing from cheek to cheek with each new step. A year from now and Cava would be the invisible man living thousands of miles away. No one would be looking for him anymore. Still, he wondered if this might not be a hallucination, or even a side effect from taking that sleeping pill last night and waking up too soon. Either way, unloading the Hummer had become a fucking nightmare.

"I'm cool," he said.

"Then let go of the camera and shake Vinny's hand."

Cava released his grip, ignoring the angry look on the cameraman's face. After another deep breath, he crossed the showroom floor. The king had hit ground level and was approaching him now. As Cava moved closer, he noticed the letters VB dangling from the king's necklace. The letters were two inches high and encrusted with diamonds. The king extended a weak hand and Cava shook it.

"My name's Vinny Bing, the Cadillac King. I heard you want an SRX Crossover in Radiant Bronze." The king turned his head, looked into the camera, and flashed a TV smile. "Let's do da deal."

People started clapping. Salesmen standing at their desks and the video crew. Cava didn't say anything, noting the cheap rings on Bing's fingers and sizing up the man as they entered the deal tent. That speck of ketchup on the side of his mouth filled out the profile pretty good. His read was so clear that it felt like it came right out of the *Encyclopedia Britannica*. Vinny Bing was an overweight, knuckle-dragging, mouth-breathing motherfucker in his early thirties. A first citizen from Generation Over and Out. Generation Done. One of the eighty-percent crew who had given up the use of utensils and ate all three meals with their hands. Given up reading in favor of watching and consuming until their brains turned into guacamole and a bowl of broken tortilla chips with too much salt.

Both video cameras followed them into the tent, along with a short, round man holding a boom mike. Bing moved behind the desk and sat down on what looked like a toy throne. Then the irritating salesman who had been hounding Cava ran in and handed Bing a spec sheet on the car.

"Where we at?" Bing said, smacking his lips. "Whatta we gots?"

Cava watched the king's eyes glide over his name on the sheet of paper. After a moment, he tossed it aside, pulled his pad and pen closer, and batted his eyes at the camera like he was ready to do big business.

"Okay," he said. "Customer Cava wants the SRX Crossover in Radiant Bronze. Are we talkin' about the V6 economy package, or the four-point-six Northstar V8? With the eight, you get three hundred and twenty horses under the hood and feel like you're in a rocket ship."

"I want the rocket ship," Cava said.

Bing smiled at the camera again. "Sweet," he said. "I like this guy. He's the quiet type, but I like him anyhow."

Then Bing cupped his left hand and jotted down a number on the pad so only he and the camera could see it. He tore off the sheet, folding it over and passing it across the desk.

"Merry Christmas," he said. "A special price 'cause you're Vinny Bing's special friend. And I'm gonna give you even more. Just say the word and the king throws in the Convenience Package, the Driver's Package, even the Seating Package. I don't care because it's Christmas. I'm throwing it all in for free."

Cava unfolded the paper and glanced at the secret number—well aware that the three packages went with the V8 and were part of the base price. He had test-driven the car at the auto strip in Glendale, researched the numbers on the Web, and knew exactly what Vinny Bing had paid for the car. The king was beginning to smell a lot like a grifter.

"What about the sunroof?" Cava said. "How 'bout throwing that in, too?"

Bing laughed. "That sunroof's part of the Luxury Premium Pack. It's an ultra-view."

"But I thought we were friends."

Bing paused a moment. "Your name's Nathan, right?"

Cava nodded, his eyes pinned on the grifter. "Nathan G. Cava."

"What's the G stand for?"

"Good."

"Anyone ever write a song about you?"

"Not yet."

Bing laughed again. "Well, we can still be friends, Nathan. But it's gonna cost you an extra five K."

Cava did the math. The package went for forty-two hundred, not 5K. The king wanted to steal another eight hundred dollars.

"What if we're talking cash," he said.

"Then we're friends again, Nathan. Real good friends. Let's do the deal while everybody's watching. Let's show 'em the cash."

Unloading the Hummer had become more than just another L.A. media nightmare. It had been painful. The back-and-forth bullshit lasted for more than an hour, so long that the shake in his hands was visible now. Even the king had mentioned it when the cameras shut down.

Cava exited the Financial Services office and followed the salesman out to his Hummer so he could collect his things. He had paid the balance between the two cars in hundred-dollar bills. Although he regretted having to buy another car so soon, he could afford the additional expense. Between the cash he'd found buried in the Iraqi desert and the money he would receive from his three-part Hollywood deal, Cava would be set for life.

It would be a modest life. Not like the generals who said they were looking for Saddam's weapons of mass destruction, the ones who always knew that they weren't there and were really searching for the man's cash. Not like his superior officers who were loading coffin after coffin with greenbacks by the millions and shipping them home with tears of joy dripping down their cheeks. But enough to lay on a beach somewhere. Enough to keep medicated and to spend the rest of his life trying to forget old memories and create new ones.

Coronaville.

Cava hit the door locks on his key ring and walked ahead of the salesman. As he emptied the glove box into his briefcase, he tried to ignore the smell of the leather seats. Tried not to look at the teched-out dashboard and stainless-steel gear shift. All the things he loved about the car. He reached over the passenger seat and cleared out the center compartment. He worked as quickly as he could, aware that his hands were shaking so hard he came off like a drunk. When he finished, he scanned the interior and spotted his Ray-Bans clipped to the sun visor. Slipping them over his eyes, he stepped back and handed the salesman his keys.

It felt more like a funeral than anything else. Watching the little guy in the cheap suit get behind the wheel of his baby and start her up. Listening to the machine purr. Facing the reality that his road-warrior days were over.

The salesman turned to him and laughed. "Hey, this thing's got less than seven thousand miles. How come you unloaded it?"

He called it a *thing.* Cava bit his lip.

"Doctor's orders," he said. "High blood pressure. I'm tired of people flipping me the bird."

The salesman laughed and shot him a look like he was crazy. Then Cava snapped shut the passenger door and watched the Hummer pull off into the bright sunlight. When it disappeared behind the building, he slipped off his shades, shouldered his briefcase, and trudged back into the building. The king was making another entrance, working that staircase again. This time the victim was a sixteen-year-old girl standing beside her father. They looked like innocents. Grifter bait mesmerized by all the lights and cameras. Cava felt sorry for them.

He checked his watch. His new wheels wouldn't be ready for another fifteen minutes. When he glanced inside the waiting room and found it empty, he walked over to the couch in front of the TV, opened his briefcase, and fished out his daily planner. Paging through the week, he made an effort to settle down and focus on his medication schedule. He kept meticulous records because he had to. He had been on the Iraqi version of the Zone diet ever since he hit the desert.

Xanax in the morning, Ambien CR at night, keeps a soldier boy from climbing out of his skin.

It was the war zone diet everybody followed because you were in real deep shit and on your own. No one could tell who the enemy was and no one could escape. When he was transferred to Eastern Europe, the pills were given just as freely, no questions asked. Just a wink and a smile with a shot of water for all the good work he was doing to save the fucking sand world.

It was Saturday, December 15. According to the notation in his planner, he had popped two milligrams of Xanax he didn't remember taking at 6:00 a.m., along with a Boniva, the once-a-month solution to maintaining strong bones he had seen advertised so often on TV. If he went by the book he'd have to wait seven to eight hours before taking another Xanax. He spent a moment looking at his hands trembling before his eyes. Then he ripped open the side pocket in his briefcase and picked through his medications. When he found the bottle of Xanax, he shook a pill onto his palm, tossed it into his mouth, and swallowed it dry.

Sometimes just taking the pill made him feel right again. Sometimes half an hour went by before the drug kicked in. He gazed around the room. The TV was switched to CNN. As his mind began to loosen up, he started thinking about Fontaine again. Once the king gave him the keys to the SRX, Cava planned on making his maiden voyage a return trip to Beverly Hills. He needed to lock in the doctor's weekend schedule and figure out how he was going to handle things with the girlfriend and those two bodyguards around. Something quiet that no one would notice for a while. And what about the witness? Now that he'd traded in his car, should he keep the witness on the back burner or amp up his pursuit?

He looked back at the TV. When he saw a photograph of the girl he'd murdered, his mind bolted to the surface. They were running the story on CNN, but the focus seemed to be on the detective investigating the case. A woman named Lena Gamble who worked out of the Robbery-Homicide Division and solved another case last year. Apparently she was trying to locate a witness to the murder. Someone who helped but hadn't come forward.

Cava jotted Gamble's name down as quickly as he could, mesmerized by the sight of her. He looked at her tangled hair. Her angular face and long body. Her hips hidden beneath her clothes. The video on the screen had been taken at night with a telephoto lens eight months ago during the wildfires. Gamble was exiting a crime scene with a shotgun in her hands. Her cheekbones glistened with fresh blood spatter. But it was the determination on her face, the smoke in her dusky-blue eyes that he found so captivating. When the report cut back to the present and ended with side-by-side photographs of the victim and her killer, he gazed at the blurred-out image of himself and realized that he wasn't shaking anymore.

"That guy looks like a goddamn ghost," a woman shouted.

Cava turned and found the woman sitting in a chair by the coffeemaker and donut tray. She was an older woman. The kind you see with a cigarette in her mouth working the slots in Vegas. He hadn't heard her enter the room. She looked back at the TV and squinted through her glasses.

"I can't tell who he is," she went on. "But I'd bet the house he's an ugly son-of-bitch."

Cava gave her a long look, then started laughing. He was feeling good again. Right again. Thanking the gods of modern medicine.

"You got that right, lady. I'll bet that guy's ugly as sin . . ."

17

Lena hit Rhodes's speed-dial number on her cell as she pulled out of the lot. After two rings, he picked up.

"Where are you?" he said.

"Just leaving the bank. Did Barrera make it in?"

"No, but Klinger's here."

She shrugged it off. "I've got news," she said. "Jane Doe made a fifty-thousand-dollar deposit six days before she was murdered."

Rhodes didn't say anything right away, but she could guess what he was thinking. Fifty thousand dollars was on the table. People had been killed for a lot less.

"You think she was blackmailing Fontaine," he said finally.

"It would explain why he lied to us."

"It would explain a lot of things."

She filled him in on her meeting with Steve Avadar, working her way through the victim's weekly deposits until she reached the check from Western Union and the kid stealing money from the ATMs one small piece at a time. The kid she believed had witnessed the abduction and walked into the lobby at Parker Center to deliver the package.

"So, our witness is a thief with a guilty conscience," Rhodes said.

"Or a greedy Good Samaritan. We need to pull the surveillance video from the lobby. He made the delivery late yesterday morning."

"I'll get things started. When are you coming in? Klinger's been asking for you."

"As soon as I run Jane Doe's photo by McBride's mother."

"There's no need," he said. "I just got off the phone with her. She saw the news last night and talked to most of her daughter's friends. The TV stations posted the pictures on their Web sites so everybody can see them now. Her friends don't know her, either. It's a dead end."

Lena tossed it over without responding. She hadn't expected a connection between Jane Doe and the real Jennifer McBride and thought that there was enough information out there for the victim to have stolen the identity outright. Still, there was always that feeling of hope flickering in the background. Hope that she might be wrong and the answers would come more quickly. She had thought it would turn out this way, but that didn't mean she wasn't disappointed.

"What about the help line?" she asked.

"Three people called to order pizza. It's a downhill ride from there."

Lena shifted lanes and made a U-turn at the corner, heading for the 10 Freeway.

"I'll see you as soon as I can," she said.

She closed her phone and slipped it into her pocket. Over the past few years it had become increasingly difficult to find witnesses willing to speak up. The trend began with gang crimes and new rounds of witness intimidation that included kidnapping, torture, and often times, murder. As the word spread through news stories and the worst of hip-hop, fear gripped the city and the witness pool for all sorts of homicide investigations began to dry up.

Snitches wear stitches.

For Lena those three words were more than the code of the street. They were a warning beacon, a reminder of how frail a society can become. How easily ignorance and ni-hilism can take root when so many people have stopped watching.

She tried to shake off the bad vibes—tried to keep her mind off the personal reasons why the one witness they knew

about probably wouldn't step forward. After hitting the
Fourth Street ramp and accelerating onto the freeway, she
found the left lane and switched on her CD player. Flipping
over to the last disc, she thought about Klinger, skipped to
track 2 and hit PLAY. The cut she wanted to listen to was
called *Stop,* a digital remaster of the album *Super Session,*
recorded by Al Kooper, Mike Bloomfield, and Stephen
Stills nine years before she was even born. She had discovered a vinyl copy in her brother's recording studio and liked
it so much she bought the CD. That was six months ago, and
the album still held a spot in her five-disc player. As the
music started, she settled back in her seat and felt her body
relax some.

The case was beginning to take shape. With Fontaine
uncovered and the discovery of the cash in the victim's bank
account, the investigation was finally beginning to move
forward. Yet, she couldn't help thinking that something was
wrong. She hadn't slept well last night, tossing and turning
in spite of the wine. She didn't understand why the detectives from Internal Affairs were parked outside her house.
Why they would risk their careers by tapping her phone. And
she wasn't sure she should mention it to anyone until she
had a better read on why they were really there. Why did
Klinger and Chief Logan feel the need to keep such close
tabs on her? Why did someone from the sixth floor—probably
Klinger himself—call the press on the night Jane Doe's
body was discovered in Hollywood? Why did he want to
make sure that everyone knew her name was attached to the
case?

The more she thought it over, the more worried she became that she was missing something important. That she
had become lost in the details of a complicated investigation
and wasn't seeing the big picture. The key ingredient that
made it all move.

By the time she reached Parker Center, she could feel the
dread following her into the elevator. She rode up to the
third floor and found the bureau empty, a picture of Fontaine from the DMV on Rhodes's desk. Hiking up the back

steps to SID, she spotted Henry Rollins, a forensic analyst from the photographic unit, working at a computer terminal equipped with a double set of flat-panel monitors. The overhead lights were off, the room darkened.

"What are you doing here on a Saturday?" she asked.

He grinned, but looked tired. "I've got your video up," he said. "I'm cutting the shots together. It'll only take a second."

Lena entered the room, pulling a chair over and handing him the DVD Avadar had given her.

"Video from the ATMs," she said.

"We'll run them side by side."

"Where's Rhodes?"

"He walked out to make a phone call."

Rollins turned back to the pair of twenty-one-inch monitors, streaming through a series of shots so quickly that the images didn't register as anything more than digital noise. He was creating a time line and pulling shots already previewed from an open window on the second monitor. The shots were no bigger than thumbnails and hard to see. As Lena moved closer, she realized that Rollins was doing more than just piecing together surveillance video from the cameras hidden in the lobby. He had taken the extra step and pulled shots from the cameras overlooking the street outside Parker Center.

She sat back in the chair and watched him finish the time line, then quickly download the video clips from the bank. She had never worked with Rollins before, but knew him because of their mutual friendship with Lamar Newton, the crime scene photographer assigned to the case. Rollins was young and lean with bright eyes and a dark complexion. He was just three years out of graduate school from UCLA. Although he never talked about it, Lena had heard rumors that the police departments in New York, Chicago, and Miami had tried to lure him away with offers of a signing bonus. According to Newton, Chief Logan had become involved and convinced Rollins to stay in Los Angeles. At the time bidding wars for new recruits were rare, but now the practice was commonplace.

Rhodes entered the room and grabbed a chair. "Are we close?"

"We're almost there," Rollins said.

Rhodes turned to Lena. "I just got off the phone with Tito," he said. "Fontaine's hired a couple of bodyguards."

"He saw them?"

"Yeah. From the neighbor's house. Two guys taking a smoke break in the backyard."

"What do you think it means?"

"I don't know," he said. "Tito's gonna knock on Fontaine's door and see if he wants to talk about it."

Their eyes met, that feeling of dread still working through her body. When she finally turned back to Rollins, he moved the cursor to the start of the time line, hit the spacebar on his keyboard, and both videos started rolling. As they watched, Lena couldn't help thinking that the edited sequence felt more like a finished work than raw surveillance footage. And there was something spooky about the images, almost as if she was watching a crime unfold before her eyes. Rollins was cutting from camera to camera, following the messenger's progress from the moment he exited the underground garage one block up and started walking down North Los Angeles Street. Although the camera angle was high, the images were in color and far clearer than the video from the ATM machines playing on the second monitor. Lena could see the package underneath the messenger's arm. She could see him turning his face away and looking at the ground as he passed two cops on the sidewalk.

"It gets better," Rollins said. "As soon as he walks inside, it gets a lot better."

Lena checked the second monitor, watching the kid work the ATM machine and steal the victim's daily cash limit. She noted the Dodger cap and leather jacket, focusing on the shape of his mouth and chin. When she turned back to the first monitor, she watched the messenger dressed in the same clothes enter Parker Center and cross the lobby to the front desk.

It was him. There could be no doubt that the messenger

was the same kid standing before the ATM machine, and most likely, the same person who witnessed Jane Doe's abduction on the night of her brutal murder. Eighteen or nineteen with long brown hair and pale skin. The thin and nervous type with dark circles under his eyes. Wasted and scared, she thought. A user in need of another hot load. Someone from the streets with a pocket full of free money and no address.

"He's rolling his eyes underneath the hat," Rhodes said.

Rollins pointed to the image. "He knows that the cameras are there, but he's not sure where they are. He's trying to find them without anyone noticing. He doesn't realize that it's hopeless. He's walking right into the shot."

Lena turned back to the monitor as the kid moved closer. The camera was right in front of him, recording every expression on his face. Every blink and every breath. Yet, he couldn't find the lens. He couldn't hide below the bill of his baseball cap. When he stopped at the front desk, Lena noticed the lunch stand in the background. The two cops taking the package were talking to another cop buying a sandwich. All three were laughing as if someone had just hit the punch line in a good joke. No one was paying any attention to the kid moving quickly across the lobby and back out the door.

Lena watched the monitor as Rollins cut back to the surveillance cameras outside the building and followed the kid up the street.

"Keep your eyes on the sidewalk," he said. "Same side. Half a block up."

She followed the sidewalk up to the corner. Two beats later, she realized that she had been picked up by the camera and was in the shot. She remembered walking back from the Blackbird Café after the autopsy and her run-in with Denny Ramira, the crime beat reporter from *The Times*. The kid was eyeing her as they finally reached each other on the sidewalk. But this time he didn't turn away. Instead, he held the look before making a hard left and vanishing into the underground garage.

What struck Lena most about the surveillance video wasn't the lack of attention paid to the messenger by the two badges working the front desk. Nor was it the coincidence of her passing the kid on the street. Both were innocent acts that carried no meaning or context without the benefit of hindsight. What struck her most was the effort the kid had made to deliver the package to her. She thought about what she found in the mailer. Jane Doe's driver's license and the short video of her abduction recorded with his cell phone. It seemed clear that the kid lived on the Westside. That he had made every effort, however unsuccessful, to avoid their surveillance cameras. So why didn't he take the easy way out and just send the package through the mail?

As Lena considered the possibilities, new questions surfaced. If the kid possessed a guilty conscience, then why was he stealing the victim's money? He would have seen the balance on the ATM machines and known that there was a lot of it. If he wanted the money, then why did he take the time and risk to hand-deliver the package? If he hadn't made the delivery he could have bled the account dry over two or three weeks before anyone noticed.

It was another loose end in a case of loose ends. Another detail that didn't make sense.

She turned back to the monitor. Rollins held the shot on the garage for another minute or two, but a car never came out. Their witness was in the wind.

"I fast-forwarded through the next thirty minutes," Rollins said. "Every car that exited the garage turned up Temple Street, but he wasn't in any of them. Maybe he just went into the food court and got something to eat."

"Or, maybe he knew the cameras were on the street and was looking for a way to disappear," Rhodes said. "How fast can you make prints of his face?"

"I've already got them. I made the prints when I pulled the shots."

Rollins reached for the photographs in the printer tray and passed them out. When he glanced at the doorway, Lena turned and saw Klinger begin walking into the room. He had been watching them. Eavesdropping. He hadn't started moving until he was noticed. Until she turned.

Rollins handed the lieutenant a copy of the image. Klinger examined the photo, then looked at Lena as if nothing was wrong.

"This isn't a serial case, is it?"

"No," she said. "Everything points to someone who's highly motivated."

"But how do you account for the fact that he dismembered the body?"

"He needed a way to get rid of her. He's doing things the way he knows how."

It sat there for a moment with Klinger tossing it over.

"Well, at least you're making progress, Gamble. Everyone understands the setbacks. I'll see if we can get this picture of the witness on the news tonight. Maybe someone will know who he is. We're due for a little luck. Maybe they'll call."

She met Klinger's eyes, thinking about the tap on her telephone and those two detectives from Internal Affairs. She tried to get a read on him, but only picked up this odd sensation of goodwill. She didn't believe it. And she didn't trust it. When his cell phone rang and he stepped away to take the call, his eyes never changed and remained clear and steady and free of any irony.

Lena let the thought go and turned back to Rollins. "What's the status of the video sent by the witness?"

"That's why I'm here today. That's what I wanted to show you."

He turned back to the computer, minimizing the open windows and launching another program. Two more windows opened on the large screen. The first photograph was the still that had been sent to the TV stations. The shot taken from the parking lot of the killer standing over Jane Doe's body in the dark of night. As Lena gazed at it, she couldn't help but feel disappointed. The man remained hopelessly out of focus. And the building with the neon sign on its roof still appeared lost in digital noise.

When she looked at the second image, she stood up and

moved closer. There were six faces on the screen. Six men with similar features and grayish blond hair. The head shots had the look and feel of a six-pack—a photographic lineup—for witnesses attempting to make an ID.

She turned to Rollins. "What is this?"

"The man who murdered Jane Doe."

Rhodes moved in beside her, eyeing the screen. "Which one?"

"All of them," Rollins said. He pointed to the photograph taken from the witness's video clip. "The image we pulled from the video may be out of focus, but the information's still there. This six-pack is a digital reconstruction of the killer's face. The six most likely ways to configure the man's face based on the information in that photo."

Klinger ditched his phone call and stepped in beside Rollins. Lena turned back to the monitor. The images were ultraclear. Ultravivid. As she examined the faces, committing them to memory, it seemed too good to be true. The young forensic analyst had everyone's attention now.

"The man you're looking for resembles each of these six faces in some fundamental way," he said. "We won't know how close they are until you actually find him. But I'll make you this guarantee. When you finally meet this guy, he'll look familiar. Very familiar."

"Like they came from the same mother," Rhodes said. "Different but the same."

"Exactly. Variations on a theme of murder."

Lena traded quick looks with Rhodes. "None of these head shots look anything like Fontaine. We'll need to get a copy of this six-pack over to USC Medical Center. If he trained there before going overseas, this might be enough to trigger an ID."

Klinger shook his head. "Barrera already briefed the chief on a possible connection with the hospital. That the man we're looking for has a medical background. The chief wants to handle this on his own. That means any mention of the medical center never leaves this room."

Lena and Rhodes exchanged another look. But this time

she agreed with Klinger and understood the chief's motive. The doer's only connection with the medical center would have been through a program sponsored by the Department of Defense. There was no reason to jeopardize the hospital's reputation just because someone may or may not have spent a few months working in the emergency room. The situation could be handled quietly, detached from the homicide, and achieve the same result.

Lena turned back to the forensic analyst. "Is there anything more you can pull out of this original?" she said. "Anything that would help point us to its location?"

Rollins grinned. Then he grabbed the mouse and zoomed in on a large white spot in the blue-black sky over the building.

"I've been working on it all morning. This spot is actually a jet making an approach with its landing gear down. When I reconstructed the shadow and counted the number of wheels, I realized that it's a big plane. The only airport that can handle something this size is LAX. So this place has to be somewhere directly east of the airport. Somewhere within a mile or two of LAX."

"It's the Cock-a-doodle-do," Klinger said.

Everyone turned to the chief's adjutant. His eyes were riveted to the photo.

"It's the Cock-a-doodle-do," he repeated with certainty. "The best chicken pieces in L.A. It's east of LAX and right under the flight path just off the one-oh-five on Prairie Avenue. Internal Affairs has been watching the place for two years. Cops go there for takeout."

Lena shot Klinger a look. "Why is Internal Affairs so interested in where cops go for takeout?"

"Because it's a whorehouse," he said.

18

The murder of Jane Doe was suddenly more complex.

Lena may have been green, but she had enough experience to know that the art of closing any case was to keep things simple. To let her imagination and gut instincts light the way, but only move forward with what she knew.

Dr. Joseph Fontaine was trying to hide the fact that he knew the victim. When questioned about the murder, he lied, threatened to hire an attorney, and rented two bodyguards. Jane Doe had stolen an identity and deposited fifty thousand dollars into her checking account six days before her murder. The source of the money had been intentionally hidden, pointing to blackmail. Based on a series of computer-generated images, the man who abducted her from the parking lot didn't necessarily resemble Fontaine. Yet, the man who actually committed the murder and cut up the woman's body shared Fontaine's medical background and military experience.

Lena spotted the neon rooster on the roof as she swept around the exit ramp. After getting an update from his partner, Rhodes closed his cell phone and leaned against the passenger door.

"Tito just left Fontaine's house. The doctor refused to talk."

"Did he see him?"

Rhodes shook his head. "Fontaine wouldn't let him on the property. He didn't get past the front gate."

"How did he think Fontaine sounded?"

"He couldn't get a read. Fontaine's neighbors told him that they used to be friends, but something happened a couple years back. He got weird and dumped everybody. The wife next door remembers walking into the kitchen at a party. Fontaine was having a full-blown conversation with himself. Tito says she used the words, *Dr. Jekyll and Mr. Hyde*."

"Then everybody in the neighborhood thinks he's crazy."

"Sounds like it," Rhodes said. "Have you thought about what could happen when Klinger releases that photo of our witness and the TV stations pick it up?"

He didn't need to ask. It had been on her mind ever since they left Parker Center and she still felt uneasy about it. They were giving the killer a heads-up. Once the photograph of the witness was made public, the kid's life would be in jeopardy. It was unintentional, of course. The only real way of locating him unless they got lucky and either caught him using the ATM card again or driving the victim's car, which remained unaccounted for.

"He's not coming in on his own," she said.

"No, he's not. There's too much money in that bank account."

She could hear the worry in Rhodes's voice, but tried to ignore it. They were passing the Cock-a-doodle-do on the other side of the street. She drove down to the end of the lane divider, then made a U-turn and floored it back up the block. The property was hidden away from the world, nestled in between Prairie Avenue and the 105 Freeway. As she pulled into the entrance and glided down the hill, the place seemed more like a family restaurant than a brothel. It wasn't until she pulled forward and noticed a second building behind the restaurant that she realized Klinger had been right. It looked like a low-end motel without a AAA rating. And the girl leading a man into a room on the second floor wearing stiletto heels and a sheer top didn't appear to have luggage or a maid cart.

"The best chicken pieces in L.A.," Rhodes whispered.

He wasn't watching the couple enter the room. He was reading the words on the neon sign over the restaurant. But

she caught the smile and laughed, guessing that he was trying to make her feel better. Then she turned and spotted the
Dumpster underneath the trees at the rear of the parking lot.
Her file was on the seat between them, and she pulled a copy
of the still photograph taken from the witness's video clip.
Glancing at the image, she measured the angle and passed it
to Rhodes as they got out.

The lot was nearly empty. The air, cool and breezy. She
looked up into the sky and saw a jet trying to find its balance
in the wind. Its wheels were down, the airport just a few
miles west. As she moved around the car and gazed back at
the buildings, she had all the verification she needed.

This was the site of the abduction. All the pieces were in
the right place. Everything was in focus now.

Rhodes passed the photograph back, reaching for his cell
phone. "Looks like we need SID."

She didn't say anything. While he made the call, she
walked over to the Dumpster. The lids were open, the container empty. Taking a step back, she calculated the approxi-
mate location of Jane Doe's body. She knelt down and
examined the broken asphalt, the patches of weeds and dead
grass. The trash had probably been picked up every day since
the abduction and murder, but the ground could still yield
enough trace evidence to confirm that the crime started here.

"They're on their way," Rhodes said.

She looked up and saw the detective standing in the sunlight.

"Klinger was right," she said quietly.

"I guess everybody gets it right once in a while."

The door to the restaurant opened. When they turned, a
young waitress was staring at them from the top of the steps
and appeared concerned.

"Is there anything I can do for you?" she said. "There's no
loitering here, and we're not really open yet. This is private
property."

"This is a crime scene," Lena said.

"It's a what?"

She stood up and called out, "A crime scene. We need to talk to you."

The waitress's face changed. Even from across the lot, Lena could see her body freeze up. Returning to the car for her file, she slipped the photograph inside and joined Rhodes and the girl at the top of the steps.

"I'm only a waitress," she said in a shaky voice. "That's all I do. Just wait on tables."

Rhodes glanced at Lena, then back at the girl, everything nice and easy.

"Relax," he said. "We're not here for that. Let's go inside and talk."

The girl searched their faces. Lena wondered if she didn't see a sense of expectation in her blue-green eyes. A certain reach as if she already understood why they were here and always knew that they would come.

"What's your name?" Lena said.

"Natalie Wells."

"Let's talk inside."

Rhodes swung the door open. As they entered the restaurant, they were met with a rush of warm, fragrant air. Lena could smell the chickens roasting from the pit behind the counter. To the right she noted a wood-burning fireplace, already lighted as they prepared for lunch, and dinner, and whatever came after that. A row of booths lined the far wall. Another two waitresses were setting the tables in the center of the room.

What struck Lena most about the place was that it didn't meet her expectations in any way. Large black-and-white photographs of the city from the 1950s lined the freshly painted white walls. The floor was planked hardwood, buffed and finished to match the fireplace mantel and the molding around the doors and windows. And the tablecloths and napkins the waitresses had set down weren't made of paper. They were linen. As she took a step to her right, she spotted a Hammond B-3 organ, a set of drums, and three mike stands. By any standard the Cock-a-doodle-do wasn't a dive. The place was clean and inviting and they played jazz here.

A door opened from the kitchen and a middle-aged woman stepped out in black slacks and a white blouse. She appeared well groomed and well kept. Although her features were fine, even delicate, Lena could tell from the expression on her face that she made them for cops even before the door rocked back and closed. As she approached, her gaze shifted to the waitress.

"What is it, Natalie? Is there a problem?"

"We're from Robbery-Homicide," Rhodes said. "Are you the manager?"

The woman turned to him. "Catherine Valero," she said. "I own the restaurant. How can I help you?"

Lena opened the file, displaying their photograph of the victim. "Last Wednesday night this woman was abducted from your parking lot. You may have seen it on the news. Her body was found in Hollywood."

Valero studied the picture and appeared concerned. "I take Wednesdays off, but Natalie was here."

Lena turned to the waitress. Her arms were crossed over her chest, her body, even tighter than before. And that reach was still burning in her eyes.

"I waited on her," she whispered.

Lena traded a quick look with Rhodes, feeling the adrenaline kick through her bloodstream. Then Rhodes turned to Valero.

"We can talk later," he said. "Would you mind if we spoke with Natalie alone?"

"Of course not. Sit down and relax. Would you like something to drink?"

"We're fine," he said. "Thanks."

Valero walked back through the kitchen door. Rhodes glanced at the other two waitresses and pointed to a table out of earshot by the fireplace. As they sat down, Lena opened her file to the photograph and noticed that Natalie Wells was trembling. She couldn't have been more than twenty. Her body was small and curvy. Her hair, the kind of brown that lightened in the summer. Sizing her up, Lena couldn't help but notice that there was something soft and exceedingly gentle about the girl.

"Why are you so frightened?" she asked.

"I'm not."

"Did you know her?"

Wells shook her head, lowering her gaze with her arms still shielding her breasts. "I just waited on her."

"This is more than a restaurant, isn't it?"

"Yes, it is," she whispered.

"Was she a regular?"

"I've been thinking about that. She seems familiar, but I don't think so."

"How long have you worked here?"

"A couple of months."

"Just in the restaurant?"

Wells paused, her eyes dancing over the place setting before her. "No," she said finally. "Not just in the restaurant."

The words hung there for a moment, along with the image of that second building off the parking lot and what went on there.

"Okay," Lena said. "You were working on Wednesday night. You were waiting tables."

Wells's eyes finally rose up from the place setting. "She ordered a cup of coffee."

"She was by herself?"

Wells shook her head. "She came in alone. Then some guy sat down with her. When I brought the coffee over, he ordered a glass of ice water with lemon. He called her Jennifer."

"Did she use his name?"

"No. But I got the feeling that they knew each other and had been together before. That happens a lot. Guys wanting the same girl."

"Did you overhear anything they were saying?"

"Just small talk."

"Were they here for very long?"

"Maybe half an hour. They got up like they were ready to leave, but then he changed his mind and said he wanted to finish his ice water. She walked out and he stayed for a while. It looked like he enjoyed making her wait."

Lena glanced at Rhodes. He was sitting back in the chair, quietly taking notes. A ray of muted sunlight from the window brushed against his face and she could see a certain degree of emotion in his eyes.

She turned back to her file and found the DMV photo of Fontaine that Rhodes had added to the stack before they left Parker Center.

"That's not him," Wells said. "He was younger. Better looking."

Lena flipped the photograph over to the shot of their witness stealing money from the ATM. Wells paused for a moment, her mind going.

"I've seen that face before," she said. "But that's not him."

"We think he was here that night," Lena said.

Wells glanced back at the photo. "Like I said, we were busy."

Lena pushed it aside for later review and pulled out the six-pack Rollins had created on his computer. "What about any of these?"

The girl's eyes drifted over the six faces. "They look familiar, too. But I can't place them."

"All of them look familiar?"

"I'm sorry," she said. "Lots of people come through here. None of these look like the guy she was with."

Lena set the six-pack beside the shot from the ATM. Remaining quiet, she let the din of the room take over and gave Wells a long look. The girl was still nervous. Too nervous. After ten minutes any embarrassment over what she did for a living should have subsided. Yet her arms were still wrapped tight around her chest. Her body remained stiff and locked up.

"You're holding something back," Lena said finally. "You're not telling us the truth. When you walked outside ten minutes ago, you knew who we were and why we were here."

Wells stared back at her in silence.

"Are you afraid you'll lose your job?" Lena asked. "Did you see the abduction? Is someone pressuring you?"

"No," she said. "I saw the story on TV, but didn't call in."

"Okay, so you feel guilty. But this is more than that. A lot more. You're holding something back. Something that you know is important."

Without a word Wells got up from the table and crossed the room. Her purse sat on the counter beside a cup of tea, a paperback, and a newspaper that had been read and folded in half. Retrieving the paper, she returned to the table, found the business section and opened it. Lena gave Rhodes a quick look, then watched as Wells set the paper down in front of them and pointed to a photograph.

"That's who she was with," she said. "Him."

19

Lena sat in the passenger seat gazing at the photograph in the paper as Rhodes wheeled the Crown Vic toward West Hollywood. According to the article, I-Marketing Institute was conducting an open focus group at their offices on Melrose Avenue this afternoon. The first thirty people to survive the screening process would pocket $350 at the end of the day.

Justin Tremell owned IMI, Inc., and would be directing the marketing session with his business partner.

She turned and looked out the window at the city racing by. While SID combed through the parking lot collecting trace evidence that yielded hair, fiber, and a stain on the asphalt that one criminalist believed was blood, she and Rhodes had interviewed the entire staff at the restaurant. Of the fifteen people they spoke with, two busboys and another waitress had been working on Wednesday night. All three identified Tremell and said that they remembered seeing him with the victim. And all three seemed as nervous about it as Natalie Wells.

Lena understood their concern. Justin Tremell was a rich kid with rich-kid problems. Speeding tickets, DUIs, bar fights, celebrity girlfriends, a sex video with an actress on her way to nowhere that had made the rounds on the Internet, dramatic breakups with rumors of violence, time spent in rehab relaxing by the pool on Xanax and mineral water over ice, pretending to fend off the paparazzi even though he needed them and wanted them because it meant regular appearances on the Hollywood rag shows, a father ten to twenty fortunes beyond rich only too willing to bail out his troubled son.

She understood their concern because she felt the same way. And when she turned and gazed at Rhodes's face, she could tell that he was feeling it, too.

"This could get tricky," he said.

"Tricky?"

"How much do you know about Justin Tremell?"

"Just the things you can't help hearing on news radio and what's in this article. It says that he got married a couple years ago. It says he's changed."

Rhodes shrugged, making a right turn on Melrose at the Pacific Design Center, then slowing down as Tremell's office came into view. It was a three-story building on the right with its own parking lot in back.

"But do you know why he's changed?" Rhodes said.

"No idea."

"No one does because it didn't go through the courts. His father hired a judge and the trial was handled privately behind closed doors. You know what I'm talking about, right?"

She nodded. It was the same reason why no one heard about Michael Jackson's custody battle with his ex-wife after his trial and acquittal for child molestation. Private trials held in upscale conference rooms were the wave of the future for the rich and famous.

"You were still in Hollywood," Rhodes said. "I didn't work it, but because of who Tremell is, the case ended up downtown. He beat some girl up. Wrecked her face and put her in the hospital. She wanted to press charges for the assault. A week later she changed her mind and the assault suddenly turned into a *dispute*. A week after that Tremell's father bought a judge and everything evaporated into thin air. You get the picture?"

"Got it," she said. "That's my boy."

Rhodes grinned at her, then pulled the battered Crown Vic into the narrow drive between the buildings. The lot was full, a limo with tinted glass idling before the building's rear entrance. Lena could see the driver—an old man with gray hair and dark wrinkled skin—wearing a cap and uniform behind the wheel. He was keeping an eye on them as they circled the lot, and appeared a little worried when Rhodes decided to park the unpainted car right beside him in front of the doors.

Lena gave him a look as they got out. He was a small man, easily past sixty. His uniform seemed out of date, even odd. But his gaze quieted some when he looked her over and spotted the badge clipped to her belt.

"Who are you driving for?" she said.

"Mr. Dean."

"You're his personal driver?"

"For the last thirty years. Yes, ma'am, I expect so."

"Who's Mr. Dean?"

The driver smiled. "The man who writes the checks."

"Thanks."

"Have a nice day," he said. "And God bless."

She glanced at the driver as they entered the building, then turned back to Rhodes. "Who's writing the checks?"

"Dean Tremell," Rhodes said. "The kid's father. Anders Dahl Pharmaceuticals. That's what I meant by tricky. The minute he sees us, ten lawyers clock in, the kid walks, and you and me are history."

They were standing before a rear staircase, the lobby at the other end of the hall. An attractive brunette sat behind the reception desk talking to two young guys in suits and ties who looked preppie and were probably interns. When the brunette noticed them, she beckoned them down the hall with a friendly smile and a wave of the hand.

"I'm sorry," she said as they reached the lobby. "We've already made our selection. But here's a personal gift for taking the time to come down on a Saturday."

Her voice was just above a whisper, her demeanor more than pleasant. As she set a gift bag on the counter, she glanced across the lobby. Lena followed her gaze to the set of double doors and could hear someone talking on the other side—probably Justin Tremell or his business partner running the focus group. Turning back, she sized the woman up and guessed that they were about the same age. Her sleeves were rolled up to her elbows and she didn't have the look or feel of a receptionist.

"Sorry," the woman repeated when their eyes met.

Rhodes pushed the gift bag toward the two interns. "We didn't come for the focus group. We'd like to speak with Justin Tremell. Is he here?"

She nodded and offered another gracious smile. "I'm his personal assistant, Ann. They're just getting started. I couldn't possibly interrupt him right now. Would you like to make an appointment for next week?"

Lena watched Rhodes pull out his badge, saw the two interns take a nervous step back, caught the brunette's eyes lighting up, and felt the air being sucked out of the lobby as if it had suddenly become a vacuum in one smooth motion. Rhodes didn't look like a man willing to wait until next week.

The brunette stammered. "I can't interrupt him. It would ruin everything."

"I appreciate that you're caught in the middle," Rhodes said. "But this isn't a social visit. We're investigating a homicide. Either you pull him out of that room, or I do."

If there had been any air left in the lobby, Lena figured that it was gone now. Just a lot of preppie wheels turning. Three sets of glassy eyes darting back and forth like flies trying to poke through a window.

"I need to speak with someone," she said, reaching for the phone.

Rhodes shook his head. "Not on the phone."

"Okay, then I'll be back in a minute."

He shook his head again. "We're going with you."

All of a sudden the brunette looked like she was having a really bad day. She grabbed her keys and trudged down the hall in her high heels, then stopped at the first door on the left where a sign read OBSERVATION ROOM. Releasing the lock, she pushed the door open revealing a private lounge. The furnishings were luxurious—everything modern and high-end. There was an entertainment center built into the far wall. Beside the couch on the right a caterer had set up a buffet table that appeared untouched. Lena eyed the variety of fruits and cheeses laid out on a silver tray, the coffee and teapots that stood in waiting beside several unopened bottles of Pellegrino water. Down the short hall to the right she could see a private bathroom that included a hot tub.

She watched Rhodes take it all in, wondering if the space didn't double as some sort of executive fuck pad for Tremell. Letting the thought go, she turned back to his assistant slogging her way across the lounge in those heels. She was headed toward the door on the far left. A red light mounted on the wall above the molding flashed in warning. Curiously, the woman stopped and took a deep breath with her head turned. Then she tapped lightly on the door and yanked it open.

Lena stepped aside for a better view. The observation booth was dark, but not dark enough to hide the white-haired man in the leather chair turning toward the intrusion with a harsh scowl on his face. Tremell's assistant didn't enter the room, but leaned into the shadows while holding the door open. Her voice wasn't much more than a shaky whisper. And nothing she said seemed to change the look on the man's face. He didn't understand why she was interrupting him. Even with two homicide detectives standing behind her, he appeared confused and incensed by the intrusion.

When the brunette finally ran out of words, he let out a sigh and waved everyone into the booth. Lena glanced at Rhodes and caught the look in his eyes. No doubt about it, the man in the leather chair was Tremell's father. The man who wrote the checks.

"Let me see your ID," he said.

Rhodes handed over his badge. Dean Tremell snapped on a low-wattage lamp and slipped on a pair of reading glasses. As he examined Rhodes's ID and photo in the dim light, Lena glanced at the suit he was wearing, his handmade shirt and silk tie, measuring the quality of the fabrics. In spite of his age, Tremell's father looked strong and vigorous and was built something like an overgroomed bull. His face was pock-marked, and weatherbeaten, and ruined from too much time

spent in the sun. His thick white mane had been meticulously styled, his fingernails buffed and polished. But when
he passed the badge back, Lena was struck by his easy
gaze—the intelligence in his gray eyes—and the gentle sound
of his voice. He wasn't angry anymore. Far from it. He
seemed curious and surprised.

"Homicide," he said. "What's this about?"

"We came to speak with your son," Rhodes said. "We
believe that he may have witnessed a crime."

Lena kept her game face on, trying not to reveal anything
as Tremell turned and gave her a long look. Rhodes had
called his son a possible witness instead of a probable suspect. A very real person of interest. He had played it just right,
and it looked like Dean Tremell was buying it.

"Do I know you?" he asked her.

"I don't think we've ever met."

"That story in the paper," he said. "I remember it now. If
my son witnessed a murder, he would have said something
about it."

"He may not have had enough information to know what
he was seeing," she said. "That's why we're here."

Tremell thought it over, his eyes still on her, not Rhodes. "Is
there any way we could put this off until the end of the day?"

"If you've read the newspaper," she said, "then you know
that the crime was egregious. We believe that your son can
help us. It's already past three. Time is of the essence."

He held the look with something churning behind his
eyes. Lena imagined that he was probably chewing over the
short list of good reasons to pick up the telephone mounted
on the wall and dial his attorney's worn-out number from
memory. Oddly enough, he didn't. Instead, he broke the
long gaze and searched for his son's assistant waiting in the
gloom behind them.

"Ann," he said. "Get Justin."

"Yes, sir."

The brunette scurried out of the booth. As the door closed,
Lena noticed the monitors and speakers and realized that the
room on the other side of the one-way mirror was wired for

video and sound. The space was set up like a classroom, the microphones and cameras hidden. Thirty people were seated at desks with pads and pens as a soft-spoken man dressed in a sweater and slacks stood before the blackboard. If the article in the newspaper was correct, the man directing the session was Justin Tremell's business partner.

Lena scanned the classroom, but didn't see Tremell. When the door off the lobby opened and his assistant hurried to the back of the classroom, she spotted him leaning against the rear wall. Whether by choice or happenstance, Justin Tremell had claimed perhaps the only spot in the entire room that was out of his father's line of vision.

She found this curious, watching his assistant deliver the news that his father wanted to see him. She kept her attention focused on his reaction. He was a tall, lean kid with long dark hair and a sullen face. Although he shared his father's gray eyes, there was something different about them. Something lost or missing. Still, he took the news with a decisive nod and headed for the door with his assistant in tow.

While they waited, Lena tried to follow what was going on in the classroom but found it difficult to listen to. Even disturbing. She turned and looked at Dean Tremell's face. By all appearances he was concentrating on the focus group, trying to recapture his place in the session before they interrupted him. All the same, he could have just as easily been plotting his next move. There had to be a reason why he didn't kick them out. Lena figured that he wanted more information—wanted to know how deep a hole his son had fallen into—and felt more than confident that he could pull the plug whenever he wanted to. This was a fishing expedition. Both parties were seasoning the water with chum and running out line.

"What is it you're trying to do here?" she said.

"I should be asking you the same question, Detective. But if you really want to know, we're preparing to launch a new drug."

"What's it called?" Rhodes asked.

"We're not that far along yet. That's why these people are

here. We're hoping they'll point us in the right direction. The release of a new medication is more art than science these days."

The symptoms were listed on the blackboard and Lena could hear Justin Tremell's partner running the session over the speakers. He was asking the audience if they ever walked out of the house and couldn't remember if they turned off the coffeepot or locked the front door. If they ever ran into an acquaintance and couldn't remember his or her name. If they ever woke up in the morning and felt like they needed another hour of sleep. Questions everyone in the room could answer yes to because they were something everyone experienced in life.

She turned back to Dean Tremell. "These are symptoms?"

The man shrugged. "We think they are. We think we can improve people's quality of life."

"What are you calling the disease?"

He sensed the irony in her voice and seemed amused. "We don't really use that word anymore because of the negative connotations. *Medical issue* is a far more positive form of expression."

"What are you calling it?"

"Cognitive Lapse Disorder is the working title. We like the acronym CLD, but we're concerned that the name may sound too negative. We're testing a new word that we hope will replace the word *disorder*. People are generally unwilling to talk about or admit that they have a disorder. But if it's a syndrome, they're more likely to ask their doctor about it."

"And that means more sales," she said. "You don't try to reach the doctor anymore. It's all about hooking the end user."

He looked her over and grinned a little. "That's the way it works, yes."

"So why don't you just change the name to Cognitive Lapse Syndrome? Why go through all this?"

That quizzical look was still in his eyes. "Because of the acronym," he said. "If you told someone that you had CLS, they might ask if you're going to die."

His grin widened and he seemed pleased with himself.

Pleased with the demonstration of his intelligence and knowledge. Lena glanced at Rhodes, wondering why Tremell's son was taking so long to get here. For some reason she thought about a weekend seminar she had attended on drug intervention sponsored by the FBI. Before reaching the homicide table in Hollywood, Lena had spent her first two years as an investigator working narcotics. The event was held in Nashville, and offered a complete view of drug use worldwide that proved invaluable. But equally fascinating was the historical data the FBI provided. Although morphine had a very real medical purpose in pain management that continued to this day, there was a time in the mid-1800s when the drug had been marketed and prescribed as a cure for alcoholism. In 1898, a major pharmaceutical company introduced heroin as a cough medicine. For $1.50 you could order a bottle out of a department store catalog and have it delivered to your door. When reality sank in, when the party was finally over, the miracle of cocaine hit the world and was mixed in countless foods and drinks.

It was the miracle of the snake-oil salesman. The miracle of one concoction after the next brought to the marketplace with good intentions. The miracle of fruit rotting on the vine. The miracle that ended in a trail of misery.

It seemed clear enough that the list of symptoms requiring any of these drugs matched the symptoms listed on the blackboard for the focus group. As Lena thought it over, what Tremell was talking about smacked of disease mongering. The fact that he wanted to market his drug directly to patients and sell them on the idea seemed a mile or two beyond dangerous. Nothing had changed in more than a hundred and fifty years. Except for her mood, which had suddenly turned very grim.

The door finally opened, and Justin Tremell stepped into the darkness. He was alone, staring at his father. The man who writes the checks.

"Is there a problem?" he asked in a quiet voice.

"Have a seat," his father said. "These detectives would like to talk to you. They've said they believe you witnessed a crime, but I suspect that it's more than that."

The room went silent. Justin Tremell turned to them, but remained on his feet. Although he glanced at Lena, his attention was focused on Rhodes.

"Witnessed what?" he said.

Rhodes turned to his father. "Is there any way we could speak with him alone?"

Dean Tremell laughed. "Not on your life. I own the place."

"I thought your son did."

"I'm staying," the man fired back. "I'm his father."

Lena pointed to a chair and Justin finally sat down. "We're interested in your relationship with a woman calling herself Jennifer McBride."

"What relationship? I'm married."

Lena pulled the victim's picture from her file and handed it to him.

"You don't know this woman?" she asked.

He made a cursory glance at the photo, checked in with his father, then looked back and shook his head. All things being equal, Lena regarded his performance as the ignorant bystander unworthy of an award, and guessed that he may have picked up his poor technique from some of the lowlife actresses he'd fucked or beaten up in his so-called former life. She noticed his hands as he held the picture. They were unusually soft. So soft and unlined that they could have been a woman's. Even more telling, they were rock steady. He wasn't nervous and he should have been. As she looked him over, she wondered why she thought of him as a kid. Justin Tremell was at least two years older than her, yet his demeanor appeared frozen in time. Almost as if he was locked into his teens and unable to move forward. After a second look, she began to wonder if it wasn't an act. That just maybe Justin Tremell was a better actor than she first thought. He wasn't playing the ignorant bystander. He was playing the good son.

Rhodes snatched the photograph away from him and held it in front of his face. "You've never seen this woman before in your life? Is that what you're saying?"

Justin Tremell shrugged. "I don't know her."

"I didn't ask that. I asked if you had ever seen this face."

He looked at Rhodes like he was bored. "This is getting pretty technical, isn't it?"

"It's a simple question," Rhodes said. "Have you seen her or not? Yes or no?"

The kid smiled at him. "Uh-uh."

Rhodes stepped back, the veins in his neck throbbing. When Lena turned to check on the father, she caught him staring at her. His eyes were roaming up her thighs and hips and lingering on her breasts. As she moved to her right and broke his line of vision, he looked back at her face without any sign of embarrassment.

She shook it off because she knew that she had to and turned to his son.

"Where were you Wednesday night?" she said in an even voice.

"Home," he said. "Where the heart is."

"A woman was murdered, Justin. Do you think this is funny?"

"Not at all."

"So where were you Wednesday night?"

The kid shrugged. "Home."

Lena rolled a chair over and sat down in front of him. "You know something, Justin. I wish that I could believe you. I even want to believe you. It looks like you've got it made. Like you're living the perfect life. But we've got a problem. Actually, it's your problem, too, because we just left a handful of witnesses who said that you were at the Cock-a-doodle-do last Wednesday night. Even better, they said that you were sharing a table with Jennifer McBride. Talking and drinking with a woman you just claimed you don't know and have never even seen. A young woman who ended up dead a couple of miles down the road."

"Witnesses?" he said.

"That's right."

"Then they must be mistaken, because I was at home."

His father cleared his throat. "What the hell is a Cock-a-doodle-do?"

Lena turned and looked at him. The curiosity had left his

eyes and he no longer appeared to be undressing her in his mind.

"It's a whorehouse," Rhodes said.

"A what?"

"A whorehouse by the airport."

"You mean that you're here asking questions about a prostitute?"

"That's right," Lena said. "Your son was one of the last people to see her alive on Wednesday night."

The man who wrote the checks suddenly appeared dumbfounded. Lena realized that she had crossed the line and shown her anger. The truth was that she didn't care. They were an inch away from being thrown out and her suspicions had already been confirmed. Justin Tremell would continue to lie, using his father as a shield. And the motive for the murder remained in play. She didn't know how the pieces fit, but this was still about blackmail. As she tried to get a read on the kid, his face didn't reveal concern, remorse, or any emotion at all. His expression was completely blank, like he didn't have a worry in the world.

Dean Tremell leaned forward in the leather chair, the overgroomed bull pointing a steady finger at her. "Let me tell you something about my son," he said in an exceedingly soft and slithery voice. "Justin's a happily married man. A new father with a newborn son, Dean Jr. It may have taken a while, but he's a responsible member of society now. I don't know who your witnesses may or may not be, but I've got a good idea where they came from. And I'm not going to sit by while you take the word of a lowlife—ruin my son's reputation or possibly even mine—then make some weak apology when you realize that it was all a mistake. Believe me when I say that you need to proceed with great care. Do you understand what I'm saying?"

Lena glanced at Rhodes. Dean Tremell finally reached for the phone.

"Then get out," he said.

20

Her eyes snapped open. She caught a glimpse of the empty wine glass standing beside the murder book on the coffee table, then the shelves on the far wall filled with hundreds of vinyl records and CDs.

She could hear music—Buddy Guy's live version of "Sweet Little Angel" playing softly in the background. Not from her CD player, but from the computer wired into her audio system. As her mind began to clear, she remembered logging onto 88.1's Web site and listening to the station out of Long Beach over the Internet. The winds had been strong last night. Too strong to pull the FM signal out of the cold air sweeping through Hollywood Hills.

The Santa Anas were back. The Devil Winds.

Her eyes meandered across the ceiling, following the shadows into the kitchen. The wall clock over the stove read 7:30 a.m. She was still dressed. Still lying on the couch after a short and troubled sleep. And her cell phone was vibrating. On the table and bouncing up and down.

She sat up and checked the screen. Although the caller had blocked their ID, she flipped it open anyway, said hello and listened.

"Lena Gamble?"

It was a man's voice. Smooth as silk. Someone she didn't recognize and couldn't place.

"Is this Lena Gamble?" the man repeated.

"Yes."

"Lena, it's Buddy Paladino."

She was awake now. All the way awake.

Buddy Paladino represented their primary suspect in her last case. But he was more than that. A criminal defense attorney who made his mark championing underdogs and attacking the LAPD after the '92 riots. He enjoyed his work and he was good at it, bleeding taxpayers for hundreds of millions in damages. Most of his cases read like fiction, but Paladino had a special talent for picking a prosecutor's case apart—no matter how solid—finding its primal weakness and winning a jury over with his soft voice and trademark smile. His million-dollar smile. That was more than fifteen years ago, his reputation as a dangerous attorney just taking flight. Now Paladino was in another league, a slippery heavyweight who represented only those clients who could afford his exorbitant fees.

"My apologies for calling on a Sunday morning," he said. "I hope I didn't wake you."

Lena grimaced. If Dean Tremell had hired Paladino to represent his son, they could have picked a better time to tell her. Still, Paladino was the perfect choice.

"You didn't wake me," she said. "How did you get my cell number?"

"A mutual friend who wasn't really a friend and is no longer with us."

Although it sounded like Paladino doing another one of his convoluted dances usually reserved for trial, it wasn't. She knew the friend who wasn't a friend and was glad the attorney hadn't used his name.

"What is it?" she said finally.

"We need to meet, Lena. We need to talk."

"About what?"

"I'd rather not say too much over the phone. But it's important to me and I would regard it as a personal favor. I would be in your debt. Given the state of the world, you might need me someday. I need you right now."

Lena walked over to the slider, looking out at the city but not seeing it. Paladino was speaking in code. Something was wrong. She moved to the counter and grabbed a pen.

"Where?" she said.

He gave her an address in Hollywood and she jotted it down. Barton Avenue was off Gower, just north of Paramount Studios, directly across the street from the Hollywood Memorial graveyard.

"Thanks, Lena," he whispered before hanging up. "See you as soon as you can get here. It's important."

She looked at her phone, spooked. But as she left the room, she felt a certain degree of relief that Paladino had used her cell number. Internal Affairs had spent another night outside her house. Although she was still forwarding the home number to her cell, the detectives monitoring her calls would hear the first ring before the telephone company's computers rerouted the signal. Rhodes had called last night as he drove up to Oxnard to see his sister through her surgery on Monday. Lieutenant Barrera had checked in. And Matt Kline, a detective from Pacific Division, called to confirm that she received his Field Interview cards after canvassing the neighborhood in Venice and interviewing the victim's neighbors. Kline had also taken the time to change the lock on the victim's apartment. The new keys had been delivered with the FI cards. Sooner or later, the guys from Internal Affairs would figure out what she had done with her phone.

She took a quick shower and changed, then grabbed a salted bagel. As she pulled to the end of the drive, she paused a beat and searched out the Caprice. She could see it through the tree branches, off the road to her right and around the bend. She could see it fading away in her rearview mirror as she turned left and hit the accelerator. Her mind was shifting gears faster than her Honda. She could feel her heart beating as she thought about the sound of Buddy Paladino's voice. How strange it was that he had called her.

Barton Avenue was a straight shot two and half miles down the hill from her house. When she reached the graveyard, she made a right and started looking for the attorney. The neighborhood had been lost a long time ago, hidden behind graffiti-covered walls and miles of razor wire. A mix of cheap apartment houses and pueblo-styled homes cut against single-story shotguns with wood siding and a full front porch. They were called shotguns because they were narrow, boxlike structures no more than one room wide. It was said that if you fired a shell from the front porch, the shot would make a clean exit through the back door. But the history of the neighborhood had more to do with the glory days of Paramount Studios and the need for low-cost housing. This was the place where set builders and lighting technicians and all those extras who made up the cast of thousands once lived. Now the neighborhood was in a state of ruin. Left behind by a world that had moved from black and white to color before going digital.

Lena spotted a car that had been jacked up and left on cinder blocks. The windows were punched out, all four wheels stolen. As she pulled around the wreck, she saw an Acura RL parked on the right a few houses this side of El Centro. Buddy Paladino was stepping off the porch and waving at her.

He wore a pair of khakis, an Oxford shirt, and a leather jacket. She had never seen him dressed casually before. Never seen him in public or print looking so bleak, so worried and concerned.

She pulled in front of the RL. When he reached for the door handle, she popped the locks and watched him climb in.

"Thanks for coming," he said.

"Are you representing the kid?"

"What kid?"

She looked him over. The defense attorney with the million-dollar smile was visibly nervous.

"Maybe you ought to tell me what this is about," she said.

Paladino nodded, then looked past her through the driver's side window. "You see that house over there?"

Lena followed his gaze to the shotgun across the street. The wood siding appeared warped and blistered from too much wind and sun. Two windows needed to be replaced and the screen door had rusted out and was hanging off its hinges.

"I grew up in that house, Lena. I spent five years of my childhood in this neighborhood before we moved north. And you know what? It was better back then, but not that much better. The only people left are the Andolinis."

He turned and gazed out his own window at the Andolini's house. A garage stood at the end of the driveway, but Lena couldn't really see it. Although the lawn had been cut and the place appeared clean and neat, the roof needed to be replaced and the house was five to ten years past needing a decent paint job. Like every other house on the block, security bars had been installed over the doors and windows. Lena imagined the view for the people inside wasn't that much different than the view from a prison cell.

Paladino cleared his throat. "To tell you the truth, I didn't know that they still lived here. I didn't even know that they were still alive. I guess when you're only a boy everybody seems old. My family didn't have much. Mrs. Andolini used to love to cook. Her door was always open. To this day I think of her every time I eat a slice of pizza. Nobody makes it as good as her. I've met a lot of people since then. No one's ever been nicer."

Lena released her seat belt and turned toward Paladino. She let him talk it out, but it was difficult. A lot like watching a black funnel cloud on the horizon and counting the minutes until it arrived. Something horrible was waiting for her at the end of this conversation. She could see it on the man's face.

"The reason I called you, Lena, is that these people are part of my life. They're good people. They're poor people, and they're very old. You've been through enough that I thought I could count on you to treat them right."

"What is it?" she said. "What's wrong?"

He met her eyes. "Let's take a walk back to the garage."

They got out and started up the narrow gravel drive, the feeling in her chest growing stronger. As the garage behind the house came into view, she noticed a door cracked open on the right side of the building.

"They rented the place out," Paladino said. "They were afraid to call the cops because they thought they might get into trouble."

"Why would they get into trouble?"

He didn't really need to answer her question because they were ten feet away from that open door now and she could smell it. The harsh sour odor of tainted blood. Judging the foul stench by its strength, Lena guessed that there was a lot of it inside the dilapidated garage.

Paladino stepped aside and let her pass. "They saw that photo on TV," he said. "I guess the shot was so bad they couldn't be sure it was him. The guy they rented it out to paid for the year in cash. Like I said, they're poor. They needed the money and wanted to keep the cash."

"So you came down to check it out."

"They found me. I'm glad they did. I can help them now."

Lena's eyes were fixed on the door as Paladino stayed behind her on the lawn.

"The lock's been replaced," she said. "Who's got a key?"

"The guy changed everything when he rented the place."

"Does this guy have a name?"

"He didn't sign anything, but he called himself Nathan Good."

A moment passed with Lena thinking it over. Nathan Good.

"How'd you get the door open?" she said.

"I gave it a hard kick."

"You go inside? You touch anything?"

"The door won't open any more than that. I couldn't fit. Besides, I know what death smells like. I talked it over with the Andolinis and gave you a call. I've been waiting on the front porch ever since."

She turned and measured his face, certain that he was telling the truth. Behind him she could see the old couple staring through the kitchen window. They looked frightened. Thin and frail and more ancient than old.

She turned back to the door and noticed that the foundation

had risen over time and the door wouldn't budge. After taking a deep breath, she squeezed through the opening and peered into the gloom. As her eyes adjusted to the darkness and details became more visible, she made an effort to slow down her heart but couldn't get past the chills. A meat hook hung from the rafters. Against the wall she spotted five buckets filled with a dark murky liquid. She didn't need a criminalist to know that the buckets were filled with blood.

The foul odor was so intense in the closed space that she became worried that she might faint. She turned around but couldn't see Paladino through the crack in the door.

"You still there?" she called out.

"I'm here," he said.

"You got a handkerchief?"

"How 'bout paper tissues?"

"I'll take them."

A long beat went by before his face appeared in the doorway and he passed them through.

"Is there a body?" he asked.

"I'm guessing she's already at the morgue."

"You okay? You want to open the garage door?"

She had thought about that, but a breeze might disturb something important. She couldn't take the chance.

"I'm okay," she said.

Her voice died off. She had just noticed the table on the other side of the garage. Covering her mouth and nose with a tissue, she located the switch by the garage door and flipped on the lights with her elbow. The table turned out to be a 4×8 sheet of plywood set on a pair of saw horses. She moved closer. One step after the other—her efforts to keep her heart rate down not working very well. She noted the massive bloodstains on the wood's surface. The gashes left behind by a razor-sharp knife. The additional spotlights mounted on the rafters overhead.

It was a makeshift operating table. Underneath the plywood, a 4×8 sheet of linoleum had been laid over the concrete serving as a blood catch.

Her eyes flicked back to the meat hook swaying in the

foul air. The five buckets filled with tainted blood. When she turned back to the operating table, she began to pick up patterns in the stains. Wisps of the victim's hair, an arc of fingertips, and the stamp of a palm—impressions from the body so clear that they looked as if they had been silk-screened onto the wood.

Something glistened in the light. She caught it out of the corner of her eye. Inching her way to the other end of the table, she found a carving knife laid out on top of a li-quor carton. She looked at the knife without touching it. The drops of blood. Two smaller knives were here as well, along with a black Sharpie.

She paused a moment, adjusting the tissue over her nose.

The garage had been cleaned, the floor swept. Whatever belonged to the Andolinis looked as if it had been moved to the back of the garage and stacked beside a workbench. When Lena spotted the trash can, she moved closer and gazed inside the plastic liner. Several pairs of vinyl gloves had been discarded, along with a smock, a pair of goggles, store-bought rags, and numerous sets of paper booties.

Her eyes skipped across the workbench. She took a deep breath and pushed the foul air out of her lungs. Felt the chills begin to swarm her spine and shake it. There was a roll of parchment paper here. But even worse, a meat grinder had been mounted to the surface with a thumb screw.

She closed her eyes and stepped back, thinking that she might be sick. Gathering her strength, she shook the thought out of her head and turned away. And that's when she no-ticed the coat rack on the wall. She had walked right by it. Missed it as she took the horror in.

The victim's clothes were here. Everything hanging neatly from the hooks on the rack as if it belonged in the woman's bedroom closet. A pair of jeans and a simple white blouse. A sweater. Her bra and panties. On the floor her shoes had been set side by side, her socks folded and carefully placed on top.

Lena moved closer, picking up a light scent of perfume—the same fragrance that managed to cut through the stench at the morgue during the young woman's autopsy. As her eyes swept across the rack, she spotted a string of Rosary beads hanging from the last hook.

A moment passed. A long stretch of oppressive silence broken up by the sound of her heart pounding in her ears. She was thinking about Jane Doe, the young woman who had stolen Jennifer McBride's identity and walked into this nightmare. She was playing back her last few moments of life in her head. She was thinking about what Art Madina had told her on Friday. That the killer had kept her alive for as long as he could. That her death hadn't been quick or easy.

The man the Andolinis knew as Nathan Good.

Her mind surfaced. She noticed her breath as she exhaled. She could see it dissipating in the cold air as it passed through the tissue. Her body was shaking now, but she couldn't tell if she was shivering or trembling anymore. Couldn't tell if it was the December air working through her body or this living vision of hell closing in on her.

She shook it off and headed for the door. Squeezing through the narrow space, she stepped outside and moved away from the garage as quickly as she could. The winds had changed direction. She could smell moisture in the air, the promise of rain. She could hear a door opening.

"Come in and get warm."

She looked up and saw Paladino on the porch, but it took a moment to register.

"I'll be there in a minute," she said. "Where are the Andolinis?"

"Resting. I went through it with them before you got here. They're tired. I figured you could talk to them later. You don't look so good, Lena. Come in and sit down."

She took a deep breath, trying to get a grip on herself. After several moments she climbed the steps and followed Paladino into the kitchen. The room was small but clean, the appliances dated. Moving to the sink, she turned on the hot water. As she splashed her face, she couldn't help noticing all the prescriptions lined up on the windowsill. There must have been at least thirty different medications. A small house plant broke the line of pill bottles into two groups. An African violet in bloom. Taped to the sill on the left and right were the words HIS and HERS.

Paladino gave her a look, his voice quiet and gentle. "What was it like in there?"

"Exactly what you think it was like," she said.

"Then this is the crime scene."

"This is it."

She turned off the water, her heart still pounding in her chest as she tried to think.

"Your friends," she said. "If they couldn't get a read from the picture on TV, what prompted the call?"

"Wednesday night. That's the night of the murder, right?"

She leaned against the counter and nodded.

"He shows up here around eleven. Backs his car up to the garage. The lights wake them up. They told me he spent four hours in there. Didn't leave until after three in the morning. He carried a trash bag out and it looked heavy."

"Did you ask them what kind of car he drives?"

"A red Hummer. But they didn't get the license plate. They didn't have any reason to. They saw the story on the news Friday night. Yesterday they put it together."

Lena glanced at the coffeepot.

"The mugs are in the cabinet behind you," Paladino said. "But it's not very good. I couldn't drink it."

She didn't care. All she really wanted was to shake the chills. She turned to the cabinet above the sink and swung the first door open.

"The other one," he said.

She heard him, but kept her eyes on the cabinet. The shelves were empty except for a single can of tuna and half a box of rigatoni. She shot Paladino a look, then glanced back at the prescriptions on the sill. The Andolinis needed food and medication to stay alive, but couldn't afford both. Something was wrong.

21

It had taken fourteen hours to process the crime scene on Barton Avenue. Fourteen hours to photograph it and dust it. Fourteen hours to log the evidence in, break it down, and carry the mess away. For Lena, it had only taken a split second to understand that the thoughts and images she collected and endured would haunt her for the rest of her days.

It was after ten, the streets wetted down by a light rain. As she reached Beachwood Canyon and started up Gower Street past the Monastery of the Angels, the road leading to her house appeared more desolate than usual. The night, three or four shades darker.

Lena had shown the Andolinis the six-pack that Rollins had created on his computer—the six faces generated from the image recorded by the witness on his cell phone. Working with a sketch artist, a single image emerged and was fine-tuned. Remarkably, Rollins had come close to depicting the killer's actual face. Using the nose from one image, the mouth from another, the eyes and ears from the next two—it all added up to the man who rented the garage. The man calling himself Nathan Good, who didn't seem to exist when Lena made the call and Barrera ran his name through the system. The man no one saw or wanted to remember seeing when she canvassed the neighborhood in search of a witness. The man with the meat grinder who drove a red Hummer and lived below the water line.

She pulled into her drive. The outside lights were off. As

she lugged her briefcase through the darkness, she felt the cool rain misting her face.

On the plus side, if there could be a plus side, the depravity of the case was out in the open now. The gruesome reality was no longer reserved for Art Madina and herself as they examined the victim at the autopsy on their own two days ago. Somehow, word of what they found had traveled down Barton Avenue to the press staging their cameras in front of the graveyard. Perhaps because of their grim location, perhaps because of the foul weather, or perhaps because SID couldn't back their truck up the narrow drive and everyone got a good look at that makeshift operating table being carried out—an almost palpable current of fear swept through the press corps. More important to Lena, it was a Sunday and details had already risen to the brass on the sixth floor. Already reached them in their warm and comfortable homes. No one would be dropping the case because Jane Doe No. 99 had worked in the sex trade. Nor was there any threat of delay at the crime labs. SID had moved the investigation to the top of their list.

Lena unlocked the front door, pausing a beat as she sensed something was wrong. She pushed the door open and peered into the darkness.

The phone was ringing inside the house. Not once before bouncing over to her cell, but in succession as if she hadn't turned CALL FORWARDING on.

She hit the lights and crossed the living room. When she saw Denny Ramira's name and number on the screen, she grabbed the phone before her answering machine picked up.

"I've gotta call you back," she said.

"Call me back? We've gotta talk right now."

"Can't do it, Denny. I'll call you back in five minutes."

She switched off the phone before the reporter could say anything someone might hear. Although his voice sounded shaky, she couldn't think about it right now. Her friends from Internal Affairs had figured out what she was doing with the phones. Obviously they had been inside the house.

She noticed the cold air and turned up the heat, then

unlocked the slider and legged it around the house. As she expected, the tap and wireless transmitter had been removed. But she could hear something. Footsteps on gravel fading onto soft earth. She looked ahead and caught a glimpse of two men moving quickly through the brush toward the road. Rushing up the path, she climbed the bluff and saw the two men hurrying back to the Caprice parked thirty yards down the road. The first was familiar to her, the same clean-cut man with the young face and short brown hair she had seen before. But it was the second man who shook her up. She got a good look at him as he turned to get in the car. His lean, rigid body. His short gray hair and wounded eyes.

It was the chief's adjutant himself. Ken Klinger.

She took a deep breath and exhaled. She didn't have time for this.

Sliding down the hill, she ran back to the house and shut the slider. Nothing that she could see appeared out of place, but she expected this, too. She picked up the phone, stepped into the kitchen, and pried off the faceplate with a knife. Lifting away the speaker, she spotted a small black cylinder with metal coils buried in the wires. She was familiar with the device and knew that the microphone inside could pick up anything in the room whether she was on the phone or not. A radio transmitter went with the low-tech bug and would be hidden somewhere away from the television and her audio equipment in the living room. But what worried her was Klinger. Because he worked for the chief, he knew that she would have been tied up at the crime scene all day. He would have had time to wire the rest of the house. This was obviously the bug she was meant to find—the *feel-good* bug that was supposed to make her feel safe after she located the device and discarded it. They could have planted anything anywhere. Internal Affairs owned the equipment and supposedly knew how to use it.

She closed the handset and returned it to her charger, leaving the bug in place and wondering why they hadn't turned CALL FORWARDING back on. As she thought it over, she realized that they probably turned off the service in order to test their handiwork. Once the service was off, there would have been no way to restore it without calling her cell. Lena would have seen her home number when the call came in and figured it out. Instead of taking the risk, they were probably counting on her not remembering whether she'd turned the service on this morning.

All in all, it added up to poor planning and sloppy police work. Klinger, the man who thought of himself as an expert at crime detection but hadn't worked a single day in his entire life as an investigator, couldn't even wire up a house right.

She hoped he liked good music because he was going to hear a lot of it.

Lena switched on her receiver, moved to the computer, and logged on to WRTI's Web site, a jazz station out of Philly. Klinger was in luck. According to the playlist, the station would be dedicating the entire night to Coleman Hawkins and his tenor sax. First up was a digital remaster of the LP, *At Ease with Coleman Hawkins*. One of Lena's favorites, "Poor Butterfly," was on the album. But as she played the cut back in her head, it occurred to her that Klinger wasn't worthy of the music. Returning to her bookmarks, she switched over to KROQ's Web site and checked their playlist. She smiled as she scrolled through the long list of heavy metal bands. Tonight was theme night. Twelve hours of great headbangers from the past.

Perfect.

She found the LISTEN LIVE icon on the screen and clicked it. Then she turned up the volume, grabbed her leather jacket, and walked out onto the back porch. Moving away from the slider, she leaned against the side of the house and gazed at the pool. The lights were off, the rain breaking the water's smooth black surface like stones falling out of the sky.

She flipped open her cell. Ramira from *The Times* would have to wait. When she found the medical examiner's home number in her address book and hit ENTER, Art Madina picked up on the first ring.

"It's me," she said. "And I need a favor."

"What is it? And what's that in the background? It sounds like we've got the same station on."

She smiled again. She knew Madina listened to rock and still went to the clubs on weekends. She knew that he had been a fan of her brother's music as well.

"I need a favor," she repeated.

"Tell me what I can do."

"I want to take another look at Jane Doe's body."

"That's easy. She's in the cooler. Come over any time you want to."

"I don't mean a quick look," she said. "I don't know what your schedule's like, but I really think we need to do it as soon as possible, Art. How's tomorrow morning sound?"

"Hold on a second."

She heard him set down the phone, then shut off the music at his end. When he finally came back, his voice had changed.

"What's going on, Lena? Tell me what you're looking for."

"We need to make sure that she's all there."

A moment passed. She could still see that meat grinder on the workbench.

"Why wouldn't she be all there?" he asked.

"I can't answer that," she said. "It's something we need to check."

"How much would be missing?"

"I don't know."

Another moment passed. Longer. Heavier. Both of them thinking it over. She could feel the wall vibrating beneath her back from headbanger's night on KROQ. She could see the lights from the Library Tower, the tallest building west of the Mississippi, flickering in the rain clouds. She kept her eyes on the tower—the city's beacon standing tall. For a moment it felt like she was riding out a storm in heavy seas, steering the bow of a disabled ship toward a lighthouse on a rocky shore.

"Can we do it?" she asked. "Can we take another look?"

"You bet we can. First thing in the morning."

"See you then," she said.

She closed her phone, wondering if it wasn't too late to call Rhodes. She had held back all day, not wanting to break in on his time with his sister. Just one call in the morning, letting him know that they had found the crime scene and SID was processing the evidence. No need for him to change his plans and return.

Deciding to wait, she scrolled through her address book searching for Bobby Rathbone's number. She needed another favor tonight, help from an old friend, and hoped that his cell number was still good. But before she could make the call, her cell started vibrating in her hand. She checked the display and saw Denny Ramira's name pop up. She had forgotten to call the reporter back.

"You said five minutes," he shouted over the phone.

"I don't have time for this, Denny."

"Five minutes," he repeated. "It's been more than twenty. When I called the house, all it did is fucking ring."

"You leave a message?"

"No. I called your cell. I'm in trouble, Lena. Big trouble. I need your help. We need to meet and talk this out."

She shook her head. She needed to reach Rathbone, not waste time on a reporter worried about making his deadline. She wanted Rathbone to sweep the house tonight. She wanted to know exactly what Klinger had done.

She lifted the phone back to her ear. "Talk about what, Denny? There's nothing to say. We processed a crime scene. End of story. Call your friend on the sixth floor."

"It's not about that. It's about saving my fucking life. I've got information. We need to meet tonight."

His voice had reached a fever pitch. Ramira sounded frightened.

"Information about what?"

The reporter didn't say anything.

"Information about what?" she repeated.

"That body you found in the trash."

22

Lena switched on the wipers and made a left at the end of the drive. The rain had picked up and the road felt slick.

Ramira had insisted on meeting in person and wouldn't say anything over the phone. Wouldn't even give her a hint. She finally agreed to see him—agreed to meet at the Blackbird—based on his word that whatever he had was worth a late-night trip downtown.

She checked the rearview mirror, the asphalt beginning to glisten behind her. Somewhere around the bend a car was on the move. Probably Klinger and his sidekick—the dynamic duo—heading out for coffee and donuts after a busy day wiring her home and breaking the law that was no longer a real law anymore.

She started down the hill, picking up speed and listening to the rain pound against the car. As she rolled into the next curve, she checked the mirror again and caught the headlights just rounding the bluff fifty yards back. Measuring the car's speed, she watched the bright lights spread across the rear window as the glass fogged.

They were in a hurry—the distance closing fast.

It occurred to her that Klinger may have stepped up his demented surveillance efforts, deciding to keep closer tabs on her. But if he was following her, why would he be so obvious about it? Particularly on a Sunday night during a rainstorm when they were alone on the road. Why play it so close?

Her car filled with more bright light, the glare wiping out

her mirrors. They were on top of her now, a few feet back on the slippery road.

For some reason she couldn't explain, her thoughts turned to that pack of cigarettes Rhodes kept in his car. She had been thinking about them off and on for most of the day, but managed to beat back the urge and keep going.

She blew through the stop sign at Scenic Avenue, accelerating all the way down the hill to Franklin. Ignoring the freeway, she hit the overpass and raced down the street until she reached Gower Gulch. When the headlights kept up with her and actually followed her into the strip mall, her jittery nerves hit overtime. She found a place to park in front of the Rite Aid and got out. Hurrying through the rain, her eyes swept across the lot searching for the Caprice in the milieu of cars. But as she reached the sidewalk beneath the overhang, she couldn't find it.

Instead, she watched a black Audi pull into an empty space across the lot in front of Denny's restaurant. Two men got out in the rain. They glanced at her, a beat longer than maybe they should have, then turned away and headed into the diner.

Lena stood there until the door closed. Ironically, she knew who they were. Everybody did. Jack Dobbs and Phil Ragetti had been partners—two cops from the old school who were forced into early retirement after beating the life out of a murder suspect. Both detectives had advanced to the Robbery-Homicide Division before getting the boot and leaving the department in disgrace. Lena wondered how they had managed to escape jail time and keep their pensions. From where she stood, they looked more like a pair of middle-aged bruisers with chips on their shoulders. Ragetti lived in a house overlooking the reservoir in Hollywood Hills, a mile up the road from Lena. She had heard rumors that he lost everything in the wildfires last spring and had decided to rebuild.

She walked into the pharmacy and bought a pack of cigarettes. Stepping outside, she tore through the cellophane and lit one. Lena had never been a regular smoker. Half a pack eight months ago when things got really tough with her last case. She drew the smoke into her lungs and blew it out into the cold night air.

But her eyes were locked on that black Audi. Dobbs and Ragetti had burned down three years before she ever got near RHD. Yet the look they had given her was the same one she gave them. Recognition. They had read her as a cop the moment they saw her. The moment they got out of the car. It went with the job—something you learned on the beat wearing a uniform. Us and them.

She took another pull on the cigarette.

Seeing the two ex-cops felt like a bad omen capping off a rough day. A sign of what things could be like for her if she fucked up. Hitting a diner in Hollywood on a Sunday night. Landing hard after a long fall.

She took a last drag on the smoke, flicking it into the torrent of rain and watching the fire go out as she climbed into her car. Pulling out of the lot, she turned up Sunset heading for the freeway ramp to downtown.

The drive took twenty minutes. When she entered the café and didn't see Ramira, she ordered a cup of the house blend and found an empty table with a view of the door. Before leaving the house she had managed to reach Bobby Rathbone, who agreed to meet her at midnight. She had an hour to kill, and wanted to spend it reviewing her day and what it actually yielded.

She lifted the top away from the cup and held her face over the steam. As she took a short sip and felt the hot brew warm her stomach, she opened her notebook on the table and pulled out her pen.

Jane Doe, aka Jennifer McBride, had been abducted and murdered by the same man.

She knew this now and had the evidence to support it. A man calling himself Nathan Good. She knew what he looked like, had a rough idea of his age and build, and unless he ditched it, knew the make and model of his car. The condition of the woman's body matched the horror found in the garage he rented on Barton Avenue. SID would probably confirm the match within the next twenty-four hours.

But she also knew that Nathan Good was profoundly twisted. And everything that she had seen today indicated that Art Madina was right to conclude that he had a medical background. Everything she saw pointed to a depraved individual. A motherfucker with brains.

She checked the door. When she still didn't see Ramira, she turned back to her pad and skimmed through the notes she had made last night after meeting Justin Tremell and his father.

People with money pay other people to do the heavy lifting. There was no doubt in her mind that for everything Nathan Good had done, he was a paid player.

This was about Justin Tremell. The rich bad boy trying to right the wrongs of his past. The kid who got married, had a son, and didn't want his father or anyone else to find out that he was still a piece of shit and doing a young prostitute. The kid under fire with the unusually steady hands who claimed that he didn't know Jennifer McBride. That the witnesses who saw him with her were mistaken because he spent the entire night with his wife and son at home.

She thought about those steady hands. Nathan Good's depravity cut against the way Justin Tremell handled himself during their interview. She thought about both of them for a long time. Tremell and Good were approximately the same age. Paying Good whatever he asked for wouldn't have been an issue in his life.

But this was also about the woman who cast spells. The woman calling herself Jennifer McBride, who met Tremell, knew exactly who he was, and probably figured that she could make some real money. Maybe enough to get out of bed. And the fifty grand in her checking account wouldn't accomplish that goal. It wouldn't come close.

As Lena tossed it over, she realized that no matter how much progress she was beginning to make, her questions still outweighed her answers. And no matter how much time she'd given it, she still didn't understand how Joseph Fontaine fit in. The Beverly Hills doctor had known McBride was dead before they even told him about the murder. When asked about his relationship with the young prostitute, he hid behind his assistant, lied, and threatened to call his attorney.

Fontaine was involved. She just couldn't see it yet. Couldn't put it together.

She checked her watch and looked up. Ramira was walking through the front door. Actually, it was more of a breeze than a walk. And as he spotted her and approached the table, she knew in an instant that her drive downtown would bear little fruit. Forty-five minutes ago, the crime beat reporter had sounded panic-stricken. All that appeared gone now.

"What do you have to say, Denny? Why are we here?"

"Let me order a cup of coffee."

He was stalling. Trying to come up with an excuse and save himself. She didn't know who was worse, Ramira or Klinger. Both were chewing up time she couldn't afford to lose.

"You can have mine," she said.

"It looks cold."

She shook her head in disappointment. "You said you were in trouble. It's a Sunday night, and it's been a real long day. Tell me what happened. Tell me what's wrong."

Ramira's face reddened and he finally sat down. "I'm sorry, Lena. I didn't mean it to sound like that."

She gave him a long look. "You said we needed to talk. You said that you had information about the murder. You were specific. That's why I came."

"I didn't say anything over the phone. All I said was that I wanted to meet."

"That's right. And you were talking about the victim. The woman in the trash. This is a murder investigation, Denny. It's more important than your next story. If you're holding something back, then you're committing—"

"I'm a reporter, for Christ's sake. Back off, Lena."

"I don't care who you are. If you're holding out and you print the story, I'll bust you."

"I don't know anything," he said.

She pushed her coffee across the table. He stared at it for a while, thinking something over. Something that appeared deep and troubling enough to cloud his eyes.

"You're fucking up, Denny."

"When I called I thought that I knew something. But since then I found out that I don't."

"Knew what?" she said.

"Nothing. I was on the wrong track."

"About what?"

He paused a moment—the clouds back in his eyes.

"About what?" she repeated.

"Who she was," he said. "I thought I knew, but I didn't."

"Who did you talk to? Who said you were wrong? Who knew enough about it to say that you were wrong?"

He shook his head and remained silent.

"Does this have anything to do with that book you're working on? Who's feeding you information? Is it Klinger? What about Senator West on the commission?"

Ramira seemed surprised. "What about him?"

"Is he your source?"

"Source for what? West gets along with the chief about as well as you do. You should know that better than anyone over there. Listen to me: I made a mistake and I'm sorry. I'm sorry I brought you out tonight."

He pulled the cup of coffee closer and took a long swig as if he needed it. As if the brew was strong enough to bring the sun out in the dark of night. Lena watched him lower the cup, then remove his glasses and wipe the lenses with a napkin.

"You said your life was in the balance," she whispered.

He shot a blind gaze her way before slipping his glasses back on. He looked tired. Road-weary. After another hit of coffee, he reached into his pocket for his pad and pen.

"I was wrong," he said. "But as long as we're here, is there anything you can tell me about what happened today on Barton Avenue? Anything on the record I can use? We saw that piece of plywood come out of the garage. Paladino won't let anyone get near his clients. He took them away and said they don't live there anymore."

She bit her lip, staring at the man. "This is about more than who the victim was," she said. "More than thinking you know something and finding out that you don't. How did you put it on the phone, Denny? I'm in trouble, you said. Big trouble. I'm trying to save my life. I've got information about that body you found in Hollywood. Only now you don't have the information. Now you're making excuses and hoping I won't see through your smoke."

Ramira lowered his pen. Lena checked her watch and got up from the table.

"You gave me your word," she said.

"I swear I'll make it up to you."

"But I won't be there, Denny. Never again."

She walked out, bristling with anger and disappointment and thinking about the clouds she had seen in the reporter's eyes. Something had happened. Something Ramira now wanted to hide.

As she drove home, she couldn't help thinking that Ramira was just as pressed for time as she was. The reporter was too smart to call her out for a meeting this late unless he had a good reason. Too smart not to cancel if his reason dried up. Too smart to jeopardize his relationship with her and burn everything down over a hunch, a guess, or even a maybe that wasn't pinned down. By the time she reached Hollywood Hills she became convinced that Ramira had been telling her the truth over the phone. He knew something about the murder. And he was in trouble.

She pulled into her drive and spotted a silver 911 Carrera parked in front of her brother's recording studio. Skidding to a stop, she ripped open the door and saw Bobby Rathbone walk out from the porch behind the house.

"What's got you so lit up?" he said.

She shrugged off the question, the two of them standing in the rain. "Thanks for coming on short notice."

"No problem," he said. "What do I need to know before we get started?"

"They left a couple of hours ago. They would have had all day to do whatever they've done."

"Pros?"

She shook her head. "It's not the Special Investigation Section. These guys are from Internal Affairs."

"What's with the music?"

She paused a beat, the sound bleeding through the house. She recognized the song by Megadeth and hoped Klinger was enjoying it.

Killing Is My Business . . . and Business Is Good.

"I thought I'd give them something to listen to," she said.

Rathbone laughed. They had met at her brother's record company and known each other for almost a decade. Rathbone owned a counter surveillance business that dealt exclusively with the music industry. Sweeping a recording studio for bugs had become common practice as corporations bought smaller labels out, left the music behind, and sought an edge that might translate into higher returns for their stockholders. Rathbone was only thirty years old, but had earned a reputation as one of the best techs around. He worked in Los Angeles and Seattle. The last time she saw him he was opening a branch office in Nashville. Lena knew that he planted as many bugs as he found, and that this was part of the business, too. That he was living off the grid and making a fortune doing it.

"Let's get started," he said.

He walked over to the Carrera, disabled the alarm and pulled out a black aluminum attache case. She looked at his long dirty-blond hair and blue eyes. His jeans and T-shirt and leather jacket. The scarf around his neck and his thin frame. No matter how shady his business, he brought back good memories and she was glad to see him.

"Open up the house," he said. "Keep the music on. I'll meet you around back."

As Rathbone headed for the porch, Lena unlocked the

front door, walked through the living room and threw the latch on the slider. By the time she got the door open, Rathbone was already strapping a small electronic device to his chest. He reached inside the attaché case for a pair of headphones. Slipping them over his head, he motioned her outside. Then he grabbed a screwdriver and a flashlight, and entered the house.

He started in the kitchen. As he reached the telephone, she noticed the LEDs on the device blinking in sequence. Once he disassembled the handset, he glanced at the contents and moved on. He worked slowly and methodically, paying special attention to her audio equipment and the way the components were cabled. Every so often he would stop at an electrical outlet, remove the faceplate, and examine the receptacle and box inside the wall. He made two passes through the living room before disappearing into her bedroom. She couldn't see what he was doing from her position outside the slider. But after ten minutes he walked out and headed upstairs. Five minutes later he returned to the first floor and stepped outside onto the porch.

He smiled at her, brought his mouth up to her ear, and whispered under the music. "I need to get something out of my car. Do me a favor and turn off all the lights on the first floor."

She watched him remove the device from his chest and run down the steps through the rain. Then she walked inside and switched off the lights. When she returned, Rathbone tossed another aluminum case on the chaise longue and flipped the locks to reveal several pairs of night-vision goggles.

He pulled a set out, switched on the power, and handed them to her.

"You'll want to see this," he whispered. "We'll talk after we come out, but this was done by a rat, Lena. Total garbage."

He helped her get the goggles on, adjusting the lenses in front of her eyes. Grabbing the second set, he slipped them over his head and led the way into her bedroom. They were walking in total darkness, yet the room had every appearance of being filled with light. An eerie green light. She could see Rathbone in front of her, vanishing around the corner as if a ghost, then reappearing in front of her closet. She could see him waving at her, working his way toward the bathroom. They stepped inside and her friend pointed to the electrical outlet by the sink. He unplugged her hair dryer, and used his screwdriver to remove the faceplate. Waving her closer, he loosened the screws on the receptacle and pulled it away from the wall as far as the live wires would stretch. Then he pointed at a small black square set between the two receptacles. It was about the size of a thumbnail and exceedingly thin.

Lena stared at it for a moment, her heart pounding as she finally picked out the microscopic lens.

Rathbone met her goggled eyes and shook his head. Then he turned his back to the outlet and extended his arms out from his body like a film director. Her friend was giving her a rough idea of the view. Lena didn't need to look, but watched just the same. The view from the camera hidden in her electrical outlet hit all the sweet spots. Her changing area. Her shower and bath.

She followed him out of the house. But as he pulled the slider closed—as if on cue—the music stopped inside the house and the night suddenly turned all too quiet.

They yanked their goggles off, Rathbone staring at her. "What just happened?"

Lena didn't reply, looking over the hill in amazement. The lights to the entire city were shutting down. One block after the next like a set of dominoes heading for the skyscrapers downtown. When the Library Tower went dark, she listened to the silence for a moment, then counted the seconds before the first siren broke into the night. The first burglar alarm running on auxiliary power in Hollywood.

It was a rolling blackout, the second in as many weeks. According to the power company, the strain on the grid came down to Christmas lights. But the excuse was more lame than real because no one was using their air conditioners this time of year. The system overload was just another ruse. Another way of tapping people for more cash.

Lena turned and watched Rathbone light a cigarette and look out over the basin. The only lights left in the city came from the cars on the roads. The life force of Los Angeles. And the result looked like eye candy. Red and white lights glittering in the blackness as they flowed through the streets and freeways like blood rolling through a human body.

Rathbone tapped the ash of his smoke in the air, then sat on the wall by the chaise longue and looked at her. "We need to keep our voices down," he said. "Half of what they've added to the house runs on batteries."

Lena understood and stepped closer.

"You moved your brother's stuff upstairs," he said.

"A while ago."

"The upstairs is clean, Lena. The bedroom. The bath. There's nothing there. You can talk all you want with the door closed and they'll never hear you."

"Thanks for doing this, Bobby. What about downstairs?"

He took another drag on his smoke. "They may not be pros, but they're using good equipment. All high-frequency stuff. Everything well over the FM band. The only loser is the one in your telephone. If you made your own sweep, that's the one you'd find."

"I already did," she whispered. "That's why I called."

"I'm glad you did because they've made some additions. Your phone's plugged into an outlet over the counter, and you've got a three-way adapter feeding the lamp and your cell charger. There's a bug in the outlet, Lena. And there's another one in the three-way adapter. Both are good enough to cover anything anyone says in the kitchen or living room. Even out here if the slider was open."

Lena slipped her hands inside her jacket pockets, feeling the bite in the moist night air. Perhaps because of the late hour, perhaps because of the way she had spent her day, her emotions remained in check. It was enough to know what Klinger had actually done. Enough to have someone she trusted like Rathbone gather the information for her. The *why* would come later.

"You okay?" he whispered.

"I'm good," she said. "Keep going."

"They covered the other side of the living room the same way. Your audio gear and computer are plugged into a surge protector."

"There's a bug inside."

He nodded. "And in the outlet as well. The same thing's going on in your bedroom. There's an outlet behind the dresser and another one by your bed where the clock radio's plugged in."

"So, I should assume they can hear everything."

"It's not an assumption, Lena. It's as true as a straight line. They can hear everything you say or do on the first floor. A pin could drop and they'd know which side of the room it fell on."

"What about the bathroom?"

He paused a moment and gave her a look. "You saw the camera. It's a TVC-X9 with a transmitter onboard. Full color. The signal's strong enough to cut through ceilings and walls up to five hundred feet. Fifteen hundred if they had a clear shot. It's the only camera in the house. And it's working on a private frequency. That's why I called whoever did this a rat. The camera's not there for business. It's there because one of your friends is a perv. Probably watching on his laptop while he beats the fuck off."

It hung there. An image of Klinger watching her and beating off.

When she turned away from the house, the image finally began to dissipate. The city below Hollywood Hills was still cloaked in darkness. She could see the headlights and brake lights congealing into rivers and streams and flowing all the way to the horizon. All the way into the black.

"Why are they doing this to you?" Rathbone whispered.

She glanced back at her friend and caught the worry in his eyes. The questions were all there. She just didn't have the answers yet.

23

Nathan G. Cava pulled in behind the Ford Explorer at the red light on Beverly Glen. Fontaine had just made a left on Wilshire Boulevard, stranding his bodyguards at the corner. Cava could see the Beverly Hills doctor looking back at his escorts like he didn't know what the fuck to do. After shouting something through the glass no one could hear, Fontaine gave up with an angry shrug and continued down the street toward his office alone.

Either the two parties had never discussed how to stay together through an intersection, or the doctor was a complete doofus. Cava suspected both possibilities were true.

The light changed. Cava followed the Explorer onto Wilshire, found the right lane, and let the SUV speed ahead. All he really wanted out of the early morning trip was confirmation that the doctor was going to work. Confirmation that his i-Mansion on South Mapleton Drive would be empty for a few hours. He could do this and keep his distance.

Besides, he was still dealing with his anger. New waves of worry and self-doubt.

Yesterday had been a bad day on almost every front. The garage in Hollywood had been found. Not that it mattered much—he hadn't left anything important behind. But the cops had talked to those poor old people he rented it from and worked up a sketch of his face. He had seen it on the news. Although the artist got his nose wrong—his eyes looked too narrow and he rarely walked around with a scowl—the overall likeness appeared too close for comfort. Anyone with a decent imagination might put it together and say *bingo*.

But even that wasn't really the issue.

In the end everything came back to the girl. The pretty one with the brown eyes who had smiled at him last Wednesday night. Part one of his three-part Hollywood deal. Finding his operating room—what they were calling the crime scene on TV—had kicked off a new round of stories. More questions about the victim and who she really was. Cava watched interview after interview with her neighbors. Then a fresh batch with waitresses and bartenders at restaurants in Venice where Jennifer McBride was known as a regular. Every interview went exactly the same way, and none of them added up.

It didn't sound like the girl had been killed for the greater good. Nor was her death being seen as a contribution to a better world, as he had been told it would. Instead, it was beginning to smell like personal gain. Like the players were playing with the facts and maybe even playing with him.

Cava tried to let it go, but couldn't.

After watching two local news broadcasts back to back, he'd worked himself into a frenzy—bought his ticket on the guilt train—and required medication in order to chill. The last thing he remembered was popping a sleeping pill and getting in bed. But when he woke up at 3:00 a.m., he found himself sitting behind the wheel in a long-term parking lot at the Bob Hope Airport in Burbank. He was dressed in his pajamas and had apparently eaten an entire box of Lucky Charms, waking up only after he had opened the toy at the bottom of the box.

A shiny red Hummer . . .

Cava cringed as he played back the night in his head. He didn't eat sugared foods, and had no idea how he acquired the cereal or drove to the airport. All he knew was that the experience, detailed on the label of his prescription as a possible side effect, had fucking become true. And nothing about it did much for his confidence. Not even the toy he won in the box of cereal.

He felt his body shiver with anxiety and tried to focus on the traffic. The here and now.

He could see Fontaine's Mercedes rolling down the ramp beneath his building into the parking garage—the men in the SUV passing their client and continuing east toward Hollywood. Cava followed the Explorer for two more blocks, guessing that the bodyguards wouldn't be back until lunch or even late this afternoon. When he spotted the pharmacy up ahead, he watched the Explorer disappear in traffic and found a place to park.

Before his meltdown last night, Cava had written two new prescriptions for himself and called them in. He had seen the ads on TV five or six times during the news broadcast. As a result, he felt certain that he was suffering from restless leg syndrome and an untimely bout with chronic dry eyes. The more he thought it over, the more aware he became of his symptoms. If he hadn't been lucky enough to see the ads, he probably wouldn't have even noticed the discomfort. He could have easily been plagued with both conditions for months or years, perhaps the rest of his life. Thank God for TV.

He walked to the back of the store and was pleased when the pharmacist told him that his two new prescriptions were ready, along with his seventeen refills. Even better, his one-month supply of meds came in at less than a grand. He took the news as a good sign, then returned to the SRX Crossover and dug out his daily planner.

In the back of the book he kept a master list of the medications he used and their possible side effects. As he added the new drugs to his list, the eye drops didn't even appear noteworthy. He could handle burning sensations, redness, discharge, eye pain, itching, and stinging. Although he wasn't too crazy about foreign body sensations or blurred vision, these were only listed as *possible* side effects and he hoped that he would do better than last night and beat the odds. But when he read the list for restless-leg syndrome, things became more tricky and he paged through his primary medications looking for a conflict. According to the pharmaceutical company, there was a chance the drug could make him feel faint, or dizzy, or even sweaty if he stood up. He could become nauseous and possibly vomit, or fall asleep in unlikely places. If he began to experience new or increased gambling, sexual, or other intense urges, it was recommended that he call his healthcare professional immediately.

Cava stared at that last one for a long time, wondering what they meant by *other intense urges*. Whether or not the intense urges he already experienced on a daily basis could be considered *other*. And if not, whether they were listed in the fine print or posted on the pharmaceutical company's Web site.

After careful consideration and review he decided that the risk was worth the benefit just like they said on TV.

Ripping open the kit, he skimmed through the dosing instructions, tossed a pill into his mouth and knocked it down with a sip of green tea. Then he opened the dry eye medication, tilted his head back, administered a single drop in each eye, and blinked.

He let out a deep sigh, filling his lungs with air and waiting for the grim reaper to knock on his door. After five long minutes of nothing, he made a mental inventory of his body, wiggled his toes and noticed that those funny sensations in his legs were gone. He sat up and leaned into the rearview mirror. His eyes felt cool and clean, almost as if he'd just received a new set. Even more important, his mind had cleared. When he examined his hands, they weren't rock steady or even kill steady. But the tremors appeared nearly imperceptible.

He might not be the road warrior anymore, or even the skilled surgeon who showed so much promise at med school. But he was in the zone again. On the diet and feeling good again. Locked and loaded and walking away from the wreckage like an action figure with no back door and bullet-proof skin.

Cava gazed through the wrought-iron gate at Fontaine's house, calculating the risks before making his move. It was still only 7:30 a.m. Because the break-in would be performed in broad daylight, entering the property from the golf course around back wasn't a viable option. The only way in was to drive up to the house in his SRX like he belonged there. Get out in his suit and tie, and walk to the back door without hesitation. That meant climbing the six-foot wall and opening the gate manually. About thirty seconds of exposing himself to actual danger.

He looked through the gate and spotted the control box tucked away in the garden. Then he turned and scoped out the neighborhood. Directly across the street was the empty lot with the wall and that pile of high-end dirt no one had stolen yet. To the left and right, the mansions were barricaded by fences, dense shrubs, and trees with no real view from the street unless you were sitting on the upper-deck of that shitty tour bus.

The risk was minimal.

Cava climbed out of the car. Lifting himself onto the wall, he dropped down on the other side and found the control box. While most security gates had a lever on the outside for easy access, this one was on the inside of the unit and painted a bright orange. Cava flipped the switch and watched the gate open, then pushed it back. Returning to the SRX, he glided up the drive and pulled in front of the guest house.

He waited a moment, letting that imaginary target between his shoulder blades fade into oblivion. The one that he had worn on his back while overseas. The gate was closing behind him and he could feel a certain rush. When he got out of the car, he scanned the property and realized his good fortune. Fontaine's neighbors couldn't see him through the shrubbery. Their view was limited to the lower terrace and the tables where he had seen the bodyguards smoking cigarettes Saturday afternoon. It didn't seem to include the pool or hot tub or the terrace and gardens running against the back of the house.

Cava was invisible. He owned the place now.

He climbed the steps, moving swiftly across the flagstone and peering through the glass door into the kitchen. His good luck held as he spotted the alarm on the inside wall, eyed the control panel, and noticed that the system hadn't been armed. Even better, the doorknob looked as if it was as old as the house. An ornamental brass number that rattled when Cava shook it.

Raising his foot, he gave the door a decent kick and watched it pop open. It had been easy. Almost too easy. As he stepped inside, he examined the doorjamb and wondered why Fontaine hadn't thrown the deadbolt. From where Cava stood it looked like the man had a lot to protect. Still, it was another good omen. There was no visible damage. No sign of forced entry. And no sirens approaching in the distance. If anyone stopped by, he could talk his way out of it.

But that didn't mean his heart wasn't pounding.

He closed the door and spent five minutes perusing the kitchen. The appliances appeared new and expensive, the room extraordinarily well equipped. He noted the eight-burner stove with the built-in grill. The crystal glassware in the cabinets and the fine china. But when he got to the knife drawer, he stopped and stared at the contents for a long time. The blades were dull and this surprised him. No matter what he might think of Fontaine, no matter what he might have been told by others, the man had a reputation as an experienced surgeon. Yet, his knives were old and didn't look as if they were well maintained. He even kept an electric knife in the drawer—what amounted to a wood saw with a safety switch—as if he had no idea or training and couldn't carve a piece of meat without electricity.

Cava shrugged it off, exiting the room and cruising through the first floor with little interest. Except for that drawer, everything in the house was rich and luxurious. And it was more than obvious that the Beverly Hills doctor enjoyed living large and showing off to his friends. He looked at the art on the walls. A collection of Fabergé eggs in a display case. A small but well-laid-out gym with its own entrance to the hot tub on the rear terrace. When he reached the den, he glanced at the Christmas tree beside the TV but didn't see a desk.

Disappointed, he hurried up the circular staircase, legged it down the hall, and found the doctor's desk in a study overlooking the pool and a view of the golf course. It was a long narrow room with a gas-burning fireplace and built-in bookshelves lining the walls. A comfortable room, if it hadn't been so chilly, with a couch, two reading chairs, and a row of casement windows providing plenty of natural light.

But the key word was privacy. The room had the look and feel of a place reserved for Fontaine, and only Fontaine, and this was what Cava had been hoping for.

He suddenly became aware of his heart pounding again. The need to not tempt the Fates and get out of the house as quickly as he could. After checking his watch, he sat down at the desk and rifled through the doctor's papers. He found a handful of patient files, along with a three-ring binder that contained the results from a research project on asthmatic children conducted over the past few years.

He set the binder down, his eyes sweeping across the bookshelves. What he needed to find was a reason worth killing for. Some verification that Fontaine deserved the title as the world's next dead man. He could feel it. Every instinct told him that Fontaine deserved his fate. But this time he needed to see it with his own eyes and not rely on the tainted words of others. He needed to find it. A tried-and-true reason good enough to stand the test of time, not something that would fall apart in a few days and become a guilt engine, following him to that beach in Coronaville where he knew Jennifer McBride's ghost was already waiting for him on the next chaise longue. Batting her pretty brown eyes and haunting him for the rest of his days.

He slid open the top desk drawer, spotting Fontaine's checkbook beside a stack of unpaid bills, and another, thicker pile that looked like receipts. He thumbed through the bills first. When he flipped to an invoice from Hollywood Shadows, Inc., he pulled the slip of paper out and grinned. It was an estimate from the security firm Fontaine had hired to protect his life. And just as Cava had guessed, Hollywood Shadows hadn't been smart enough to ask for their money up front. According to the estimate, all they wanted was a two-hundred-and-fifty-dollar deposit. A down payment made in good faith that occurred last Saturday—the notation written by hand and initialed by one of the losers following Fontaine around.

But even better, it looked like Fontaine had signed up for the economy plan on the nowhere network. The two guys in the Explorer were part-timers. Fontaine feared for his life, yet was too cheap to buy the whole day.

The thought lingered. It all felt good. Reaching for the checkbook, he paged through the register, found a pad and pen, and started to write things down. The only deposits came from Fontaine's practice and were made every other week. By all appearances he was doing better than well with an annual salary just over a million dollars. After taxes the doctor probably cleared six or seven hundred thousand. More than enough money to pay for his toys and impress his friends, or even buy a decent set of knives, upgrade the windows in the house, and hire a pair of real bodyguards.

But as Cava began to focus on the money going out, he sensed that maybe a million in gross pay wasn't enough to cover the man's heavy-duty lifestyle. It looked like Fontaine was taking a lot of vacation time. That he was spending everything he made with little or no margin for error. Even worse, it looked like Fontaine was spending everything he made on himself.

The revelation smelled like pay dirt. His first impression of the man had been the right one.

He pulled out the stack of receipts as if they were a set of X-rays and tilted them into the window light. He was seeing it now. Everything was beginning to jell. Fontaine was paying for too many things with cash. That eight-burner stove with the built-in grill in the kitchen. A new treadmill for his gym. Two paintings from a gallery in West Hollywood. When Cava checked the dates on the receipts against the check register, there was no record of any withdrawals from his account.

Pay dirt.

If the purchases had been legit, Fontaine would have used a credit card or written a check. Instead, every single invoice in the stack was marked PAID IN CASH.

Fontaine was supplementing his bullshit world with free money. He wasn't a nickel and dimer. It was all about greed and living in the material world. And all of a sudden part two of Cava's three-part Hollywood deal was righteous.

He looked at his hands. The tremors had vanished. He looked at them for a long time, turning them in the window light. Everything rock steady, everything kill steady—in spite of the cold air.

He turned back to the room, chewing it over. The doctor was living a secret life and obviously on the take. It occurred to him that he might just be stupid enough to keep his cash in the house rather than a safety deposit box at a bank. Everything that Cava had seen so far pointed to him being a certifiable idiot. An amateur. Based on the man's spending habits, the pile of cash had to be substantial.

But where would he hide it?

Cava began searching the room, certain that if the money was in the house it could only be in two places. The two most private places. Here in the study or down the hall in the master bedroom. He found a pair of filing cabinets in the closet. After locating the keys in the desk drawer, he opened them up and had a look. He checked behind the paintings for a wall safe. Unzipped the cushions in the couch and chairs. Looked behind every book.

And then his eyes came to rest on the fireplace.

There was something wrong with it. Something odd about the way the firebox was cut into the wall. It almost looked as if the house had settled into the ground at an angle and thrown the level of the room off.

Cava felt a tinge in that space between his shoulder blades. He found the switch on the wall below the mantel and pressed it, then looked down at the fake logs. When nothing happened, he hit the switch a second time and watched the ignition spark. In spite of the season, in spite of the draft from the casement windows, Fontaine hadn't bothered to turn the gas on.

Why? Particularly when it was so obvious that he spent a lot of time in the room.

He took a step back, eyeing the firebox and following the gas line into the floor. The level was definitely off, but he suddenly realized that it had nothing to do with the fireplace. Instead, it was the small sheet of marble laid to the side of the hearth. The stone wasn't seated into the floor properly.

He checked his watch again. It was only eight-thirty. Less than an hour had passed and the Fates had left him alone.

Sinking his fingers into the seams, he pried the stone up and lifted it away. As he peered into the darkness, he felt that rush again. That anxious feeling in his chest. The gas pipes were here and so was the shutoff valve. But nestled between the floor joists was Fontaine's secret. Counted and wrapped in one-inch packets of hundred-dollar bills.

Cava dug the money out of the floor and counted it, wondering what the doctor had done to earn one-point-three million dollars in cash. He shook his head, staring at the pile. Knew it would go a long way in Coronaville, and wished that he could see the doctor's face when he realized that his stash was gone.

He took a deep breath and exhaled, the scent of all that money filling his lungs. Then he pinched himself, hoping that he wouldn't wake up in his car at the airport with an empty box of Lucky Charms. When the cash was still there, when his world didn't turn to shit, he felt his heart slow down. The muse dancing with his soul.

He still had a seat on the guilt train. All this money wouldn't change that. But dealing with Jennifer McBride's ghost would be easier now.

He spotted a gym bag slung over a chair and got to his feet. Ripping it open, he dumped Fontaine's workout clothes on the couch and scooped up the money. Then he reset the piece of marble, double-checked the floor, and hurried out.

He could smell the cash riding his wake. He could feel

the dollar signs buzzing around his head even though he thought that he was immune. But as he reached the landing, he stopped. There was something else in the air. Another fragrance just as fresh and strong.

Perfume . . .

Cava spun around. He could hear something.

Tightening his grip on his bounty, he eased down the hall to the next set of double doors. As his view cleared, he took a step back and realized why the alarm hadn't been armed.

Fontaine's girlfriend from the office was still in the house. She was standing before him in her underwear. A black bra and panties. The kind Cava liked to look at because he could see through them. He heard the TV going in the room. Some guy from one of those early morning news shows was doing the weather and laughing like a fool at his own joke. She seemed to like it, though, and kept turning back to watch as she made the bed.

But Cava kept his eyes on her body. It had been a long time since he'd been with a woman. Her breasts looked soft and round and jiggled every time she turned. Her hips were wide and curvy. When she bent over to fluff the pillows, he felt his dick get hard and push against his pants. He had seen her before, but only from a distance. Only wearing a business suit or jacket to protect her smooth tan skin from the cold. From what he could tell, she didn't appear too thin. All things being equal, the blonde in the black underwear smoothing out the silk sheets was just about perfect.

For some reason a memory from his youth surfaced. A good one.

Cava had grown up on the East Coast, just a few blocks from the prep school Holden Caulfield was rumored to have attended in one of his favorite books, *The Catcher in the Rye*. Beneath the railroad bridge in the center of town, a barber kept his shop in a small space he rented over the movie theater. Cava could remember his mother dropping him off with his best friend every six weeks or so. How the strange old man took two hours off in the middle of the day and laid on the floor to rest. How he showed everyone the weird box doctors had placed inside his chest to keep his heart beating. How he liked to talk about women when no one's parents were around.

He tried to think of the old man's name, but couldn't place it. Still, he remembered the day that he and his best friend were alone in the shop. The day the barber had told them that the art of a great fuck was a matter of physics. And the whole thing came down to how much meat a woman had on her bones. He liked full-bodied women, he said. The more full-bodied, the better because there was nothing good about a woman's hip bones. And he liked doing it on the floor. He called it the secret to his success. The key to making it all work. Losing the soft mattress and doing it with a full-bodied woman on the floor.

Cava remembered giggling. That feeling of racy uncertainty because he and his friend were still too young to really know what the word *fuck* meant. From the electricity in the air, the dreamy smile on the old man's face, it seemed more than likely that anything to do with getting laid was a good thing. All the same, it was a new world still lingering on the horizon. Still too far off to touch. It would take a few years before Cava understood that the old man had been a wise man and everything he taught them that day was true.

The thought vanished. Chased away by a sudden rush of panic.

The blonde was staring at him. Frozen in her tracks and standing on the other side of the bed. Fixated on him with her mouth open and her blue eyes as wide as blue eyes go. Cava had seen it before. That look that she could tell the future. That things were about to get dramatic.

Even worse, his meds had kicked in just as his luck ran out. He could feel his chemistry coming to a boil. An overwhelming bout of foreign body sensations mixed with a heavy case of those intense urges he had read about in the car—sexual urges coupled with *other* urges. If he went by the book it was time to call his healthcare professional immediately.

She took a step toward the bedside table. But instead of

reaching for the phone, her hand dipped down to the drawer. Cava lunged across the bed, spotting the gun as the drawer slid open. Wrapping his arms around her chest, he yanked her away from the weapon and they tumbled onto the floor. She yelped and started punching him as he rolled on top of her. Soft glancing blows weakened by fear and trembling. He could smell her skin. Her soft beautiful skin. And as he tried to quiet her legs and figure out what the hell to do, he thought about the hour he had spent searching the house while she was getting ready for work. He wished that he hadn't seen her. Wished that he hadn't caught the scent of her perfume from the top of the stairs. Wished that he didn't have to do what he knew he had to do.

She would be a casualty of war, he decided, a domino in the middle of the pack that had no more meaning or relevance other than its position and timing. Its need to fall. There would be more guilt to deal with. More medication and more sleepless nights. Another ghost on another chaise longue on that beach in Coronaville.

He looked down at her face, everything in slow motion now. She had ripped open his shoulder bag and was tossing the money all over the room. She was saying something to him. Something he couldn't quite hear with so much going on. Curiously, the scissor kicks had stopped and she had wrapped her thighs around his buttocks. As he tried to concentrate, tried to lock in on the Zen moment, he became aware of his erection again. It was still there. Still hard as a rock. And when he gazed into her wild eyes, he caught the fire in them and knew that she could feel his dick, too.

She grit her teeth. Ran her fingers down his arm and dug her nails in. Took a swing at him.

All of a sudden life was complicated again. A hodgepodge of mixed signals that he didn't have time to figure out. The Fates had arrived and he needed to make his move. He needed to end this. If the guilt got too crazy, he could always spend the night counting hundred-dollar bills . . .

24

Lena had been late for her meeting with Art Madina. Fifteen minutes late. Not from the drive downtown, but from an unexpectedly long sleep. A big dreamless sleep so heavy and so blank that she had no idea how she finally broke back to the surface and opened her eyes.

She had gone to bed before the power was restored and fallen asleep before she could reset the time on her clock radio and switch on the alarm.

And it had been late. Long after Bobby Rathbone had given her the bad news and gone home. Long after two glasses of wine and another half a cigarette helped her think it all through.

She had come to a decision last night to leave the bugs in place. Her house would remain hot-wired except for the low-tech bug in the handset. The *feel-good* bug that she was meant to find. After ripping it out of the phone, she killed it with a hammer on the kitchen floor. And when the electric company got around to turning the juice back on, Klinger and his sidekick would no longer be burdened with loud music. By all appearances, everything would be back to normal, and the dynamic duo could listen in and think that they were outsmarting her.

For Lena, this was the quickest way back to her case and what really mattered. And it was easy enough to avoid Klinger's camera by using the shower upstairs in her old bathroom.

But none of that was really on her mind as she followed Art Madina inside the cooler and the door snapped shut behind them. None of what happened last night really mattered right now.

Madina switched on his flashlight, checking toe tags in the darkness and rolling gurneys out of the way as he searched through the crowd of dead bodies. The dank air was just above freezing, her breath vaporizing before her eyes and thick as smoke. After ten long minutes, they found Jane Doe resting in the far corner beneath a thin sheet of translucent plastic.

Madina handed over the flashlight and pulled the plastic away. Time, even in a temperature-controlled setting, had a way of changing things. Although Lena's first instinct was to turn away, she held her ground and looked at the corpse.

"If something was missing, how much would it be?" Madina asked in a low voice.

"I don't know."

"What did he do with it?"

"We found a meat grinder in the garage."

Madina turned and gave her a long look. "You're not serious."

"We can't tell when it was last used," she whispered.

Several moments passed. Then Madina took charge of the flashlight and panned the beam over the victim's wounds.

"My problem with all this is that it's such a neat job, Lena. So surgically precise. This guy went to med school."

The door opened, the space flooding with light. Two men were peering into the cooler. When they spotted Lena standing beside the pathologist, the man in the lab coat stepped away and the second man entered on his own. He was holding a manila envelope and seemed as uncomfortable by the setting as Lena was. She recognized him as Martin Orth from SID, but they had never been formally introduced. Orth was a division supervisor and it appeared strange to see someone so high in the food chain off-site and making what looked like a delivery.

"Lena Gamble?" he asked.

All three shook hands and introduced themselves. Then Orth handed the envelope to Lena, straining to keep his eyes on her and away from the victim.

"You were right," he said. "It's her."

A moment passed—SID's confirmation giving the depravity new life and breadth.

"You're absolutely sure," she said.

Orth nodded. "We ran side-by-sides from the blood samples taken in the alley last week, the parking lot at the Cock-a-doodle-do on Saturday, and the garage on Barton Avenue. Everything matches. It's her. It's Jane Doe. That's where she was killed."

His voice trailed off, his gaze finally moving to the victim. Lena could see the pain in his eyes as he measured the woman's battered face and skimmed over her wounds. A certain amount of determination lingered in his jawline as he turned back to her.

"We're twenty-four-seven on this, Lena. Weekends and holidays. Forget about the backlog. Anything you want, you get until this guy's in the ground."

She wished the case was that simple. One man acting on his own.

"What about the meat grinder?" she said.

"We found trace amounts of muscle tissue, but we don't think it's human. There's enough rust to indicate that it went through a dishwasher. We're not really sure what it is."

Lena traded looks with Madina, then turned back to Orth.

"What about the rest of the garage?" she said.

"It's gonna take a while," Orth said. "Everything we pulled looks like it came from the victim, not the doer. Hair, fiber, fingerprints. But there's still hope. There's still a long way to go."

"What about the trash can by the workbench? He left behind a smock. Everything he wore Wednesday night."

"We're concentrating on the gloves for touch DNA. There's a chance we might luck out and lift a print, but I wouldn't count on it. They're vinyl."

Lena understood the odds, but remained upbeat. Nathan Good would have been wearing the gloves long enough to have left a fair amount of perspiration behind. Although touch DNA, or low-copy DNA, was still new, still not legislated in all fifty states, the science had evolved and could yield a positive result. But lifting a print from inside a vinyl glove would be more difficult. While it had been done before, success depended on the conditions being just right. Still, they were inching closer. And when she caught the glint in Orth's eye, she realized that there was more.

"What is it?" she asked.

"He left something behind," Orth said. "It's not as good as a fingerprint. It's not something that we can key into a database and pull out his name and address. But it's almost as good. That sheet of linoleum underneath the operating table?"

"You lifted a shoe print."

Orth grinned with pride. "About three-thirty this morning," he said. "It was invisible, but we found it. It's amazing what florescent powder and a black light can do. I called and they said that you were here, so I came down. The placement on the linoleum couldn't be reached once the plywood was clamped to the saw horses. I figure he left the print when he was setting up and didn't have his booties on."

"You got the entire print or just a piece?"

"Take a look. A copy's in that envelope. We lifted the whole thing, but it gets better. He was wearing Bruno Maglis just like O.J.: a size-ten Magdy boot. It's a lace-up dress shoe with a rubber sole. List price: four hundred eighty-four dollars and ninety-five cents."

She pulled the photograph out of the envelope and gazed at the shoe print. Everything crystal clear.

"He has money," she said.

"He's got more than that. Look. He's got a small Phillips head screw embedded in his right heel. Maybe he stepped on it in the garage. Maybe not. Either way, you get the deal."

She found the screw in the photograph. "The shoe puts him away forever."

"Like I said, Lena, it's not a fingerprint. But in court—"

"It'll work just as well."

Her cell phone started vibrating. When she checked the screen, she knew that she had to take the call. It was Klinger, dialing in from Chief Logan's office.

"He wants to see you," Klinger said. "I told him that you'd be here in fifteen minutes. That was ten minutes ago, so you'll be late."

The chief's adjutant didn't give her a chance to respond. Before she could say anything, he hung up on her again.

25

District Attorney Jimmy J. Higgins hustled out of the chief's office and rolled down the hall toward the elevator. As he passed Lena, he kept his eyes fixed on some invisible object ten feet ahead, scratched the back of his overly groomed silver hair, and muttered the word *bitch* under his breath.

Lena didn't stop or turn or even question whether or not she'd actually heard it. She kept walking until she reached the door at the end of the hall.

Klinger looked up as she entered. He was seated at his desk, installing software in a new laptop computer. The carton and packing materials were on the floor. Checking his watch, he smiled and pointed at Chief Logan's office.

"You're late," he said.

Lena ignored him and tapped on the door. Bracing herself for the main event, she took a deep breath and walked in.

"Close the door behind you," the chief said.

She followed the chief's instructions. When she turned, she noticed Lieutenant Barrera leaning against the windowsill and caught the imperceptible shake of his head. He was here, and he was her ally. But he was also trying to warn her. Keep cool. Trouble ahead.

Chief Logan cleared his throat. "Did you see the DA on his way out?"

"Yes, sir."

"Did he say anything to you?"

"He called me a bitch."

A beat went by. She had been matter-of-fact in her delivery. Then the chief shrugged from behind his oversized desk.

"The man's pissed," he said. "A lot of people are. Welcome to the real world, Gamble. Now take a seat."

He was studying her, measuring her with those dark eyes of his. As she moved toward the chair, she noticed an M21 sniper rifle mounted behind glass and hanging on the near wall beside his medals from the Vietnam War. Several black-and-white photographs were on display as well, one that included the chief sitting beside a .50-caliber Browning machine gun in the jungle. She remembered reading something about the chief's war record in *The Times* after his interview with the police commission. He had been one of the first to use a .50-caliber weapon in a sniping role, and had recorded the second farthest confirmed kill during the war. She couldn't remember the distance, but thought that it was over two thousand meters.

"Why do you think the DA's pissed, Gamble?"

She turned back to the chief, considering his question. She wanted to say that Jimmy J. Higgins was pissed off because he had become a pig, but didn't. She wanted to say that the district attorney had let the high-profile job go to his head. That he would do or say anything for a political campaign contribution or a decent headline. That he loved having a limo and a driver and hanging out with celebrities. That he campaigned on ending the dangerous practice of keeping score on wins and losses like so many other cities had, but never followed up on his promise to see justice through no matter how it turned out.

But the truth was that she knew why Higgins had called her a bitch the moment it slipped out of his sloppy mouth. The DA was taking heat from both the press and his political rivals for backing down on a young TV actor who crashed his Land Rover and killed his teenage friend sitting in the passenger seat. The actor's blood alcohol level was four times over the legal limit. An ample supply of cocaine had been found in his system as well. Detectives working the case wanted to charge the actor with gross vehicular manslaughter, which carried a prison sentence of ten years. Instead, the kid went to *rehab*. This was the second incident in as many months where a celebrity had been responsible for the death of an innocent person while driving drunk. The second time in two months that Jimmy J. Higgins had looked the other way because he had so many celebrity friends.

She could have said a lot of things. But when the chief repeated the question and asked her why Higgins was so pissed off, she said, "Because Dean Tremell made a contribution to his campaign and this is strike three."

The chief's compact body tightened up. She had struck a nerve and could see his wheels turning. Her answer had been the obvious one. Dean Tremell was using his political muscle in an attempt to protect his rotten son. And the DA was in a jam.

"When does Stan Rhodes get back?" the chief asked finally.

"Tomorrow."

"Did either one of you bother to find out exactly who Dean Tremell is?"

"His son's name came up on Saturday afternoon," she said. "Yesterday the crime scene was located. Today that's been confirmed."

"I understand that you've been busy. But that's no excuse for fucking up."

Lena glanced at Barrera standing by the window. Then the chief leaned over his desk.

"Stop looking at your supervisor, Detective. He can't help you now."

She turned back, the chief glaring at her. "Yes, sir."

"That's better," he said. "You fucked up. You didn't do your homework, so now I have to do it for you. Anders Dahl Pharmaceuticals employs thousands of people in this city. There are more full-time employees working at Anders Dahl than any two movie studios combined. The company is an important part of our city's economy. You're right, Dean Tremell is one of the district attorney's biggest contributors. If you had bothered to check, you would have learned that he's also made contributions to every member of the city council. It's business, Gamble. And he's a player. A mover and a shaker. Do you understand what I'm saying? The man counts."

She didn't respond. She tried to let the words sink in, but couldn't. Even the concept felt dirty.

"You got a problem, Gamble?"

"I thought everybody counted," she said.

"Stop feeding me your bullshit. The man deserves your respect. I deserve your respect."

The chief finally took his eyes off her and leaned back in his chair. She could see where the conversation was headed. It was in her best interest to keep quiet—in her best interest to take the blows and walk out in one piece. And she probably would have followed her own advice if her eyes hadn't come to rest on the chief's telephone. The intercom light was on. Klinger was listening. The high-octane pervert who installed the camera in her bathroom and just bought a new laptop computer was listening to her take the chief's verbal beating.

"This isn't about Dean Tremell," she said. "This is about his son. He was the last person seen with the victim before she was murdered."

"You haven't been listening," the chief said. "You're not hearing me."

"Justin Tremell lied about being there. He's more than a person of interest."

"What are you trying to do? Fuck me up so that I can be like you? I don't want to be like you, Gamble. You should have checked with me before you barged in on them Saturday. And you should have had more than the word of a part-time prostitute working at a whorehouse off the one-oh-five fucking freeway. This isn't a drunk-driver case. This is a homicide investigation. What if you got it wrong? What if your asshole friend over at *The Times* printed your fuck-up in his newspaper? You could have ruined Justin Tremell's life. And the story would have followed him around forever. Zero plus zero equals zero, Gamble. And this is the Los

Angeles Police Department. We work with evidence here. Not hopes and dreams. Empirical evidence. Quantifiable evidence. You don't walk in on people like this half-cocked and try to wing it. You're not ready for prime time. You're a fucking disgrace."

Lena tried not to show any emotion. Tried to find her game face. She remembered what Ramira had said to her less than a week ago when the reporter followed her into the Blackbird Café. You're in a rough business, he said. And you need friends. Everybody knows that you're on the outs with the chief and his band of self-righteous Boy Scouts. It's all about your last case. You were right and he was wrong and everything went down in public. I know that you didn't mean to embarrass him, but you did. The bottom line is that no matter how much he'd like to, he can't transfer you to the Valley and he can't fire your ass to oblivion. His hands are tied, and he can't get rid of you. But I'll bet he thinks about it. I'd bet the city he spends a lot of time thinking about it. And that's why you need friends. You're in a rough business, Lena. Shit happens . . .

The chief banged his fist on the desk. "Are you still with us, Gamble? Or are you dreaming about the way things could have been?"

"I'm still here."

She tried to pull herself together. Her voice was breaking up, her cadence shaky. Like all of sudden she was a boot just out of the academy. As she thought it over, she couldn't believe how easy it had been for the chief to peel the years away and knock her down. And she could still imagine Klinger at his desk, reveling in her jagged fall. She remembered Barrera's initial call on Thursday afternoon. She remembered him saying that Chief Logan had specifically asked for her to investigate the case. Now she knew why. And now she understood why they had wired her house for video and sound. Another reason more insidious than just keeping tabs on her. Ramira had been right. They were trying to distract her. Trying to break her. They were hoping that she would fuck up. They wanted her to quit and run away.

And if she didn't?

Then what Ramira had been inferring might be more right than she had first thought possible. She was caught in a dangerous business. Shit happens.

Her gaze returned to the photographs on the wall. The chief in Vietnam with his machine gun. She was thinking about statistics now, feeling the beads of sweat begin to percolate on her forehead. A cop goes down in the line of duty every two days in this country. If a cop wanted to get rid of another cop and ran out of options—the possibility, the horror—all of it was there. If they couldn't push her out, then they might be looking for the opportunity to take her—

She couldn't face it. Couldn't think it.

The chief cleared his throat again, his sniper eyes sharp as glass. "I've lost my confidence in you," he said. "I'm sorry, Gamble. Things just don't seem to be going right. Lieutenant Barrera gave me an update while we waited for you. There seem to be a number of loose ends. Have you located the victim's car?"

"It's a black Toyota Matrix," she said.

He reached for a pen, then glanced at a list jotted down on his legal pad. "Lieutenant Barrera told me what kind of car it is. I asked you if you located it."

"Not yet."

"Then it was probably stolen on the night of the murder?"

"If it's on the road and the plates haven't been changed, we'll find it. The bulletin went out as soon as we heard back from the DMV."

"What about the part-time prostitute you interviewed? Did you run a background check?"

A moment went by as she thought it over. The chief was doing everything he possibly could to make things difficult for her. Keying in on the minutia. Standing in her way.

"Which is it, Gamble? The girl pointed her dirty finger at Justin Tremell. For all you know she hates rich people. Did you run a background check or didn't you?"

"Not yet, sir."

The chief glanced back at his legal pad as if he knew the

answers before he asked the questions. "What about the lost witness?"

"He's still lost," she said.

"Is that a crack?"

"No, sir. It's a statement of fact. The witness is still missing."

Somehow her voice had returned. Her cadence, steady as a west wind. Everything fueled by an intense anger burning in her gut.

"The department released the witness's photograph to the press on Saturday," the chief said. "I understand that he's hit several ATMs and stolen money from the victim's account. What else are you doing to find him?"

"If we locate the victim's car, we think we'll find the witness. He has the keys and everything else that was in her purse."

"Is that it?"

"No, sir. We're working with the bank as well."

"What can they do that we can't?"

"Monitor hundreds of ATMs."

"You mean you didn't close the account, Detective?"

She hesitated a moment. The chief should have known better. She was surprised that he didn't.

"No, sir," she said. "The number on the card has been restricted and won't work in any ATM that isn't owned by the bank. The cash limit has been cut in half and the account can't be accessed except during normal business hours. If he tries to use the card, every bank in the city has his photograph and knows what to do."

"Who made the call? You or them?"

Lena ignored the sarcasm in his voice. The decision had been made before she left the bank on Saturday. Steve Avadar wanted the witness as much as they did.

"Both," she said. "We share the same interest. They're tracking her credit card as well."

The chief gave her a hard look. "What about this doctor in Beverly Hills? Joseph Fontaine."

"What about him?"

"What did you do to piss him off?"

The question was insane, and she didn't know how to respond. As she gazed back at the chief, she realized that the anger coursing through her veins had nothing to do with his rank or position. Like Klinger, something was off. Something about the moment was wrong.

"What did you do to piss the doctor off?" the chief repeated. "Is he a legitimate person of interest or not?"

Before she could respond, Barrera broke in.

"While Detectives Gamble and Rhodes were processing the crime scene at the Cock-a-doodle-do on Saturday, we made an attempt to reach him. He refused."

"Who made contact?" the chief asked.

"Tito Sanchez," Barrera said. "He was canvassing the neighborhood and learned that Fontaine had hired a pair of bodyguards. We thought there might be a chance he'd want to talk about it. He didn't."

The chief took a moment to think it over.

"He's involved in the murder," Lena said. "We just don't know how yet."

"Well, until you do, leave him alone. His attorney sent a letter over by messenger this morning. I don't want to get another."

The chief reached for a file. As he pulled out a sheet of paper, Lena risked a quick glance at Barrera, who didn't appear to be having a good day, either. When she turned back, the chief was holding the sketch they had worked up with the Andolinis of the man calling himself Nathan Good.

"Is this the most up-to-date version?" he asked.

Lena nodded. "It was released to the press last night."

The chief returned the sketch to his file, grabbed his legal pad, and slipped everything into his briefcase. "Okay," he said. "Lieutenant Klinger and I have a meeting at USC Medical Center this morning. We'll pass the sketch around and see what happens. If he received his training in the trauma unit before shipping overseas, then we've lucked out. If he didn't and no one can identify him, then we'll regroup. But until this plays out, Gamble, until further notice from this office, your job is to clean up the loose ends we just spoke about. That means crossing Justin Tremell off your list. That means leaving the kid alone. And it means any contact with Fontaine is prohibited without my okay as well. Just the loose ends, Gamble. You think you can handle that?"

She was speechless. The case was almost a week old. In the past few days they'd made up a lot of ground and now the chief wanted to shut them down. But Dean Tremell had pressed the right buttons. He had the ability and resources to protect his son. Like the chief said, the man counted.

She watched the chief close his briefcase, then glance at the door indicating that the meeting was over.

"I'm no counselor," he said in a lower voice. "But I think you should start thinking about your future here, Gamble. And talking about department business with a reporter like Denny Ramira probably isn't going to help your cause. Now get out of my office. Get out and do your job. And if you come up with a lead on that witness, you better make sure that I'm your first call."

26

Keep cool. Trouble ahead.

She lit a cigarette and cracked the window open. The radio was tuned to KFWB, but she wasn't listening. Instead, she was staring through the windshield, her car idling in the rusted-out garage across the street from Parker Center. She took another drag on the smoke, hoping that the nicotine would settle her nerves. But it wasn't enough—not near enough. She could see Chief Logan exiting the building with Klinger, his car and driver waiting for them in the VIP lot by the door. She could see both men laughing.

Keep cool. Trouble ahead.

Lena watched them drive off, thinking about the number of blows she had taken. Most of them felt like head shots, her mind still numb. Her career, dead on arrival.

She tapped the ash out the window, then focused on a Lincoln pulling into the lot and parking in a space reserved for members of the police commission. Senator Alan West got out from behind the wheel and walked over to the cop in the guard shack. It looked like the senator was showing him the pin he wore on his lapel. The gold fire engine he had received from the LAFD after 9/11. As she watched, she remembered what he had said to her less than a week ago when they met and he showed her the same pin.

This is Los Angeles. Chiefs come and go. If I can do anything for you, I'll try my best.

She reached inside her pocket. West's business card was

still there and she gazed at it. Looking back, she followed his progress across the lot until he reached the door and vanished inside the building.

Lena knew with absolute certainty that going to West was not an option. Not if she still hoped to remain a detective anywhere near Los Angeles. Any contact with West would be suicide. He might be one of the good ones. There was even something reassuring about the fact that he drove his own car. But like every other commissioner, he wasn't a member of the club. No one would ever trust her if she went outside the blue curtain. No one would ever work with her again. Being right had about as much relevance and worth as half a dollar bill. She couldn't buy anything with it. And she couldn't save it for a rainy day no matter how big the storm.

Her cell started vibrating. Glancing at the display, she saw Lieutenant Barrera's name and flipped it open.

"You okay, Lena?"

"Since when did we stop following leads?" she said. "It must have been in a department bulletin I missed."

Barrera didn't say anything right away. From the lack of background noise, she guessed that he was in the captain's office with the door closed.

"Something's up," he said finally. "I told you that last week. I wish I could tell you what it was."

"What's up is easy," she said. "They're looking for a way to give Tremell's kid a pass. How did the chief put it? The girl pointed her dirty finger at him. Her finger isn't dirty, Frank. And we didn't move with just one eyewitness. Four people put him with the victim that night."

"That's what you said. What's so bizarre is that the chief knows it, too. After we talked Saturday night, I called and gave him a complete briefing. It's a disgrace, simple as that. He's fucked up. The whole thing's fucked up, so don't let it get to you. Don't let it get inside you. Don't let it fuck you up, too."

"So, what comes next?"

"Fuck him, Lena. That's what comes next. You're a cop. Do what you gotta do."

She pulled the phone away from her ear—Barrera shouting. Switching over to speaker, she turned the volume down. She had never heard him so upset before. It occurred to her that the meeting must have been just as tough on him. Maybe even worse because he couldn't say anything, and had to stay after she left. Barrera was a fair-minded man who began his career in a patrol car just like every other cop. He had risen through the ranks on his own and worked the homicide table long before his promotion to lieutenant. Long before Chief Logan ever dreamed of moving to Los Angeles and starting at the top. Barrera had the support and respect of every investigator he supervised. And everyone on the floor knew how much he despised department politics. But what the chief was doing amounted to more than that. He and the DA were breaking a cardinal rule.

"Follow the evidence," Barrera said in a firm voice. "And I don't care where it leads or who it fucks up. You know what the Groucho is, right, Lena?"

He was referring to the way SWAT teams entered a hostile location. The way they bent their knees and kept their backs straight so that they could aim their shotguns and rifles, and fire on the move. Because the posture mimicked the way Groucho Marx often walked in his films, the tactical move was often called the Groucho.

"I've heard of it," she said.

"Then keep it in mind. Stay low and push forward. After what just happened, if you want to take the day off and get drunk, I'll say okay to that, too. I'll buy the first and last round. But I'm hoping you won't. I'm hoping none of this bullshit really matters to you. Either way, Lena, be careful and keep me in the fucking loop."

He hung up. Lena stubbed her cigarette out, lighting another and thinking it over. What the chief had done was already inside her. Already fucking her up. She couldn't help that. But Barrera didn't need to buy her a drink, either.

Something clicked and she became aware of the radio. A story on the news.

A dead body had been found in an apartment on Willoughby Avenue early this morning. An old man who once ran a hotdog stand in West Hollywood had been discovered by a maintenance worker. According to the investigator from the coroner's office, the old man was found sitting in a chair in his living room. He had been dead for more than a year, his body mummified by the dry air. When authorities entered the apartment, the TV was still on.

It was another L.A. story. A sad and horrific story. But what resonated for Lena was the fact that the old man had died alone. That no one had checked on him or seemed to care. That he didn't have a lifeline—some connection between himself and the outside world.

Chewing it over, she wondered if she had a lifeline. Someone who checked on her and seemed to care.

She pulled out of the garage, the story following her into the bright daylight—that feeling of loneliness lingering in the smoky air as she stubbed out that second cigarette. Winding her way around Parker Center and through the city, she reached the 10 Freeway and decided to head west. She wanted another look at Jennifer McBride's apartment on Navy Street. A quiet look on her own. But she needed to get away, too. She needed a time-out to regroup and put things in perspective.

The freeway was moving, the drive across town taking no more than half an hour. As she found a place to park two doors down from the building and got out, she spotted the patrol car at the end of the street. Pacific Division was keeping a loose eye on the place just in case the witness showed up. No one thought that he would. Even though the kid had retrieved the victim's purse and everything inside it at the Cock-a-doodle-do, the risk of breaking into a murder victim's apartment seemed over the top. She had forgotten to mention it to the chief. But things had been so bad, she didn't think that it would have made a difference if she had.

She let the thought go, fishing through her briefcase for

the keys. When she got the lobby door open, Jones was waiting for her.

"Why did you put that stupid lock on the door?" he shouted.

She looked up and saw him glaring at her. The small, troll-like man with the damaged eyes hadn't bothered to dress. He was standing by his door in his boxer shorts and that old tank top. Even from a distance, Lena could tell that he still needed a bath.

"It's a crime scene, Jones. Go back inside."

"When can I get rid of her shit and rent the place out? She's dead, isn't she? What the fuck's the difference now?"

"Go back inside."

"But I want my money," he said. "I need it."

She started up the steps, then turned back when she remembered what Jones had done to Jennifer McBride's rental application. That bottle of Wite-Out he used to erase her security deposit and pocket the cash.

"You already got the money," she said.

"What are you talking about?"

"Did you really think that we wouldn't notice?"

"Notice what?"

"Her rental application, Jones. You altered it. You stole her security deposit. Two thousand bucks."

His face reddened. He didn't say anything.

"There's a cop down the street," she said. "Do you want me to call him? Do you want to spend the next two years in jail? Or are you gonna go back inside, get your copy of her application out, and fix what you did?"

"But she's dead."

"Your choice, Jones."

He didn't spend much time thinking it over. When the door slammed, Lena took a deep breath and trudged up the steps to Jennifer McBride's apartment. The door had been sealed with crime scene tape. And Kline had added a hasp and padlock. Just enough to set Jones off.

Lena got inside and closed the door behind her. As she stood in the dark foyer, she took another deep breath and wondered if she had made a mistake by coming here. The place was too quiet. Too black. And the day had started off with an overdose of the abhorrent. Two experiences with two people so foul that she could taste it in her mouth.

But there was something else here. Something more. As she first entered the apartment, she became aware of the victim's scent. It only lasted for a split second, dissipating in the air just as she noticed—but it had been there. And it wasn't the soap the woman had used, or even the perfume that Lena had smelled twice before. It was her person, lingering behind. Her body. Her physical being, six days gone.

Lena didn't know whether she could handle this right now. Like maybe the timing was off and five or six shots of tequila with salt and lime would do her good.

She switched on the lamp and gazed through the French doors into the living room. She had forgotten how barren the place was. Not a single photograph. Not a letter from a friend. Just the basics. One set of sheets and a pair of bath towels. Enough clothing to pack a suitcase. Enough lingerie to fill a duffel bag so that Jennifer McBride could make a buck.

Lena glanced inside the bedroom, deciding to enter when she spotted the snow globe on the bedside table. She picked it up and gazed at the snow falling over Las Vegas. The Bellagio Hotel and Caesar's Palace. All the streets painted a bright gold. Although Barrera had managed to get the story on five stations in Nevada, the response from viewers matched the response here in Los Angeles.

Lena rubbed her thumb over the glass, thinking that its meaning for whoever Jane Doe really was didn't point to where she came from. It would have been too easy if it had. Instead, the object was probably nothing more than a souvenir from a weekend visit. Or, maybe only a gift from a client or a friend.

She set the snow globe down and returned to the living room. Moving to the couch, she opened her briefcase and pulled out the murder book. The Field Interview cards Kline had sent with the key to the padlock were in the back. She pulled them out, sorting them on the coffee table. Her sole interest was with the tenants living in the building, not the total number of people contacted when Pacific Division canvassed the neighborhood. Other than Jones and the victim, there were six names, and Kline had told her that he conducted these interviews himself. She trusted the detective. They had gone through the academy together and he had played a role in her last case. She skimmed through the cards, rereading his notes. But every card was exactly the same. Every interview, almost identical. The young woman calling herself Jennifer McBride lived a private life. No one in the building knew her. Over the past year, no one really talked to her. She was attractive, had a great smile, but kept to herself and was always seen alone.

Lena set the cards down, that story on KFWB resurfacing in her mind. The story about the old man who died in his living room and sat for a year in front of his TV before anyone noticed. The man without a lifeline.

She lay back on the couch, thinking it over and wondering why this mysterious woman—the woman who cast spells—didn't have a lifeline, either. No connection between her real identity and the life that she was living under another name. No connection left behind just in case something went wrong.

The more Lena considered the circumstances, the less sense it made. The victim had obviously been too smart, her theft of Jennifer McBride's identity too thorough. The life she was living had been too risky to not include some sort of an out pitch, some kind of an insurance policy. A lifeline back to the real world and the people who knew her and loved her.

She woke up in the dim light, her body flinching as it broke the surface. She turned and looked back at the lamp on the foyer table. Sat up and stared at the fire escape outside the windows. Night had fallen, the marine layer had rolled in—and she was still in Jennifer McBride's apartment.

She checked her watch. It was seven-thirty and she'd been asleep for hours. She didn't understand it. The loss of control worried her.

Lena got up and crossed the room to the window, sorting through the events of the day she couldn't seem to face. But as her eyes climbed the brick wall on the other side of the alley, everything came to a sudden stop.

That man with the wool cap and the binoculars was staring at her through the fog. Staring at her and not looking away.

She glanced back at the couch, calculating the angle. When she realized that his view included most of the living room, she stopped calculating and drew the curtains. She didn't really need to do the math. The day was already too rich, too good.

She stepped into the kitchen, splashing her face with warm water. Her mind was still going, and it felt like a migraine was waving at her from an hour or two down the road. She thought she remembered seeing a bottle of Tylenol when she and Rhodes made their initial search. Switching on the overhead light, she found it in the cabinet beside several bottles of vitamins.

The Tylenol was new and she picked out the cotton. After filling a glass with tap water, she popped two caplets and noticed a piece of scratch paper on the counter beside the stove.

It was a grocery list. Lettuce, yogurt, bread, and cheese. Four or five basic items the victim had jotted down before her death.

For some reason she found it hard to look at. She thought about her meeting with the chief again. Her confrontation with Jones in the lobby. The pervert with the wool cap watching her sleep. As the moments faded, her eyes drifted back to that grocery list that had been left behind and was no longer needed. She felt the sting and wondered why it was always the small things about a victim's life that brought a murder home.

Lena flipped the paper over in frustration, but froze before she could shake her head. The grocery list hadn't been scrawled out on a piece of scratch paper. Instead, the victim had used the back of a script from her doctor.

She whisked the paper off the counter, holding it closer to the light and trying to keep her emotions in check. She saw Jennifer McBride's name and a drug called Synthroid. The words were barely legible, but they were here. The name of the doctor who prescribed the medication was here as well, along with an office address and phone number, printed neatly at the top.

Everything about the script looked legit.

She packed up the murder book, locked the door, and hustled downstairs. Hitting the sidewalk, she saw Jones keeping watch with his ruined eyes from the window. The clouds were tumbling in at street level, the air, pitch-black and raw. She knew that he couldn't see her in the fog, and even if he could, she didn't care.

Her car was parked two doors down. As she picked up her pace, she noticed another man exiting the next building. His body was silhouetted in the darkness, but she could see him shouldering a book bag. In spite of the cold, it looked like all he had on were a pair of jeans and a T-shirt. He crossed the street, moving away from her into the mist. His gait appeared smooth and easy, like he didn't know that she was even there. Still, she kept an eye on him and watched as he clicked the remote on his key ring. She heard the alarm chirp and saw the headlights blink. And that's when she spotted the wool cap.

"Hey, you," she shouted.

He stopped and turned from half a block away, his face lost in the gloom. Lena searched for the patrol car at the end of the street, didn't see it in the wall of fog, and turned back. Then the man jumped into his car and pulled out.

Her eyes flicked down to the license plate, but the car seemed new and she didn't think it was there. She heard the tires screeching on the wet asphalt—watched the car shimmering in and out of the darkness and ghosting as it picked up speed. It was an SRX Crossover. When it rolled beneath a street light, she caught a glimpse of the color before it vanished into the December night. She had seen a similar color on a Lexus SC coupe and liked it. Radiant bronze. At least the perv had taste.

27

Doctor Ryan is with a patient," the nurse said. "She won't be long. You can wait in here."

Lena followed her into the doctor's office. When the nurse left, she took a seat in front of the desk and looked out the window. The medical building was on Sunset at the very end of the Strip and she could see the rays of early morning sunlight burning through the mist. She had spent most of the night on her computer, catching up on Justin Tremell's exploits and researching Synthroid on the Internet.

The woman living as Jennifer McBride had an underactive thyroid gland, yet at the time of her death was only twenty-plus years old. The medication she was using amounted to hormone replacement therapy. It was a simple fix for a condition that affected both men and women. From what Lena had read, people whose families originated in countries close to the Mediterranean Sea appeared more susceptible to the disease than those who didn't. But the condition had no real boundaries, a long list of possible causes, and could affect anyone.

Lena stood up as Dr. Sue Ryan entered, introducing herself and shaking hands. She watched the doctor move around the desk with Jennifer McBride's file under her arm, a blonde in her mid-forties with gentle eyes and a round figure that seemed to fit her well. Lena could tell from the expression on her face that the nurse had given her the news. There was no reason to explain why she wanted to talk.

"I'm sorry to hear about Jennifer," the doctor said. "I've been so busy, I didn't know."

"How long was she a patient?"

"Only about two months. I'm afraid I didn't even recognize her name. I had to skim through her file before I remembered her."

Lena tried not to show her disappointment. She had been hoping for more.

"I need to look at that file," she said.

The doctor hesitated. "I've never been through anything like this before. She signed a privacy agreement."

"I understand, but I need to see the file. She's not a suspect, Doctor. She was the victim. She's dead."

The doctor thought it over for a moment, then slid the file across the desk.

"Thanks," Lena said.

She leafed through the pages quickly, skipping over McBride's brief medical history. Instead, she wanted to look at the personal information forms the victim would have filled out before her first appointment. The names and phone numbers she would have listed in case of an emergency. When she found them, she pulled the murder book out of her briefcase and located the rental agreement McBride had submitted for the apartment on Navy Street.

The information forms were two pages long and exactly what Lena expected—a mirrored copy of the rental agreement the victim had given Jones. Her social security number was here, along with her mother's name, address, and phone number. Everything she had stolen from the real Jennifer McBride, the girl who had been murdered in a bank robbery two years ago.

Lena made a second pass, comparing the two documents side by side. Nothing she saw pointed to the woman's real identity. Jane Doe No. 99 hadn't left a lifeline.

"Is there a problem?" Dr. Ryan asked.

"Not really."

"But you were looking for something and it's not there. You're disappointed."

Lena met the doctor's eyes, then noticed that the murder book was distracting the woman. A crime scene photograph taken of the victim in the alley was partially visible. She closed the binder and casually returned it to her briefcase.

"I was just wondering about the medication you prescribed."

"Synthroid."

"I found the script in her apartment."

Dr. Ryan leaned back in her chair. "Jennifer had an under-active thyroid gland."

"I understand that. But why not the generic? When I looked it up on the Internet, the generic was prescribed more often than the original."

"I'm sure that's true," she said. "Most of my patients use the generic. Let me see the file."

Lena passed it over, watching the doctor turn directly to her notes. After a moment, the woman found what she was searching for.

"Jennifer said that she didn't want the generic. It was a specific request."

"Any reason why?" Lena asked.

"None that I can think of. The only difference is cost."

"But I noticed that she didn't list an insurance company. That would mean that she had to pay for everything herself."

The doctor glanced back at her notes and started reading. "She told us she just changed jobs. She was supposed to call in and update her records, but I can see that she didn't."

"She seems so young," Lena said. "Is this condition common for someone in their early twenties?"

"It's not as uncommon as you might think. For someone in her situation, you'd be surprised."

"What situation?"

Dr. Ryan lowered the file to her desk and looked at her. "Her thyroid problems began with a pregnancy."

It hung there, in the silence between breaths. Lena didn't say anything as the doctor continued.

"I guess I should be more precise. Jennifer didn't realize that she had a thyroid problem until after her pregnancy.

Sometimes it's hard to separate the two. Fatigue and weight gain are symptomatic of both."

"Do you know when she had the child?"

The doctor shook her head. "I'm not even certain that she carried it to term. If I had to guess, I'd say that she didn't."

"You mean she aborted it."

"Or lost it. She wasn't my patient at the time. She came to me with these symptoms. After a blood test, the results were obvious. She was due for a more thorough exam next month. All I have are my notes from her first visit."

"Then why are you so certain that she didn't see the pregnancy through?"

"Because she didn't want to talk about it. What new mother doesn't want to talk about having a child? I've been seeing patients for fifteen years. I haven't met one yet."

Lena sank back in the chair as the doctor went on. But she wasn't really listening anymore. She was thinking about Justin Tremell and the many reasons why he wanted to keep his relationship with Jennifer McBride hidden. She was thinking about why he claimed that he didn't even know her. But even more, she was thinking about the fifty thousand dollars they found in McBride's bank account, and a pregnancy that may have come to an untimely end.

28

She didn't want to get too jazzed. Didn't want to run out too much line or acknowledge that given what she knew and had just learned, things were beginning to make sense.

It was 9:30 a.m. Lena sat in her car, working the phone from the parking garage at the doctor's office. According to Justin Tremell's assistant, he never arrived at work before eleven. According to Lieutenant Barrera, Tremell lived just ten minutes away in Pacific Palisades—a neighborhood Lena was familiar with just off Sunset and Brooktree Road. She jotted down the address in her notebook, thanked Barrera, and closed her phone. Then she slipped the personal information forms Dr. Ryan had given her into the murder book and pulled out of the garage.

She had walked out of the doctor's office with the originals, not photocopies. The actual forms that Jennifer McBride had handled and spent time filling out. Documents that Lena could take back to the lab because she thought she'd noticed something.

Sue Ryan, MD, didn't have to be that nice, but she was. Nor did Barrera, who knew Lena had been ordered to cross Justin Tremell off the list, but never mentioned it as he looked up Tremell's home address and gave it to her.

She blew through the first traffic light. For a split second she thought about her meeting with the chief yesterday. Just long enough to push it back and bring the car up to speed. The road coiled through the hills like a warped spring. As she slid into the curves, she tried to keep an open mind and not connect the dots—even though the dots seemed to be connecting themselves. Within ten minutes she found Brooktree, made a left and coasted down the hill. When she crossed the stream at the base of the canyon, she made another left, saw Tremell's house, and started down the private drive.

The house had been set in a meadow that stretched across two or three acres of open land in a city that wasn't supposed to have any open land. She could see the stream winding through the tall grass and a barn with two horses beside a small pond. When the drive split, she spotted a pickup truck and several cars in a parking area and stayed to the left.

There was something idyllic about the property. Something remote and unreal. The house was smaller than she would have guessed, but just right for the setting. It was an eclectic mix of stone, wood, and glass with a vaulted roof line and a modern feel that took advantage of the views without overpowering the landscape. As she pulled beside the pickup and got out, she noticed the ladders leaning against the back of the house. A handful of day laborers were taking a break in the warm sun beside three palates of roof shingles. She caught the laughter in their eyes. Someone was whispering in Spanish while another giggled with his head down. Lena looked for the contractor that went with the pickup, but didn't see him around.

She crossed the gravel lot and stepped onto the rear porch. The door was open. Cupping her hands, she gazed through the screen into the kitchen and saw an older couple sitting at the breakfast table. And the infant was here, too. Tremell's new son, Dean Jr. The woman was cradling the baby in her arms, patting his back, and still holding the empty bottle of formula in her free hand.

At first glance, the scene inside the kitchen seemed just as pastoral as the trip down the driveway from the road. But after a short time, it struck Lena that the older couple had no intention of acknowledging her presence. They had seen her approach the door, yet they hadn't moved or said anything. They just sat there, staring back at her.

She reached for her badge and pressed it against the screen. "I'd like to speak with Justin Tremell."

A beat went by before the man finally spoke in a weak voice. "He's not here."

"Where is he?"

"He belongs to a club. He goes there before work. He won't be back until late tonight."

There was something odd going on. The way they were sitting, the timid, even forced sound of the man's voice. And the woman was patting Tremell's son like a robot, her life-less eyes stuck on the floor just below the screen door.

"Who are you?" Lena asked.

The man shrugged. "Eve's parents."

"Then you're Justin Tremell's father-in-law?"

He seemed to need time to think it over.

"Is something wrong?" she asked.

He didn't answer the question. Lena felt certain that they were frightened and made the decision to enter. But before she got halfway into the room, she stopped and thought that she knew what the problem was.

She could hear it. The sound of the couple's daughter from the master bedroom. The sound of an a.m. fuck session filtering down to the kitchen from the second floor. It wasn't hot and heavy, but it was there.

Lena thought about the contractor she didn't see outside and looked back at the couple. It wasn't fear in their eyes. It wasn't even pain. It looked more like sadness. The kind that keeps you up at night and eats away at your soul.

Lena drew a business card from her pocket and set it down on the table. "I'd like to speak with your daughter."

The man's eyes skimmed over the card, his head remaining still.

"I'll be waiting outside," Lena said.

She stepped onto the porch, thought about lighting a smoke but decided against it. She could see the roofers eyeing her from the lawn. She could see them trying to get a read on her. Trying to figure out whether or not she got it and knew what was really going on.

She turned away, walking to the end of the porch and over to the fence. As she gazed at the horses, she thought about the way the couple had been dressed. They didn't come from money. And they had to live with whatever hell their daughter was putting them through. It didn't look easy.

She turned and leaned against the fence, gazing back at the house. She was at the far end, well out of the roofer's line of vision. And she could see Justin Tremell's young wife checking her out from a window on the second floor, her fuck session with the help apparently over. She hadn't covered up and was holding her breasts in her arms. But Lena was surprised by her face. She appeared melancholy, even wounded, not arrogant. When she stepped away from the glass, Lena thought about the hollow look in her eyes and wondered if she wasn't calling out for help in some way.

It was an uncomfortable feeling, and Lena tried to shake it off. Glancing at the pickup beside her car, she continued walking around the circular drive toward the pond. But as her view cleared the corner, she noticed a limo parked in front of the house, recognized the driver, and suddenly knew exactly what was going on. Justin Tremell's young wife wasn't doing the roofing contractor. Someone else was doing her.

It took a moment to settle in, then another few seconds to play back what she had seen in the kitchen and through the window. The images were raw and dirty, and she couldn't help feeling stunned. When they finally died off, she approached the car and gave the driver a long look.

"Waiting for someone?" she said.

He couldn't look back at her and squirmed in his seat. "Yes, ma'am. I expect so."

"The man who writes the checks?"

"That sounds about right," he said.

"Dean Tremell?"

He tipped his cap, still unable to make eye contact. "That's right. Mr. Dean will be along any time now."

"What's your name?"

"Louis."

"How often do you come out here, Louis?"

"I just drive, ma'am. It's what Louis does. He drives and he keeps his eyes on the road. At the end of the week, he collects a paycheck and goes home."

"I get it, Louis. But how often do you come out here?"

Dean Tremell cleared his throat from behind her. "Whenever I tell him to."

She turned and watched Tremell getting into his suit jacket as he approached. He was moving quickly, eating up ground in meaty chunks like a feisty bull. It seemed like whatever he'd done to his daughter-in-law had put him in a good mood. Oddly enough, there wasn't even a hint of embarrassment. Just a slight grin stretching across his weatherbeaten face, an ironic grin laced with curiosity.

"What are you doing out here?" he said.

"Looking for your son. How 'bout you?"

He paused to think it over, running his fingers through his white mane. When he was ready, he met her eyes, cocked his head, and lowered his voice.

"I've always believed that a man doesn't choose his needs. His needs choose him. That's why I've made it a practice to never apologize for who I am. What you see is what you get. Life's simpler that way, don't you think?"

"How's your son feel about that?"

"I'm sure that he'd be upset if he knew. Who wouldn't?"

"What about his wife?"

Tremell didn't answer the question, and Lena instinctively took a step back. She was thinking about Justin Tremell's exploits and what she had read on the Internet last night. It seemed clear that the kid had been home-schooled: Justin Tremell had learned everything from his father.

Tremell cleared his throat again. "I had a long talk with the district attorney Saturday night. We spoke after you left. He gave me every assurance that he would take care of this."

"Maybe you didn't give him enough money."

Tremell laughed. "It's not what you think, Detective."

"It isn't?"

"Not by a long shot."

Lena glanced at the house, then turned back and decided to take a chance.

"I know about the abortion," she said.

"What abortion is that?"

"Jennifer McBride got pregnant."

"The dead whore?"

A moment passed. Dark and sick and beyond the pale.

"Yeah," Lena said. "The dead whore."

Tremell leaned against the car. Who he was didn't match what she saw in his eyes, and it bothered her.

"I'm sorry, Detective. I should've had more respect. It sounds like she lived a dangerous life on all counts. It's always hard to watch when life bites back. Let me make it up to you."

"How would you do that?"

"I know a place downtown. Actually, I own it. Let me buy you an early lunch."

She shook her head. "I don't think so."

Tremell grinned. "Come on, Detective. Meet an old man halfway. You've got your point of view, and I've got mine. They may not be as different as you think. Isn't it worth talking about? Let's have lunch. The chef's the best in L.A."

Lena looked back at him, offering a tentative nod. Then Tremell smiled and gave her the name of the restaurant. Although it didn't ring a bell, she knew the street and block number, and agreed to meet him there in an hour. When he climbed into the limo and reached for his cell, she walked around the drive to her car. The roofers were back at work on top of the house. None of them were laughing anymore.

29

I hope you like squab," Tremell said.

"I can't say that I've ever had it before."

Lena watched the sous-chef set down their plates. The roasted pigeons were served whole and appeared undercooked. Tremell thanked the man and watched him return to the kitchen as he sipped ice water from a crystal glass.

They were sitting at a table by the fireplace. And they were alone. The restaurant didn't open for lunch. Lena counted only twenty tables when she first arrived, with two private rooms. The bar was small but elegant and carved out of solid walnut—an antique that had been meticulously restored and probably imported from the East Coast. The art on the walls was magnificent.

"It's potluck around here," Tremell said. "There aren't any menus, and if we were here for dinner and drinking, the wines would be preselected. Gérard makes one twelve-course meal for each seat in the house. You pay for your place, not the food. You pay for the privilege. The waiting list is six months long."

Lena was listening, but considered herself immune. She had agreed to come for no other reason than the fact that Tremell had made the offer. It seemed clear that he made it for a reason. She thought that she knew what it was, but needed to be sure. Until then, she felt certain that she could take anything he tried to do to throw off her balance. This included the pigeon that she was about to eat.

She picked up the knife and made her first cut. The meat looked raw.

"It's not chicken," Tremell said. "It's supposed to be served like that. If they were roasted any longer, the meat would taste like liver."

She took a bite and had to admit that it tasted good. Maybe even better than that. And she could tell that Tremell enjoyed watching her. He seemed amused, even confident, that he was pulling off whatever he had caged up in his demented mind.

He started eating, attacking the small bird on his plate like a man with a big appetite.

"Now that we're here," he said, "why don't you start by telling me exactly what you think my son did?"

"What would be the point when the DA has probably told you everything already?"

"As a matter of fact he has. But let's face it, nothing Jimmy J. Higgins ever does will make the world a better place than it was before he got here. He's a lawyer and a politician. That's a pretty bad combination if what you want in life really needs to get done. You're in charge, aren't you? It's your case, right?"

"The last time I checked."

"Well, I'd like to hear your version of the story. From the horse's mouth, so to speak."

Lena watched him take another swig of water. She wasn't surprised that Higgins had talked to Tremell. She assumed as much from the things Chief Logan had said. Still, hearing Tremell talk about it so openly felt something like being part of the actual crime. Her revulsion was a reflexive move, an act of self-defense against a district attorney who had crossed the line tens times over and may have given their case away to the father of a suspect. It was more than dishonest. It was reckless.

"I've got a better idea," Lena said. "Let's start with the baby I saw in the kitchen. Why don't you tell me who the real mother is?"

He lowered his fork and gave her a long look. She didn't

detect a change of mood—didn't see any sign of anger on his face—and this surprised her, too.

Tremell reached for his napkin. "I thought you said the girl had an abortion."

"I did. But things are still fluid and that's not the question right now."

"We're talking about my grandson."

"That's right. Who's the mother?"

"My son's wife, of course. Eve."

"Can you prove it?"

He picked up his fork and started eating again, his wheels still turning. "You're a suspicious woman, aren't you?"

Lena met his eyes but didn't respond, waiting for his answer.

"I'll save you some time," he said. "But only because I don't want to hear that you've been poking around. And I don't want to see this turn into something it isn't on television. You don't either, unless you want to meet my attorneys."

"Save me some time."

"Eve gave birth to Dean Jr. at UCLA Medical Center. It was an extended stay that cost a fortune. I'll call my assistant. You'll have copies of everything faxed to your office within the hour. Good enough?"

"Good enough."

"Now tell me what you think my son did."

Lena didn't need to think it over. "He strayed and picked the wrong woman."

"And you're guessing that he knocked her up."

"Maybe. But it wouldn't really matter who the father was, would it. It's the threat that counts. She knew who he was and what he was worth."

Tremell understood and nodded as he sliced the meat away from the bird's rib cage. "She would have known that he was trying to avoid the rag sheets. That his life had changed and he couldn't afford to let the story get out. Higgins told me that you found fifty thousand in her bank account. You're guessing that it wasn't good enough. That she wanted more."

Lena wasn't about to follow the DA's lead and talk about details. At the same time, what Tremell just said was obvious enough that it deserved an answer.

"Probably a lot more," she said. "Enough that you might notice."

"So, my son decides that the only way to get rid of his problem is to get rid of his problem."

Lena didn't respond and didn't need to. Tremell was putting it together himself.

"Justin lures her out to that whorehouse," he said. "The Cock-a-doodle what?"

"The Cock-a-doodle-do."

"He lures her out to that place with the promise of another payday. Someone he knows or hired is waiting in the parking lot. Justin waits inside. She walks out. And the man hiding behind her car takes care of the details. Is that pretty much it?"

"There may or may not be other ways of looking at it," she said. "But yes, I'd say that's pretty much it."

The sous-chef walked out to check on them. After eyeing their plates, he glanced at Tremell and disappeared into the bar. A few minutes later, he returned and set a glass down on the table. She watched Tremell reach for the drink and take a short first sip.

"Bourbon," he said. "Would you like one?"

Lena shook her head. "No thanks."

The sous-chef walked off and they were alone again.

"Do you hate rich people, Detective?"

"Not at all. Why?"

"But you hate the pharmaceutical companies," he said. "I could tell on Saturday. You hate being bombarded by all those TV ads. You think that they're stupid, maybe even dangerous because they encourage self-diagnosis. You hate all the talk about money, stock options and year-end bonuses that add up to hundreds of millions of dollars. I've been around long enough to know the rap. Fifty percent of the population makes less than thirty-five thousand dollars a year. Twelve million kids in the United States aren't just hungry, they're starving to death. Executive compensation isn't related to performance. Companies stumble, lay off everybody, and then renege on billions of dollars in pension obligations. It takes one and a quarter years for the average salaried employee to earn what most CEOs make in a single day. You hate me because of what I stand for. And that's the reason, isn't it? That's the real reason why you're going after my son. You want to take the one thing away from me that I can't buy. The one thing in my whole life that I truly love."

Tremell's voice trailed off. He pushed his plate away and took a longer pull on that glass of bourbon. Lena was glad that she had come. Glad that she understood what was motivating him—the reason he wanted to talk. Tremell was frightened that he might lose his only son. Talking to the district attorney wasn't good enough because he couldn't count on the man. Tremell would make his pitch to everyone involved. He would do whatever he could. Whatever it took.

"I don't hate anyone, Mr. Tremell."

"You're a beautiful woman, you know that. And you look good in this room. You look good in black."

A moment passed, the two of them staring at each other.

"No one's going after your son," she said finally. "A young woman was murdered. Like any other investigation, we're following the evidence."

"But I don't want Justin to pay the price for who I am or who you might think I am. Do you understand what I'm saying?"

"How much are you worth?"

"Eighteen billion, but the stock's down. On a good day, twenty-three."

A beat went by. The kind that follows the word *billion*.

"Then why are you fucking his wife?" she said.

"I thought we already went through that."

"You've got more money than a hundred people could spend in ten lifetimes. You could have half the women in Los Angeles on any terms you want no matter what their age. Why are you doing it?"

"It's more complicated than that."

"How complicated could it be? You said you love him. Why do you need to beat him? That's what it's really about, isn't it? How hard is it to stay away from your son's wife?"

"The situation isn't what you think it is. And it would take too much time to explain. All you need to know is that my wife's gone and my son is all I have left. That's why I don't want to see the progress he's made over the past few years destroyed by accusations or innuendo. By the word of someone working at a whorehouse who thinks she saw this or that but really isn't sure who she saw or even what day it was."

Lena looked at her plate, then back at Tremell. "Have you been out there? Have you been talking to the girl?"

Tremell shook his head. "No. But in the grand scheme of things, how reliable is an eyewitness compared to circumstantial evidence? If you had to go to court, Detective, which would you rather build your case on?"

"The evidence."

"Why?"

She gave him a look before answering. She could see the intelligence in his gray eyes and sensed that he was leading the conversation in the exact direction he wanted it to go.

"Because eyewitnesses make mistakes," she said. "What they saw or thought they saw needs to be corroborated. In this case we've done that. Four people saw your son with Jennifer McBride on Wednesday night."

"According to Higgins, eight other employees say they didn't see him at all. That leaves two busboys and another waitress, all with criminal records. The only real witness you've got is the part-time hooker, Natalie Wells."

"Higgins ran background checks and gave you the information."

He nodded and took another sip of his drink. "I don't believe that my son was there. I don't believe that he knew her. And even if he did, I don't believe that he'd do the things you think he did. He'd have no reason to. You were right about the money I have. The well's too deep to ever run dry. But the same thing goes for Justin because he's my flesh and blood. He wouldn't throw his life away—he wouldn't take the risk—for something he could buy his way out of by writing a check. It wouldn't have mattered how much Jennifer McBride wanted. He could have afforded any price and never looked back. Do you understand where I'm going?"

Lena didn't say anything.

"We share the same goal, Detective. You're looking for a witness. The one who sent you those pictures. The only one we know with certainty who was there, saw the abduction and shot the video to corroborate the facts. A young man who knows exactly what happened and what the murderer looks like. A young man who might be able to clear my son's name. Finding that witness is more important to me than it is to you."

"I understand, but—"

"But nothing, Detective. I'm offering you my resources. I'm offering you everything I have. I'm offering you free access to the well."

30

She didn't see the traffic backup on the 110 Freeway until she reached the top of the ramp and there was no way out. No way but forward, one or two feet at a time.

She didn't mind. She was still trying to process what Dean Tremell had said to her at lunch.

Her cell started vibrating, but she couldn't dig it out of her pocket in time. As she tossed it on the passenger seat, the phone triggered a memory maybe ten years old. An interview that she had heard on either KPCC or KCRW—two NPR affiliates that crisscrossed the city from Pasadena to Santa Monica. It was an interview with the CEO from one of the country's biggest engineering firms, a company that made everything from dishwashers to jet engines. The man had been known as an innovator, was on the verge of retiring and had written a book. When he was asked how he came up with so many great ideas, his answer was something Lena never forgot. He said that his best ideas usually came while performing mundane tasks. Cooking, gardening, cleaning up his desk. But his biggest breakthroughs came while driving his car. There was something about the act of driving to and from the office, being alone with himself, letting his mind wander. He said that when the cell phone came out, he knew that ingenuity would take a measurable hit. No one would be on the road by themselves anymore. No one would have the quiet time to think about what they were doing and where they wanted to go. Instead, everyone would be on autopilot, jabbering away about nothing.

Lena remembered the interview because she agreed with the man and respected him. But as the traffic started moving, her mind appeared stuck in neutral. It would take a longer road—a lot more miles—to come to terms with what Dean Tremell had said to her.

She hadn't expected him to ask her for help. She didn't foresee the setup or realize that this had been his purpose all along.

Lena bailed out at the first exit, then cut across town to Parker Center. Pulling into the dilapidated garage, she hoped that it wouldn't fall down until she found a place to park. As she ran across the street, her cell lit up again and she flipped it open. Innovation might have taken a hit, but at least she knew that the caller was a friend.

"Where are you?" she asked.

"Watching you cross the street from the third floor," Rhodes said. "I just got back."

She looked up and found him in the window. "How's your sister?"

"Doing great. Her doctor thinks she's out of the woods."

Lena could tell that Rhodes was still worried. She could hear it in his voice.

"I'm glad she's okay," she said. "I'm glad you're back."

"Me, too," he said. "I can't find Barrera, and no one's around. I need to catch up."

"I'll be there in ten. I've gotta drop something off first."

She slipped the phone into her pocket and shouldered her briefcase, wondering if Rhodes could hear the worry in her voice. Whether or not he knew her as well as she knew him. Entering the building, she rode the elevator up to the fourth floor and walked down the hall to the Questioned Documents Unit. Irving Sample ran the unit, but wasn't in. Fishing through her briefcase, she found the forms Jennifer McBride had filled out at her doctor's office, along with her application for the apartment on Navy Street. Then she wrote a note that included her cell number and left everything on his desk. Sample had examined McBride's driver's license and was already familiar with the case.

Deciding against the elevator, she took the stairwell down to the third floor and entered the alcove outside the captain's office from the rear. None of the administrative assistants were here, and she didn't see Lieutenant Barrera through the plate glass window. When she glanced at the bureau floor, she didn't see Rhodes or anyone else at their desks. She checked her mail slot and found a manila envelope. The papers inside were still warm from the fax machine. As she glanced at the cover sheet, she realized that they had come from Dean Tremell's office.

Her cell started vibrating again. She flipped it open thinking that it was Rhodes. Instead, Irving Sample was back at his desk.

"I just read your note," he said. "What am I looking for?"

"I left two sets of forms with you. The first is a single-page application the victim filled out for an apartment. The second is a two-pager from her doctor's office."

"I can see that," he said. "If you want to know if they were written by the same person, it's an immediate yes."

"I understand," Lena said. "But it's that two-pager from the doctor's office that bothers me. It's probably nothing. It's just that it looks like she rushed through the first page, then slowed down to fill out the last. If I hadn't seen her application for the apartment, I wouldn't have noticed."

Sample didn't respond. She could hear papers rustling in the background.

"I see what you mean," he said finally. "There's a difference. It's subtle, but I see it. They handed her these forms at the doctor's office and she ripped through the first page writing as fast as she could. But what are you getting at?"

Lena lowered her briefcase to the floor and gazed out the window. "Why would she start fast and end slow? Most people in a hurry pick up their pace at the end, right? Most people see the clock ticking and rush to the finish line. When I saw them side by side, I thought that it might be worth checking out. You think it's ridiculous?"

Sample didn't say anything for a while. When he finally spoke, she heard the hesitation in his voice.

"This girl wasn't like most people, was she."

"No," Lena said. "I don't think she was."

"Let me see what I can do," he said. "I'll let you know either way."

She closed her phone, feeling embarrassed as she imagined Irving Sample shaking his head at her from the fourth floor. She was grabbing at straws and he was being polite. Her request, an obvious lack of ingenuity due to too much time spent on a cell . . .

She shrugged it off and sat down at her desk. She noticed that Rhodes had hung his jacket on his chair and wondered where he went. After a moment, she settled down and reviewed the papers Dean Tremell's office had faxed over. A copy of the child's birth certificate was here, along with his daughter-in-law's release from the hospital. A copy of the bill was also included with all personal and financial information blacked out. Just the length of stay and what it cost. Still, Dean Tremell had made the call to his office just as he promised. And he had saved her some time. There could be no doubt that his daughter-in-law gave birth to a son. In all probability, the woman living as Jennifer McBride did exactly what her doctor guessed that she had done. Her pregnancy ended with a miscarriage or an abortion. Either way, there was no child.

Lena heard someone and turned around to find Barrera exiting one of the interrogation rooms. Rhodes was behind him, closing the door. Both looked concerned as they spotted her on the floor and approached.

"Lena," Barrera said. "You've got company."

She glanced at Rhodes. "Yeah, we spoke ten minutes ago."

"Not Rhodes," Barrera said. "Justin Tremell."

A moment passed, both men studying her.

"He's been waiting for more than an hour," Barrera said. "He won't talk to anyone but you. When I saw Rhodes, I brought him in. The kid shook his head and said just you. What's going on that I don't know about?"

Lena hesitated. She didn't want to mention her meeting with Dean Tremell because the data was still raw and she hadn't come to any conclusions yet.

"You want to call upstairs and record this?" she asked.

Barrera slipped his hands in his pockets and checked the empty floor. "Tapes already rolling and he's been read his rights. I talked to Lamar. He's got the monitors shut down so no one upstairs will know that the kid's here. You heard what the chief said yesterday. If anyone upstairs finds out that you're in an interrogation room with Justin Tremell, your world turns to shit and so does mine."

She glanced at Rhodes. He had been away for three days and didn't know about her run-in with the chief. She could see him trying to put it together.

She turned back to her supervisor. "Let's see what he wants."

"Do it quickly," Barrera said. "We'll figure out how we're gonna get him out of the building later. I'll update Rhodes. We'll be in the captain's office."

Lena's briefcase was on the empty desk beside her. As Rhodes reached for the murder book, he looked at the papers Dean Tremell had faxed over.

"What about these?" he said.

Lena picked the papers up and stuffed them in her briefcase. She didn't want them to be part of the record. And she didn't want to take the chance that her inquiry about the legitimacy of Tremell's grandson might be made public.

"They're irrelevant," she said. "A dead end not worth talking about."

Lena pushed open the door and found Justin Tremell sitting in the far chair staring at the ceiling. When he saw who she was, he jumped to his feet and shook her hand. He was being gracious and polite. And as Lena measured him, she immediately recognized that he was nervous. The sullen face that she had seen when they first met on Saturday was no longer sullen. And those steady hands weren't so steady anymore. Tremell looked wasted. Like all of a sudden, the tall, lean kid with rich-kid problems was dealing with a real-life crisis.

Lena watched him sit down and took a chair on the other side of the table. The room was cramped, the bright florescent lights buzzing overhead.

"I just spoke with your father," she said.

"I know. That's why I came."

"If you wanted to talk, why didn't you ask Lieutenant Barrera to call me?"

"I knew that you were with my father. I didn't want to interrupt."

Lena kept her eyes on him. He seemed sincere.

"Do you want an attorney?" she asked.

"No. I'm fine, thanks."

"Do you need an attorney?"

Tremell met her eyes and lowered his voice. "I don't think so."

She settled back in her chair, everything quieting down.

"So tell me why you're here, Justin. What do you want to talk about?"

Tremell didn't respond, shifting his weight and wrestling with his thoughts. He took a deep breath and exhaled. When he finally spoke, it wasn't much more than a whisper.

"I knew her," he said.

A long moment passed—everything in the small room becoming perfectly still.

"I was there that night," he said. "I didn't say anything on Saturday because my father was in the room. I'm sorry if I caused you any trouble. But I knew what he would think, and I didn't want to let him down. I didn't want him to know what I'd done."

Lena let the thought settle, the silence in the room becoming truly silent again. Just those lights buzzing overhead.

"What did you do that you didn't want your father to know about?"

Tremell sighed. "Jennifer was my friend."

"Your friend?"

"My wife was pregnant. It was a tough pregnancy—the last three months spent in bed—and I couldn't handle it. I needed an outlet. I found Jennifer's ad in the *L.A. Weekly*. It started out as a massage, then became something else. I liked her and she was nice to me. I don't expect you to understand this because I don't understand it myself. I'm still very much in love with my wife, but I fell for Jennifer. If my father finds out, he'll have a shit fit."

"Did she know who you were?"

"Sure, but she didn't care about things like that."

"She didn't ask you for any money."

He shook his head. "I paid for the first few massages. But when things changed, all that stopped and I'd give her things instead."

"What kinds of things?"

"Flowers. Dinner. Books. Things you'd give a friend or lover."

"So she wasn't blackmailing you? She didn't tell you that she was pregnant?"

Tremell sat back in his chair and looked at her like someone who was hearing something for the first time. Everything about his behavior appeared true and authentic.

"Jennifer wasn't pregnant," he said. "At least not when I knew her. She was menstruating. She'd get headaches, and cramps, and everything else."

"Maybe she called it a loan," Lena said. "Maybe she asked you to help her out."

"If she had, I would have given it to her, no questions asked. But she didn't. She never asked for anything."

Lena took a moment to think it over. She had been moving slowly. Making Tremell feel comfortable and at ease. She didn't see any reason to change course.

"Why were you at the Cock-a-doodle-do on Wednesday night? If Jennifer was your friend, why meet her there?"

Tremell pushed his seat away from the table, leaning his elbows on his knees and looking up at her. She had been wrong about his eyes as well. They were the same color gray as his father's and just as vibrant.

"You guys keep records," he said. "I'm sure you know more about me that even I do. The speeding tickets, the DUIs and bar fights, some of the women I went out with in the old days who spent most of their time trying to get noticed and get picked up by those crappy entertainment shows on TV. It wasn't the fake trips to rehab that saved me. And it wasn't the warnings from the judges I faced, or the embarrassment you might expect that I felt when I woke up in the morning. I didn't feel embarrassed. I was too high. What saved me was meeting my wife. She was the one who opened the door to the possibility that I might step out of my father's shadow and become something on my own. I got a late start. And I'm not all the way there yet. But she was the one who opened the door."

"How's she get along with your father?"

Tremell grinned. "Not very well. But he knows what she's done for me, so I guess that's good enough. He tolerates her, and she tries to be nice to him."

Lena gave Tremell a long look, studying his face and re-laxed posture. He didn't know. He didn't know what his father was doing behind his back. When it clicked, she let the thought go and moved on.

"Okay," she said. "So, why were you meeting Jennifer?"

"I needed to end it, but I didn't know how. I was planning to tell her that night. My wife had given me a son. She was feeling better. There was no reason to keep seeing Jennifer except that I still liked her. And that's not really good enough."

"Why there?" Lena said. "Why take the risk that some-one might recognize you?"

He laughed. "That's probably the one place in this city where no one would. And even if they did, they'd keep quiet about it because someone might ask them why they were there."

She could see his point. If the murder hadn't taken place, there was a good chance no one would have mentioned it.

"That place isn't exactly what it looks like," he said.

"Especially if you like music. The food's good and the woman who owns it isn't a phony. We met there because Jennifer had an appointment in Torrance. We met halfway."

"How did she react when you gave her the news?"

"I never did. I couldn't get the courage. And she had to leave for another appointment. I stayed for a while. When the band finished their set, I split."

Lena sifted through her memory of the interview she and Rhodes conducted with Natalie Wells. Everything Tremell was saying seemed to match what the waitress said.

"What about her job?" Lena said. "You obviously knew what Jennifer did for a living. Were you ever jealous?"

Tremell's face reddened, his voice quieter now. "You're a woman, so this is kind of hard."

"Believe me. There's nothing you could say that I haven't heard before."

He spent a few moments tossing it over, then sat up and shrugged. "The truth is that I kind of liked it. It turned me on. That probably means I'm still fucked up, but that's the way it was. And Jennifer didn't talk about it that much. It was just kind of there in the background. It wasn't like she was gonna do it forever. She told me she met someone who wanted to help her out."

"Who?"

Tremell shook his head. "She didn't say, but I could tell that he was a client. She called him her personal patron."

"And you still weren't jealous."

"Maybe a little," he said. "But I think I was secretly hoping that it might be an easy way out of all this. If she ended it, then I wouldn't have to."

"She never mentioned the guy's name? She never told you anything about him?"

"No, but I got the feeling that he was older. Maybe even a little kinky. He bought her a nurse's costume and made her wear it. That's all she said about him. He liked nurses and he was from Beverly Hills."

It hung there. The two of them looking at each other. Then the door snapped open and Barrera rushed in.

"I'm sorry," he said. "But you'll need to pick this up later. Lena, I need a word with you."

She walked out and saw Rhodes waiting in the alcove. Barrera shut the door and lowered his voice.

"Something's come up," he said.

"Fontaine?"

Barrera seemed surprised. "No," he said. "The guy who rented the garage on Barton Avenue. We've got his name and address."

31

"What's his real name?" Lena shouted.

Rhodes brought the Crown Vic up to speed, hit the Christmas lights, and rolled up his window. "Albert Poole. He's renting an apartment in Hollywood. The building manager says he's home."

"Tell me what happened."

"Someone recognized him from that sketch and called it in. Another doctor, I think."

"So our guy got his training at USC."

Rhodes shook his head. "The call came from the trauma center in Inglewood, less than a mile from the Cock-a-doodle-do. Poole got back six months ago and showed up looking for a job. He spent four years in Iraq as a combat field surgeon, so it looked like a perfect fit. Only now Poole's back and he's got issues. He worked one weekend in Inglewood, then flaked out."

"What issues?"

"Sounds like a head case, but we'll see when we get there. The manager's a vet. He said they talk once in a while. Poole got shipped from Iraq to Germany and ended up at Walter Reed."

"As a doctor?"

"As an outpatient. From what the manager said, he got lost in the bureaucracy at Walter Reed. They spit him out before he was ready and never said thanks."

"You talked to him yourself?"

Rhodes nodded, then picked up the file on the seat and handed it to her. Inside, Lena found the composite sketch they had worked up of the man calling himself Nathan Good. Underneath were copies of Poole's driver's license and photo ID from the trauma center in Inglewood. The likeness was unmistakable, even in the dim afternoon light. Although his eyes were set wider apart in the photographs, his hair less blond, and he wore a smile instead of a frown, she could see it.

She turned and looked out the window. The cars on the Hollywood Freeway appeared to be standing still. Frozen in time and somehow disconnected. When she glanced over at the speedometer, the dial was pegged at ninety and Rhodes's eyes were glued to the road.

"Barrera told me what happened," he said.

Lena didn't say anything. She wasn't thinking about the chief anymore.

"What about Tremell?" he said. "Why did he come in?"

She gave him a summary of her day. Rhodes listened without interrupting. At one point he opened the glove compartment and reached for his emergency pack of cigarettes, then rejected the idea and slammed the door shut.

"You think the kid would've agreed to a polygraph?" he asked.

"I needed more time," she said. "I didn't get the chance to ask, but that's the direction things were going."

"What about Fontaine? The chief said hands off. Is what Justin Tremell said enough to open the door?"

Lena thought it over. In a rational world, it was more than enough. In the chief's world, up was down, left was right, and green lights meant stop. Nothing would be good enough because strings were attached.

Rhodes gave her a look. "Are you okay?"

"The back and forth," she said. "Something's gotta give, Stan. And we still need to talk to Fontaine."

Rhodes exited off the freeway at Beachwood Drive and made a left on Franklin. By the time they reached Poole's apartment building and found a place to park, the winter sun had already slid behind the hills, the streets bedded down in a dusky blue light.

Lena could feel the fresh charge of nervous energy in her chest and gazed at the building as she crossed the street. The modern design stood out from the rest. It was twelve stories high with balconies on all four corners and a gated parking garage underneath. She guessed that it had been built within the last twenty-five years and that rents were high because the place was clean and well maintained.

They reached the lobby and found the building manager waiting for them at the door. He seemed just as anxious as they were, only he was showing it. He introduced himself as Chess Washington. Dressed in khakis, an Oxford shirt, and a light down vest, Washington was a thin man in his late fifties with a dark complexion and bright green eyes.

"Do you live here?" Rhodes asked.

Washington pointed to apartment 101. "Right there," he said.

"What about Poole's? What's the layout like?"

"Same as mine, twelve floors up."

"Would you mind if we had a look at your place?"

Washington shrugged. "No problem at all."

Lena realized that Rhodes was anticipating trouble. He wouldn't have made the request otherwise. Poole was obviously lethal—someone living on the edge who hadn't just murdered Jennifer McBride, but cut her up. Mapping the layout of his place before they got there was the smart move. They entered Washington's apartment and stepped into a small foyer. To the left was the living room, to the right, a long hallway to what looked like a den. Rhodes held the door open, blocking the view down the hall and turned to Lena.

"The door hinges on the right and opens in," he said.

Lena got it. Doorways were called *vertical coffins* for good reason. That's where you were most vulnerable. That's where the highest risk was. Passing through them.

"He'll be in the den," she said. "Behind the front door."

Rhodes met her eyes and nodded. When he turned to

Washington, his voice was calm and easy and didn't betray his emotions.

"You said you talk to Poole once in a while. You were in Vietnam, right? You trade stories."

"Not very often, but once in a while, yes."

"Do you know if he owns a gun?"

"As a matter of fact, he's got several. So do I. But I think you guys got it wrong. Albert's a war hero. And he's the quiet type. Doesn't bother people and keeps to himself."

"I'm sure you're right," Lena said. "What kind of guns does he keep, and how many are there?"

"He's only shown me three or four, ma'am."

"What kind?"

"He's got a Spencer Repeating Carbine and a flintlock pistol, but both of them are mounted on the wall and behind glass."

Lena met the man's eyes. "What else?"

"A Mossberg shotgun and a Glock .40 pistol with a fifteen-round magazine. The shotgun's an autoloader. I think he keeps it underneath his bed. The Glock's in a drawer by the front door."

"That's it?" Rhodes asked.

"He collects knives. Mostly from the Civil War. He's got a lot of them."

Lena and Rhodes traded looks, then made a sweep through the rest of Washington's apartment. The hall to the right led to a den, then turned left. They passed two bedrooms on their right before the hall made another left, feeding them into the dining area and kitchen, then returning to the living room, foyer and front door. The floor plan was essentially a loop. The only other way in or out was the slider leading to the balcony off the living room.

"How's his furniture set?" Lena asked.

"Same as mine and everybody else's," Washington said. "The place is built so it only really fits one way."

Lena glanced at the couch and chairs, noting the walking lanes. Then Rhodes ran out to the car and brought back two vests.

They followed Washington into the elevator. When they reached the twelfth floor, the building manager pointed at apartment 1201 and stepped back around the corner. Lena and Rhodes approached and took each side of the door. They drew their guns and looked at each other. She could see the fire in his eyes. The life in his face. Through the door she could hear Poole talking with the TV going in the background. It sounded like he was on the phone. His voice was high-pitched, his cadence awkward and crazy. As she readied herself, she felt the rush of adrenaline swell through her body and bit her lip.

On Rhodes signal, she knocked on the door.

Poole immediately stopped talking. She could hear the patter of bare feet moving toward the door. She kept her eyes on the light feeding through the peephole, then looked back at Rhodes after it went dark.

"Who is it?" Poole shouted. "Show yourself. Why are you hiding out there?"

He sounded frightened and pounded on the door.

"Police," Lena said. "We'd like to speak with you, Albert."

He didn't set the phone down. He dropped it on the floor. Then Lena heard him pull open a drawer, followed by the unmistakable sound of the man jacking the slide on his Glock.

"About what?" he screamed. "Why me? Why are you fucking with me?"

It wasn't going well. Lena watched Rhodes turn back to the building manager peeking around the corner.

"Something's wrong with him," Washington said. "That's not the way he usually sounds."

Rhodes grimaced. "Toss over the keys. Then go downstairs and call nine-one-one. Don't come back."

Washington dug a key ring out of his pocket, removed two and slid them across the floor. When they heard the elevator doors shut, Rhodes spoke up.

"Come on, Poole. Calm down. All we want to do is talk."

Poole slammed another fist into the door. "How many of you are out there? Why are you whispering? How will I know who you are? Show me your ID."

"I'm gonna do it, Poole. I'm gonna do it right now. Are you looking through the peephole?"

"Show me your ID."

Rhodes stayed to the side of the door and didn't move. "Here I go."

Lena zeroed in on that peephole, saw the light come back, and heard the sound of the Glock firing. Three rounds burst through the wood, ripping through the wall into the elevator shaft behind them. She could hear Poole screaming at them and running away.

She grabbed the keys and hit the locks. Still on his knees, Rhodes inched the door open with his gun. Then three more shots rang out, drilling through the wood at chest level into the living room wall. Rhodes gave her a look and took a deep breath, then scurried into the foyer on his knees. When Lena followed, she slammed the door behind her and caught a glimpse of Poole rushing out of the den toward the bedrooms. It was more of a blur than anything else. And the man was still screaming, still out of his skin.

They raised their guns and started down the hall, pausing at the corner. The two bedrooms were on the right. He could be in either one, or he could have run around the loop, hoping to hit them from behind. Lena slipped into the den, spotted Poole in the second doorway, and fired two rounds into the near wall, knowing that her .45 would punch out the other side at head level. The sound of her .45 was louder than the Glock. More menacing and primitive. She met Rhodes's eyes and waited a beat. If Poole hadn't moved before she fired, he was dead.

"You there?" Rhodes called out. "You still with us, Poole?"

Poole lunged out of the bedroom doorway, his pistol flashing as he zigzagged down the hall and around the corner. He was laughing now. Cackling. Lena bolted down the hallway, ducking into the bedroom. As she looked around and turned back to the door, Rhodes slid into the bathroom across the hall. She heard Poole slam another mag into his gun as her eyes flicked around the bedroom. She had seen something when she first entered, but it hadn't registered.

She found it on the bed. A bag from a pharmacy. She opened it and dumped out the contents, revealing too many meds to count.

She turned back, eased into the hallway and peeked around the corner. She didn't see Poole, and figured that he might be hiding in the kitchen. But when she looked behind Rhodes toward the den, she saw the light change on the wall and ran back down the hall. He was coming in from behind, ready with a full load. Lena started firing before she even turned the corner. Punching out the plaster in the wall, rounding the bend, holding up.

She could see Poole backing out onto the balcony. She caught the grim smile on his face, his zombie eyes. He lowered his gun, grabbed hold of the railing, and jumped up onto the wall. As he turned to fire, their eyes met and he started laughing again. Then he lost his balance and began to teeter. His grin vanished, his face flushed with fear. Lena saw his gun drop onto the floor and then Poole disappeared.

She heard a woman scream. Heard glass shattering followed by a heavy thump. Sirens approaching in the distance.

Running out onto the balcony, she looked over the edge with Rhodes. By all appearances, Albert Poole, aka Nathan Good, wouldn't be shedding any light on the case. He wouldn't be answering any questions, or telling them who had hired him. What was left of his body was lying on the grass twelve stories down. And the ride hadn't been very easy. It looked like he had hit the glass ceiling in the lobby and bounced off the steel beams into the front yard.

They rushed downstairs, Lena feeling the heat now. They raced through the lobby and onto the lawn. Washington was already outside, standing over Poole's body and shaking his head.

"He was a war hero," the vet was whispering. "A fucking war hero, for Christ's sake. One of the guys who made it back and got treated like shit. It's a disgrace. You hear me? It's a fucking disgrace."

Lena moved in and gazed at the body. The ground was soft from all the rain over the past month and Poole had sunk a good six inches into the soil. But as she studied his face—examined it from less than a foot away—she was overcome with a horrible feeling. She looked at Rhodes, who didn't seem to understand. Cops were running up the sidewalk. People crowding in to gawk.

Lena flashed her badge at the cops. "You need to get these people out of here." She glanced at Washington, then turned back. "Him, too."

Rhodes nudged her. "What is it?" he whispered. "What's wrong?"

"You said a doctor made the ID and called it in. Did you talk to him?"

Rhodes shook his head.

"Who brought this to you? Barrera or the sixth floor?"

"Chief Logan's office," he said. "Klinger came down while you were in the room with Tremell. He briefed us and gave me those photographs."

She shook her head and felt the burn. The terror. Then she dug into Poole's pocket and fished out the dead man's keys.

"Come on," she said. "Hurry."

She led the way down to the garage, ripped the door open and peered through the darkness. There were too many cars. Too many SUVs. Too much gloom to fight through. She hit the clicker, disabling the car's alarm, and turned when she heard the chirp. As her eyes locked in on Poole's car, she knew that she was staring into the abyss again. Tasting its rotten fruit. It wasn't a red Hummer. Instead, it was a ten-year-old Toyota Camry parked in the far corner.

Now a war hero was dead.

32

It was just before midnight. The marine layer had rolled in, low and thick and burying the City of Angels in the clouds. Rhodes was wheeling the Crown Vic back to Parker Center so that Lena could pick up her car. Forty-five miles an hour on the Hollywood Freeway. It felt like they were alone on the road. Just those occasional beams of light zipping by like UFOs, the sound dampened by the heavy steam.

"It's my fault," Lena whispered. "You were away. You didn't know."

"It's not your fault or my fault. It's Klinger's."

"I should've paid more attention," she said. "I lost my focus."

"Klinger did this, Lena. And he should pay for it."

Lena slipped her hand into her pocket and wrapped it around the pack of cigarettes she bought Sunday night. She wouldn't light one. She'd save that for later. It was enough just to know that they were there.

She turned and looked at Rhodes. "Klinger won't pay for this, Stan. The chief won't, either. That's not the way it'll work."

"Then how the hell is it gonna work?"

She paused for a moment. She had spent the last three hours grappling with it. Seeing what had happened for what it was and what it would be. They had searched Poole's apartment and found things—medals, honors, remembrances. But it was the letters recovered from his desk that told the real story and defined the man. Letters written by soldiers whom Poole had risked his own life to save. Letters from their wives and parents, their husbands and children. A diary that he'd started after a roadside bomb wounded more than a hundred civilians and Poole was the only one at the scene with medical experience. Poole had been a combat surgeon with enormous talent, but also a medic in the field. He was someone who gave it his all, but then buckled under the strain. Someone who had given, then given even more until he reached the point where he needed something back. But no one answered the call. No one lent him a helping hand. All they did was write scripts and feed him more pills.

Lena let the thought go, staring into the wall of fog but not seeing it.

"One of two things are going to happen," she whispered from a place deep inside herself.

"What things?"

"They're going to say that we cleared the case tonight. That we got our man. That Albert Poole was Nathan Good and everything ends with him. Poole will take the fall so there won't be any reason to pursue Fontaine, or Justin Tremell, or whoever's put the fix in with the chief and the DA. They're gonna close the case, Stan. It's either that or they're gonna say that I'm the one who totally fucked things up. That I killed a war hero tonight without justification. A man who helped others and didn't deserve to die. It'll be one or the other or some combination of both. Either way, the chief can do whatever he wants to me now."

Her voice faded into the muted sound of the Crown Vic cruising through the clouds. Floating in the dark mist. After a long moment, Rhodes broke the silence, his voice barely audible.

"Poole may have been a war hero, Lena. But we didn't start shooting. He did. And Klinger probably knew enough about the guy to guess that he would."

Lena didn't say anything, even though she agreed that Klinger and Chief Logan had done their homework. The setup had been perfect. Barrera had warned her on the first call. She had known that something was coming all week.

And when it finally did, she missed it. Now an innocent man, however troubled, was dead.

"What's important," she said, "is that you need to distance yourself from me."

"That's not gonna happen."

"Yes, it is. You're gonna keep your job and let me take the fall. And you're gonna stay away from Klinger."

Rhodes looked at her with those eyes of his. "Fuck you," he said.

33

Nathan G. Cava crept up the stairs and moved silently down the hall until he reached the study. When he peeked in, he saw Fontaine on the floor by the fireplace and damned himself for being ten minutes late.

The Beverly Hills doctor had just discovered that his cash stash was history.

Cava had to admit that the show was still pretty good. There was some crying going on—some fist-pounding and weeping. Even some grunting and swearing, weak as it may have been. Still, he'd missed the big moment. The existential moment. The beat of all beats. He'd hoped to see the greedy little bastard move the rock away and peer into the darkness. He'd hoped to witness the moment when the man realized that there was only *nothingness*.

Fontaine crawled over to his desk and lifted himself onto the chair, still unaware that Cava was watching him from the doorway. He was cradling his head in his arms and feeling sorry for himself. His shirt was wrinkled and soaked through with sweat, his hair in disarray. After a good five minutes, Fontaine reached for the phone and dialed a number.

Cava felt the cell begin to vibrate in his pants pocket. The phone belonged to Greta Dietrich, Fontaine's love interest and fuck object. Cava had kept the phone since Dietrich hit the finish line yesterday morning. Curiously, Fontaine had been calling the number every hour as if he didn't fucking get what was going on. The constant barrage of phone calls had become something of a nuisance for Cava. He had spent the night at Greta's apartment in Santa Monica. Slept in her bed and got lost in the scent of her body as he grieved over her loss and tried to repent for the things he'd done. Greta didn't deserve her fate, but Fontaine did.

The phone was still buzzing in his pocket. Cava pulled it out, deciding to take the call.

"Hello," he said.

"Who is this?" Fontaine asked with suspicion.

"Your new best friend."

"Where's Greta? Put her on."

"She's busy. She can't come to the phone right now."

Cava tried not to laugh. Fontaine's head was still buried in his arms. The guy was so distraught, so inside himself, he hadn't picked up Cava's voice in the room. For Cava it made it all worth it—like all of sudden he was playing with house money.

"Who are you?" Fontaine shouted into the phone. "Where are you?"

"Over here, Doc. Standing by the door."

Fontaine finally lifted his head and looked over, then flinched as he got it.

"Where's Greta? Where's my money?"

Cava closed the cell phone, trading it for a .38 revolver. "Which is more important to you, Doc? The money or the girl?"

"We're talking about over a million dollars."

Cava grinned. "I thought so. Now, be real good and sit still."

"What are you gonna do? Shoot me?"

"Not if you sit still. I promise."

Cava crossed the room, opening his briefcase behind the doctor's back. He found the five-pack of auto-injectors, opened two, and removed the red safeties. Each device delivered a fixed dose of 10 milligrams of morphine. One would probably be enough, but Cava wanted to ease Fontaine's worries and make the ride feel good.

"You're wearing latex gloves," Fontaine said.

"That's right. I'm a physician."

"You're joking."

"I'm afraid not," Cava said. "Now roll up your right sleeve."

He walked around the desk. Fontaine's eyes got big when he spotted the auto-injectors.

"Please," he said. "I can get my hands on more money. Please don't do this."

"It's morphine, Doctor. The White Nurse. Morpheus and the Greek god of dreams. You see the dosage. It won't hurt you, and we need to talk. It's either the needle or the gun. Pleasure or pain. There's no other choice tonight."

Cava could see the beads of sweat percolating on the man's forehead as he wrestled with the decision. He placed the auto-injectors beside the doctor's hand, aimed the .38 at his head, and sat down in the chair in front of the desk.

"Where did you get these?" Fontaine said.

"The U.S. government. They come with the uniform, Doctor. The morphine will make you feel better. It will help you deal with your loss. The safeties have been removed. Now press the purple ends against your arm and shoot."

Fontaine's face lost its color. After several hard moments and three or four looks at the .38, the man held the injectors against his arm, closed his eyes, and pushed. One after the other.

It wouldn't take long. Just a few minutes. Less than an hour to reach the moon.

"Good," Cava said. "Now place the injectors on the desk and push them toward me."

Fontaine did as he was instructed, then sat back in his chair and let out a loud gasp. His body had already begun to relax. The lines in his face were vanishing, his eyes just starting to become lazy.

"How do you feel?" Cava asked, his voice smooth as glass.

"Stoned," he whispered. "Why are you doing this? Where's my money? Where's Greta?"

"I can't show you your money, Doctor. But Greta's in the

basement. If you'd like to see her, we could go down and take a look."

"The basement? What's Greta doing in the basement?"

"Not that much, actually. Would you like to see her?"

"No. She ran off with my money. Tell her to give it back."

"I'm your best friend, Doc. I'll see what I can do."

Fontaine smiled, drooling a bit as his mouth opened. "That gun looks familiar."

"It should," Cava said. "It's the one you kept in the bedside table. You gave it to me. Don't you remember?"

Fontaine rocked his head up and down. "That's right. I did. I forget when, though."

"You gave it to me for Christmas. It's a toy gun."

"I like toys. Does it make a sound?"

"No," Cava said. "It's a toy. It just clicks. Watch."

Cava turned the revolver to his own head, pressed it against his temple and pulled the trigger. When the gun clicked, Fontaine erupted in laughter, nervous laughter that he couldn't stop. The man was feeling joyous. In the zone and rolling with the morphine. Still making the climb toward the top.

"Do it again," Fontaine said.

"I'd be happy to. It's a fun game."

Cava pushed the gun against his head and pulled the trigger a second time, smiling at his prey.

"You're a funny man," Fontaine said. "A funny friend. I wanna try."

Cava nodded, leaning forward and calmly loading the weapon behind the desk. Fontaine reached out and began to whine.

"I wanna try," he said. "It's my turn now."

Cava passed the revolver over. Fontaine was beside himself with glee and fighting off the giggles. Once he finally settled down, he met his new friend's eyes and raised the gun to his own head. He flashed a big wide smile, and Cava smiled back.

"It's your turn, Doc. You're free."

Fontaine giggled and pulled the trigger.

34

Lena ignored the Caprice hiding in the mist and pulled into her drive. Somewhere along the way home her priorities had changed. That included the idiots from Internal Affairs watching and listening to her house when she wasn't even there. Somehow they had become irrelevant. They didn't seem important anymore.

She pushed open the front door, didn't bother switching on the lights, and headed straight for the kitchen. Inside the freezer she kept a fifth of Skyy vodka. She didn't drink it very often. But tonight she needed it. Tonight the blue bottle looked like medicine.

She poured a glass over ice in the darkness, then headed outside onto the back porch with her cigarettes and sat down on the steps. There was no view tonight—just the fog tenting the city and glowing from the lights underneath.

She held her glass up as if to make a toast, then took a long sip that burned her throat. As she lit a cigarette, she felt the vodka reach her stomach and ignite.

This was what the fall felt like. Sitting alone in the darkness. Unable to see the city lights even though she knew that they were right in front of her.

Her cell started vibrating and she thought about throwing it into the pool. When she saw Steve Avadar's name on the display, she took a drag on the cigarette and decided to take the call.

"I'm sorry, Lena. I know it's late. Did I catch you at a bad time?"

She tried to pull herself together. "Everything's good, Steve. What's up?"

"It's about the witness," he said. "I'm worried."

She looked over the hill into the gloom. Everything seemed so far away.

"What's happened?" she asked.

"He tried to use McBride's ATM card on Sunday."

"Where?"

"Fourth and Arizona. The same branch we met at on Saturday. When that didn't work, he hit an ATM at a convenience store in Venice."

Lena took another pull on the drink, pressing the ice against the glass with her fingers so Avadar wouldn't hear it. "I thought you said that the card would only work inside the bank during business hours."

"That's all still good," he said. "He didn't get any cash. But here's the problem. Yesterday there were no attempts to use the card at all. Same thing happened today, and that's why I'm worried. Usually they keep trying. The machine doesn't eat the card. The screen they get gives them their balance, branch locations and tells them to try again."

"And this guy hasn't tried again."

"It's a first, Lena. There's a lot of money in that account and he knows it. I think something's going on."

She took another drag on the smoke. A lot was going on.

"Let's see what happens tomorrow," she said.

"I'm just giving you a heads-up. I'll call if anything changes."

"Thanks."

She slipped the phone into her pocket and doused the cigarette in the wet ashtray. It seemed fitting that Avadar would call this late and give her the news. Albert Poole was stretched out on a gurney at the morgue and now it looked like their witness was in the wind.

The chief and his adjutant were probably celebrating. Probably out there somewhere in the fog with the DA.

Lena looked back at the drink in her hand, then dumped it out on the lawn. She got up, heading inside to make a cup of coffee. She didn't want any more vodka. The blue bottle wasn't working tonight.

35

It was 5:30 a.m. Lena disconnected the charger on her cell and glanced at the display, expecting the worst. Good calls didn't come this early in the morning. When she read Irving Sample's name, it threw her. Sample was calling from his desk in the Questioned Documents Unit at Parker Center. Either he was getting an early start, or like Lena, he hadn't gone to sleep yet.

She opened the phone and pulled a stool over to the counter, no longer concerned that anyone was listening. Two hours ago she had walked outside and heard the Caprice drive off. Her life as a homicide detective had hit the drain. No one was listening anymore.

"I've got the answer," Sample said.

"The answer to what?"

"The forms the victim filled out at her doctor's office. I've got the answer to your riddle. I know why she rushed through the first page and slowed down on the second. It took a while, but I figured it out. And you're not crazy, Lena. You noticed something no one else did."

The words were coming rapidly. She could hear the excitement in his voice.

"Okay," she said. "What's the answer? Why would Jennifer McBride start fast and end slow?"

Sample laughed. "Because she didn't," he said. "She made a mistake on the first page and crossed it out. When she finished the second page, she asked for another copy of the first

and filled it out twice. She did just what you said. She followed human nature. She started slow and picked things up
at the end."

"You're saying that there were two first pages?"

"That's right. And the pen she used left impressions from
both on the second page."

"What did she cross out?"

"A phone number. The one they need in case there's an
emergency."

Lena grabbed the pen off the counter, barely able to
speak. "What's the number?"

Sample read it to her. After writing it down, she read it
out loud just to confirm.

"That's it," he said. "And that area code's Las Vegas."

"Yeah," she managed. "Vegas."

"Then it's important. I wasn't sure."

"I can't thank you enough."

"I didn't do the work, Lena. You did. I'm just glad I could
help."

She closed her cell and stared at the phone number on the
pad. She could imagine what happened with perfect clarity.
The woman living as Jennifer McBride had thyroid problems
and needed to see a doctor. After filling out the forms, she
would have checked her work just to make sure it mirrored
the real Jennifer McBride's history and contact information.
When she spotted the Las Vegas number, she realized her
mistake and crossed it out.

But the number must have been too important to her. There
could be no other reason why she decided to take the extra
step and ask for another form, or even why she made the mistake itself. The woman living as Jennifer McBride had left a
lifeline after all.

Lena thought about that snow globe she had found beside
the victim's bed. The snow falling over Las Vegas. Most
likely it wasn't a gift or souvenir, but a remembrance. And
there was a decent chance that it pointed to home.

She turned and looked outside. The sun was still hidden
below the horizon. The city, still buried in the marine layer.

She dialed the number anyway, lifted the cell to her ear, and listened. After three rings, a man picked up and said hello. His voice was low and gruff, but not groggy. In spite of the hour, he hadn't been sleeping.

"I'm trying to locate Jennifer McBride," she said.

His hesitation was unmistakable. "Who?" he asked finally.

"Jennifer McBride."

Another beat went by. When he spoke, she sensed the undercurrent of emotion in his voice and knew that she had just struck a nerve.

"I'm sorry," he said. "There's no one here by that name. You must have dialed the wrong number."

She listened to the man hang up. Then she moved over to the table by the windows. Her computer was already logged on to the Internet. She found AutoTrack in her bookmarks and entered her user name and password. When the search window popped up, she typed in the phone number and hit ENTER. Almost immediately a man's name appeared on the screen. Mike Bloom from Las Vegas, Nevada.

Lena jotted his address down and started reading. Until four years ago Bloom had been employed by the Las Vegas Police Department and carried a badge. He was only thirty years old, so he couldn't have retired and she already knew that he wasn't deceased. Every job he had ever worked was listed. Every address ever used and every phone number. Yet, the lack of information about the man was striking. Everything was listed as it should have been until four years ago when everything in the man's life seemed to stop. Everything went dark except for the registration on his Ford F-150 pickup.

She made a second pass, rereading Bloom's history and thinking it over. She didn't want to call him back and she didn't necessarily want to inform the LVPD. After what happened last night, she didn't want to spook the guy or possibly warn him. Still, Bloom's past four years had as much detail as a black hole feeding on the universe.

She crossed the room, opening a cabinet below the bookcase. Inside were a variety of LAPD forms she kept as backup when working at home. Most of them were blank reports that made up a murder book. But now she was looking for a letter. The one she needed to get her firearm through security at the airport. Vegas was only an hour away from Burbank. And after one week, she finally had a lead on who the victim might actually be. A real name to go with the woman's dead body.

36

She had tried to catch some sleep on the plane, but couldn't shake the way Albert Poole had died. The man's fate had followed her to Vegas. And she knew with certainty that he would follow her home when she returned to Los Angeles. No matter what happened to her career, no matter how Chief Logan decided to rewrite what went down, Poole would be with her for a long time.

Just like the woman who cast spells. The woman without a name who was driving her, pushing her. As Lena walked down the aisle to her rental car, she understood that her need to know the victim's true identity had become an obsession—but also her saving grace. If she could just find out who she really was, Lena thought she stood a fair chance of living with whatever came next.

She climbed into the car and unfolded the map on the passenger seat. Bloom lived in the desert, northwest of the city off Kyle Canyon Road. After deciding on her route, she powered up her cell phone and checked for messages. There were three. The first call had been made by Rhodes an hour ago. He said that he had checked in with Barrera. There was no word from the chief's office yet. Barrera thought that it would be a good day to lay low and see what happens, maybe work on that loose end list. Rhodes had been away and didn't know about the chief's list, but promised to call back later.

The next two messages surprised her. Both were left by

Denny Ramira from *The Times*. And both calls were made within the last fifteen minutes. Ramira sounded upset again and wanted to talk. But like the last time, the reporter didn't give her any details. Just more smoke.

Lena tossed her phone on the passenger seat and pulled out. As she exited the garage and hit the bright sunlight, she could feel the dry heat and still air. According to the thermometer on the dash, it was already seventy-five degrees. A winter day in the desert wasn't usually so warm or forgiving.

It took about half an hour to clear the city and suburbs. Once the city finally vanished in her rearview mirror, she spent another fifteen minutes on paved roads, then more than ten miles on gravel. It was brighter here, warmer—the open desert, raw and untouched. As the road dipped and curved and seemed to melt into the sand, she finally spotted a mailbox. But as she got closer, she saw the burned-out house and kept moving. After five more miles, another mailbox appeared on the right. This time the house that went with it was still standing. She could see it a hundred yards off the road.

She pulled behind a sand dune, looking at the dust trail she had just left. If Bloom was anywhere near a window, then he knew that someone was here.

She got out of the car, trying not to think about it. Climbing the dune, she lowered her body onto the sand and peered over the top.

The house shimmered in the distance, its windmill standing motionless in the still air. She could see Bloom's pickup parked in front of the garage. Behind the house she noticed a shed. From this distance everything appeared weather-beaten. Dried out, windswept, and so quiet and undisturbed that it didn't feel right. All she could hear was the sound of her own breathing. The rhythm between her breaths.

And then something started rattling in the car.

Lena slid down the hill and looked inside. It was her cell, beating against the map on the passenger seat. She checked the display and flipped it open. It was Ramira again, and he sounded panic-stricken.

"I need to see you," he said. "The shit's hitting the fan."

Lena moved back to her position on top of the sand dune. "What is it, Denny?"

"The shit's hitting the fan. What more do you fucking need? How soon can you get here?"

"Where's here?"

"My place. We need to meet and I'm ready to talk."

"Why don't you start by telling me what this is about?"

Ramira paused just as Lena expected he would. She looked back at the house.

"I can't reach my contact," he said finally. "I think they got to him. I think he's dead."

"The senator?"

"Not West. My contact."

"Who's your contact, Denny?"

Ramira shut down again. Lena was losing her patience and thought about hanging up.

"I get it," she said. "You're still not ready to talk."

"It's not that. It's just that I can't tell you the guy's name. I'm a reporter."

"What difference would it make if he's dead?"

"But I promised. And I don't know that he's dead."

"Like I said, Denny, you're not ready to talk. And I'm out of town and too busy to fool around. If the shit's really hitting the fan, you know what to do. Hang up and call nine-one-one. If it can wait and you change your mind and really want to talk, I'll be back sometime late this afternoon."

He didn't respond. Lena waited a beat, then slipped the phone into her pocket.

Smoke.

She looked over the dune, scanning the property and trying to put Ramira out of her mind. She took in the house and shed—the Ford F-150 parked in front of the garage and the windmill that wouldn't turn. The place reeked with bad vibes. It felt too remote. Too much like the last stop on the train. Too much like a place someone would live if his life had gone dark four years ago just like Bloom's had.

Lena checked her wristwatch. It was still early enough

that she had options. She no longer wanted to approach him here. She could drive down to the end of the road and spend a few hours waiting him out, then follow his pickup to the market or the bank. Any public place would be better than here. If he stayed home, she still had time to drive back to Vegas and work the meeting through the LVPD.

She turned away from the house. Turned and heard the slide rock back on a semiautomatic pistol. Turned and saw the man standing beside her rental car.

"Are you the one who called?" he said. "The one asking for Jennifer McBride?"

Lena's eyes zeroed in on the gun Bloom was holding. It was another Glock—a .40 or a .45. Either way, she knew that he only needed to fire a single round.

She nodded, hoping her voice wouldn't betray her fear. "Did you know her?"

Bloom's eyes narrowed. He motioned her toward him with the gun, then slammed her body against the car. He was bigger than her, stronger than her, at least five inches taller with dirty-blond hair and sunburned skin. He looked like he hadn't shaved in a couple of days. Like he didn't get much sleep. He spun her around and frisked her. His search was quick and professional and left nothing to chance. He pulled her gun and ID and slipped them into his pocket. He found her cell and tossed it inside her car. Then his large hands rolled over every inch of her body, from her neck down to her ankles. Satisfied that he had found everything, he pointed the gun at her and backed away from the car.

Lena turned and watched him light a Marlboro. Bloom stared back at her like he meant business.

"Jennifer said that if anyone ever asked for her and used that name, they were trouble."

"I'm a police officer," Lena said.

"You think I give a shit? Welcome to Vegas, bitch. Now, get in the car and drive."

"Where?"

He moved around the car, limping slightly, then climbed into the passenger seat with the gun on her. "Down the driveway to my pickup," he said. "This piece of shit won't go anywhere in the sand."

37

She pulled the rental car up to the garage, unable to ignore the dread weighing her down. As they got out and walked over to Bloom's pickup, her legs felt weak and mushy. She couldn't think her way out of this. Nothing was coming. Just Mike Bloom with his Glock.

"Get behind the wheel," he said. "You're driving."

She climbed in, then watched Bloom enter. He tossed over the keys, pointing at the desert that began at his driveway and didn't seem to end.

"That way," he said. "Now let's roll."

She pulled off the gravel into the sand, trying to keep Bloom's house in the rearview mirror for as long as possible. She checked the odometer, noting the mileage. She could see her fingers trembling as she gripped the wheel. When she tried to say something, he told her to shut up.

They drove in an eerie silence. Pushed forward over the brush, crossing a dried-out stream bed and bouncing over the rough terrain. She knew that her only real chance of surviving was to appeal to Bloom on some personal level. But as she glanced over at him and saw the madness in his eyes, the brutal determination on his face, the hope flickered out and died. About two miles into the desert, she steered the pickup around a hill and came to a clearing.

"This looks like a good spot," Bloom said. "Pull over and get out."

Lena did as she was told, watching the man grab a shovel out of the bed and throw it at her.

"Start digging," he said.

She picked up the shovel and stared at him, calculating the distance between them.

"I know what you're thinking," he said. "Your eyes are all big. You're breathing heavy. You're all revved up because you're about to die. And now you've got that shovel in your hands. You're thinking maybe this is your chance to take me out. Well, forget it, bitch. It takes one-point-five seconds for a human being to travel twenty-one feet—the same amount of time it would take me to draw my weapon and fire. It's called the twenty-one-foot rule. Only you're more than twenty-five feet away, and this gun's out and ready to rock and roll. Now start digging."

She drove the shovel into the sand, keeping her eyes on him as he sat down on a boulder and grimaced. He lit another Marlboro and started rubbing his right leg. If Lena was looking for a weakness, it had to be his leg. There was something wrong with it. A pulled muscle in his lower thigh. Or maybe a blown ligament in his knee.

She tossed another load of sand out of the hole, feeling the sun on her back. She paced herself—not too fast or too slow—just steady enough to not be noticed and keep things going. Maybe buy enough time to come up with something out of nothing. It suddenly occurred to her that she hadn't told anyone where she was. Other than Ramira, no one knew that she had left Los Angeles.

"You used the past tense," Bloom said after a long stretch of silence.

Lena stopped digging and gave him a look.

"Back at the house you used the past tense," he said. "What happened to her?"

"She was murdered. Wednesday night. Exactly one week ago."

She watched him take it. She saw him lower his eyes and shake his head. The pain he felt was deeper now. But more important, it seemed real.

"I know that you used to be a cop," she said.

Bloom met her eyes, but remained silent.

"I looked you up when I found the phone number," she said.

"How'd you find the number?"

She watched him smoke the cigarette. He'd asked her a question, but didn't seem to care if she answered it.

"She left it with her doctor."

"Now I know you're full of shit," he said. "Jennifer would never do that."

"I'm a homicide detective. I'm trying to figure out who she was."

He shrugged. "Who do you think she was?"

"A prostitute working in Venice. Someone trying to hide what she was doing by using someone else's name."

"Is that it?" he asked.

"Pretty much."

"Then I'd say you know all you need to know. Shut up and dig."

She got back to work with the shovel. After a while she looked up and saw him whispering something into his cell phone. But the call didn't last very long, only three or four minutes before he clicked off. When he noticed her looking at him, he waved the gun at her and she turned slightly. Bloom was lifting his pant leg. As he pulled it over his knee, she knew what the problem was and had a better than good idea of what the man had been doing for the past four years.

Bloom had a prosthetic right leg. There was something wrong with the fit around his thigh. Something that required an adjustment. After a moment, he looked over and caught her watching him again.

"Don't get any crazy ideas," he said. "I don't need two legs to shoot a stupid bitch like you."

Lena shrugged it off. "You were in Iraq. That's why you left the department."

He didn't say anything, still working on his prosthetic leg.

"You signed up?"

He laughed. "Yeah, I bought the lies and signed up. And

if I could go back I would. Not for the idiot politicians who started it and wanted it, or the ones who watched and sat on their butts. Not for the chicken-shit TV reporters who've had their heads stuck up their asses since nine-eleven and don't give a damn about the truth anymore. Not even for my fucking country because I don't know what that means right now. But I'd go back if I could for the guys I met and everybody else who got screwed by people like you. I'd go back to help the people who lived there and got fucked. I'd go back to fix the lie and everything else we broke."

His voice died off. His anger and bitterness seemed to subside as the silence returned.

"Is there a problem with the prosthetic leg?" she asked.

"The leg's fine," he said. "It's the liner. I should have changed it today, but didn't."

Bloom fixed his jeans and stood up. Then he planted his right leg in the sand and pivoted his body. The adjustment he made seemed to work. His grimace was gone, and he sat back down on the boulder and lit another Marlboro.

"You need to keep digging," he said. "It's okay the way it is, but the coyotes will sniff out anything above three feet. If you don't wanna be eaten—if you wanna rest in peace—you've gotta go deeper."

She kept her mouth shut. Slamming the shovel into the sand, she lifted out another load. Then she heard his cell phone ring and watched him dig it out of his jacket. He didn't say much. From what Lena could hear, it sounded like he was answering questions, not asking them. When he clicked off the phone, he stared back at her and smoked that Marlboro. He seemed more nervous now. More edgy. And he didn't say anything. He just sat there, measuring her progress and smoking.

After another ten minutes and another cigarette, he got up and walked over.

"That's good enough," he said. "Get out of the hole."

She started shaking. Struggling to catch her breath. She stepped out of her grave and gave him a long look—then watched as he reached into his pocket, trading his own gun for hers. She wasn't sure if she should close her eyes or not. She was thinking about her brother who had been murdered six years ago. Thinking about her father's death, and the mother who had abandoned them. She was thinking about a lot of things that had nothing to do with this murder case or the desert she would end up in.

Bloom stepped closer, gun in hand, everything over. When he finally reached point-blank range, he stopped and tossed the spent Marlboro in the sand. Lena could hear her watch ticking in the silence. Time streaming by.

Then Bloom handed over her gun and reached into his pocket for her ID.

"My sister wasn't a whore," he said. "We need to go back to the house and talk."

38

Lena needed to sit down. Bloom pointed to the table in the kitchen, but anywhere in the house would have been just as good. She needed time to compose herself and collect her thoughts. Time to let her emotions catch up to where she stood.

She wasn't dead. She hadn't been executed in the desert and left in a shallow grave for the coyotes to feed on. But there was more. Jane Doe No. 99 was no longer a Jane Doe living under the stolen identity of Jennifer McBride.

She had been Mike Bloom's sister. And as they drove back to the house, he had given Lena her legal name: Jennifer Bloom.

Lena watched Bloom pour two cups of coffee and join her at the table. Although the sadness remained, his rough edges were gone. Even his voice had changed.

"I thought it was important that she keep the same first name," he said. "I didn't want her to blow it."

"You mean you created the identity for her?"

He shrugged. "I'd been a cop, so I had access to the information she needed and knew how to use it. But finding someone with the same first name took some time. When I finally hit on Jennifer McBride, I had certain misgivings because the girl had been a murder victim in a bank robbery. But almost everything else about McBride was perfect, so we went with it. They didn't look alike, and I saw that as an advantage. There was so much background information available. So many stories about McBride's life on the Internet. It made the job much easier. It gave the identity detail."

"What about your sister's driver's license? The DMV says it's real. When we ran McBride's name through the system, she didn't come up as deceased."

"I thought my sister needed one piece of identification no one could question. I had a friend at the DMV who agreed to work with me on McBride's history. He made a few deletions. Then Jennifer walked into a DMV and had her picture taken, took the test, and walked out."

Lena sat back in the chair, her head spinning. She looked around the house. It was an open floor plan not much different than her own house in Hollywood Hills. And she was surprised by the art on the walls and the number of books in the living room.

"I'm sorry," Bloom whispered. "The way I spoke to you out there. The way I treated you. I didn't know what was going on. I had to make sure you were okay."

Lena took a sip of coffee, trying to steady her hand. Then Bloom pulled out his cell phone and showed her a picture that he had taken of Lena digging her own grave. After a moment he clicked to another picture of her that had been sent to his phone by whomever ran the background check. For a split second, but only a split second, she thought about cell phones again and how Bloom's had saved her life.

She looked back at the man, taking in his brown eyes and sunburned skin. The emotion on his face that she had misread as madness less than half an hour ago.

"The question is why," she said. "Why did you do all this?"

Bloom thought it over. "If you'd ever had the chance to meet Jennifer, you'd know. But I guess the answer is that she used to be married. She loved the guy and I did, too. He was with me when I lost my leg. He lost more than that. And she did, too."

A moment passed. Jennifer Bloom had lost her husband in the war.

"It tore her up pretty good," Bloom said. "But she was a

strong-willed woman. Lots of spirit. The kind that lights up a room. Somehow she got past it and moved on."

"Then why did she need to steal McBride's identity?"

"Follow me."

Bloom crossed the living room, then led the way upstairs. Lena could tell that his leg was bothering him again as they walked down the hall. When they reached the room at the very end, Bloom stepped aside. It wasn't a bedroom. It was a nursery.

"She got past her husband's death," Bloom said. "But she couldn't get past this one. I'm not sure any mother who loses a child ever does."

It felt like the floor was moving beneath her feet, the air charged with electricity. Lena looked at the crib. The changing table. A mobile hanging by the window. Her mind was suddenly razor sharp. Jennifer Bloom had gone to see Dr. Ryan because she had a thyroid problem. Ryan believed that her patient had been pregnant, but didn't carry it through because she didn't want to talk about her child.

"Is something wrong?" Bloom asked from the doorway.

Lena shook her head. "Tell me what happened."

He entered the room and walked over to a chest of drawers. Lena's eyes zeroed in on a framed picture of Jennifer with her husband and baby. It looked like the photograph had been taken in the backyard by the windmill. Three people with their futures ahead of them—a moment in time when everything was good.

"She had a son," Bloom said. "A little boy just a year and a half old. He had health issues, though. He was asthmatic. It wasn't constant. The attacks seemed to come and go. But they were scary."

Bloom was having trouble talking about it. Remembering it. He became silent for a while, then reached for a plastic bag on the chest and handed it to her.

"This was the medication the doctor prescribed. He died about twenty minutes after his mother gave it to him. One minute he was breathing. The next minute he wasn't. I guess a lot of kids have had the same kind of luck. The drug got pulled off the market, but it took a while. The FDA's still trying to sort it out."

Lena noticed the nebulizer on the chest, the child's face mask, then examined the medication that had been sealed in the plastic bag. As she read the label, it felt like she was still standing over her grave in the desert. Like Bloom still held the gun in his hand and had just pulled the trigger. The drug manufacturer was Anders Dahl Pharmaceuticals. Dean Tremell's name was even listed in the fine print.

Jennifer Bloom had never been a whore. She had been a mom. Another fallen hero like her husband. And the case was radioactive now.

39

She could see her house on top of the hill as the jet eased over the Valley toward Burbank and glided with the wind. She could see it in the blue light. Her small house standing over a city that spanned as far as the eye could see. Her anchor. After the plane landed, she walked down the rear steps onto the tarmac and out the airport exit to the parking garage just across the street.

She had spent the last hour staring out the window and letting her mind wander. Being alone with herself and watching the loose ends drop away on their own. The same way her brother used to tell her he could feel the moment for what it really was and improvise on his guitar.

The smoke Dean Tremell had sent up about this case had been the best money could buy. The best Lena had ever known or read about or could even imagine. As she paid her parking ticket and exited the garage, she couldn't help but find Tremell's expertise and attention to detail something to behold. Every possibility had been accounted for. Everything rigged so well that Jennifer Bloom never stood a chance.

The fake ad in the *L.A. Weekly* and the messages on her answering machine that it harvested after her death. The bag of tricks left in her closet filled with lingerie and sex toys, scented oils, and plenty of prescription drugs. He even gave her a company line. *The woman who cast spells.*

Lena had seen the bait and snapped at the hook. She had bought it. All of the above.

And then there was the *almost* bought, but smelled bad . . .

Justin Tremell's heartfelt story about his friendship for the victim that turned into something else. Dean Tremell's bullshit act as the concerned father. And what about the fifty thousand that wound up in the victim's bank account?

The deception had been so complete, so thorough, so brilliant. A command performance by every participant on every front.

It worked, of course, because somehow Dean Tremell had uncovered Jennifer Bloom's secret. At some point he found out about her stolen identity and would have understood that he was working with an empty canvas. After her murder, Tremell would have known that he could define Bloom any way he wanted and make the crime look the way it did.

She could see Tremell standing in his boardroom sipping bourbon from a crystal glass. She could see him working out the logic for his demented plan. Deciding what it should look like and who would take the fall. Jennifer McBride would no longer be a mother who had lost her son. Once the transformation was complete, all anyone would ever see was a greedy whore. A whore blackmailing one of her wealthy clients—or so the bullshit went.

The scope of the crime took Lena's breath away. The brutality. The audacity. The sickness.

She flipped open her cell, found Denny Ramira's number and hit ENTER. She thought she finally knew what the reporter's book was about and why he had been so reluctant to talk about it. And she thought that she knew who his contact was. The one who wanted to remain anonymous. It had been sitting out there all along. The way the pieces fit. It had been hidden behind a veil of money and power and absolute barbarism. Hidden in a stolen identity. She saw it now.

Ramira wasn't picking up his cell. Paging through recent calls, she found his house number from earlier in the day and clicked it. When she hit his message service, she began to get a bad feeling and pulled over to the side of the road. Her address book was in her briefcase. Lena punched in

Ramira's number at *The Times*. After nine rings, a woman finally answered but sounded rushed.

"I'm trying to reach Denny," Lena said.

"I'm sorry, but he's not in. Could you try back later? We're busy."

"It's important," she said. "I've tried the house and his cell. Where is he?"

"We were wondering the same thing. Denny didn't come in today."

Lena felt her heart sink. "Does he still live in Silver Lake?"

"As far as I know. Why?"

Lena snapped her cell shut without answering the woman. Pulling back onto the road, she brought the car up to speed, blew through a red light, and jumped onto the 5 Freeway. It was 4:30 p.m. with just enough traffic to spike her blood pressure. She worked the road hard and fast and dipped onto the shoulder when she needed it. By the time she reached the reservoir and found Ramira's house off Edgewater Terrace, the sun had set and every house on the block had its lights on.

Except for Ramira's. Even worse, his car was in the drive.

She grabbed a pair of gloves, found a small flashlight in the glove compartment and walked up the drive. It was a California Craftsman with a long front porch and large windows. When she reached the steps and got picked up by the motion detectors, the sudden wash of bright light spooked her.

She could feel the tension, the heat in the cold air. And when she moved to the window and peered through the glass, she could feel the terror.

Something was swaying from the banister on the second floor. After a moment, she realized that it was Ramira's Chihuahua, Freddie. She had met the dog eight months ago when she gave the reporter her account of the Romeo murder case. She hadn't been to the house since, but remembered that his dog barked a lot and had plenty of attitude. It looked like someone had tied the leash to the banister and let the choke chain do the rest.

She backed away from the window, digging her cell phone out and hoping she wouldn't remember what she had just seen. Rhodes picked up before she heard a ring.

"Where are you?" she asked.

He must have sensed something from her voice. "Doesn't matter," he said. "Give me the address."

"Ramira's house. You remember. We were here last spring."

"See you in twenty minutes."

"Don't say anything, Stan. Everything's different now."

He paused a beat. "See you in twenty minutes," he repeated.

She closed the phone, then tried the front door. When she found it locked, she moved around the house looking for a breach. There was no sign of a break-in. Every window and door appeared undisturbed. She glanced at her watch, then returned to the backyard. She had noticed a small window the first time around and seemed to remember that it opened to a powder room. Removing her jacket, she wrapped it around her arm and drew her gun. Then she punched out the glass with her .45, reached inside for the lock and raised the window.

She climbed in and froze, listening to the silence and getting a feel for the house. She could hear the fan from the heater running. The ice maker filling with water. As her eyes adjusted to the darkness, she saw Ramira's dog hanging from the stairs and felt the chills hit the back of her neck again and coil around her spine. Below the dead dog she could see blood pooling on the floor.

She shook it off and stepped into the hall. Moving silently past the dog, she checked the living room but didn't see anything. Same with the dining room. When she entered the kitchen, she noticed the long shadows on the floor and switched on her flashlight.

Ramira's body was here, lying beside a fallen bag of groceries. Her heart fluttered in her chest as she ran toward him. His eyes were pinned to the ceiling in a thousand-yard stare, his mouth still open as well. As Lena struggled to hold the light steady, it seemed obvious from the wounds on his face that the reporter had been beaten to death with a blunt instrument. That the end had been painful and difficult. She panned the light across his body. When she spotted the meat thermometer buried in his chest, the chills got worse and she shuddered.

She tried to pull herself together. Tried to picture Jennifer Bloom's mysterious journey and courage. Tried to draw on her reserves even though it felt like she didn't have anything left.

No matter what the reason may have been for Ramira holding back on her, he had been a good man. It had been Denny Ramira who wrote the story about her brother's murder, forcing the brass on the sixth floor at Parker Center to walk a straight line and tell the truth. It had been Ramira who stepped forward when she needed him. As the memories rose to the surface, she wondered why he hadn't called 911 this morning. She hoped that he hadn't been waiting for her. Counting on her.

She knelt down beside him, pushing her thoughts away. She could take it, she repeated to herself. She could handle this.

She looked back at the meat thermometer that had penetrated Ramira's heart, noted the lack of blood, and realized that it had been an afterthought. He was dead before the stabbing, so she ignored it and pressed forward.

Lena understood from her work with Art Madina that there was no way to tell the time of death by studying the core temperature of a dead body. That probing the liver with an instant-read thermometer much like the one in Ramira's heart looked good on TV, but was essentially ridiculous. There were too many variables. How much clothing was Ramira wearing? How much body fat? What was the temperature of the room? Or Ramira's body temperature when he was beaten to death? Was he feeling well or was he ill with a temperature of more than 100 degrees?

She knew that she had talked to Ramira early this morning, so the murder went down sometime within the last eight hours. Digging the receipt out of the grocery bag, she tilted it into the light and found the date/time stamp. Ramira had checked out his groceries three and a half hours ago at one-thirty-seven this afternoon. Although the market was only five minutes away, that didn't mean that he had come straight home.

She moved back to the body. Ramira's left fist was clenched in a death grip. She noted the defensive wounds on his knuckles, the cuts and scratches, then tried to pry his fingers open but couldn't. She knew full well that this was a chemical reaction and not a result of rigor mortis. That when rigor mortis finally came and went, his hand would relax. Still, she needed a better sense of timing.

She smoothed her gloved hands over his wrists and arms. They were still loose and free. Moving up his body to his shoulders and neck, she could feel the tightness beginning to set in. When she tried working his jaw, the muscles were frozen in place.

She took a deep breath and exhaled as she thought it through. Ramira spent most of his time sitting in front of a computer, not working out at the gym. Rigor mortis was just beginning to set in. Because of his physical condition, the murder had to have occurred sometime within the past hour or two. It was close. Real close.

The fan to the heater shut down. As the sound dissipated, the house began to take on that special kind of silence that only seemed to come when a dead body was around.

Lena picked up the flashlight and exited the kitchen. Moving down the back hall, she passed a spare bedroom and stopped in the doorway to Ramira's study. She shined her light into the darkness. The room had been trashed. Every drawer in his desk had been dumped on the floor. The closet was open, the shelves tossed.

She moved to the desk, sidestepping the debris. When she switched on the lamp, she noticed a file on the chair. Inside she found transcripts that Ramira had made from interviews he had recorded for his book. But as she skimmed through them, she began to sense that something was wrong. This file shouldn't have been here. The interviews were with the key players in the case. She saw Senator Alan West's name. Jennifer Bloom was here as well, identified as Jennifer Mc-Bride. When Lena found Joseph Fontaine's interview, she realized that her hunch had been correct. The Beverly Hills doctor was an expert in treating asthmatic children and had served as Ramira's primary contact. It had been Fontaine who managed the clinical trials for Dean Tremell and Anders Dahl Pharmaceuticals. At the time the drug's name hadn't been tested by focus groups and was simply known as Formula D.

Lena stopped reading and began listening to the house again. Weighing the silence.

The file didn't belong here because it was the motive for Denny Ramira's murder. She kept her body still and let her eyes wander off the desk, then drift to the right where a large photograph hung on the wall. It didn't take very long to spot the flaw in the reflection. The nuance in the silence that went with the file she held in her hand.

Ken Klinger was hiding behind the closet door. And he was armed.

Lena took the shock, but dug down deep and didn't flinch or move. She could see him staring at her, the glass over the photograph as clear as any mirror. His forehead was bandaged and it looked like he had a black eye. But even worse, he was cornered and appeared extremely nervous. Lena had interrupted his search, yet she sensed that he wanted to remain hidden. That he had been watching her ever since the porch lights snapped on. That he may have even overheard her on the phone and understood that Rhodes was on his way.

When she saw him lower the gun to his side, she walked out with the file and stepped into the bathroom. Locking the door, she switched on the lights and dropped the toilet seat down as if she intended to use it. Then she slipped through the open window, bolted around the house, and shuddered as she spotted Rhodes pulling down the street.

"What happened?" he said, rolling the window down. "What is it?"

Lena jumped in and opened her cell. "Ramira's dead. We need to drive out to Fontaine's place."

"I tried to reach him today. He didn't show up at work. And Greta Dietrich's missing. No one's heard from her in two days."

She gave him a troubled look, then worked the keypad on her phone. "We need to drive out anyway, but let's just sit here for a while. Turn off your lights."

"What are you doing? Who are you calling?"

"I'm blocking my caller ID, and calling nine-one-one."

Lena brought the phone to her ear, keeping her eyes on Ramira's house.

"What the hell is going on, Lena?"

She shook her head as the 911 operator picked up. "Shots fired," she said into the phone. "There's a dead body on the kitchen floor. Denny Ramira, the reporter from *The Times*. He's been murdered in his home."

The operator asked for her name. Lena gave the woman Ramira's address instead, then repeated it and ended the call.

"If Ramira's been murdered," Rhodes said, "then why go through nine-one-one? Why not just call it in?"

"We can't call it in. Everything's different now. Keep your eyes on the house."

"You mean the guy's still in there?"

"We can talk on the way out to Fontaine's. Just keep watching the house."

She could hear the sirens just beginning to bleed through the night. As she sat back and waited, she tried to imagine what Klinger was doing right now. He wanted the file she had taken, but his need to remain hidden seemed to outweigh that. She wondered if he had second thoughts. Wondered if he was waiting for her outside the bathroom in the hall with Ramira's dead dog, Freddie. Wondered if he could hear the sirens approaching.

They were getting louder. They couldn't have been more than half a mile away now. And the answers came quick.

Rhodes pointed at the house. A shadow was leaping off

the front porch into the yard and breaking through the bushes. As the figure sprinted down the sidewalk on the other side of the street, the headlights from an approaching car washed over his face. Rhodes glanced at Lena, who turned and watched Klinger vanish into the darkness. The chief's adjutant had made it. He didn't get the file, but he was still hidden. Still free.

40

The drive out to Fontaine's place on South Mapleton Drive went quickly. By the time they reached the front gate, Lena had managed to give Rhodes a detailed picture of where they stood and what they were probably about to face.

Like Ramira's house, Fontaine's mansion was the only one on the block with its lights out.

"I'm going over the wall," he said. "When the gate opens, bring the car through."

He took her flashlight, then hoisted himself up and over the other side. After a few minutes the gate opened, and Lena pulled the Crown Vic onto the property. Then they followed the drive up the hill to the back of the house.

Fontaine's Mercedes was parked in front of the garage. She traded looks with Rhodes and caught the grim expression on his face. The only light she could see was coming from the hot tub on the terrace at the far end of the house. The only sound she heard came from the water bubbling and fizzing in the night.

Lena gazed at the mansion silhouetted against the clouds in the sky. The moon was trying to break through, but couldn't. The air was raw and ice-cold. As they approached the back door, Rhodes switched the flashlight back on, shined the beam through the glass, and found the alarm on the inside wall.

"It's not armed," he said.

"Did you think it would be?"

He tried the doorknob. When it turned, he shook his head at her and gave the door a push. They were inside the house now. And Lena picked up on the silence again. The kind that went with a corpse. Rhodes hit the light switch on the wall.

"I guess it was just hope," he said. "I thought he hired bodyguards."

"Let's go find him."

It only took ten minutes to clear the first floor and work their way upstairs. Once they reached the landing, all they needed to do was follow the harsh odor down the hall into the study.

Lena switched on the desk lamp. From the condition of the body, it was obvious that Fontaine had been dead for at least twenty-four hours. He was slumped over the side of the chair and appeared to be melting into the arm. A .38 revolver lay on the floor to his right. On the desk she spotted two auto-injectors and read the labels.

Morphine. The Greek god of dreams.

Rhodes stepped over to the computer, eyed the screen saver, and gave the mouse a tap. When the computer woke up, a word processor was running that seemed to contain Joseph Fontaine's last words. Lena joined Rhodes by the monitor and read the note.

"If they think we're gonna buy this as a suicide," he said, "they're crazy."

"It would've worked if we didn't know who Jennifer Bloom really was."

"It still might, Lena. If we're out of the mix. What did Justin Tremell say to you in the interrogation room?"

She turned back to Fontaine and gazed at his corpse. "Jennifer McBride had met someone who wanted to help her. A client she called her personal patron. Someone from Beverly Hills who liked it kinky and made her dress up in a nurse's costume."

"A costume they bought and planted on their own," he said. "It's all there. They set Fontaine up and did everything except give you his name."

Lena agreed. There was no doubt about the play or what

Dean Tremell wanted them to think. Fontaine was their fall guy. Someone who talked to Ramira. Someone Dean Tremell wanted to get rid of just as much as Jennifer Bloom. And if they could turn her into a whore, then making Fontaine look like her client and victim was easy. The one who sent her the fifty thousand dollars and hired a hit man to take her out. A doctor with a guilty conscience who took his own life six days before Christmas.

"Let's check the rest of the house," Lena said.

"You think Greta Dietrich's here?"

"Where else could she be?"

They searched the rooms on the second floor, then made a sweep through the third-floor bedrooms and attic. The exercise proved fruitless and burned up almost half an hour. Returning to the kitchen, Rhodes located the door to the basement and they headed downstairs. The footprint seemed to mirror the exterior of the house and had been divided into separate rooms. They found a wood shop that didn't look like it had been used in a long time. Three more rooms that probably once served as a home office, but which, like the wood shop, no one used anymore. Beside the utility room, a small greenhouse opened to the side of the house where the hill had been carved out. As they reached the end, they came to a storage room and found shelves packed with oversized items bought at Costco.

Greta Dietrich wasn't here.

They headed back toward the steps. As they passed the laundry room, Lena noticed an alcove and paused. The shelves were lined with canned goods, bins of onions and potatoes, and bottles of olive oil. And that's when she spotted the freezer in the corner. It wasn't an upright. Instead, it opened like a chest and couldn't have been more than a few years old.

She lifted the handle and pulled the door up, the frosty air rising into her face. As the mist cleared, she gazed into the ice box and tried to focus. She didn't see what she expected to see. Not a single pizza was here. Not a frozen dinner or a bag of vegetables. The longer she stared at the contents, the more she thought she might be in a grocery store. There were at least a hundred small packages carefully stacked in three rows. Each package was approximately the same size and wrapped in plain white butcher's paper. And each was labeled and dated by hand with a Sharpie.

No more than ten seconds had passed since she first opened the lid. It just felt longer because the realization was such a big step. Because she had to break through the uniformity of the packages to see the darkness and understand what she was really looking at.

Rhodes picked up a package and read the label. "Does this say what I think it does?"

Lena glanced at it. Greta Dietrich was here.

41

"We need to talk," Rhodes said. "Before anything else, we need to talk."

They were sitting in the Crown Vic. Parked in Fontaine's driveway. Passing a cigarette back and forth.

"They're wrapping things up," he said. "They're killing everybody who knows."

Lena nodded without speaking, took a deep pull on the smoke, and passed it over. It didn't feel like there was enough nicotine in it.

"You said that it looked like Ramira had been dead for a couple of hours," Rhodes said.

"Two hours. No more than that."

"Do you think Klinger's good for the murder? Did it look like he'd been inside the house for that long?"

"I don't know," she said. "But Ramira's knuckles were scratched. He fought back. And Klinger looked roughed up."

"What do you mean, roughed up?"

"I saw his face. He had a black eye."

Rhodes shook his head. "He didn't get that from Ramira."

"How could you know that?"

"After I dropped you off last night," he whispered. "After you picked up your car, I drove over to his place."

A moment passed in the darkness. Their eyes met.

"I thought you might be right," he said. "I thought they might try to close the case and stamp Albert Poole's name on it. I needed to take that off the table, so I did."

Another moment passed. Longer than the first.

"Is Poole off the table?" she asked.

Rhodes looked at her again and nodded with assurance.

Lena reached for the cigarette. "Klinger's hands are dirty, Stan. And so are Chief Logan's. But there's no proof that either one of them murdered Ramira. I didn't see it happen. I only caught the aftermath. Klinger could have been there for a lot of reasons. He was searching the place. He found the file."

"If that's what you think, then why did he let you walk out with it?"

She shook her head. "It was his moment. His call. I can't answer that."

"What else?" Rhodes asked.

"There's a theme to the murders."

"What theme?"

"Bloom was found in the trash outside Tiny's. In the garage on Barton Avenue we found a meat grinder. Ramira was stabbed with an instant-read thermometer. And now we've got Greta Dietrich on ice."

"So Ramira's murder fits," Rhodes said. "This guy we're looking for did all of them."

Lena shrugged. "I don't know."

Her voice faded. The car became quiet. She could see Rhodes thinking it over. Weighing the odds. After a few minutes, he broke the silence.

"When I was at the hospital last weekend, I met this guy in the waiting room. He was from L.A. and we started talking. After a while I asked him what he did and he told me that he was a professional seat filler."

"What's a seat filler?"

"I asked him the same thing. Do you ever watch those awards shows on TV?"

Lena shook her head.

"Me, either," Rhodes said. "So he told me that when a celebrity goes out for a smoke or needs to use the bathroom, this guy takes their seat. When they come back, he gets up and leaves."

"What's the point?"

"He said that the TV producers don't want to see empty seats when the cameras pan through the audience. They want the place to look full, so they hire professionals to fill the seats."

"Okay," she said. "So why do I need to know this?"

Rhodes took a drag on the smoke and passed it back. "He said that celebrities don't like being looked at. It makes them feel uncomfortable, and they don't like feeling uncomfortable. You have to trade places without making eye contact. If you can't pull it off, you're fired. He said it's not as easy as it sounds."

"So, this guy makes a living not looking at people."

"I know," Rhodes said. "He was an idiot. But the reason I mention it is because of Dean Tremell. That's who he is. A guy who's connected and doesn't want anyone to make eye contact. A guy who'll pay people whatever they want so that he can walk on air. How do we get to him? And other than Barrera, who can we trust?"

Two big questions without answers. Lena glanced out the window at Fontaine's mansion. The windows were dark again. They had left the place exactly as they found it.

"What you're saying is that we need to call this in."

Rhodes's eyes were on her. "And we both know what it looks like inside the house."

"It looks exactly the way Tremell wants it to look."

"Everybody's dead, Lena. Everybody who knows. Except for me and you and the witness, everybody's gone."

"Avadar thinks that the witness bolted."

"Then it's just me and you."

"There's one more," she said.

"Who?"

"A police commissioner. Senator Alan West."

"You still got the ID blocker working on your cell?"

She nodded.

"Then maybe you better call nine-one-one."

* * *

She could see the fear on his face as soon as the door opened. The two bodyguards standing beside the senator bristling with suspicion.

"Relax," West said to the men. "They're friends."

The suspicion never left the bodyguards' eyes, but they took a few steps back just the same. They were big men. Two heavyweights wearing dark suits and rough faces with no interest in hiding the fact that they were armed. As Lena entered with Rhodes, she looked around the house and wondered if two of these guys would be enough. The senator lived just north of the Strip in the hills off Hedges Place. The house was big and modern and designed to take advantage of the views.

And that was the problem. There were too many windows. And too many views.

West sent his bodyguards off and led them into the living room. The spark in his blue eyes was gone, and so was the smile she remembered when they met last week. He was dressed casually in a sweater and slacks and appeared distraught.

"I can't reach Denny," he was saying. "I've been trying all day, and I can't reach him."

Lena gave him a look as he sat down by the fireplace. "You're not going to," she said.

West became quiet after that and lowered his head.

"Tell us about the book you were helping him with," she said. "Tell us about Formula D."

West attempted to pull himself together, but not with much success.

"Why don't you tell me what happened to Denny," he said in a quiet voice.

Lena traded looks with Rhodes, who sat on the couch and reached inside his pocket for his pad and pen.

"Denny was murdered," she said. "His house, ransacked."

"Did you find anything?"

"A file."

"What was in it?"

"Transcripts from interviews for his book. We haven't had a chance to read it yet."

"Why not?"

"Fontaine's dead, too."

It hung there. The weight of the moment pressing down on them. West sat back in his chair and gazed out the window. His face had turned as gray as his hair.

"Then I guess I'm next," he whispered.

"You're a police commissioner. A former U.S. senator. We can provide as many uniformed officers as you want or need."

West shook his head. "The chief's in bed with the district attorney. The district attorney's in bed with anyone who'll write a check. You're forgetting that I know the players. One of them can afford to write a lot of checks."

"You mean Dean Tremell."

West nodded. "How close are you to putting a case against him together?"

"We've identified the girl. We know why she was murdered, but don't have much detail."

"Denny was a good reporter. Very thorough. His notes will probably carry you over the hump."

"We hope so," Lena said.

"Is there any way we could talk after you've read them? All of a sudden I'm not feeling very well."

"You were that close?"

"Jennifer's son died after using the medication," he said. "She came here to find out why. She met Tremell through his son. I don't really know the details. Denny had all that. But it sounded like she sat in on one of the kid's focus groups and got noticed. The old man has a weakness for good-looking women and fell for her. She played along until she gathered enough information to confront Fontaine. From what Denny said, she had Tremell wrapped around her finger. Once she convinced the doctor to talk, she showed up at my office. She didn't have much faith in the system, so she went to Ramira the same day. She was smart. Denny was her insurance policy."

His voice died off. His eyes were still fixed on the hills outside the window. Still fixed on the memory.

"We'll talk after we've read Denny's transcripts," Lena said.

"I appreciate the courtesy. But there's one thing you need to know before you go."

"What's that?"

"I spoke with Denny last night. I was trying to convince him that we needed help. A friend of mine works for the FBI over in Westwood. It seemed like the right move."

"What did Denny say?"

"The same thing he's been saying all along. He needs more information. It's not time yet."

"What information?"

"He wanted to confirm something, then turn over everything to you."

"Confirm what?"

"The name of the man who murdered Jennifer."

"Denny had a name?"

West turned and finally looked her way. Their eyes met.

"Nathan G. Cava," he said.

42

Nathan G. Cava was thirty years old, stood five feet ten inches off the ground, and weighed one hundred and eighty-seven pounds. He had blue eyes and blond hair—cropped short but not buzzed—and a tan complexion. From the width of his neck, he looked rugged. From the slope of his shoulders, more than just sturdy. Unfortunately, the information was ten years old. Everything after that read like a blank sheet of paper. Another black hole.

It was 7:00 a.m., Thursday morning, five days before Christmas. They had spent the night working out of the captain's office with Barrera and Sanchez. Rhodes had a call into his contact over at the DMV and was sitting at his desk on the floor. Barrera was waiting on his friends in Washington, but hadn't heard back and was snoozing in his chair. In another three hours, they would lose Sanchez because he was still locked into testifying in court.

Lena took a sip of coffee, comparing her notes with the interviews Ramira had conducted. Any doubt about the track they were on was completely gone now. The motive for the murders, ultra-clear.

Joseph Fontaine had supervised the clinical trials for Formula D. The problem was that he had a financial interest in the outcome. According to Fontaine, both he and Tremell knew that the drug was dangerous before they won FDA approval and launched the advertising campaign. Jennifer Bloom had used her body to get close to Tremell and proved more than convincing. When she put the pieces together and ended the affair, she confronted Fontaine and threatened to expose the doctor with what she knew. Fontaine realized that he would be ruined either way and decided to talk. It seemed clear to Lena as she read his interview that Fontaine was looking for a deal somewhere down the road. That he thought he would be better off if it looked like he was cooperating and felt some degree of remorse for the things he had done.

But it would have been an upward climb for the wealthy pediatrician. Had he survived, the rock he was pushing never would have made it to the top of the hill.

Fontaine had run more than one clinical trial, yet only presented the FDA with the results from a single study that turned out positive. Everything real had been buried. Articles were written and published in medical journals that amounted to pure fiction. Key members of the FDA motivated by politics and religion were paid off with cash and the withdrawal of a new morning-after pill that Anders Dahl Pharmaceuticals had been developing. Fontaine admitted that he had lied for the money. And that Tremell knew that he was selling poison, but thought that he could fix the formula while he raked in even more cash. Kids were dying, but that didn't seem to matter. From what Lena could tell, Tremell had been more concerned about his investor's expectations that the new drug would be delivered on time.

She turned back to her notes. A few hours ago Rhodes had pulled an article published yesterday in *The Times*. Apparently, Tremell was at odds with several board members from his company over his annual bonus. The board had already agreed to give Tremell seventy-five million dollars for a job well done. According to the newspaper, Tremell thought he deserved a hundred million.

Lena tried to imagine what it must have been like when Tremell learned that Jennifer Bloom had played him for a fool. That it had been Tremell himself who gave her the goods. That she had seduced the old man and won him over until she could prove that he had killed her son.

The woman who cast spells.

The words had been resurrected. Flushed with new meaning and an overwhelming power that burned clean and true.

They had their hands on the motive. But Lena knew that they still didn't have a case.

She gazed across the table, letting the reality soak in. Sanchez was sorting through the ATM and surveillance pictures of the witness. As he spread them out, Lena eyed the photos and noted the leather jacket and Dodger cap. The dark circles under the kid's eyes and the wasted expression on his face. Avadar hadn't checked in yesterday from the bank. That could only mean that their witness hadn't made another try with Bloom's ATM card. That he was still missing. Still lost—or maybe worse.

"You need to call the coroner's office," she said.

Sanchez looked up. "You think he's dead?"

"You need to make the call," she said. "Get them copies of these pictures and ask them to go through the list of ODs they've picked up over the last three days."

Sanchez agreed. Before he could say anything more, Rhodes burst into the room.

"Anyone here ever heard of Vinny Bing, the Cadillac King?"

Barrera shrugged. Lena shook her head.

"He's got a show on cable," Sanchez said. "It sucks."

"Well, he just called and said he's got Cava's Hummer."

Lena spotted the Hummer from a block away. It was hard to miss because it was parked in front of the dealership's showroom door. But even worse, two guys were outside setting up movie lights.

She glanced at Rhodes and took another hit of coffee. She hadn't slept in two nights. She was grinding now. On the move and feeling the furies in her gut. They didn't have time for this.

Rhodes pulled up to the showroom. As Lena jumped out, she turned to one of the lighting techs.

"Where's Vinny Bing?" she said.

"Inside the deal tent."

Rhodes closed in on the man. "What the fuck's a deal tent?"

The guy gave him a look. "It's inside," he said. "You can't miss it, dude."

They entered the showroom and heard Nat King Cole singing "The Christmas Song" over the PA system. It was still early and no one was around. Lena spotted the neon sign over the tent's entrance and pointed at it. LET'S DO DA DEAL. Pushing the curtains away, she entered with Rhodes.

A kid wearing jeans and a T-shirt dropped a legal pad on the table and looked up. When some weird guy standing behind the desk in his boxer shorts turned, his eyes got big and he grabbed his costume off the chair.

"What's up with all this," the guy was saying. "The cops are already here."

Lena watched him step into his king costume, noting the diamond necklace and the rings on his fingers. His face was pale, his eyes swollen. The king looked like he had a hangover.

"Are you Vinny Bing?" she said.

The kid in the T-shirt answered for him. "Who do you think he is? And why'd you get here so early? We need more time to set up."

"Set what up?" Rhodes said.

"The lights. The shots. You're blowing it, man. Don't you want to be on TV?"

Rhodes glared at the kid. "No," he said. "We don't want to be on TV. Now get out of here."

"What are you talking about? We need to shoot this, man. This'll be the climax for our whole season. This'll make the King of Caddies the King of Cable TV."

"You heard the detective," Lena said. "Police business. Get out."

The kid looked at Bing for help. After a moment Bing snapped his fingers and pointed at the door.

"Later, Mr. Hollywood. We'll do our deal. You do yours in B mode."

The kid grimaced, then grabbed his legal pad and stormed

out. Lena turned back to Bing. He was still getting into his costume. When he opened a box and clipped on a wireless microphone, Lena thought she understood what B mode meant. Tape was rolling. She glanced over at Rhodes and caught the look in his eyes. He had made the connection as well, but there wasn't time to care.

"Tell us about the Hummer," she said.

Bing smiled through a yawn. "Customer Cava shows up here last Saturday. The dude wants to do business and trade up to an SRX Crossover. Says he wants the V-8. Says he wants the rocket ship."

"Were you guys shooting video?" Rhodes asked.

"'Course we were. Customer Cava sat in that chair and showed me the cash."

Lena paused a moment, thinking about the man in the window she had seen in Venice the other night. The man who walked out of the next building and raced off.

"What color was the Crossover?" she asked.

"Radiant Bronze," he said. "One of our best."

The news settled in. Lena had seen Cava. Not his face, but the way he moved. The way he carried himself and walked away from her into the fog. Cava was the one keeping an eye on the apartment. He was looking for the witness and having the same luck they were. As she tossed it over, she made a mental note to check in with the coroner's office and see if the witness's body had turned up. Her hunch had more kick to it now.

"Tell us about Cava," she said.

Bing clipped the wireless transmitter to his belt and starting buttoning up his costume.

"The man's got the shakes," he said.

"You mean that he was nervous because of the cameras."

"No, ma'am. Customer Cava's got the shakes. The dude's a user. A space man. That's why he wanted the rocket ship."

Lena traded looks with Rhodes. Bing picked up on it, then yanked open a desk drawer and tossed a Taser in front of them.

"The guys found it underneath the driver's seat when they

were detailing the car," Bing said. "At first we thought it was a toy. You know, a Christmas toy for kids. Then I start think'n it's some kind of ray gun, man. An electric gun. I put two and two together. Customer Cava's into something weird. The parallel universe, so to speak. I got up this morning and made the call. Time for the king to do his best."

Lena drew a pen from her pocket and slid the Taser closer without touching it. It was an M-18. A third-generation Taser used by special forces and SWAT teams that ran on eight AA batteries, yet hit the subject with fifty thousand volts. Lena checked the safety. She had seen the weapon used in a demonstration just a couple of months ago. The blast of electricity lasted for five seconds. Some people took the hit and were deluged with uncontrollable muscle spasms. Some froze in a standing position, while others tumbled over and hit the ground. But what interested Lena was the data port just below the battery indicator light. The M-18 had a microprocessor. A chip that recorded the time and date of every shot.

Her laptop was in the Crown Vic. She looked past Bing out the window and found the car in the lot. Hidden behind the Hummer she could see a man with a video camera pointed at them. When she glanced back at Bing, she saw his face turned toward the window slightly and realized that they were shooting through the glass. The king was playing to the camera.

She turned to Rhodes. "I'll be right back."

She ran outside for her briefcase, ignoring the video crew by the Hummer. Returning to the office, she found a place away from the window, slipped on a pair of gloves, and connected the Taser to her computer. As the information rendered on the screen, she listened to Rhodes warn Bing that Cava was dangerous, then ask for his paperwork. When Bing picked up the phone to call the finance department, Rhodes joined her.

The M-18 had been fired five times last Wednesday night.

Five bursts of fifty thousand volts at a young woman who weighed only one hundred and twenty-two pounds. The first occurred at 10:27 p.m. The second, four minutes after that. Then nothing until 11:15 p.m. Shots four and five were logged in at 11:38 and 12:01. According to the Andolinis, Cava showed up at the garage on Barton Avenue around eleven. That meant that the first two jolts went down in the parking lot at the Cock-a-doodle-do and were used to subdue the woman. The last three were fired in the garage for other reasons.

Lena slipped the Taser into her briefcase. By the time she packed up, a timid man with bleached blond hair and black roots entered with Cava's file. They opened it on the table. As she read the contact information, she noticed Bing standing beside her in full costume. The king was pointing at the documents and pretending to be involved for his audience outside the window.

Lena turned back to the file. After a moment, the timid man with the bad dye job cleared his throat.

"That's not his address," he said. "He doesn't live there anymore. He made a mistake and wrote the wrong one down."

Lena didn't say anything. When Rhodes flipped the page over, an envelope fell out. The letter had been sent by the dealership to Cava's address and returned by the post office.

"It came back yesterday," the timid man said. "It's no big deal. It's just a thank-you letter we send out after every purchase."

Lena glanced at the envelope. There was a bright yellow preprinted label beside the address. Beneath the words RETURN TO SENDER was an explanation. Cava's application for a change of address had run out and the post office was no longer forwarding his mail. But what struck Lena was the label itself. Cava had used a real former address. At one time he had lived there.

She turned to Rhodes and caught the glint in his eye.

"He's not hiding," he said. "He lives here. He's got a home in L.A."

Rhodes gazed out the window at the Hummer. She could see him putting something together, and suddenly realized what it was.

"The navigation device."

Rhodes rocked his head up and down and turned to Bing. "Are the keys in the Hummer?"

"Yeah, sure. We just moved it."

Lena followed Rhodes out the showroom door. Ignoring the video camera, they rushed over to the Hummer and climbed in. Rhodes turned the key, then switched on the navigation device and began toggling through the menu until he reached a list of previous destinations Cava had programmed into the system. She saw Fontaine's address. Then the victim's apartment on Navy Street in Venice. But it was the list of options at the bottom of the screen that seemed the most important right now. The button marked HOME that would have been programmed by the dealership at the time of purchase for the original owner of the car.

Rhodes pressed the button. Lena's eyes zeroed in on the text. They had him. Nathan G. Cava lived in Universal City.

43

Barham Boulevard had been closed, the entire complex of four buildings, evacuated and shut down. Each building was three stories high and shaped like a box. A mix of modern and Tudor styles wrapped around courtyards that were fleshed out with swimming pools and palm trees and rows of lounge chairs. The fact that the Bates Motel from the movie *Psycho* stood just over the next hill on the Universal lot was something Lena didn't really want to think about right now.

She was waiting by the pool with Rhodes, hidden beneath Cava's unit on the third floor. Neither detective would be involved in the arrest. Lena didn't want to take the chance. They needed Cava alive. After hashing it out with Barrera at Parker Center, Lt. Chase Thomas from Special Weapons and Tactics was called in to oversee the operation. Thomas had rescued fifteen hostages from a bank robbery last year and was awarded the Medal of Valor, the department's highest award for heroism in the line of duty. He was the cream of the crop and a consummate professional. In five minutes he would lead his team upstairs to Cava's front door.

Curiously, as they planned the operation in the captain's vacant office, there had been no word from the sixth floor. Chief Logan had made no comment, offered no response, and remained strangely silent. And Klinger hadn't been seen in the building all day.

Lena didn't take any of this as a good sign.

The crime scenes at Ramira's house off Edgewater Terrace and Fontaine's mansion on South Mapleton Drive had been processed by different divisions at the local level. Both decisions had been made in the heat of the moment, both decisions born out of desperation. But from where Lena stood, the tree wasn't rotting from the ground up. The tree was disintegrating from the top down. Her best chance at getting to Tremell, her only chance, was to keep the investigations as far away from Parker Center as she could. To have faith in the department's roots and the local homicide divisions where the chief's ability to write and direct the outcome would be far less certain. It seemed obvious enough now that Logan had assigned the case to her because he wanted to destroy her. But just as important, he was in on it. He had asked for her because he believed that she would fail. By calling 911 at both locations, she had thrown a wrench into his plans. She had brought more people into the mix. Fresh eyes and ears.

So the silence from the sixth floor had to mean something. And Lena figured that nothing about it could be good.

Her mouth was dry. She turned and saw Thomas entering the courtyard with ten men behind him—each wearing helmets and body armor. Of the ten, four carried shotguns. The rest were equipped with automatic rifles. But it was the shotguns that caught Lena's eye. They were Winchester SX3s capable of firing twelve shells in less than 1.5 seconds.

The SWAT team was ready. And when Thomas gave her the nod, she moved down the walkway with Rhodes and followed their progress up the stairs. Cava's curtains were drawn. The entry team worked quickly, avoiding the windows and falling into position. Then Thomas stepped to the side and pounded on the front door.

Thirty seconds rolled out hot and heavy with no response. Thomas tried again, harder than before. Another burst of time came and went.

Lena watched as he held his ear to the door. After a third attempt, he turned and found her in the courtyard below. His shrug could only mean that there was no movement inside.

She thought about Cava's car in the garage. The SRX Crossover. They knew that he was here. And there was no need to break the door down. The keys had been furnished by the management company.

Thomas fished them out of his pocket and tossed them to a team member. Once they got past the locks, Cava's door was pushed open with the business end of a Winchester SX3.

A moment passed. Those first jittery peeks inside the darkened apartment. Then the team quickly filed in with their weapons raised.

Lena glanced at Rhodes, instinctively moving toward the stairs. Listening, watching. The waiting tearing her up inside.

After five long minutes, Thomas reappeared in the doorway and waved them up. Lena's first thought as she tore up the steps was that Cava had been killed before they got here. That the word had been out all morning that they located him, and that no one involved at any level could afford to take the chance that he might talk. When she reached the front door, Thomas pulled off his helmet like the operation was over and gave her a look.

"You need to see this," he said. "Follow me."

Her heart almost stopped beating. She entered the darkened apartment, noting the sparse furnishings as she and Rhodes followed Thomas past the kitchen into the bedroom. All ten SWAT team members were huddled around the bed. Thomas cleared a path for them. As the bodies parted, she looked down and saw Nathan G. Cava lying on top of the bed.

But he hadn't been murdered, and the surgeon-turned-hit man wasn't dead.

Instead, Cava was listening to music with a pair of headphones on and his eyes closed. Lena could hear the sound leaking into the quiet room. It was a blues cut and a good one—"Bobby's Bop," from an import album by Ronnie Earl and the Broadcasters called *Hope Radio*.

"He won't budge," Thomas said. "He's out."

Rhodes pointed to the bedside table. Six or seven empty

auto-injectors were piled up beside a fresh pack of five more. Cava was binging on morphine. The auto-injectors were identical to the two they found on Fontaine's desk.

His eyes opened.

Everybody in the room flinched.

Then six rifles and four shotguns slid forward an inch or two from the man's face. Cava didn't appear to see them. He didn't even move. He just lay there, listening to the blues and holding on to the great White Nurse in a state of bliss.

44

Lena looked at Barrera standing before the window. He was smoking a cigar and watching the last rays of orange sunlight clip the hilltops to the north. Directly west, the marine layer was already flooding into the basin.

"You've got everything, right?" he asked.

"I'm all set."

They were in the captain's office. Alone on the floor. The air fraught with electricity. Cava was waiting in one of the interrogation rooms across the way, his cosmic bliss winding down from a six-hour discharge. A doctor had examined him at his apartment and signed off on his condition. For the past hour, Cava had been alone in the small room—handcuffed to a chair with nothing to do. By now the walls were closing in on him. The ground, fertile.

Barrera turned from the window. "If you need anything, I'll be right outside the door."

Lena nodded. She appreciated his concern, but they had gone over it at least ten times. And there had been more than enough time to pin down who Cava really was, collect props, and prepare for the interview.

She gathered her files, then picked up a pair of new slip-on sneakers. Because the interrogation rooms were built almost fifty years ago and didn't include one-way mirrors or observation rooms, the session would be recorded by SID on the fourth floor. Although Klinger was still missing and Chief

Logan remained eerily silent, Rhodes would oversee the recording to make sure that no one was eavesdropping from above.

The phone rang. Barrera grabbed it and listened, then hung up and turned to Lena.

"Rhodes," he said. "They're ready. Tape's rolling."

She met his eyes, then walked out of the office heading for the interrogation room. When she pulled the door open, Cava looked up from his chair against the rear wall.

"Would you like a cup of coffee, Doctor?"

He stared at her for a moment, surprised. "Sugar, but no cream," he said in a quiet voice.

Lena left her things on the table, then poured two cups of coffee at the counter by the fax machine, added sugar, and returned to the room. As she closed the door and sat down, she could feel Cava's eyes on her. He seemed reserved, catlike. She pulled her cell out and flipped it open. When the screen lit up, she switched off the power and returned the phone to her pocket. Cava's eyes slid across the table to his coffee. Lena watched him lift the cup. His hands were trembling, and he seemed aware that she had noticed.

"Where are my medications?" he said. "And what happened to my shoes?"

She pushed the sneakers across the table. "These should fit. They're size ten."

He pulled them closer and examined them, then noticed the lack of shoelaces. "You think I'm gonna hang myself?"

She shrugged and it seemed to anger him.

"The pair you took from me were Bruno Maglis. They cost four hundred dollars."

"These cost twenty-three," she said.

He shook his head, then dropped the sneakers on the floor and slipped them over his socks. Lena used the time to open her files and lay them out on the table. As she made a few adjustments, Cava rattled the handcuffs.

"You think that I don't know what you're doing," he said.

She turned to him, but remained silent.

"You think I haven't sat in your chair before and done the same thing? You think that I'm really gonna talk to you? You think that I'm that stupid?"

He was nervous. She could see it. And he was spent. His eyes were glassy. Like a window in a gutted house, she could see the damage on the other side.

"How did you find me?" he asked.

Lena ignored the question and stared at him for a moment. "You're not a real doctor, are you?"

"What are you talking about?"

"Sure, you went to med school, Cava. But you almost flunked out. You've never worked at a hospital and you've never had any patients. You're a loser, Cava. And I've seen your military file. You're not even a real spook. You're only half a spook. The only reason the army took you into the medical corps is because no one else signed up. They were desperate. After they ran out of good guys, they came to you. They took one look and knew that you'd do their dirty work for them."

Cava laughed. "Nice try, but it won't fly. No matter how strung out I am, you will never break me down. Never ever, bitch. I'm gonna walk on this. You'll see."

"You're too sloppy to walk, Cava. You do too many drugs and you're too far in. You only see what you want to see."

"I'm connected. And I'm gonna walk out of here in these lousy shoes. I'll drop you a line from paradise when I get there."

Lena pushed her coffee aside. She didn't need it.

"But you don't live in paradise, Cava. You live in a world where it's cloudy every day. I went through your medications. You need pills to do everything that you do in this world. You take a pill to get up and another one to go to sleep. You need medication to eat, take a leak, get it up, or turn your stupid iPod on. You even take something because you can't blink your eyes on your own. You're a parasite. A follower. A scavenger and a user. You see a situation and you take advantage of it. You work it, exploit it. You don't mend things, you kill them. And I can see it in your eyes, Cava. Your dead fucking eyes. You dig it. Killing turns you on."

Cava leaned back in the chair, stunned by the barrage. "That's not true. Now tell me how you found me."

Lena ignored the question again. It was time to walk the murderer down Memory Lane. She sifted through the pictures she had selected with Barrera and Rhodes and began setting them down on the table. First up were snapshots of the Taser they recovered and the Cock-a-doodle-do.

"You don't even need to talk," she said. "Just sit back and relax."

"Fuck you."

She set down a series of pictures from the crime scene inside the garage on Barton Avenue, and the alley behind Tiny's a half block north of Hollywood Boulevard. Jennifer Bloom was finally on the table, stuffed inside a garbage bag with her lost eyes squared up to the lens. Everything was here: the makeshift operating table, the buckets filled with the victim's blood.

"We know that you shot her five times with the Taser. Twice in the parking lot, then three more times in the garage you rented. We know that you bled her out, cut her up and dumped her body in Hollywood."

"Could have been anyone."

"Like I said, Cava, you're a loser. You're sloppy. You're in over your head."

She laid down two additional snapshots. The first was taken at Cava's apartment at the time of his arrest. A close-up view of the shoes he had been wearing that included the Phillips head screw still embedded in his right heel. The second, the footprint SID picked up from the garage that made it a perfect match. Then she added three more. Joseph Fontaine slumped over his chair with a bullet in his head. Greta Dietrich sliced and diced and packed up in the basement freezer. And finally, Denny Ramira, an award-winning journalist, sprawled out on his kitchen floor beside a bag of groceries with a meat thermometer puncturing his heart. When she remembered the shot of Ramira's dog, Freddie, hanging from the stairway, she threw that on the table, too.

A moment passed. A long stretch of silence.

Four people. Four murders. Four corpses and a small dead dog.

The scope of the crime, the photographs, cut to the bone.

Lena returned to her chair and sat down, watching Cava examine the photos. "Do you really think that you're gonna walk, Cava? Are you so deluded that you think there's a way out of this? That somehow your friends can explain this away and get you off the hook? You're the only one who's expendable. The only one without power or standing. You know what's gonna happen better than I do. You're a soldier, and they're gonna throw you into the wind and run for cover. Look at these pictures. Think about the story they tell. What's a jury gonna say when they see them?"

His dead blue eyes rocked back and forth over the photos, then rose up from the table and found her in the room.

"The question isn't how long you'll be in prison," she said. "It's the circumstances that you need to worry about. They're special. You're gonna die, Cava. They're gonna stick the needle in your arm and you're gonna die. The last execution I witnessed didn't go very well. Someone screwed up and it took half an hour for the guy to die. It looked like it hurt."

He was still staring at her with those bloodshot eyes. His face had lost its color and he was perspiring. When he spoke, his voice was so hoarse she could barely hear him.

"You're good at this," he said. "Now tell me what you want."

"The man who's writing the checks. Dean Tremell and everyone else who's in on it."

"What do I get in return?"

"Have I shot straight with you?"

"Yeah," he said. "I'd say you're a straight shooter. Do you have the authority to make the deal?"

"Everything's been approved."

"What do I get?"

"Life in prison without the possibility of parole. Any place in the federal system you choose within the continen-

tal United States. A guarantee from the governor of the State
of California that you will be looked after by the medical
staff and receive any medications that you require."

"Sounds like paradise," he said.

"Beats tying a sheet around your neck and ending up in a
hole in the ground."

He paused a moment, reviewing the photos as he considered her proposition. His eyes lingered on the shot of Ramira.
Then he found the reporter's dog in the pile and looked at it
for a long time. Most juries liked dogs.

"I'm gonna need to think this over," he said.

Lena nodded. "You'll be taken to Men's Central Jail for
the night and placed in isolation. You can think it over and
we'll talk tomorrow morning. The offer's good until then."

Lena gathered the photos, returning them to her files. As
she got up to leave, Cava tried a third time.

"It's not like I was hiding," he said. "But it had to start somewhere. How did you find me?"

She turned from the door and looked at him, thinking
about Denny Ramira and the investigation that had cost him
his life.

"We'll talk tomorrow," she said.

45

Maybe it was the stars, the planets, or even some weird moon thing that crazy people talk about. Some sort of perfect astrological alignment that he didn't understand and couldn't see because the clouds covered the sky. Maybe he had an angel looking over his shoulder. A halfwit angel who took him on as a test case or lost a bet. After all, there had to be a reason why they called this place the City of Angels.

Or maybe this was the moment. The big one when the door opened and the rest of your life winked at you from the other side.

Nathan G. Cava watched Parker Center fade into the night, then turned to the two cops sitting in the front seat. He hadn't caught their names when they cuffed his wrists behind his back. And he hadn't bothered to ask who they were as they led him out of the building to an unmarked car for what everyone believed would be his last ride as a free man.

They were older guys. Seasoned veterans. At the end of their shift and making the trip before they went home. Cava didn't want to know their names because they were part of the moment, too.

The car stopped at a red light on North Alameda Street. Men's Central Jail was a brief five-minute drive somewhere up the road. The cops weren't talking to each other, so Cava had to become still.

Maybe it was just the morphine, he thought—some small amount that remained in his system, relaxing his muscles

and joints and making his body extraordinarily pliable tonight. Maybe it was his will to live. His will to spend the
rest of his days as a free man under the sun. Or, the secret
that he had kept from Lena Gamble and every other cop that
he wasn't as stupid as they thought. That all his money was
safe and secure because he never kept it anywhere near his
apartment.

Cava didn't care either way. All he knew was that he had
a chance. One last chance to squirm through the door before
it slammed shut.

The car started moving again. Cava had managed to slip
his bound wrists underneath his body and work the handcuffs behind his knees. Leaning forward slightly, he strained
to lower his hands to the floor. If he could just step through
them. If he could just manage to bring his arms forward—

A thought surfaced. The sound of a jail cell door reverberating in his skull.

Cava bent his legs and pushed his wrists lower until he
reached his heels. All he needed was another half inch. It
suddenly occurred to him that he wasn't wearing his Bruno
Maglis. That he had been given a cheap pair of slip-on sneakers. He looked back at the cops as he slid them off his feet,
then pushed down as hard as he could. His socks were
sweaty and he could feel the chain between the handcuffs
begin rolling over the moist cotton until—

He'd made it.

He leaned back in the seat, masking his smile with a
darting look out the window. His mind was a jumbled blur.
Everything crazy. He slipped his feet back into those twenty-
three-dollar shoes and felt his stomach get hot.

They had just crossed over the Santa Ana Freeway and
were passing Union Station on the right. Up ahead he could
see a series of industrial buildings marring the landscape.
The street looked darker there. One empty parking lot after
the next. He turned back to the cop sitting in the passenger
seat, trying to remember how the man's gun sat on his belt.
Cava knew that he would only get one chance. That although
he would have the element of surprise on his side, his move

would have to be decisive and smooth. But even more important, the car would have to be moving fast enough that the driver couldn't let go of the wheel and interfere. Cava estimated that he needed three seconds at over 30 mph, no more and no less.

The car stopped before another red light. The cop behind the wheel gave him a hard look through the rearview mirror.

"Everything okay back there?"

"Yeah, sure. I'm making my list and checking it twice."

The cop kept staring at him. Giving him the evil fucking eye. Cava looked away for fear the man might read his mind. When the light turned green and they started moving again, he watched the speedometer begin to rise and worked on controlling his breathing. He slid behind the cop in the passenger seat, his eyes still on the dash. The car continued to accelerate forward into the barren cityscape. Ten mph turned into 20, then became 30 and 40, until they topped out at 50 mph.

Kill speed.

Cava grit his teeth and reached deep down in his rotten gut for the courage. And then he burst through the cosmic door, swinging his arms over the man's head, grasping the gun at his waist and pulling up until he found his prey's neck and drew the chain between the handcuffs tight.

The cop struggled beneath the chain, kicking his legs into the windshield. The car started swerving, the cop behind the wheel slamming on the brakes. Cava jacked the slide on the semiautomatic, saw his own face in the rearview mirror and didn't know who he was. He jerked the gun up and to the side, pulling the trigger on the driver as he throttled the cop in the passenger seat. The gun roared, loud as a jackhammer inside the tight space. One shot after another, cut against the sounds of both men screaming. Cava could feel his arms shaking. His entire fucking body. He could see the rounds moving to the left—breaking through the windshield, the door, and then finally, exploding into the driver's face.

The car veered off the road, smashed into something, and flipped over. Skidding across a parking lot, Cava rode it out as best he could, watching the roof beneath his feet collapse in slow motion. When the car finally ground to a stop, he took a deep breath and shuddered.

He could smell gasoline in the air. A lot of it. From the glow outside the window, he guessed that the back of the car was burning but couldn't see the flames. He looked under the front seat, everything still upside down. Both cops were strapped in with their feet up in the air like a pair of dead astronauts all set for their rocket launch to heaven. Cava could hear the flames now and scurried into the front compartment. Once he found the keys to the handcuffs, he grabbed the gun and crawled underneath the cop in the passenger seat out the window.

He was hyperventilating. The flames were beginning to engulf the car. He could hear sirens breaking through the night. But as he worked his way out of the handcuffs, he heard something else. He turned to the car and looked in the window. The cop in the passenger seat was staring back at him. He was reaching out the window and moaning, his face awash in blood.

Cava checked the progress of the fire, then looked back at the cop. The sirens were getting closer, but help probably wouldn't make it in time.

He shook his head, thinking about the guilt that was piling up. The idea that once the killing started, it took on a life of its own and was hard to stop. He could feel the cosmic door closing on him and knew that he needed to find a new set of wheels and bolt. He picked up the gun with a jittery hand and put two rounds in the cop's head. Then he ran off.

46

The king was dead.

Cava gazed up at the ceiling in the garage and watched Vinny Bing's knuckle-dragging corpse sway from a rope as the heat switched on and the vents in the rafters blew out hot air. Remarkably, it looked like the king was still wearing that TV smile beneath his crown. His mouth was thrust open and he could see his yellow teeth.

Cava had been freezing his ass off outside the dealership for more than hour. Following the king's movements through the plate glass windows as he closed up for the night. It turned out that Vinny had a thing for Frank Sinatra CDs, microwaved popcorn, and glasses of bourbon. That he liked to prance around the showroom in his costume, listening to music and peeking in his employee's desks when no one was around.

Cava had caught up with him as he walked out the front door. Although the king acted surprised and things got dramatic for five or ten minutes, although the king had repeatedly bitten him like a rabid dog during the struggle, it was over now. The king and his cable TV show would wind up buried in the metro section of the paper and fade into oblivion as a rerun.

Cava looked at the cell he had removed from the man's pocket. It was encrusted with diamonds in the shape of a crown. Below the crown was his first name, Vinny. When he flipped the phone open, it played a jingle. Cava recognized the tune, but couldn't place it. Once he finally did, he almost wished that he hadn't killed the slob. It was from the Miss America beauty pageant that used to be on TV. The jingle they played at the end of the show when the winner received her crown and started to cry.

Cava shrugged it off and entered a phone number from memory. After three rings he heard her voice. Heard her say hello.

"Lena?" he asked.

She didn't say anything right away. He could see her face in his mind's eye. He could feel the shock through the radio waves in the air.

"Where are you?" she said.

"Free and clear and heading for paradise in a magic pair of cheap shoes. I told you that I'd walk."

"You're a cop killer, Cava."

"Does that mean our deal's off?"

She paused again. And he could see her face again. He liked having the image in his head and hoped that it wouldn't wear off over time.

"How'd you get this number?" she said finally.

"I saw it on the screen when you opened your cell and turned it off."

"You need to turn yourself in, Cava. Believe me. It's your best chance at surviving this."

"Stop talking and listen," he said. "I called for a reason."

"What reason?"

"My end of our deal and a rare moment of clarity. Tremell's kid didn't know anything about the murder. The old man used him as bait to get the girl out to that whorehouse. All the kid knew was that his father wanted to dirty her up and make her look like a whore."

Another run of silence. Cava thought he could hear traffic in the background. She was in her car.

"He's covering for his father," she said.

"Most sons would. But he didn't know about the murder."

"What else?"

The king's shadow drifted over the key rack on the wall.

Cava noticed it and glanced at the tags. He could have any car on the lot he wanted. It was free car night.

"The reason I called," he said. "You've missed something."

"Missed what?"

"A piece of the puzzle. You've missed it. And it's a big piece."

"What is it?"

He paused a moment, thinking it over. "I'll leave that to you," he said. "I've got your number. I'll check in when I get to paradise."

He shut down the phone and slipped it into his pocket. Then he skimmed through the key tags and picked out another SRX Crossover. Walking to the door, he turned back for one last look at Vinny Bing the Cadillac King and caught the man's horrific smile from above.

"Hang in there," he said.

47

Lena sat in her car, still parked on the shoulder of the Hollywood Freeway in Echo Park. She had pulled over as soon as she realized that it was Cava on the phone. Not because of the shock. She could handle that. She had pulled over because she wanted to hear his voice. Wanted to listen to him and concentrate on the moment.

She gazed over the concrete divider at the cars moving up and down Glendale Boulevard below the freeway. Echo Lake was almost invisible. The marine layer had pushed east from the coast, the cool mist hugging the ground and beginning to fill the basin like concrete rising to the lip of a mold.

Cava had said that she missed something. Something big.

And she had no doubt that he was telling her the truth. She had heard it in his voice. And now she could feel it in her gut. The main wheel that guided her internal compass. The thing she relied on that made it all work.

Something remained hidden. Something essential to the case.

Her cell started vibrating on the passenger seat. She read Barrera's name on the display and pried open the phone.

"Where are you?" he asked.

"Echo Park," she said. "Heading home."

"Don't go home, Lena."

The tone of his voice spooked her. "What is it?" she said. "What's wrong?"

"Don't go home," he repeated. "I'm in Hollywood. We need to talk."

"Where?"

"How 'bout the parking lot outside Capitol Records in ten minutes?"

That main wheel in her gut was talking to her again. "I'll see you then," she said.

She closed the phone with an unsteady hand. Lit a cigarette and pulled onto the freeway. The traffic was moving smooth and steady through the gloom toward the Cahuenga Pass. Almost too steady. Her imagination was playing tricks with her. Feeding on something she couldn't place. Connecting dots that might not be there. When she pulled into the lot, she spotted a Lincoln Town Car parked all the way back against the chainlink fence. On the other side of the fence was Vista Del Mar—a small road tucked away from downtown Hollywood and the exact spot where she had found her brother's dead body so many years ago.

Couldn't be good.

She got rid of the cigarette and climbed out of her car. As she crossed the empty lot and walked toward the Town Car, the rear door swung open and the interior lights switched on. Barrera was behind the wheel sitting beside a man she had never seen before. When her eyes flicked to the backseat, she froze.

It was the chief. All three were waiting for her.

She kept her eyes on them and started backing away. Then she finally turned and made a run for it. Barrera jerked the Town Car forward. Lena jammed her key into the ignition, fired up the engine, and floored it. When she hit Vine Street, she made a hard left and pointed the hood downhill into the congestion. But the Town Car was right behind her—tires screeching and pushing fast.

She blew through the light at Hollywood Boulevard and gunned it, then checked the mirror. Barrera was closing in. She tried to think. Come up with a plan. She grabbed her phone and hit Rhodes's speed dial number, waiting for him to pick up. It felt like an eternity. And she could hear the phone beeping through the ring. Someone else trying to break through. Her Honda was a stick shift. At this speed she couldn't hold the phone and work the road at the same time. Rhodes finally picked up.

"Where are you?" she said.

"Venice."

"Stay there. Keep your cell on."

"Are you okay?"

"I don't know yet. I'll call as soon as I get there."

She threw the phone onto the passenger seat and grabbed the gear shift. The Town Car could easily outrun her on a straight track. Zigzagging her way over to La Brea, she finally hit the Santa Monica Freeway but lost sight of Barrera in the rearview mirror. There were too many headlights. Too much traffic and glare. She brought the car up to a hard ninety. As she wove through the lanes, she checked the mirror searching for a pair of headlights following her path. After a mile she thought she spotted them. But when the car rocketed past her doing a hot one hundred and twenty, it was another Honda, a lowrider with neon lights along the floorboards and a straight pipe out the back.

She slid into the next lane, keeping her eye on the lowrider and following its course through the traffic. When she hit the Lincoln Boulevard exit, she made a sudden hard cut across three lanes and blew up the ramp. She checked the mirror again. The darkness and the mist. She'd lost them.

She filled her lungs with air and exhaled, thinking that she needed a place to hide while she called Rhodes back and figured out what was going on. When she finally reached Navy Street, she checked her rearview mirror again and turned back.

The fog was thicker here. Billowing off the Pacific over the buildings and streets and filling in the rough edges with more gloom.

Lena cruised past the apartment and found a place to park around the corner. Then she pulled Jennifer Bloom's keys out of her briefcase and legged it up the sidewalk and into the building.

She could hear the TV from Jones's apartment leaking into the foyer. People laughing and buzzers going off from some game show. She hadn't seen him in the window from the sidewalk and she was glad. She hurried up the steps, unlocked the door, and pushed it open. As she switched on the table lamp in the foyer and leaned against the door, she thought about Barrera.

She already knew what the word betrayal meant. The way it cut and chewed through your being. The way it tore everything up and burned everything down. She knew what it meant. What it felt like. The scars that it left behind. Still, she was having trouble catching her breath.

She switched on the lights in the living room and bedroom. Erasing the darkness didn't seem to help. As she started to walk out, she sensed something and turned back. There was something going on. Something out of place. She scanned the room and checked it against her memory. When her eyes zeroed in on the bedside table, she felt a chill flicker across her shoulder blades.

The snow globe was missing.

She glanced at the floor on the other side of the bed. Looked over at the chest of drawers. Tried to remember where it was the last time that she had been here. Snowflakes falling over Las Vegas.

And that's when she heard the noise. A floorboard creaking. Someone else was in the apartment.

Lena eased out of the bedroom, moving silently through the entry way. When she reached the French doors, she stopped and peered through the glass into the living room. It took a moment for the image to register in her brain. She could feel the rush as she stared through the glass.

It was him—wearing the leather jacket and the Dodger cap.

The lost witness—tiptoeing his way out of the kitchen toward the window and fire escape with the snow globe in his hand.

The thief with the guilty conscience who sent her the package and then tapped out the victim's bank account with the stolen ATM card. Eighteen or nineteen with brown hair and pale skin. The thin and nervous type with dark circles under his eyes. The user loser who needed more cash for more stash and another hot load.

Lena had walked in on a robbery. The witness hadn't overdosed and wasn't stretched out on a gurney at the morgue. The piece of shit had waited them out and picked his night. He was cleaning out the place.

She turned the corner and stepped into the living room. When the kid spotted her, he dropped the snow globe, and made a run for the window. It was already cracked open, but appeared stuck. Lena raced across the room and grabbed him by his shoulders. Yanking him away, they tumbled back and hit the floor. The kid groaned and appeared panic-stricken. She could feel him trying to squirm out from beneath her, thrashing his arms and legs.

But he was smaller than her. Lighter. Lena gave him a hard push, then rolled him over onto his back keeping him still with the weight of her body. She grabbed his hands and pinned them to the floor over his head. Then she reached out and pulled off the Dodger cap.

A long moment passed. The two of them lying there eye to eye. Face to face.

Lena suddenly became aware of the body underneath her. The long list of things that didn't add up. The width of his hips and the smell of his skin. His brown eyes—big and wild and staring back at her with a certain reach.

Releasing her grip, she got to her feet. The witness didn't move, looking up at her and panting. She could still hear Cava's voice on the phone. Still feel the wheel inside her gut turning. She had missed something and it was big.

She checked the face again. The body. The air in the room suddenly white-hot like a dirty bomb. She hadn't found and captured the witness. Her eyes were locked on the victim.

"You're Jennifer Bloom," she said. "And I'm investigating your murder."

48

The shock wave was still reverberating. The fallout still playing with her core.

Lena closed her cell phone after calling Rhodes and gazed at Bloom with utter amazement. She was thinking about the autopsy. The woman she had seen on the stainless steel gurney that had been cut up and dumped in the trash. The woman originally known as Jane Doe No. 99.

She was trying to picture her face.

The victim had been beaten. Disfigured. She remembered that her eyes had been spared, but not much else. That the sight of the decapitated head had been hard to look at. Yet, she seemed so vulnerable, it had been difficult for Lena to turn away.

Identification had been made based on a theoretical reconstruction of her face, a physical description that fit like a glove, overwhelming circumstantial evidence, and more than one eyewitness who saw her at the Cock-a-doodle-do on the night of the abduction and murder. Although the DMV confirmed that her driver's license was legit, certification that the thumb print on the license matched the print taken from the actual dead body was still pending. Lena remembered Rhodes telling her that it would take a week before they arrived and SID could begin their examination.

"You'll be okay," Lena said to her. "Take my hand."

She pulled the young woman off the floor and helped her over to the couch. Bloom was clearly frightened, and Lena's words didn't seem to make any difference to her. As Lena thought about the body count, Bloom had every reason to still fear for her life. Tremell had offered all his resources to help find the witness. Cava had been watching her apartment. And Chief Logan had shut down the case and made it the number-one priority on his *Loose End List*. Every one of them had wanted to find the witness at all costs. Now Lena understood why.

"You went out to the Cock-a-doodle-do with a friend," she said. "Your friend was murdered. Who was she?"

Bloom lowered her eyes. "Beth Gillman," she whispered. "She was waiting for me in my car."

Lena heard the sound of footsteps through the door. They were moving down the hallway. She checked Bloom's face, caught the edge, and stepped into the foyer. When she heard the tap, she peered through the peephole and unlocked the door. Rhodes hurried in and glanced at Bloom from a distance. Lena could see him making the connections. The shock as he got his first look and realized that their victim wasn't a ghost.

"Were you followed?" he whispered under his breath.

Lena shook her head. "I lost them. A Lincoln. Who's out there?"

"Two guys in a black Audi. I couldn't make out their faces. But it doesn't look good. They're waiting for something. Who was in the Lincoln?"

A memory surfaced before she could answer. Jack Dobbs and Phil Ragetti had chased her down the hill last Sunday night in the rain, then innocently walked into Denny's restaurant. The two former RHD detectives who got the boot for beating the life out of a murder suspect but somehow managed to escape jail time. She could remember the way they had looked at her when they got out of the black Audi. The recognition on their faces. Seeing them hadn't been an accident, she realized. They had wanted her to see them. Both detectives had left the department three years before Lena was promoted to RHD. But Rhodes was there at the time and would've known them.

"Jack Dobbs and Phil Ragetti," she whispered.

Something stirred in Rhodes's eyes. "What about them?"

"Ragetti drives a black Audi," she said. "They followed me Sunday night. How do we get her out of here?"

"Not through the front door."

Lena gave him a look and they entered the living room. Bloom read their faces and seemed all jacked up.

"What is it?" she asked. "What's going on?"

"We're not sure yet," Lena said. "This is Detective Rhodes. Why don't you tell us why you took your friend with you last Wednesday night."

She wanted to keep Bloom talking. Take her mind off what might be going on outside. Bloom appeared to buy it.

"How much do you know about Dean Tremell and Anders Dahl Pharmaceuticals?" she asked.

Lena moved to the window. "Your brother told me why you came here. We know about your son, and both of us have read Ramira's transcripts. Fontaine and Tremell lied to push the drug onto the market when they knew that it wasn't safe. We know you talked to Ramira and West."

"I've been listening to the radio," Bloom said. "Everybody's dead now. Everybody except for me and West."

"Why'd you take your friend with you?" Rhodes asked.

"Justin Tremell wanted to meet there and talk. If it had been his father I would've blown it off. But Justin was different. I didn't exactly trust him, but I wanted to hear what he had to say. I asked Beth to come with me and wait in the car. I didn't think I'd be very long and I wasn't. Justin was speaking for his father. They were making me an offer. Another bribe to not say anything and go away. But there was something about the place where we met—all these prostitutes walking in and out the door. When I asked him why he wanted to meet there, he wouldn't answer me. I started to get paranoid, like maybe something was wrong. Like maybe I'd found out who these guys were but didn't really know what they were. And so I left. I ran out to the parking lot. And that's when I saw a man standing over Beth with a gun in his hand. It was dark, but I could see her body on the ground beside my car. She wasn't moving and I didn't know what to do. I found a place to hide and shot that video with my phone, but I was freaking out. All of a sudden I knew why Beth had been murdered. All of a sudden I knew that the guy who did it thought she was me."

Bloom covered her face with her hands, the memory still too vivid. Rhodes sat beside her on the couch.

"You had blond hair," he said. "The same color eyes. Roughly the same height and weight."

"She was waiting in my car. She's dead because of me."

Lena had been listening with her back turned—staring out the window past the fire escape and looking for an anomaly. And she had found one hidden in the billowing clouds. She could see a man standing in the alley at the end of the building. The shape of his figure without any detail. She didn't need a face or a name to go with the body to understand his purpose. The gun in his right hand said it all.

She turned and shot Rhodes a quiet look. They were fucked. She tried to keep calm, keep Bloom talking while she thought about what to do.

"Okay," Lena said. "So what did you do after they left? You grabbed your friend's purse out of the Dumpster and then what? Drove your car over to her place and hid out?"

Bloom met her eyes. "Something's wrong, isn't it?"

Lena ignored the question and kept cool. "Tell us what you did."

"Beth had a garage. I got your name out of the paper. Then I delivered that package to you with my driver's license and the video clip. But I could see what they were doing. The money they deposited in my bank account and the stories on TV. I never touched their money. I only took what was mine. I knew what they were trying to make it look like. I didn't come forward because I saw what they did to Beth and knew they'd do it again."

She was speaking quickly. Her voice tight as piano wire.

"Makes sense," Rhodes said. "As long as they thought you were dead, you thought that you had a chance."

"Did you tell anyone?" Lena asked. "Anyone at all?"

She shook her head. "Not even my brother. Not Ramira, or West, or Fontaine. Beth's murder was my fault. I couldn't jeopardize anyone else. I couldn't take the chance. And I didn't think I needed to. You guys were saying that Beth was me. As long as you were investigating my murder, there was a chance you'd find them before they found me."

Lena traded looks with Rhodes. Bloom was a remarkable young woman. There was no reason to tell her that her friend had been beaten beyond recognition. No reason to mention that the man with the gun in the alley had a new buddy and that they had moved closer and were eyeing the fire escape. She drew her weapon from her belt and rocked the slide back. It was a .45 Smith & Wesson. She watched Rhodes check his Glock. Everything was copasetic. Everything tuned and amped up. There was no clean way to walk out of Bloom's apartment. No easy exit. They'd have to cut their way out.

"Why did you risk exposure by coming here tonight?" she asked Bloom.

"Why did you guys just pull out your fucking guns? You're scaring the shit out of me."

Lena noticed the snow globe on the floor and picked it up. As she handed it to the woman she realized that it wasn't snow falling over Las Vegas. The flakes were actually miniature silver dollars. And the streets outside the Bellagio Hotel and Caesar's Palace were knee-deep in money.

"It was a risk," Lena said. "Why did you take it?"

Bloom shook the globe and gazed at the silver dollars falling out of the sky. "I made a mistake," she said. "Everything was okay at Beth's place until a few days ago. Then the phone started ringing at odd hours. I made a mistake and answered it one night. I was asleep and woke up and wasn't thinking. They didn't say anything, but they heard my voice. I knew that I needed to get out of here. My husband gave me the snow globe before he left for the war. It was the only thing I brought with me."

"You drove over in your car?" Rhodes said.

Bloom nodded at him.

"Where did you park?"

"Out front."

Her words settled into the room. But only for a split second. Then someone tried to kick down the front door. They didn't make it. The lock held, but Bloom screamed.

"Get down on the floor," Lena said.

Bloom glanced at the window, panicking. "I need to get out of here. I don't want to die."

"Behind the couch," Rhodes said. "Hurry."

The door took another hard kick. When Lena checked the window, the two men were racing up the fire escape. Rhodes raised his Glock and fired a round through the front door chest high. They heard someone fall down in the hall and shout, "I'm fucking hit."

Rhodes quickly lowered his aim and took a second shot. Chaos followed as the round punched through the wood and that first voice never came back. Just the thunderclap of a 12-gauge shotgun blowing a hole out of the cheap door. It was a repeater, the muzzle poking through the hole. Then five quick shells lashed out free and clear, tearing chunks of plaster out of the walls. The sound was deafening.

Lena rolled behind the chair, keeping her eyes on the window behind them. When the two men reached the second floor, she didn't recognize them. The only thing that clicked was that they looked mean and angry. The only thing that mattered was that she knew that they were coming. She pulled the trigger on the .45 before they spotted her, felt the kick and heard the pistol roar. Three quick shots. The glass shattered and began raining down on her. But she had hit her mark. She could see their bloody faces. She could see their bodies tumbling off the fire escape and heard the thud when they hit the ground.

She turned, spotted Bloom crawling over the broken glass toward the window, and shouted at her to stay down. But the repeater was back—the shotgun on steroids—ripping away at the chair and blowing out the lights. Rhodes signaled from the other side of the couch to hold her fire and take the shelling. After another barrage, the repeater shut down and the thunder faded out.

Lena could hear them priming semiautomatics in the hall and laughing like devils. Then the front door burst open and two men entered the foyer. They stepped through the French doors, eyeing the wreckage and searching for bodies in the darkness. And that's when Rhodes reared up from behind the couch with everything his Glock had left. Thirteen rounds into the open targets. Thirteen shots finding their mark.

Lena unloaded her clip, the .45 pounding. She could see the two men taking fire and shooting at the phantoms in the room. The shadows in the night. Remarkably, they were still laughing when their pistols ran out. Still giddy until they finally dropped onto the floor. Then their bodies shuddered, their eyes blinked, and they lost their grip and passed into a sleep so dead, so silent and still, the blood stopped flowing from their wounds.

Lena gazed out the front door into the hall. A man sat on the floor leaning against the wall. She noted the wounds in his chest and stomach, the splintered wood on his suit jacket. As her eyes rose to his face, she realized that she knew him and that he carried a badge. The dead man had been Klinger's young protégé from Internal Affairs. The watcher, the listener—the one who helped Klinger do the dirty work at her house.

"You okay?" Rhodes called out.

"Yeah."

She stood up and looked over at Rhodes in the muted light feeding into the apartment. The air was thick with plaster dust and the strong smell of fresh gunpowder. As she dusted herself off, she glanced at the two dead men on the floor but didn't recognize their faces. When she turned to check on Bloom, her chest locked up.

Bloom wasn't hiding behind the end of the couch. She wasn't anywhere in the room.

Lena ran over to the window. The two guys she had shot through the glass were laid out on the ground, the fog sweeping over their dead bodies. Farther down the alley she could see a blur of motion rounding the corner.

"She's making a run for it."

"We'll cut her off," Rhodes said.

They raced into the hall, hit the stairs two at a time, and ignored Jones screaming at them in the lobby. Bursting through the doors, they looked up the street through the swirling clouds. Lena saw it and knew that Rhodes did too—Dobbs shoving Bloom into the Audi and jumping into the passenger seat, Ragetti throwing his gun on the dash and pulling out.

49

They were heading east on Westchester Parkway. Visibility was less than two car lengths through the murk, and the wipers on the Crown Vic were unable to sweep the ice-cold steam off the glass. All Lena could see through the windshield were the Audi's taillights burning through the fog, then vanishing again. Rhodes pushed forward, concentrating on the road with both hands on the wheel. Every once in a while he would check the rearview mirror, hold the glance, then look back at the road.

"Who was in the Lincoln?" he said finally.

She turned and noticed that his eyes were fixed on the mirror again. When she gazed out the rear window, she understood why. The Lincoln was behind them, cruising eerily through the night with its headlights off.

"How long have they been back there?" she asked.

"Ever since we left Navy Street. Who's in the car?"

"Chief Logan," she said.

Rhodes opened the glove compartment and reached for his emergency pack of cigarettes. When he offered her one, she shook it off and watched him light up.

"Who else?" he asked.

"Somebody I didn't recognize. Probably another empty suit from Internal Affairs."

"Anyone else?"

"Yeah," she said. "Barrera. He's driving the car."

It hung there for three or four beats. Out in the open and

sharp as broken glass. Rhodes cracked the window, working his smoke and thinking it over.

"And you thought what?" he asked.

"That this is a guerilla war and I can't tell who my friends are anymore."

"They don't call them guerillas these days, Lena. They're insurgents."

"Okay, then we've got two traitors with a hostage in front of us, and three insurgents behind us. If we try to shake the insurgents off our tail, we lose the traitors and the hostage. Does that sound any better?"

Rhodes looked at her and grinned. "Maybe we'll get a drink later. Kick back and relax. I know a good bar down this way."

The taillights broke through the fog bank, too bright and too close. Rhodes slowed down and got rid of the cigarette. They were passing signs for the Hollywood Park Casino and Race Track. The Avenue of Champions was lost in the mist just ahead. Lena suddenly thought she knew where Dobbs and Ragetti were taking Jennifer Bloom. When they made a right turn heading south, it became obvious.

The Cock-a-doodle-do was just two miles down the road.

"You see where they're going?" she said.

Rhodes nodded. "The parking lot sweeps down from the building and sits against the 105 Freeway. Prairie runs over both. Across the street I remember seeing a vacant lot. I think we should park there and come in from the back on foot."

Lena agreed. They had just reached the overpass and she could see the neon rooster glowing through the haze. As the building began to break through, she realized that the windows were dark, the parking lot underneath, empty. It was a Thursday night and the place looked like it had been shut down. Rhodes checked the mirror again. When Lena turned, she saw the Lincoln lose air speed and fade back until it disappeared.

Rhodes didn't say anything, but appeared shaken by the image. Easing into the right lane, he let the Audi pull to the end of the lane divider and made his turn. The empty lot sat beside the building on the corner. Rhodes waited at the curb with the lights out until the Audi made its U-turn and doubled back. Once he saw the car pull into the lot at the Cock-a-doodle-do, he hit the gas and parked behind the building.

Lena climbed out and drew her pistol. Rhodes did the same and they moved swiftly and silently through the vacant lot. The traffic on the freeway was so light, Lena wondered if it hadn't been shut down. She could see the pillars rising out of the mist at the back of the lot, the Prairie Avenue overpass clutching the clouds and holding them to the ground. As they approached, she saw the vapor in the air wash with bright light and realized that the Audi had driven off the parking lot at the Cock-a-doodle-do and was headed their way. Even worse, she could see a large object beneath the overpass. Something long and dark. As her eyes adjusted to the dim light, the shape took on more definition.

Dean Tremell's limo was parked in the grass beneath the overpass.

She grabbed Rhodes and pulled him behind the first column. Tremell was there with his driver. She could see his son leaning against the hood with Klinger. The fact that it looked like a drug deal seemed only fitting for the CEO of a pharmaceutical company. But Lena knew exactly what was going on. Tremell was buying Jennifer Bloom. And Dobbs and Ragetti were making the delivery. The old man needed to talk to Bloom and find out who she may have spoken with. The interview would occur here because this was where he wanted the body found when he was through.

Lena felt the adrenaline spiking through her chest. She watched Klinger wave the Audi down the hill as he walked back toward the parking lot at the Cock-a-doodle-do. The clouds lit up with the approaching headlights. Lena moved to the other side of the column, watching Dobbs drag Bloom out of the car and throw her onto the ground. Bloom screamed, but it was pointless. And after a short time, she seemed to realize it herself and quieted down.

Ragetti switched off his headlights and the darkness returned. Then he walked over to Dean Tremell and shook his hand.

"Can you hear what they're saying?" Rhodes whispered.

"No."

"I don't see Cava. Where is he?"

"Paradise," she said.

The two men were walking around the limo. When they reached the trunk, the lid popped up and Lena could see a duffel bag inside. Tremell unzipped it and pulled the bag open. Then Ragetti moved closer and examined the contents. In spite of the distance, in spite of the murk, Lena knew that Ragetti was counting his money. And from the size of the duffel bag, there was a lot to count. But in the end, it didn't really matter. Nothing did as Lena felt someone press a pistol against the back of her head and the world stopped.

"Breathe too hard and you're both dead."

It was Klinger's voice. Soft and low and rising out of the darkness behind them. He must have spotted them early, circling his way back to the Cock-a-doodle-do, crossing Prairie Avenue, and following them into the vacant lot.

"Drop your guns," he said. "Slow and easy."

Klinger pushed Lena's head into the concrete. She met Rhodes's eyes. When she heard his Glock hit the ground, she dropped her .45. Then Klinger picked them up and jammed them underneath his belt. He raised his gun and took a step back.

"Turn around," he said.

Lena gave him a hard look. His cheek was still bruised from the beating Rhodes had given him the other night. And he had a crazy glint in his eye—a vicious glow about his face that she had never seen before. Lena realized that his mask was finally off. He was out in the open and all amped up.

"Let's go," he said. "Down the hill like Jack and Jill."

He flicked his gun to the left, clenching his teeth and ushering them toward the limo. Ragetti stopped counting his money. Dobbs pushed Bloom away, switched on a flashlight, and drew his gun. Justin Tremell kept his eyes on his father. And the old man just stood there in the mist with his hands in his pockets.

Lena took it in, then turned to Tremell and sized the man up. It was too fucking late to be scared.

"Buying something?" she asked.

"You might say that, yes."

"Is it really worth it?"

"With what's at stake, Detective, I'd call it a bargain."

She glanced at Dobbs with the girl, then Ragetti with the cash. Two bruisers who couldn't make the grade.

"These guys are bottom feeders," she said to Tremell. "How much are you paying them?"

Dobbs laughed. "The cunt's got a mouth on her, huh?"

"Shut up," Rhodes said.

Tremell raised his hand for silence and seemed amused. "One million dollars."

"Tax-free?" Lena asked.

He thought it over and grinned. "I guess that's up to them. They're freelance."

Lena looked at Jennifer Bloom, then turned back. "When did you know?"

"When did I know what?" Tremell asked.

"That you killed the wrong one. That you murdered her friend."

"But I'm a businessman, Detective. I haven't killed anyone."

Lena's eyes flicked across the way and found Justin Tremell in the gloom. He was still staring at his father. From the look on his grizzled face, he didn't want to be here. She thought about what Cava had told her on the phone. The kid had been used as bait and didn't know about the murder. But that was more than a week ago and now he did. Now he seemed repulsed by his father's shadow and wanted out.

Lena turned back to the old man and rephrased the question.

"When did you know who she was?"

"Early," Tremell said.

"How early?"

"The night you met the reporter at that café. Sunday, wasn't it? Ramira spent the afternoon on the phone. He figured it out. My friends were listening. I'm surprised that he didn't say anything to you."

She thought it over. Thought about Denny Ramira, what he knew and the reasons he may have had for not telling her. And she finally understood why they had wired up her house even though she spent so little time there. It was all about who talked to whom. It was all about covering the odds. Everybody's house had been wired.

Tremell cleared his throat. "I enjoyed our lunch, Detective. You're an attractive woman. I only wish that you had the brains to go with it. I believe they call it the total package. I wish that you could have seen the situation for what it truly was. I wish that you would've agreed to work with us. Believe me, I take no pleasure in what's about to happen."

"But you're wrong, Tremell. I see it exactly the way it is. You kill people, and you're in it for the money. Little kids or anyone else who gets in your way. You're no better than any other drug dealer."

Tremell's smile faded into a grimace. When he looked past her at Klinger and spoke, his voice shook.

"It's getting late," he said. "And we need to finish our business, Ken. Take them up the hill and earn your bonus." Then he turned to Bloom. "Get in the limo, Jennifer. I'd like to have a word with you."

Lena felt Klinger jab his gun into her side, and they started walking. Not toward the vacant lot, but underneath the overpass toward the Cock-a-doodle-do. She could see his Caprice on the hilltop. It looked like he wanted to earn his bonus in the parking lot. Like the last thing she would see before she hit the void was that stupid neon rooster glowing in the fog.

She glanced over at Rhodes. Klinger was playing it smart and keeping his distance. They didn't have a move. Rhodes shrugged his shoulders and shot Klinger a look.

"You're gonna get an award for this," he said.

"Shut up, Rhodes. Just keep walking."

"They're gonna give you a medal, Klinger. Put your picture in the paper. The caption's gonna read KEN KLINGER, THE DUMBEST FUCK THERE EVER WAS."

"You're making this easy, Rhodes. You're making it fun. Keep moving."

Lena didn't think taunting Klinger would work. He was still keeping his distance and running too hot to make a mistake.

"I don't get it," she said to him. "When Dobbs and Ragetti went down, you were still over at Internal Affairs. You made the case against them, Klinger."

"So what?"

"You ended their careers. You don't think they want pay-back?"

He hesitated, but only briefly. "Money changes things," he said. "It always has."

"But who's gonna take the fall for all this? Someone's got to be held accountable. With Cava gone, you're the weak link, Klinger. You're the only one left."

"Keep your mouths shut. Both of you."

They had reached the top of the hill. Lena could feel time running out. The dark building across the lot was shimmering in and out of the grim clouds. The neon rooster on the roof, winking at her and waving good-bye.

"This is it," Klinger said. "Get down on your fucking knees."

"You sure we're facing east," Rhodes said.

"No, you piece of shit. You're heading south. Now get down on your fucking knees and smile at that fucking chicken over there."

Lena took a deep breath and lowered herself to the ground. It felt like all the blood had already drained out of her head. Everything was spinning. Everything blurry and slowed down. She glanced over at Rhodes and tried to focus on his face. He was looking back at her. She could see the sweat blistering on his forehead. His nostrils flared. His eyes big and bright and full of life. She could remember what he said in the car. How he tried to make her feel better. Maybe they'd get a drink later. Maybe they'd kick back and relax. He knew a good bar down this way.

And then she heard the sound. The loud hollow crack.

50

It sounded like a melon exploding. The blood spatter fanning out all over the asphalt. All over Klinger's Caprice in an ultra-fine spray.

Lena jumped to her feet and stared at the body beside her. Felt someone grab her hand, and looked up in horror. Met Rhodes's eyes and finally noticed that the sound of the shot was still reverberating within the fallen clouds. Still streaming through the darkness.

It couldn't have been a pistol.

And Klinger wasn't lying before them with a small hole in his head. The skin from his face had peeled away in a thin layer that reminded her of a latex glove. The image was still there, his identity intact. But everything else was gone.

She jerked her head around and looked behind them. Caught the three figures standing on the overpass behind the Lincoln. The trunk was open and she could see Barrera peering through a pair of binoculars. The chief lifting a long rifle off the handrail and passing it to the man she had seen sitting in the passenger seat.

It took a moment to comprehend what had actually happened. Lag time before the meaning reached her and finally jelled.

Chief Logan had just saved their lives—the same man who kept an M21 rifle mounted on his office wall beside his medals from the Vietnam War. For whatever reason, the former sniper had selected his target in the gloom and wiped it out with a single shot.

She watched Rhodes raise his hand in the air. She saw Barrera signal back that help was on its way. The moment was real. And even though she didn't trust it, it took her breath away.

She turned to Klinger, her stomach in her throat. Rolling his body over, she pulled his belt away and grabbed her .45 and Rhodes's Glock. Then they charged back down the hill.

The limo was still here, and so was the Audi—both cars smoldering in the cold heat. But it looked like the rats had heard the rifle shot and run for cover. Rhodes moved around the limo to the trunk, grabbed a handful of cash out of the duffel bag and tossed it in the air. They couldn't have run very far. And it was more than obvious that they had every intention of coming back.

She turned and counted twelve pillars supporting the overpass. Then she kept watch as Rhodes started working his way down the line toward the trees and brush bordering the freeway. Visibility was still less than twenty-five feet. The first two columns were clear. But when he swept past the third, something scurried out on two legs and made a run for it. Rhodes fired two shots at point-blank range, then ran forward as the figure collapsed on the ground.

The silence returned and Lena waited, keeping her eyes on the support columns with her Smith & Wesson ready. Rhodes turned the body over in the mist.

"Dobbs," he called out. "He's not gonna make it."

Lena waved back but knew that she was losing sight of Rhodes in the clouds and wouldn't be able to cover him from the limo. After a quick look around, she legged it across the grass to the first column on the far side. She could see Rhodes pocketing Dobbs's gun and patting down the man. When she checked her back, she spotted Ragetti rising out of the muck and realized that he had been hiding underneath the limo guarding the cash. Now his gun was raised and pointed at Rhodes. Directly behind Rhodes she could see Justin Tremell pulling away from his father and stepping out from behind a tree with Jennifer Bloom.

Lena turned back to Ragetti and aimed her .45, but knew that she was late on it. Knew that she didn't see it in time.

She shouted Rhodes's name, pulled the trigger, and felt the recoil. She saw Ragetti's pistol flash in the darkness and heard the loud pop. Bloom screamed and Ragetti fell down. And then Dean Tremell cried out.

Lena picked up Ragetti's gun and moved closer. No one had screamed or cried out for Phil Ragetti. And no one seemed concerned about Rhodes. He was on his feet and brushing himself off after hitting the ground.

Ragetti had pulled the trigger, missing one life and hitting another. And everyone's eyes were glued on the luckless target. Justin Tremell had been hit in the center of his chest as he tried to flee with Bloom. The kid was lying on a bed of grass. His eyes were open, his gaze stamped out.

Headlights began streaming down the hill, the space filling with a light so bright that the fog looked more like smoke now. Dean Tremell didn't seem to notice and staggered toward his son's dead body. Wilting onto the ground, the old man drew his only son into his arms and began rocking him on his knee.

Lena glanced over at Rhodes, then pulled Jennifer Bloom away and guided her toward the approaching headlights. She could hear Tremell weeping behind her. She could hear his sorrow cutting into the night. She knew the tone and cadence from personal experience. Knew what the agony felt like and looked like. Knew how much the loss of a loved one could weigh down the soul.

And so did Jennifer Bloom.

51

Lena watched two cops handcuff Tremell, read him his rights, and lead him away from his son's body in the grass. Tremell stared at the ground as they passed through the darkness. His lips were quivering, his shoulders hunched. Dean Tremell had been ruined, so there was no real reason for anyone to say anything to him. No reason to call him a piece of shit. But someone from the crime scene team muttered it anyway. Lena doubted that he heard it, though.

She looked up the hill and saw Rhodes interviewing Tremell's driver, then turned back to Barrera. They were standing by the ambulance while the EMTs prepared Jennifer Bloom for the ride to the hospital. Lena had bummed a cigarette from one of the paramedics. She couldn't help it.

"I knew that it was a bad idea," Barrera said. "I knew that when you saw the chief in the car, you'd think the worst."

"You were right," she said. "I did."

"I knew that you'd never believe me. That you wouldn't pick up your cell. It was a mistake, but he wanted to be there. He insisted on it."

"Where is he?"

"On his way downtown for the press conference."

She checked her watch. It felt like four or five in the morning. When she saw that it was only 10:30 p.m., it threw her until she remembered that she hadn't caught a decent night's sleep in three days.

"The chief wanted to be the one who told you," Barrera said. "He wanted you to hear it from him."

"Hear what?"

"It doesn't fucking matter anymore."

She took a drag on the cigarette. "What did he want to say?"

Barrera flashed a wry smile, then pulled back on it. "He wanted to warn you about Klinger. He thought that you were in danger if you went home. Like I said, Lena, it doesn't really matter anymore."

"I guess it doesn't," she said. "Who was the guy in the passenger seat?"

"His new adjutant."

"Hand-picked from Internal Affairs?"

"No. Abe Hernandez from Pacific Division. I've known him for ten years. He's a good man."

Barrera's cell started ringing and he stepped away to take the call. Lena turned back to Jennifer Bloom. She was strapped down on the gurney and about to be lifted into the ambulance. She reached out for Lena's hand and held it. Bloom didn't say anything. Just met her eyes.

"It's okay," Lena said. "Everything's good now. I'll stop by tomorrow so we can talk. You want me to call your brother?"

"It might be a shock if he hears my voice. He's been through a lot."

"I'll take care of it."

Bloom released her hand. Lena stayed until the ambulance drove off. Then she walked halfway up the hill and sat down in the grass. She was watching the criminalists from SID swarm the crime scene and trying not to think about what a hot shower might feel like. Trying not to think too much about climbing into bed. Her ears were still ringing from all the gunshots. Her body was so sore it felt like someone had tossed her out of a moving car.

The investigator from the coroner's office hadn't arrived yet and the bodies were still laid out the way they fell. Justin Tremell was too far off to really make out, his corpse muted by the fog. But she could see Dobbs and Ragetti clear enough. One face up, the other face down.

She took another drag on the cigarette, the body count preying on her mind. As she got to her feet and looked up the hill, she saw the coroner's van backing into position at the edge of the parking lot. Ed Gainer hopped out and spotted her in the haze, then motioned her up to the van.

"What's with your cell, Lena?"

She pulled the phone out of her pocket and checked it. The battery was dead.

"What's up?" she asked.

"Madina was trying to reach you," he said. "He had something he wanted you to see."

She followed Gainer to the back of the van and watched him open up. It looked like he had made a stop before this one. A single body bag was already onboard.

"What's he want me to see?"

Gainer shrugged. "I don't know. He said that when you saw it, you'd understand what it meant. You know what Madina's like, Lena. Sometimes he goes cryptic on you like just maybe he did one too many autopsies that day. After a while it would have to get to anyone. All those dead bodies. It sure as hell gets to me."

He laughed, then rolled the body bag closer to the rear doors.

"What are you doing, Ed?"

He turned and gave her a look. "He wants you to see this. It's Denny Ramira. He got started on the autopsy, then stopped and said you needed to take a look first."

Lena tried to pull herself together. She had already seen enough. She needed the day to end and needed it bad. Taking another look at Denny Ramira's corpse felt like it was pushing her over some psychological edge. She watched Gainer unzip the bag, then pull the plastic open. Saw Denny's battered face and eyes. That meat thermometer still in his chest. But even worse, she caught the odor venting out of the plastic and thought that she might lose it.

Gainer reached inside the bag and fished out Denny's left

arm. Then he switched on his flashlight and turned over the dead reporter's hand. All of a sudden, Lena was wide awake. Her mind, clear as a day with the man in the moon.

"Do you know if they took a picture, Ed?"

Gainer nodded. "It's documented. It's a matter of record. After they got the shot, Madina stopped the autopsy and loaded him in my van. What is it?"

Lena zeroed in on the pin stuck in Denny Ramira's left palm. The palm that she couldn't see when she found his body in the kitchen because he had clenched his fist in a death grip. Denny had been a crime-beat reporter and a good one. He would have known from experience that by clenching his fist at the time of his death he was unleashing a chemical reaction in his body. That his fingers would be locked like a bank vault until rigor mortis set his body and finally released it. That he could keep his secret for more than a day. And that he could buy enough time to tell Lena exactly who murdered him by jabbing the pin into his own palm and holding on to it for the rest of his life.

Just the sight of it cut to the bone.

She parted the body bag and gazed at Ramira's face for a long time. Her doubts about his murder had begun the moment she set eyes on that meat thermometer. She had known from the lack of blood that it had been an afterthought. A play that followed the murder but had nothing to do with it. Ever since that moment she had suspected that Cava probably wasn't good for it any more than Klinger could have been. Over the past hour she had come to the conclusion that Dobbs and Ragetti made the kill. The two bruisers seemed to fit the bill. The two ex-cops with a history of physical violence. The two thugs whom Tremell had said were listening to Ramira's phone calls.

But now she knew with certainty that it was none of the above. That the play had been a weak attempt to link Ramira's murder to the rest and let Cava take the fall for everything. After all, the play explained why Cava spent so much time staring at the picture of Ramira's dead dog during their interview. He was looking at the photograph the same way anyone would have if they were seeing it for the first time. But even more, it explained why Cava had needed time to think her offer over. And it explained why he had called her on the phone. The things he had said to her and his reasons for saying them.

Nathan G. Cava had seen it, too.

52

She caught the flashing lights as she made the turn off Sunset and looped up and around the hill. Ten patrol cars from the Sheriff's Department in West Hollywood were lined up in front of Senator Alan West's house. A Chevy Suburban with tinted windows was backed into the drive with its rear gate open. Every window in the house was lit up, and the front door stood open. As Lena got out of the car, she counted five uniforms standing around on the porch and wondered if she wasn't too late. She hustled up the front steps. When the five uniforms stopped talking, she clipped her badge to her jacket and picked out the deputy who looked like he was in charge.

"Is the senator around?"

"Is he expecting you?"

"We're friends," she said. "What's up tonight?"

The deputy shrugged. "We're making an airport run. We were supposed to leave ten minutes ago."

Lena entered the house. One of West's bodyguards was rushing down the stairs with a suitcase. When she turned, she saw West exiting his study with his second bodyguard in tow. West smiled at her. The two bodyguards didn't.

"What are you doing here, Detective?" West said.

"Just stopped by to talk. Where are you headed?"

"Washington," he said. "It's just for a week. Can it wait?"

Lena glanced at West's bodyguards. The two heavyweights

with rough faces and dark suits who appeared utterly calm and heavily armed. She turned back to West.

"I don't think it can, Senator."

West slipped into his suit jacket. "We're gonna miss our plane. You'll have to ride with us over to Burbank."

Lena followed them out the door. West hurried toward the Suburban with his bodyguards. The deputies from the Sheriff's Department were climbing into their patrol cars. When the last suitcase was tossed into the SUV, Lena got a look at the driver before he closed the gate. He was young and thin and Latino, no older than twenty with shy eyes. And there were a lot of bags. A lot for a week in D.C.

She walked around the Suburban and was ushered into the rear seat. One of the bodyguards sat beside her without saying anything. Then West took the seat in front of her, and the second bodyguard sat down beside him. The Suburban was linked to the patrol cars with a temporary radio sitting on the dash. As the driver adjusted the volume, Lena could hear the deputies discussing their route. Laurel Canyon over the hill to Sherman Way. Once they received confirmation, the caravan started rolling. Five patrol cars led the way. The remaining five covered their backs.

Lena turned to West. "I see you took my advice."

The senator smiled. "The cavalry? Yeah, I made the call. Can't be too careful. And I was losing too much sleep."

"Over Denny," she said.

He turned to her and nodded. His blue eyes glistened from the ten sets of flashing lights. He looked better than the last time she had seen him. His face had regained its color. He seemed fresh and relaxed, even relieved.

Lena kept her eyes on him. "His murder upset you, didn't it, Senator."

"Denny didn't start out as a crime reporter. He covered politics. I bet we went back ten years."

"I bet you did."

"Is everything okay, Detective?"

Lena glanced at his jacket. "Where's your nine-eleven pin? I don't see it on your lapel."

West stared back at her as if he hadn't heard her over the sound of the SUV.

"Your gold pin," she said. "The one the fire department gave you for being such a great guy. The one that you said you wore every day. What happened to it?"

As Lena watched West squirm, she realized why she had never looked to politicians for the answers in her life. Without a script to follow, politicians couldn't quite find the right words. Without a lift across the water, most of them would probably drown.

"What happened to your nine-eleven pin, Senator?"

West rubbed his finger over his lapel. "It's in a safe place, Detective."

"I agree with you. Your pin is in a very safe place."

"How would you know?"

"Because I saw it less than an hour ago."

"Oh, yeah?"

"That's right. You lost it."

"Where?" he asked.

"Denny Ramira's house. You lost it when you murdered him, Senator. Denny hid it before he died. That's why Klinger was there, right? The file I took was a bonus. He let me walk out with it because it made you look good. Nothing inside pointed to you. But the pin would, and you needed to cover your tracks. You sent Klinger over to Ramira's house to find your pin."

A long moment passed. Tight, and heavy, and dark as midnight. Everyone in the SUV was making lots of eye contact and trading secret messages. Lena noticed the driver's gaze riveted on her in the rearview mirror. The kid looked scared.

West didn't say anything right away, staring out the window as they reached the top of the hill and started down the winding road into the Valley. There was absolutely no reason for the senator to hide anymore. The pin that he had received for his support of the rescue workers after 9/11 had been handmade by an artist living in South Pasadena. The three-dimensional work of art depicting an LAFD fire engine set at ground zero was one of a kind. And there could be only one explanation for how the gold pin wound up in Denny Ramira's hand.

West cocked his head and looked at her. "Do you have it with you?" he asked.

"No," she said. "It's still in Denny's hiding place."

"And where's that?"

Lena met the senator's eyes. "You might say he palmed it."

West grinned at her, then spoke slowly as he thought it through. "Denny Ramira was a great reporter. He didn't care much for politics, though, and he was glad when the chance came his way to move on. He always used to say that we didn't get it. That the world couldn't be divvied up into left or right. That you couldn't distinguish people by their god, their tribe, their size or shape. You couldn't even break them down by the things they liked to eat. Something was either right or it was wrong, he'd say. A person was either decent or indecent. And that was the key to his work. That was his secret. If you had to pick a side, you better make sure there was more right to it than wrong."

"Which side did you pick, Senator?"

He shrugged, still gazing into the past. "I can tell you this, Detective. I gave as much as I got. And if some say that I got more than I gave, well—I did better than most."

"I'll keep that in mind when I talk to the families who lost their children because they thought Formula D was safe. The people who put their trust in you, Senator—you and Tremell and the FDA. Thanks for making sure the clinical trials were straight and true."

He held the glance but didn't say anything. Lena pressed forward, still trying to understand.

"When Jennifer Bloom first came to your office and told you what happened to her son, it didn't move you?"

"She didn't use her real name, Detective."

"What kind of a response is that? When she told you how her son died, that it had been a deliberate act on the part of Tremell, a pharmaceutical company, and a handful of government lowlifes who were bought and paid for, you weren't moved by her story?"

"Of course I was. Who wouldn't be?"

"When she walked out, how long did it take before you called Tremell? A day? An hour? Or was she still on her way out the door? You're the one who called him. You told Tremell who Jennifer Bloom really was. You're the one who told him that she played him for a fool."

She could see his soiled mind working behind his eyes. The gears inside his head spinning 'round and 'round even though they were warped and bent and out of alignment.

"He couldn't keep his dick in his pants," West said. "Ten percent of my stock portfolio was wrapped up in his lousy company. The share price had already nose-dived because of all the rumors. If Bloom's story had been made public, it would've taken years for the price to bounce back."

Lena stared at him in disbelief. "That's why you ratted her out? Because of your stock portfolio?"

"That's right, Detective. For the money. For *my* money. She didn't trust me to see it through. A former member of the United States Senate. She walked out of my office, met Ramira, and told him everything. And I mean everything. And so I made Denny Ramira my new best friend. It was the only way I could keep an eye on him. He had this thing for you, you know. He felt guilty about what happened to you last year. That story you gave him about your brother's murder. He felt guilty that he won so many awards and you nearly lost your career. He wasn't holding out on you because of the book or anything he was doing for the paper. He wanted to hand you this one on a plate. Everything wrapped up and ready to go. He thought he owed you that. But as you can see, timing is everything in life. Denny waited a day too long."

The SUV made a right turn onto Sherman Way. They were less than two miles off, approaching the airport from the rear. Lena glanced at the patrol cars. West's bodyguards didn't seem concerned that they were surrounded and she turned back to the senator.

"Denny was ready to talk," she said. "So you went over to his place. What clinched it for him? And don't tell me that it was because he ID'd Cava. Denny didn't ID Cava. You fingered him to cover yourself."

West smiled at the memory. "The lost witness," he said after a moment. "Denny thought he'd figured it out last Sunday. That the witness was really the target. That the witness was Jennifer all along."

"But it took until Wednesday before he confirmed it," she said.

"That's right. It took three days to find her. She was living at a friend's house, the one that Cava murdered. She made a mistake and answered the phone. Denny heard her voice."

"And you called Tremell again. You sold her out twice."

"That's right. I let everybody know. Then I went over to Denny's and tried to convince him to wait. I told him that we needed to find her and talk to her. But he wouldn't listen and he got angry. When he reached for the phone to call you, things got out of hand. Then I cleaned out his office, and drove home. Obviously, I missed a single file. The one Klinger found. But you're right, the pin was more important to me than the file. And that's why I sent him there."

Lena shook her head, silently counting the number of people who had lost their lives because this man was worried about the price of a share of stock. This man who had served three consecutive terms in the U.S. Senate representing the State of California. This man who had been appointed to the police commission by the mayor of Los Angeles and approved in a unanimous vote by the City Council in an attempt to restore public trust in the department.

This horrible man sitting right in front of her. Somehow he had managed to rat out Jennifer Bloom twice. And he'd ratted out Cava, too.

"What about Cava?" she said. "How did you make contact?"

"I was a senator at the time. I spent a few days in Iraq, then toured a facility in Eastern Europe. Cava was there and we met."

"What facility? Are you talking about the secret prisons? The Black Sites?"

West eyed her face, choosing his words carefully. "It was a facility," he said. "Cava had been transferred there as a medical officer. His role changed over time, but he didn't have the temperament for it."

"You fucked him up is what you're saying."

"I didn't do anything to him."

"How did you talk him into killing for you?"

"I told him what you tell every soldier. That his efforts would be for the greater good. That his sacrifice would be seen as contributing to a better world. Then Tremell backed it up with cash. Cava was so fucked up he bought it. At least in the beginning he did."

The van slowed down and Lena watched as the five patrol cars in front of them shut down their flashing lights and pulled ahead. When she looked out the window, she saw the five cars behind them passing on the left and vanishing up the street. The kid driving the Suburban switched off the radio, making a right turn into a parking lot, passing a guard at the gate, and cruising swiftly onto the tarmac. Lena spotted the private jet, felt the burn, and read the sign on the hangar.

BARNES AVIATION.

She turned back to West and caught the broad smile on his face.

"Did you really think we were flying Southwest?" he whispered.

The senator's bodyguards chuckled. As the van stopped, Lena tried to pull herself together. She could see a handful of private aviation companies on this side of the runway, but every one of them was closed. The lights from Burbank Airport were cutting through the light fog a half mile across the tarmac. West's pilot was inspecting the jet, and after circling the plane, appeared ready to go. Then the young driver climbed out of the Suburban and began helping a member of the grounds crew transfer the bags.

Lena turned back to West. His eyes were on her. He had been watching her take it all in.

"My apologies for keeping you in the dark," he said. "I'm sure you understand that it was the only way. You thought that you could rely on the Sheriff's Department once we reached the airport. You thought that you could milk what happened out of me, and West Hollywood's finest would back you up. And just like Denny Ramira, you got your story but guessed wrong."

Lena had been holding her .45 in her hand ever since she set eyes on the jet. Now she lifted it out of the darkness and pointed the muzzle at West's face. The senator laughed at her.

"It won't work, Detective. You're a hell of a man, but it won't work."

The two bodyguards drew their pistols in unison. Another stretch of silence passed with everyone making eye contact and trading heavy secrets.

West shrugged. "It really won't work here, Detective. You're outmanned and you're outgunned. Bringing me in to face my sins just isn't in the cards tonight. And let's face it. It isn't worth losing your life over when you could live to fight the fight another day. You better hand me that. My friends get nervous and even a private aviation company has a thing about people pointing guns."

Lena didn't move, her Smith & Wesson up and ready. "Where are you going, West?"

"Paradise," he said. "Now, hand over the gun. There's no sense dying tonight."

She took a deep breath and exhaled. After a long stretch, she passed the gun over and felt her body shudder. The senator grinned, but took a deep breath, too.

"That's better," he said. "Much better."

The driver returned to the Suburban and climbed in behind the wheel. "Everything's ready," he said. "You're all set, sir."

West offered the kid Lena's .45. "Thanks, Juan. Thanks for everything. You'll need to keep this until we take off. Maybe we'll see each other again sometime."

The kid stared at the weapon and was clearly nervous. But when West handed him the gun, he looked at Lena and pointed it at her.

She sat back in the seat, watching the two bodyguards file out ahead of West. When the senator turned back and shot her a parting glance, she remembered the card in her pocket and dug it out.

"You forgot this," she said.

West didn't seem to understand, but stepped closer as she extended her hand.

"Your business card," she said. "I won't be needing your help anymore."

He glanced at the card, then slipped it into his pocket and smiled at her.

"You never know," he said.

And that was it. Lena sat in the van keeping one eye on the nervous kid with the loaded .45 in his hand, and the other on the jet taxiing down the runway en route to paradise. After about five minutes she heard the roar of the engines and looked out the window as the jet rocketed down the short runway and strained to make the steep climb out over Hollywood Hills. It sounded a lot like thunder. A lot like a passing storm. When it was over, when the jet carrying West and his bodyguards finally faded into the heavens, the kid tossed her the .45 and asked if she wanted a lift home.

53

She had spent the last four days thinking it over and couldn't decide who was worse. Both Tremell and West were responsible for the murders. Both had been motivated by greed and had a hand in the deaths that resulted from the marketing and use of Formula D. The only real difference between the two was that West sold out everybody. That Tremell was in a jail cell on suicide watch, while West was free and clear and probably living large.

It was Christmas Eve. A cold, grim afternoon in Hollywood Hills.

Tracking West's escape over the past few days had proved fruitless. The jet flew directly to the Cayman Islands. According to the pilot, who returned to Burbank the following morning, West and his companions boarded another plane waiting for them on the tarmac. No flight plan was available—the plane never returned—and the FBI had taken over the case.

Lena closed the tray on her CD player and adjusted the volume. She had loaded it up with some of her favorites. Nat King Cole because it was Christmas Eve. Mike Bloomfield, Al Kooper, and Stephen Stills's *Super Session* for reasons she couldn't explain, Gerry Mulligan and Astor Piazzolla because she was thinking that West probably made a run for South America and the music might trigger something in her imagination that would help, and that import CD she had heard Cava listening to. *Hope Radio* by Ronnie Earl and the Broadcasters. She had ordered the album on the Internet three days ago and had been listening to it ever since it arrived.

She sat down on the couch and looked at the Christmas tree on the porch outside the slider. The tree was alive. Although she didn't have any ornaments, she had spent the afternoon stringing white lights through its branches. The tree was a rental from a company in Hollywood who delivered it to her door and would pick it up after the new year. The rental fee covered their expenses for planting the tree in the hills that had been destroyed by the wildfires last spring.

But her mind wasn't really on the holiday right now. There were still too many things to remember. Too many things that she could learn from. And too many images she wanted to forget.

Rhodes was with his sister in Oxnard, so she didn't really have anyone to talk to. Jennifer Bloom had been released from the hospital and was with her brother in Vegas. The family of Beth Gillman, the girl Cava had abducted from the Cock-a-doodle-do and murdered in the garage on Barton Avenue, had been located in Portland and notified of their daughter's death. And Vinny Bing the Cadillac King had been found hanging from the garage at his dealership, his cable TV show still running because network executives thought that they might get a ratings boost.

It might add up, Lena thought. But it played havoc with the soul.

Someone knocked on her front door. She walked over and pulled it open, then gazed at her visitor for a long time.

It was Chief Logan, dressed casually in a sweater and a pair of slacks. And he was holding a bottle of Pinot Noir in his hand.

"A friend of mine lives just west of Pasadena," he said. "He's got a great wine cellar. He said that he knows you and thought you might like this. I guess you ate dinner together in the kitchen at Patina once. He was celebrating the birth of his grandkids. I was hoping we might share it."

She looked at the label trying to buy time. It was a bottle

of Williams Selyem—out of her price range and hard to find. And she could remember the man the chief was talking about. It had been an evening of great food and conversation with someone who had changed the face of the city. Lena hadn't been aware that the two men were friends. When she finally spoke, her voice cracked.

"Come in," she said. "Please."

A warm smile spread across the chief's face as he entered the house. She didn't know what to make of it, and switched over to automatic pilot. She managed to set two wine glasses on the counter without breaking the stems. Then she watched the chief pull the cork and marveled at the rich color of the grapes as he made the pour. They clinked glasses and took their first sips. It may have been the best first sip she had ever tasted.

"Would you mind if we drank this outside?" he said. "I'd like to sit by your tree and enjoy the view."

Lena shook her head. "Not at all," she managed.

The chief opened the slider and set the bottle on the table. As he grabbed a chair, Lena pulled the grill over, loaded it up with charcoal, and lit a fire to keep them warm. She took another sip of wine and opened the pack of cigarettes. There was only one left, and she remembered the night she had bought them. The night she ran into Dobbs and Ragetti in the parking lot. The last time she saw Denny Ramira alive. She knew that it would be her last cigarette for a long time.

"You watch much television, Lena?"

She shook her head. "Not really."

"Me either," he said. "How 'bout movies?"

"I like them a lot."

"How many times have you seen *The Godfather*?"

"More than ten."

"Then maybe you'll understand why the first thing I did was make Ken Klinger my adjutant."

He turned and looked at her with those dark eyes of his. And for the first time since they had met, she got a decent read off them, caught the spark, and everything clicked like a crystal ball.

"Keep your friends close," she said. "But keep your enemies closer."

The chief raised his glass as if making a toast to her.

"I knew that Klinger was a piece of shit the moment I met him," he said. "I'd been waiting for something to happen. I never thought that it would break this big. That so many lives would be lost. But that's the way it is, I guess. When he told me that he thought you should be assigned to this homicide case, I knew that something was up. But most of all, I knew that Klinger was a moron. He wanted you because he, and the DA, and his lousy friends at Internal Affairs all thought you were incompetent. I agreed to give you the case and called Barrera because we knew that you weren't. After the way you handled yourself last year, I knew that I could trust you. That I could count on you. That once you got started, you'd put yourself on the line and see it through. That you could take the bullshit I had to deal out for what it really was. A high-stakes gamble by a new chief to clean up our house. That's why I gave you all those Officer Involved Shooting cases. It wasn't punishment. I needed to know who was who. And that's why I had to be so hard on you in my office. Klinger was listening. I needed his confidence, and he needed to hear me knock you down. All I can offer is my apology. By the way, you'll be receiving the Medal of Valor for this, Lena. No chief has ever been more proud."

She heard his voice break and felt something deep inside her give way. She tried to hang tough. Tried to keep her game face on. But none of it was working this afternoon. She jammed the unlighted cigarette into the pack and turned her face away.

"Cava's a cop killer," she said. "And West's a former senator. The water's cloudy, Chief. Both of them got away."

"For now, at least. But we've started to clean house. And sleeping with one eye open every night takes its toll. The world isn't as big as it used to be, Lena. Sooner or later they'll run out of road."

She took a sip of wine, then sat back and finally lit her last cigarette. She looked at the chief's chiseled face, his gray hair, the intelligence in his eyes, and felt herself begin to relax.

"What about the DA?"

The chief set down his glass. "He's friends with Tremell. The press can already smell blood in the water. I don't think he'll survive. And even if he does, I doubt he'll be reelected. Before I came over, I checked on Tremell. He's off suicide watch."

"That was quick."

The chief grinned at the thought. "He's hired one of those consultants to the stars to help him cope with prison life. You know, learn to blend, don't ask for favors, and don't make friends with the guards."

His voice suddenly faded and Lena followed his gaze off the porch to the city below the hills. Something was falling out of the sky. At first she thought that it might be ash from another wildfire. But when it seemed to pick up, she realized that it was snow.

She watched the flakes touch the ground and melt away. She looked at it with amazement and thought about Jennifer Bloom's keepsake from her husband who died in the war.

It was snowing in Los Angeles. Anything could happen here.

"I love this city," the chief whispered. "Maybe it's because I wasn't born here. Maybe that's why I can't take it for granted."

Lena's cell began vibrating. After checking the display, she turned the phone so that the chief could read the name.

VINNY BING, THE CADILLAC KING.

The chief gave her a look. "When a dead man's on the other end of the line, I guess you've gotta take the call."

Lena flipped the cell open and switched on the speaker phone, then listened as Nathan G. Cava said hello.

"Where are you?" she asked.

"It doesn't matter because I won't be here for very long."

"Then why did you call?"

Cava laughed. "To let you know that I figured it out."

"Figured what out?"

"I know how you found me."

"I thought you said that you weren't hiding."

"I wasn't. But I needed to know and now I do. Someone gave you my name. And I found out who."

Lena glanced at the chief, then leaned closer to the phone. "Do you know where he is?"

Cava laughed again. "In a small bungalow on a hill facing the beach. He thinks he's found paradise. In a few minutes he'll probably change his mind, though."

"This isn't the way to handle it, Cava. You need to turn yourself in."

"A guy like me needs to do a lot of things," he said. "And you were wrong."

"Wrong about what?"

"Killing," he said. "When we met, you said I liked it. Maybe we'll talk about it someday."

The phone clicked off. Lena stared at the snowflakes drifting down onto Hollywood, then turned to the chief as he filled her glass.

"You were right," she said. "The world isn't as big as it used to be."

54

Cava slipped Vinny Bing's cell into his pocket and glanced at the two bodyguards. They were sitting on the floor in West's bedroom, their oversized bodies propped up against the wall on either side of the bathroom door. Their head wounds had stopped bleeding while he was on the phone. Still, the wall would need to be wiped down before he left. And something would have to be done about the stain on the carpet.

Only Alan West would think that paradise came with wall-to-wall carpeting.

Cava looked at the clothes laid out on the bed as he listened through the door to West taking a shower. He had forgotten to pop a Flomax this morning and needed to take a leak. The sound of the senator soaping it up in all that water wasn't helping much. At the same time, life had its rewards. Within the next few minutes all business would be concluded. In another day, Cava would be a thousand miles away picking out his chaise longue in Coronaville.

In another day he would be invisible.

The two bodyguards had gone down as easy as a couple of dead trees, and this surprised Cava. When he saw them in L.A. they looked so rough and tough in their black suits. Each one of them had to weigh in at over two hundred and fifty pounds. Maybe it was the change to Tommy Bahama sportswear that weakened them. Maybe the flowers on their shirts lowered their guard. Or maybe it had something to do with the suntan lotion on their meaty white legs and their big red noses.

Cava didn't really give a shit what it was. He had been watching the house for a day and a half and the only thing that mattered was that it had been easy. One round each from a .22 pistol stuffed inside an empty half-gallon Pepsi bottle to dampen the noise. They never did see the gun. Just the Pepsi bottle. Just Cava's friendly smile and wave.

But even better, Cava was certain that West didn't remember that he had actually talked about this place six months ago when they discussed what might happen if things went wrong. West had talked it up and even pointed it out on a map. An oasis, he called it. A safe haven with maid service, satellite TV, access to the Internet, and all of the amenities a U.S. senator in hiding might require.

Cava lifted the KitchenAid Pro mixer out of the box and set it down on the table. Attaching the meat grinder, he estimated that he would be working with more than seven hundred pounds of raw product and hoped that the 325-watt motor was up to the job.

He could hear the senator singing a show tune now. West seemed to know all the words to "Singin' in the Rain," but couldn't quite manage to stay in key. Cava shook it off, setting a box of butcher's paper beside the meat grinder and laying out a fresh roll of masking tape.

He was ready. Everything he needed was here. And the senator sounded like he was in a good mood.

He looked down at his lucky shoes. The cheap pair of sneakers that Lena Gamble had given him not knowing that they would play a crucial role in his escape. He wiggled his toes and smiled.

He wouldn't be using the .22 this time. It wasn't tactile enough and the moment had too much meaning. West had needed him and lied to him about everything. After the good senator had killed that reporter and his little dog, he turned on him and gave him up. When that didn't work, he made a run for it.

Alan West was a worm.

Cava thought about what he had just said to Lena Gamble on the phone. That he didn't like killing. He knew in his heart that his words rang true. But maybe not this time. Not when it came down to Alan West. He wouldn't even be using a knife because the moment was so special. So important to his psychological recovery.

The senator finally stopped singing and turned off the water. Cava pulled out his razor-sharp scalpel and wiped it on his shirt sleeve. Satisfied that the instrument was nearly sterile, and if not sterile, clean to anyone who might be observing, he glanced at the two dead guys on the floor and pushed open the bathroom door. He could see the senator through the steam. His hair matted down and his loose body dripping wet. He could see the man's beady eyes on him penetrating the tempered glass. The shock and awe on his face. The fear and loathing. Although Cava had only been here for a short time, the people living in town looked hungry. Beef tacos were everywhere, but he noticed many people eating cheeseburgers as well. . . .